THE LOST KEYS OF ST. PETER

Patrick Reis

Encounter Publishing

The Lost Keys of St. Peter by Patrick Reis

Paperback ISBN: 979-8-9995497-4-7
Hardcover ISBN: 979-8-9995497-7-8
E-book ISBN: 979-8-9995497-5-4
Audiobook ISBN: 979-8-9995497-6-1

Cover image © 2025 Encounter Publishing
Design by Encounter Publishing

Published by Encounter Publishing
In operation with Encounter Ministries
730 Rickett Rd
Brighton, MI 48116

encounterministries.us
encounterschool.org

Dedicated to my dear friend Aziz Maakaroun and the Encounter leaders across Lebanon and the Arab world. Your friendship, devotion to Christ, and vibrant testament of life in the Holy Spirit have deeply inspired and shaped my journey.

Contents

Preface

I never expected a single footnote to upend two millennia of assumptions—but that is exactly what happened in the spring of 2025, while I was gathering sources for my follow-up to *Supernatural Saints: A School of Ministry from the Saints* (2023). The new project was meant to examine the genius of the Early Church Fathers in providing our generation with inspiration to live in the life, power, and gifts of the Holy Spirit. Yet halfway through reading Pope Gregory the Great's letters, I stumbled upon an arresting line. Writing to Patriarch Anastasius of Antioch in A.D. 597, Gregory says—almost in passing - **"Furthermore, I have sent you the keys of the blessed Apostle Peter, who loves you. These keys are known to perform many miracles when placed on the bodies of the sick."**

I froze. The keys given to Peter by Jesus (Mt 16:19) were more than metaphor? Gregory treated them as tangible, healing relics and claimed to have sent them across the Mediterranean! Centuries of commentators had glossed over the phrase, assuming a symbolic flourish. Here, laid bare, was evidence that sixth-century Christians believed the "Keys of the Kingdom" were physical objects that could be boxed, couriered, and venerated.

My first instinct was to contact trusted historians and theologians. Not one had ever heard of a credible tradition asserting the keys were literal artifacts. Their collective silence told me two things: (1) the scholarly consensus had a blind spot, and (2) I had just been handed the research question of a lifetime.

I abandoned the tidy outline of my original book and plunged into a deep historical excavation. Step by step, the world of late-sixth-century Christendom opened like a cryptic mosaic:

Healing and Deliverance - not only were there claims of miraculous healing power, but there was also conviction that evil spirits could afflict those with malicious intents.

The Lombard invasions - Their lightning conquest of northern Italy explains how Pope Pelagius II first received (and nearly lost) the keys before Gregory ever re-routed them east.

Rome and Constantinople - Pope Gregory's diplomacy reveals a Church walking a tightrope between a fading Western empire and a resurgent Byzantine court.

Antioch on the brink - As Persian armies under Khosrow II swept west, relic-hunting became statecraft.

Geopolitics of relics —The Persian seizure of the True Cross, the lance of Longinus, and other treasures shows that kingdoms were willing to kill for objects they thought could sway heaven itself.

Every chapter of that investigation pressed the same question: If the keys were real, where are they now?

The results of that search fill the pages ahead. Every date, every place, every quotation has been sifted against primary sources - Gregory's letters, Byzantine chronicles, Lombard annals, and the historical record of the Persian invasions. Conjecture is flagged as conjecture; archival fact stands as fact. What remains is a tapestry of intrigue that bridges ancient basilicas and modern battlefields, shattered domes and covert digs, saints and soldiers.

Yet research alone cannot convey the wonder I felt each time a fragment linked Gregory's Europe with Anastasius's Antioch, or when a forgotten chronicle confirmed that the healing power upon St. Peter, whose shadow healed the sick (Acts 5:15) was imparted into these physical keys. Those moments convinced me this story needed to be told not only as history but as living narrative—a suspense-driven tale that invites readers to feel the stakes as sharply as the people who risked their lives for two pieces of hammered gold.

So, turn the page with one guiding thought: the object at the heart of this novel is not legend. It is the set of keys Jesus pressed into a fisherman's hand, keys emperors coveted for their power to heal bodies, sway armies, and- just possibly - unlock the fate of nations. Whether they lie forgotten beneath Anatolian dust or await discovery in some Byzantine vault, their legacy is already rattling the present.

May the journey enthrall you as deeply as the research enthralled me - and may you never hear the phrase "the Keys of St. Peter" the same way again.

—Patrick Reis

ONE

The Keys of St. Peter

A raw wind blew through the gaping doors of the cathedral in Mantua, Italy, that chilly evening in the year 583. The city had only just fallen to the Lombard King Autharith, but the clamor of the siege still seemed to echo in the cold stone walls. Dirt and debris trailed in behind the single Lombard soldier who hurried inside, casting nervous glances over his shoulder. He carried a torch, its flame bobbing and sputtering in the drafty interior as he made for the sacristy door.

He slowed only once to listen for the sounds of pursuit. The king and the other men were behind him in the city, but he'd gained a good head start. Grinning to himself, he pushed the heavy wooden door open and slipped inside.

His name was Gundric, a soldier of rough origins and an even rougher temperament. He was known among his comrades for an unquenchable greed—gold, silver, whatever he could pocket. And here, in a conquered city, he knew there would be loot for the taking. He had heard rumors from a captured cleric about a crypt beneath the sacristy that held unimaginable riches. That was all the encouragement Gundric needed. "Let them celebrate taking the city," Gundric muttered under his breath. "I'll collect my prize first."

Gundric had always been a force to be reckoned with, a towering figure whose presence on the battlefield inspired both awe and fear. His courage was legendary among the Lombards, a testament to his indomitable spirit and unmatched prowess in combat. On the day Mantua fell, it was Gundric who led the charge, his battle cry rising above the clamor of war like a clarion call. With unyielding strength, he wielded his axe as if it were an extension of his own arm, cleaving through defenses and scattering foes with ruthless efficiency. His eyes burned with a fierce determination that seemed to draw strength from the very chaos around him, and his comrades followed his lead, galvanizing their attack with the force of a tidal wave.

It was through Gundric's sheer might and strategic acumen that the Lombards breached the city walls, a feat that seemed insurmountable to many. He was a whirlwind of destruction, his every move calculated to sow terror and confusion among the defenders. His reputation for invincibility only grew as he single-handedly drove out scores of inhabitants, clearing the way for the Lombard forces to flood into the city. There was no hesitation in his actions, no sign of doubt or fear; Gundric was the embodiment of martial prowess, a soldier without peer whose physical and mental fortitude made him an unstoppable force on the battlefield. In the aftermath, as the city lay in the grip of the conquering Lombards, none could deny that Gundric was among the most capable and fierce warriors of his time.

Inside the sacristy, wooden furnishings were in disarray. Empty candelabras lay tossed aside, half-burnt candles scattered across the floor. The city's nobles and clergy had withdrawn in haste; clearly, they hadn't managed to secure every precious object. Yet none of that interested him. He had heard that the real valuables sat below, hidden in the crypt. He found the narrow staircase and descended, the torch throwing flickering light against damp stone walls.

At the foot of the staircase, a heavy iron gate loomed. Gundric jammed his shoulder against it. The rusted hinges groaned but yielded. He ducked through and stepped onto the crypt's cold floor. Motes of dust danced in the torchlight as he scanned the shelves and chests around him.

Small boxes lay scattered, likely containing chalices or minor religious articles. But in the corner, beneath an arch carved with Latin inscriptions, a trove glimmered: gold-plated reliquaries, jeweled goblets, silver censers. Gundric felt his pulse pound. He raised the torch higher. "So, this is it," he said with a wolfish grin. "Riches fit for a king—my king."

He took a step forward, scanning the shelves. Various items caught his eye, but one object in particular burned brightest in the torchlight: a large set of two golden keys. They lay atop a small marble plinth, partially covered by a dusty cloth. "Interesting," he murmured. "Never seen anything like that before."

He lifted the cloth away, revealing the keys in their full splendor. They were more ornate than any he'd beheld. A faint inscription carved into the stone overhead read: CLAVES PETRI.

He whistled low under his breath. "Peter's Keys." The name meant nothing to him beyond potential value. "This might fetch a fortune."

Gundric removed his leather backpack and tried to fit them inside, but the keys were too large. He huffed. "That's fine. I'll make 'em smaller."

Drawing his knife, he placed the blade at the thick golden bow of one key, expecting to slice off a sliver or two. As soon as metal scraped metal, an unnatural hush fell across the crypt. The shadows in the corners seemed to shift. He froze, holding the torch at arm's length.

His heart hammered. The flicker of his torchlight revealed shapes—no, not shapes, but a darkness that slithered like living smoke. He backed up, stepping on a loose stone, nearly stumbling.

He licked his lips and spoke aloud, as though to ward off whatever threat he sensed. "Who's there?"

No voice answered. But the darkness moved closer, winding around him with a deliberate, creeping motion. He tried to run. His body refused to obey. His breath caught. In a single moment, an icy dread flooded his veins.

A whisper—soft, indistinct—filled his ears "furetur, mactet, perdat" - "steal, kill, destroy" - over and over - with the keys still tightly grasped in hand, the dark presence overshadowed him, its essence pressing down like a tangible weight. Desperation surged through him, and he swung his knife at the encroaching darkness, but it was futile. The blade sliced through the air, meeting only emptiness as the shadows coiled and writhed, unhindered by physical barriers.

The presence descended upon him, an eerie chill seeping into his bones. It was as though a liquid shadow was being poured into him, filling every crevice of his being. His muscles convulsed violently, and he collapsed to the floor, limbs twisting into unnatural contortions. His back arched, and his fingers bent at impossible angles, the keys jangling in his rigid grip.

For a brief moment, he lay still, his chest barely rising, the room silent but for the distant drip of water echoing in the crypt. Then, abruptly, his eyes snapped open, wide and unseeing, pupils dilated with an unearthly darkness. His mouth gaped, a void of blackness from which the words came forth, disembodied and chilling: "furetur, mactet, perdat," the mantra spilling into the air with a resonance that seemed to vibrate through the stones themselves. The hand gripping the knife whipped around. With a sudden, savage force, the hand of Gundric drove the blade into his own throat. The torch fell, sputtering, as blood sprayed across the stone floor. His legs buckled and he collapsed, dead before he hit the ground.

The golden keys remained locked in his stiffening fingers.

Hours later, King Autharith and a cadre of men entered the cathedral and made their way to the crypt to investigate the treasures of the city. Tall and broad-shouldered, his armor clinked as he took a few cautious steps into the gloom. His gaze swept across the scattered relics until it landed on the bloodied body crumpled on the floor.

A hush fell over the men behind him. The atmosphere in the crypt pressed down on them, a suffocating heaviness. Autharith and his men advanced cautiously, their torchlight flickering against the cold stone walls of the crypt. As they drew nearer, the dim glow revealed more of the scene—a glint of metal and the dark stain that pooled around the body. Gundric lay sprawled on the floor, his eyes wide open but unseeing, a cruel knife embedded in his throat by his own hand. The blood still fresh, painting a grim pattern on the ground.

One of the men gasped, an involuntary sound that echoed harshly in the silence. The others stepped back instinctively, a ripple of fear passing through the group. The torchlight trembled in unsteady hands, casting shadows that danced ominously around them.

Autharith's face remained impassive, though his eyes were sharp and calculating. He crouched beside the fallen soldier, inspecting the wound with a practiced eye. The men shifted uneasily behind him, their earlier confidence shaken by the brutal reality laid bare before them. The crypt seemed to close in around them, the air thick with the metallic scent of blood and the weight of their own mortality. Autharith's eyes narrowed. Autharith's voice broke the oppressive silence, his tone laced with disbelief. "Gundric, the unyielding, felled by his own hand? This cannot be—it defies all reason," he murmured, his mind grappling with the impossible.

"There is evil here," the king muttered. Even the torchlight seemed muted, as though the shadows themselves pushed back against the flame. King Autharith's mind raced as he surveyed the scene, his thoughts a turbulent mix of anger and unease. Gundric had been a seasoned warrior, not one to fall easily. The very air seemed charged with a malevolent energy, whispering secrets that eluded his understanding.

What madness drove you to this end, Gundric? he wondered, a bitter taste in his mouth. The crypt felt like a living thing, watching, waiting. It was as if the ancient stones themselves conspired to hide the truth, mocking his authority.

Autharith clenched his fist, the metal of his gauntlet biting into his palm. He could feel the weight of his men's eyes on him, seeking guidance, but beneath his stoic exterior, doubt gnawed at him. The treasures of the city were close, but at what cost?

With a deep breath, he steeled himself against the oppressive dread. Whatever dark force lurked in the shadows would not deter him. He was king, and this crypt would yield its secrets.

The king stood in heavy silence, then looked to his men and jerked his chin toward Gundric's corpse. "Take those gold keys out of those hands."

His warriors exchanged wary glances. None moved to obey.

Autharith's tone sharpened. "Cowards." King Autharith surveyed his men, his expression a blend of frustration and resolve. The flickering torchlight cast long shadows on the crypt walls, making the air feel even more oppressive. He knew his men were brave, but the fear of the unknown, of whatever malevolent force lurked in the darkness, was palpable.

"Is there no one among you with the courage to take these keys?" the king demanded, his voice echoing off the stone walls with an authority that brooked no dissent.

The men shifted uncomfortably, their eyes darting away from the king's intense gaze. A tense silence stretched on, until finally, one of the soldiers stepped forward. His name was Leofric, a grizzled veteran with scars that spoke of countless battles.

"Sire," Leofric began hesitantly, "there is only one among us who might be suited for this task. A man of faith, who knows the old ways and the power they hold. The only Catholic in our company—Minulf."

Autharith considered this for a moment, the weight of the decision heavy on his shoulders. Minulf was a quiet man, known for his almsgiving and piety. If anyone could face the unknown with courage, it would be him.

"Summon Minulf," the king commanded, his voice firm. The soldiers moved quickly to carry out the king's orders, their relief evident in their swift compliance. As they waited for Minulf to arrive, Autharith allowed himself a brief moment of reflection. Within moments, Minulf appeared, his expression calm yet serious. He approached the king and knelt, awaiting his orders. Autharith studied him for a moment, gauging the resolve in the man's eyes. "Minulf" the king said, "we have just found Gundric lying dead here by his own hand, clutching these golden keys in his other hand. No one here is willing to take these keys. What do you make of this?"

Minulf investigated the scene and found the former resting place of the keys and the CLAVES PETRI inscription. "That inscription—it says Claves Petri. The Keys of Peter."

Autharith frowned. "The ancient apostle of the Christians?"

"Yes, my lord. The Church teaches that Christ Himself bestowed the keys of heaven upon Peter, and the Bishop of Rome, his current successor, Pope Pelagius II, is the rightful owner of these keys. These keys are... extremely sacred. Misusing sacred objects can invite evil, your majesty."

"Minulf, take these keys from Gundric's hand."

Minulf knelt, murmuring a brief prayer as he carefully pried the keys free from the hands of Gundric. His eyes darted about, as if expecting something to strike him down. But nothing happened. No swirl of malignant shadow. No bone-chilling whisper.

He stood and held the keys up, arms trembling slightly. "Sire, we cannot keep these keys or else we could invite the same kind of evil upon us that Gundric experienced. I believe we should send these keys to Pope Pelagius in Rome."

Autharith fixed him with a hard stare. "Is that your counsel?"

"Yes, sire. He is the current successor of Peter."

Autharith exhaled slowly. "Very well. To Rome it shall go."

TWO

From the Crypt to the Campus

(Setting: Modern Day – University of Notre Dame, South Bend, Indiana)

Professor Joseph Scanlon stood at the podium, a PowerPoint slide showing an image of the Lombard King Autharith. The heading read: *Conquest of Mantua (583) and the Keys of St. Peter.*

He leaned on the lectern, addressing his students. "That, dear class, is how King Autharith came into possession of the legendary Keys of St. Peter and sent them back to Rome - providing us the first historical evidence that the keys of Peter were indeed real artifacts. The only reason we know these details is thanks to a surviving letter of Pope Gregory the Great. He flicked to the next slide, a scanned Latin text side-by-side with English. "This is the letter from Pope Gregory the Great to Theoctista.

A certain Lombard, upon entering a city in the region beyond the Po, found it and, paying no regard to it as Saint Peter's keys but wanting to make profit from it for himself, since he saw it was gold, drew a knife to cut it. But immediately, seized by a spirit, he thrust the very knife with which he meant to cut it into his own throat, and in that same hour fell down dead. When Autharith, king of the Lombards, and many others with him came to the place, they found the man who had stabbed himself lying dead in one spot, and the keys on the ground in another. Great fear then fell upon all, so that no one dared to lift the keys from the ground. Thereupon a certain Lombard named Minulf, a Catholic known for prayer and almsgiving, was called, and he himself took it up from the ground. But Autharith, in view of this miracle, caused golden keys to be made and sent them, along with the original keys, to my predecessor of holy memory, proclaiming what sort of miracle had happened through it. Therefore, I have resolved to send Your Excellency these same keys, through which Almighty God cut off a proud and unbelieving man, so that by means of it you who fear and love Him may gain both present and eternal well-being.[1]

As you can see, Gregory explicitly mentions the circumstances of how King Autharith found the Keys of St. Peter, including the story of a soldier's mysterious demise through the intervention of an evil spirit."

Another student, Marcus, ventured, "But why did the soldier kill himself? I get that the letter mentions an evil spirit, but c'mon... do we believe that literally?"

---

[1] Pope Gregory I. Epistle XXVI: To Theocista, Patrician. Translated by James Barmby, Nicene and Post-Nicene Fathers, Second Series, Vol. 12, edited by Philip Schaff and Henry Wace, Christian Literature Publishing Co., 1895.

Scanlon gestured back to the text on the screen. "Look at this line: *'But immediately, seized by a spirit, he thrust the very knife with which he meant to cut it into his own throat, and in that same hour fell down dead.'* The text attributes this to a spirit - in context a demonic spirit. Whether or not you believe in evil spirits, it's in the historical record. My job, folks, is to present the historical documents. It would be scientifically unsound to rule out all possibilities—evil can take many forms. Whether the soldier was seized by madness, or something worse, the source attributes it as supernatural."

A short silence fell. Finally, a young woman, Caitlyn, raised her hand. "What happened to the Keys, then? If it was so important, how did it end up?"

Scanlon brightened. "Excellent question. Although Pope Gregory himself recounts in the letter that King Autharith had the original Keys of St. Peter—and a replica—sent to Pope Pelagius II before Gregory became Pope, we see that it was the replica set that was then sent as a gift to Theoctista, the Byzantine emperor's sister."

At this point, a slight commotion at the back of the room drew Scanlon's attention. The Dean of Academic Affairs, Henry Briggs, slipped in and gave the professor a conspiratorial wink. Scanlon returned the grin, then turned back to the class.

"As to the real keys," he continued, "In another letter, written by Pope Gregory in November 597 to Bishop Anastasius of Antioch, we see the following line, as he projected it onto the large screen:

'I have given instructions to Boniface the guardian, who bears these presents, and I have sent you keys of the blessed apostle Peter... which shine forth with many miracles when placed on the bodies of the sick.'[2]

"This letter, dated 597, provides a crucial piece of evidence," Joseph explained as he pointed to a specific passage. "Here, Pope Gregory the Great explicitly states again that not only were the keys of St. Peter real physical objects but were also imbued with supernatural healing powers. This isn't just a symbolic reference or a metaphorical expression. It's direct evidence of miraculous properties associated with these keys."

The students leaned forward, some jotting notes, others whispering among themselves. Joseph's eyes swept over the class, a sense of satisfaction mingling with the gravity of the historical implications.

"This passage," he continued, "is pivotal because it directly links the physical keys handed down through the church to tangible, supernatural effects. It's evidence that the people of the time believed—and witnessed—these miracles, which further cemented the keys' importance in the history of the Church."

A girl in the front row—Dani, the popular one who usually scrolled through her phone—actually looked up now, interested. "Professor Scanlon, I've got one question—actually two. First, how can a

---

[2] Pope Gregory I. *Epistle XXVI: To Anastatius, Bishop.* Translated by James Barmby, **Nicene and Post-Nicene Fathers, Second Series, Vol. 12**, edited by Philip Schaff and Henry Wace, Christian Literature Publishing Co., 1895.

key heal people? And second, why would the Pope give the keys of Peter away to some bishop in Antioch?"

The professor chuckled. "Two questions, indeed. Let's start with the second: Why send it away? In 597, Rome was under siege and in threat of falling. Pope Gregory the Great took responsibility for defending the city—both physically and spiritually. He likely feared that if Rome fell, the Church might lose lives and priceless treasures, including the Keys. So, he sent his servant Boniface to Antioch, which was part of the more secure Byzantine Empire. Antioch's Church of the Golden Dome was a known repository for relics, including part of the True Cross and the lance of Longinus, which pierced Jesus' side on the cross. In Gregory's mind, those keys would be safest there."

Dani persisted. "But the healing powers?"

Scanlon nodded, rummaging under the lectern. He withdrew a richly bound Bible, the leather glistening under the lecture hall lights. "All right, folks, let's see if any of you can tell me which Bible verse references Peter receiving the keys."

Silence. No hands.

Scanlon blew out a breath. "Notre Dame students, come on! Matthew, chapter 16, verses 18 to 19." He flipped to the passage and read aloud: "*And I tell you, you are Peter, and on this rock I will build my church... I will give you the keys of the kingdom of heaven...what you bind on earth will be bound in heaven*"

He let the words hang in the air. "For centuries, Christians interpreted this mostly as metaphorical—the spiritual authority of the

Church - which is absolutely true, but absolutely incomplete. This sixth-century letter I just showed you is the first strong evidence that there were physical keys in addition to that spiritual dimension. Not only did Jesus work miracles, but in John chapter 14 verse 12 he promised his followers would do even greater works. Pope Gregory simply believed that relics connected to Peter had extraordinary power, including healing."

A handful of students muttered among themselves. One young man, leaning forward in his seat, asked, "So is it like... the relic itself has power? Or is it the faith behind it?"

"Perhaps both," Scanlon allowed. "If you believe in sacramentals and relics, you know the Church teaches they're conduits of grace—but God remains the ultimate source of power. Now, if you want biblical precedent for miracles connected to Peter specifically, let's turn to Acts chapter 5." He flipped to another page, reading: "*Yet more than ever believers were added to the Lord... so that they even carried out the sick into the streets... that Peter's shadow might fall on some of them as he came by... and they were all healed*"

"Wow," murmured a student near the aisle. "That's intense."

"It is intense!" the professor agreed. "So not only was Peter so imbued with the power of God that his shadow healed people miraculously, but in the early Church they found that by laying Peter's keys on the sick, they start getting healed. So, if we accept that Peter's presence or relics once held miraculous potential, it's not too far a leap—at least in the worldview of the time—to believe these Keys carry the same miraculous properties."

Another student, arms folded, raised his hand. "If these Keys are so miraculous, why haven't we heard more about them? Where are they now? I know a lot of sick people who could use a miracle."

Scanlon closed his Bible carefully. "That's the billion-dollar question—one I tackled for my doctoral dissertation at Oxford. After Pope Gregory sent them to Bishop Anastasius in Antioch, the keys apparently remained there, likely in the Church of the Golden Dome... Sorry, students, but Notre Dame was not the first place in the world with a Golden Dome." The students chuckled. As they laughed, he saw his friend Henry smiling in the back.

He continued, "When the Persian Empire under Khosrow II invaded in 611, Antioch eventually fell in 613, and the Persian army deliberately seized the city's Christian relics. They burned the Golden Dome to the ground. Although the Persians made off with many artifacts, they never found the keys. Bishop Anastasius was kidnapped and taken to Persia in exile and there was no more historical record of him. The Keys were never seen again. As the city was rebuilt over centuries, all traces vanished."

He paused. "I've devoted years trying to track them. My best guess is that they were either destroyed or remain hidden beneath layers of rubble somewhere in modern-day Antakya, Turkey. And yes, that's precisely where I did my post-doctoral archaeological work—and where I met my wife."

At the mention of his wife, several students whistled and whooped in good-natured fun. Someone yelled, "Dr. J's got some game!" Another joked, "Serious Riz, Professor!"

Scanlon shook his head, smiling. "All right, settle down. Let's keep it scholarly."

As the students laughed and made jokes about the professor's love life, images of all the intertwining paths that had led him to this lecture hall came to his mind like a rushing wind. His father, Michael Scanlon, had been a beacon of knowledge in church history at the University of Notre Dame, instilling in Joseph a profound respect for the scholarly pursuit of religious truths. His mother, Joelle, brought a different heritage—a Lebanese Catholic who had fled the civil war as a teenager, bringing stories of resilience and faith that echoed through Joseph's childhood. Joseph stood at the front of the lecture hall, his mid-thirties frame, with an olive complexion and dark, wavy hair that hinted at his Lebanese heritage. His deep-set green eyes, a gift from his Irish American father, contrasted sharply with his angular middle eastern features, allowing him to easily pass as fully Lebanese. Though strikingly handsome, with a chiseled jaw and an effortless charm, Joseph never relied on his looks, preferring the substance of his intellect to speak for him.

Summers spent in northern Lebanon, near the historic complexities of the Syrian and Turkish border, had opened young Joseph's eyes to the living tapestry of faith and history in the Middle East. The ancient churches there, guardians of countless relics, told stories of a faith that shaped civilizations. It was these stories, so vividly shared by his mother, that grounded his academic pursuits.

At Notre Dame, Joseph dove into Theology and History, his fascination with Late Antiquity growing with each lecture and text.

This era, marked by the decline of the Roman Empire and the rise of Islam, was a crucible of cultural and religious transformation, and Joseph's fluency in Arabic allowed him unprecedented access to primary sources that were out of reach for many scholars.

His advanced studies took him to Oxford, where he honed his focus on the geopolitical and religious currents of the sixth and seventh centuries. Post-doctorate, he joined an archaeological dig in Antakya, modern-day Antioch, a site as rich in history as it was in relics. It was there, in the courtyard of the small Catholic Church that he met Salma. Her quick wit and deep roots in the region captivated him, and their spirited exchanges over formal Arabic and local dialects marked the beginning of a profound partnership.

Proposing to Salma in Antakya symbolized the merging of their lives, much like the relics they both cherished brought together stories from the past. Their subsequent marriage was a testament to the enduring connections formed by shared faith and heritage, despite the shadows cast by their struggles with infertility.

Just then, the campus bell rang, a cheery electronic chime that signaled the end of the class period. Students began shutting laptops, stuffing notebooks into backpacks. Scanlon raised his hands to get their attention.

"For those who want more details, my dissertation on JSTOR is titled *The Lost Keys of St. Peter: Relics and Geopolitics in Late Antiquity.* And don't forget, finals are next week—study hard, folks."

He closed his notes and turned off the projector. The students trickled out, some lingering to ask quick questions or to shake his hand.

A moment later, Henry Briggs stepped down the aisle, arms wide open. "Joseph, my friend, that was quite a performance. You know how to capture a crowd."

Scanlon grinned, shaking Henry's hand. "All thanks to you for letting me teach this course in the first place."

Henry nodded. "Well, I loved two parts in particular—first, you looked like you were having fun. Good job weaving history and faith together. Second, your quotes from Gregory's letters and the evidence about the keys having healing power really got the students attention. Nicely done."

"Only two? I'll have to work on impressing you more next time."

Henry chuckled. "Come on, wise guy. Let's get some lunch at Legends. I reserved a table for us at twelve-thirty. My treat."

"Sounds great," Scanlon replied, gathering his notes.

They headed for the exit together, leaving the lecture hall behind. As they stepped into the corridor, students bustled around them—some wearing Notre Dame sweatshirts, others sporting headphones. The campus hum was in full swing.

Henry steered them toward a side door, leading out into the crisp Indiana air. Sunlight glinted off the golden dome of the main building in the distance. Scanlon took a moment to appreciate the campus he'd grown up with, the place that had shaped him as much as any ancient city he'd traveled to.

"I'll never get tired of that view," he said, eyes on the iconic dome.

Henry followed his gaze. "Nor I. And you know what? It's good that we cherish our own golden dome. Keeps us mindful that no matter how ancient or distant some relic might be—like those Keys you speak about—there's still a legacy we carry here."

Scanlon gave a soft laugh. "Nicely put. I might just quote you on that in my next class."

"You better footnote me," Henry joked, pushing the door open.

It was 11:30am. Henry noted that he had to make a quick stop back in his office and would meet him at 12:30pm on the dot. As Henry walked through the campus, students thronged around him, discussing weekend plans, sports, and upcoming exams. Amid the normal humdrum, Professor Scanlon allowed himself a brief, inward smile.

THREE

Shadows of Empire

Joseph arrived at Legends Café fifteen minutes early, choosing a quiet table by the window that offered both a view of the bustling university campus and the café's mounted television. Settling in with a steaming cup of coffee, he surveyed the room, his gaze occasionally drifting to the TV where a news anchor was detailing the latest geopolitical tensions. The report on the mounted TV screen displayed a bold caption—"Winter Offensive." For two years now following the United States departure from NATO, Russian President Igor Volkov's campaign to reclaim lands of historical Russian influence had rattled all of Eastern Europe.

As he waited, the screen showed David Mitchell, a seasoned Fox News anchor, reporting on significant Russian military advances in Eastern Europe. "In the war in Eastern Europe, Russian forces have made notable gains in Poland, Lithuania, and Finland," Mitchell reported, his voice underscored by images of maps marked with advancing troops. He outlined three tactical reasons for these successes: the unexpected rapid movements of Russian armored divisions, disruptive cyber warfare impairing NATO communications, and the advantage of harsh winter conditions familiar to Russian forces.

The conversation shifted as Mitchell introduced his guest, British foreign policy analyst Oliver Carrington, to discuss the broader implications of these movements. "With the U.S. out of direct NATO involvement and the remaining NATO countries lacking resources and clear unity, Russian President Igor Volkov has been bold in his advances. Oliver, what's driving Volkov's strategy?"

Carrington adjusted his spectacles before replying, "President Volkov has openly referenced his desire to restore Russia to the borders of Catherine the Great's empire. This era represented Russia at one of its most expansive moments, stretching far into Eastern Europe. Volkov could see regaining these territories as a matter of historical pride. I think there is more to it than that. I believe that these territories create a broader buffer zone to future Western encroachment upon Russia. Geographically, Russia's current western borders, particularly along the East European Plain, are relatively flat and open. Many Russian strategists consider it a traditional invasion route used against Russia through history. By pushing those borders outward, Volkov aims to secure what he views as critical strategic depth."

Mitchell leaned in, pressing further, "And how does Volkov's personal faith play into his political ambitions? He's tying this expansion not just to Russian history, but to the resurgence of the Russian Orthodox faith."

"Despite his morally ambiguous past, Volkov is a devout member of the Russian Orthodox Church," Carrington explained. "He likely views his faith not just as a personal commitment but as a political tool to consolidate power and reinforce national identity. It's an appeal to a sense of divine sanction for his actions—something that might be difficult for Western secular democracies to fully grasp."

Mitchell nodded but circled back to the military implications. "You mentioned the East European Plain and the vulnerability it poses. Can you go into more detail on that?"

Carrington leaned forward. "Historically, Russia's lack of natural defensive barriers to the west has been a major concern. Invaders, from Napoleon to Hitler, have swept across those plains. After the Soviet Union dissolved, Russia lost many buffer states that once cushioned it from potential European threats. With NATO's expansion eastward, Volkov believes Russia's current frontiers are dangerously exposed. Restoring a sphere of influence akin to Catherine's era is, in his view, not just historical romanticism—it's a strategic imperative. By controlling more territory, Russia can better position its forces, develop advanced defense systems, and ensure that NATO bases remain further from Russia's heartland."

Mitchell, with a concerned expression, posed his next question to Carrington. "Given the current situation, is there any hope for de-escalation? Is there a way this conflict could be resolved without further violence?"

Carrington sighed, considering the complexity of the situation. "There is a glimmer of hope, David. One key figure in the Russian military establishment is General Alexei Morozov. He's a seasoned strategist and has been a close confidant of President Volkov for years. However, unlike some of the more hardline elements in Volkov's inner circle, Morozov is known for his pragmatic approach to international relations and his belief in diplomatic solutions when he's been given the chance."

Carrington continued, "General Morozov has a background in both military and diplomatic circles, having served as a military attaché in several European capitals earlier in his career. His moderate views and understanding of the West position him as a potential stabilizing force within the Russian hierarchy. There are whispers among some Western diplomats that if Volkov were to fall from power—either through internal dissent or external pressures—General Morozov could be the one to guide Russia towards a more conciliatory stance. His leadership could pave the way for negotiations and possibly an easing of tensions, as he might seek to balance Russia's strategic interests with a more cooperative relationship with NATO."

Mitchell nodded thoughtfully, "So, while the situation is tense, there might be a path to peace if the right leaders emerge."

"Indeed," Carrington replied. "It's a delicate situation, but in geopolitics, the right mix of pressure and diplomacy can sometimes open unexpected doors."

At this point, Henry Briggs hurried through the café door, looking slightly disheveled and apologetic. "Joseph, sorry I'm late. Got held up at the office," he said, settling down across from Joseph.

"No problem at all, Henry," Jospeh responded with a warm smile, glad for the company of an old friend. He then quickly filled Henry in on the news segment, setting a familiar context for their catch-up.

"It's relentless, isn't it? Every day, something new," Henry sighed, glancing at the screen before turning his attention fully to Joseph.

Henry nodded and then reminisced, "Reminds me of our Notre Dame days, doesn't it? You and I, challenging each other academically, and on the fencing team. Your dad was my professor and still your toughest competition," he chuckled, stirring a sense of nostalgia.

Joseph laughed, a spark of the old competitive spirit in his eyes. "You know, I've always suspected you were his favorite student. And about that fencing match—when are you going to admit that last point was a fluke?"

Henry grinned, teasingly replying, "A fluke? That was skill, my friend. But I'm up for a rematch anytime you say. Ready to defend your honor?"

Their banter eased them into a comfortable rhythm, a testament to years of friendship that had started on campus and endured beyond. This camaraderie was a welcome prelude to more serious discussions, grounding them in shared history as they navigated the complexities of their current realities.

Henry's tone sobered as he turned the conversation back to current events, "Speaking of challenges, this situation with Russia isn't going away any time soon, is it? What's your take on all this, Joe?"

With a deep sigh, Joseph shifted in his seat, ready to dive into deeper waters with his trusted friend, discussing global issues that were as complex as they were distant from the simplicity of their college days.

Seeking a lighter topic, Henry shifted the conversation to Joseph's morning lecture. "Back to your earlier lecture - definitely your best stuff. But there was something I never thought about... do you really believe an evil spirit is what caused the Lombard thief to die?"

Joseph took a deep breath, appreciating the shift away from global politics to historical mysteries. "It's a question of faith and inter-pretation, isn't it? The accounts from that era were steeped in su-pernatural understanding. If we take the text at face value, we must consider all possibilities—despair-driven suicide or demonic influence. My mother, Joelle, used to share stories from Lebanon about spirits and exorcisms in Lebanon that were quite vivid."

Henry listened, fascinated by the blend of personal history and academic analysis. "So, you lean towards believing the demonic influence theory?"

"I do," Joseph affirmed. "Especially considering the context. Those keys weren't ordinary—they were believed to be handed down by Christ himself. Misusing such sacred relics could indeed invite dire consequences, at least according to the beliefs at the time."

Henry chuckled, shaking his head slightly. "I suppose that's one way to keep people from touching things they shouldn't."

The conversation then turned towards Joseph's personal life, particularly his and Salma's ongoing struggle with infertility. Henry's tone softened, "How's Salma holding up with everything?"

Joseph's eyes dimmed a little with the mention of his wife. "She's incredible, Henry. Keeping us both hopeful. We're still undergoing treatments—NaproTechnology. It's been tough, but her faith... it's something else."

"And your mom, still doing those novenas to Saint Charbel for you two?" Henry asked, knowing how much Joseph valued his family's support.

Joseph laughed, a sound tinged with affection and slight exasperation. "Every day. Our house has more icons of Saint Charbel than a church. I dare not move them—mom would never forgive me."

As they neared the end of their meal, Henry's expression turned serious. "Joe, there's another reason I asked you here today. I got a call from Father Ryan this morning. He wants to meet with you at 3:00 p.m. today, and he suggested I could be there with you if you want."

Joseph's fork clattered to his plate, his concern palpable. "What? Why does Father Ryan want to meet with me? Do you know what it's about?"

Henry shook his head. "I honestly don't know, Joe. But I'm sure it's nothing bad."

Joseph looked unconvinced, but he nodded, trying to mask his anxiety. "Okay. Thanks for being there, Henry. I appreciate it."

They finished their meal in a thoughtful silence; each man lost in his own concerns as they prepared to face whatever the afternoon at Notre Dame might bring.

FOUR

Crossroads

Joseph Scanlon arrived at the office of the president of the University of Notre Dame fifteen minutes early, a routine that had always served him well in his academic career. However, today his punctuality was met with an unexpected wait as he found himself seated in the finely appointed waiting area, watching the minutes tick slowly by. After thirty long minutes, Father Ryan's secretary finally opened the door.

"Professor Scanlon, Father Ryan will see you now," she announced with a professional smile.

Joseph stood, adjusting his jacket, and followed her into the spacious office where Father Ryan, a man whose commanding presence was softened by a pastoral gentleness, stood waiting. The president of the university greeted him with a firm handshake, his grip strong but his eyes warm.

"Joseph, good to see you. Before we sit, would you mind if we say a quick prayer?" Father Ryan's voice was inviting, making it clear that this was more than just a formality.

"Of course, Father," Joseph agreed, feeling a slight relief in the face of spiritual support.

Father Ryan clasped his hands and bowed his head. "Heavenly Father, grant us wisdom and peace as we discuss the matters at hand. May Your guidance illuminate our path and Your grace be with us. Amen."

"Amen," Joseph echoed, finding a momentary peace as he took a seat across from Father Ryan's large, oak desk.

The room was quiet for a moment before Father Ryan began with personal inquiries, his tone warm. "How's Salma doing?"

"She's well, thank you," Joseph responded, his answers brief but polite, his mind anxious about the real reasons behind the meeting.

"And your father, how is he holding up?" Father Ryan continued, showing genuine concern.

"He's managing, Father. Thank you for asking," Joseph replied, his responses succinct, eager to get to the heart of the matter.

Father Ryan nodded, a reflective look crossing his face. "You know, I owe a great deal to your father. When I was just starting out here, he supported my first research grant. He went out of his way when no one else would. I've never forgotten that favor."

Joseph felt a sense of pride for his father's longstanding impact but remained tense, sensing the conversation was about to take a serious turn.

Father Ryan sighed, the weight of his position evident. "Joseph, I wish our discussion today were under better circumstances. It's about the Late Antiquity Studies program."

Joseph's heart tightened, a chill running down his spine. "Yes, Father?"

"The board has made a decision to phase out the program, effective at the end of this academic year," Father Ryan delivered the news with a heavy heart.

"But the program has been thriving. Why would they decide to cut it now?" Joseph's voice was tinged with disbelief and frustration.

Father Ryan leaned forward, his expression somber. "It's a decision that doesn't make sense to many of us. Ever since the university became board-led, we've seen an increase in decisions driven more by financial metrics than educational values. There's been a push from certain powerful board members, and unfortunately, they've swayed the majority this time."

Joseph struggled to process the news, his mind racing with implications for his career and his students.

"There is, however, a potential opportunity that could be a good fit for you," Father Ryan continued, hoping to offer a silver lining. "Dr. Alexei Lavrov, the director of the Center for Russian Orthodox Studies, is very interested in having you join their team for a significant project. They're looking for someone to lead one of their archaeological digs in the Middle East."

Joseph, still reeling, barely managed to nod. "What kind of opportunity?"

"It's a prestigious project, and Alexei believes your expertise would be invaluable," Father Ryan explained. "He's currently in Chicago but will be driving to South Bend tomorrow. He would very much like to discuss the project with you over breakfast, if you're open to it."

The offer hung in the air, heavy with both opportunity and sudden change. Joseph hesitated, his future uncertain, yet the potential to continue his work in a new capacity was enticing.

"I'll think about it, Father. It's a lot to consider," Joseph admitted, the weight of the decision pressing down on him.

"I understand, and I encourage you to meet with him. Despite the circumstances, this could be a valuable step forward," Father Ryan assured him, his tone both empathetic and encouraging. "Remember, Joseph, Notre Dame has always taken care of its own. We will support you through this transition, and I believe that this new path could lead to great things."

Joseph nodded, a mix of gratitude and apprehension in his heart. "Thank you, Father. I appreciate your support and your prayers. I don't see what could go wrong with a meeting with Dr Lavrov. I will be very grateful for you to set the meeting up."

"You got it Joseph. I'll make sure that my secretary gets everything set up. As always, I'll be praying for you, Joseph. God works in mysterious ways, and perhaps, this is a door opening where an-other has closed," Father Ryan said, standing to escort Joseph to the door with a reassuring smile.

Joseph left the office feeling a tumult of emotions but held onto a thread of hope, buoyed by Father Ryan's faith and the unexpected opportunity that awaited his decision. As he stepped out into the crisp afternoon air, his path was uncertain, but the next steps were beginning to form, one prayer and one decision at a time.

FIVE

Gifts and Secrets

Joseph pulled into the long, winding driveway leading to his parents' colonial-style home, the headlights carving a path through the early evening darkness. Gravel crackled under the tires. Salma smoothed her hair in the passenger seat, catching Joseph's eye for a moment—she smiled, a playful glint that never failed to raise his spirits.

Salma, in her mid-thirties, had an air of timeless beauty and a presence that was unmistakably her own. Her Chaldean heritage was evident in her striking features: deep-set, almond-shaped eyes framed by thick, dark lashes, holding a warmth and depth that seemed to tell stories of ancient lands. Her skin, a rich olive tone, glowed with vitality, accentuating high cheekbones and a graceful, slightly aquiline nose that lent her an air of elegance and strength. Her hair, a cascade of dark, lustrous waves, framed her face perfectly, adding to the uniqueness that made her unforgettable. The combination of her features created a harmony that was both beautiful and distinct, ensuring she could never be mistaken for anyone else.

The house glowed with warm lights in every window, and the front porch was awash in a welcoming amber hue. Still, Joseph's stomach fluttered with the distinct mix of comfort and nerves that always hit right before a dinner with his parents.

"Oh, you look tense," Salma teased, leaning over and stroking his arm. "Afraid of your mother's cooking or her attention?" As Joseph navigated the final turn in the driveway, his mind churned with conflicting thoughts. He felt the weight of the secret he was carrying, the burden of losing his job. The urge to confide in Salma was strong, to share the truth and unburden his heart. But each time he considered it, a knot of anxiety tightened in his chest.

He convinced himself that he didn't want to worry her unnecessarily, not when there was a promising interview just around the corner. It seemed pragmatic to wait, to spare her the stress until he had a clearer picture of their future. Yet, deep down, he knew this reasoning was a flimsy veil over the real issue—his own shame. Admitting the loss felt like admitting failure, and the thought of seeing disappointment in her eyes was unbearable.

Joseph glanced at Salma, her laughter a soothing balm to his troubled mind. He told himself that soon, once he had good news to share, he'd let her in on everything. For now, he tucked away and decided to evade.

"Definitely not her cooking," he joked. "The attention, on the other hand, is a force of nature."

They stepped out and made their way up the porch steps. Before Joseph could even knock, his mother, Joelle, swung open the door. Her chestnut hair, streaked with silver, was pulled back in a tight bun, and her eyes twinkled with exuberance. The moment she caught sight of Salma, Joelle let out a cry of delight.

"My sweet Salma!" Joelle's voice rang out through the hallway. She grabbed Salma's hands, practically pulling her inside. "Come in, come in! You must be so tired. I have everything prepared."

Joseph moved to embrace his mother in greeting, but Joelle was too fixated on Salma, looking her up and down like a curious seamstress taking measurements. She clucked approvingly. "My goodness, you're radiant tonight. And your hair—just beautiful."

Salma laughed, the sound mixing amusement and affection. "Thank you, Joelle." She tilted her head. "I'm not sure what makes me so radiant, maybe the excitement of dinner with you?"

Joelle patted her cheek with motherly confidence. "Nonsense. You've got something going on." She rummaged in her apron pocket, producing a small glass vial. "I'm going to bless you and your future children with the holy oil from Saint Charbel's tomb."

Joseph exhaled, half in amusement, half in exasperation. "Mom, you don't have to do this every single time." Joelle gave Joseph a knowing look, her eyes twinkling with conviction. "Oh, Joseph, never doubt the power of Saint Charbel's intercession. Every demon would flee when he invoked the name of Jesus."

Ignoring him, Joelle uncorked the vial. The scent drifted upward as she dabbed a bit on her thumb. "Joseph," she said sharply, "breakthrough only comes with persevering faith. We don't do things halfway in this house, especially not prayer." She turned back to Salma with a kind but intense smile. "Close your eyes, habibi."

Salma did as she was asked, a slight grin betraying her amusement. Joelle made the sign of the cross on Salma's forehead, then pressed her thumb lightly on her abdomen. "Bless this woman's body, Lord," she prayed, eyes closed in deep reverence. "Grant her the gift she desires in Your good time."

Joseph shifted from foot to foot, feeling equal measures of love for his mother's steadfast devotion and embarrassment at the spectacle. When Joelle finished, Salma opened her eyes, a mischievous spark dancing there. She shot Joseph a flirtatious glance that all but said, "You'll never understand us Middle Eastern women."

"And you," Joelle said, eyes now on her son, "you behave yourself. Let the Lord handle what's beyond your control."

Salma slid her hand into Joseph's. "He tries, Joelle. Believe me, he tries," she teased, then turned to him with a fond, mocking sigh. "You'll never fully understand Middle Eastern women, my dear" saying out loud what he already saw in her eyes. Joseph loved how clever she was. He chuckled. "I'm starting to see that."

Joelle stepped back to admire them both, clearly satisfied. "Now, Salma, come to the kitchen with me. I've got fresh kibbeh waiting, and the tabbouleh could use another taste-tester."

Together, Salma and Joelle disappeared down the hallway, leaving Joseph alone in the foyer, inhaling the aroma of roasted lamb and spices that wafted in from the kitchen. He shook his head, chuckling to himself—he truly would never fully grasp his mother's boundless energy.

Just then, he heard heavy, familiar footsteps behind him. He turned to see Michael, his father, standing in the living room archway. Michael was a wiry man in his mid-sixties, but his bearing gave the impression of something iron-forged. Dressed in a flannel shirt and jeans, he looked like the retired outdoorsman he was, the hints of white in his beard marking him with a stately, rugged air.

"Son," Michael greeted, stepping forward to shake his hand, though Joseph pulled him in for a quick embrace instead.

"Dad." Joseph inhaled, noticing the faint smell of gun oil that always clung to his father's clothes. "How's retirement?"

Michael grinned, leading Joseph through the living room and toward the back door. "Not so retired when you've got a property like this to manage. Good thing I love the wide-open space." Joseph noticed the tightness in his father's face that evening, a faint pallor that seemed more pronounced than usual. Michael waved off Joseph's concern, insisting it was just a headache from all the yard work, but the uneasy flutter in Joseph's stomach didn't subside. He glanced down the hallway toward the kitchen. "I got everything set up outside. Wanna head out back for a bit?"

Joseph nodded slowly. "Sure, Dad. Let me guess—shooting range?"

Michael's eyes twinkled. "Like you even have to ask. I've got new targets lined up."

They slipped through the sliding glass door, stepping onto a large wooden deck that overlooked a sprawling backyard. Moonlight reflected off a row of silhouettes and steel gongs arranged in the far corner of the field. Joseph stuffed his hands in his jacket pockets, memories flickering of the times he'd stand beside his father, the crack of rifle shots echoing in the distance.

"When I bought this place in Niles," Michael explained, "I did it for one reason: to have enough space for target practice without someone calling the cops every time I fired a few rounds." He let out a small laugh that didn't entirely reach his eyes. "South Bend was too cramped for a man with my hobbies."

Joseph recognized the nostalgia in his father's gaze. "Remember when you first took me shooting?" he asked quietly, the memory drifting into the present. "I think I was eleven. The rifle nearly knocked me on my butt, but you said I had good form."

Michael's laugh this time was more genuine, a deep rumble. "You did have good form—and you turned out to be a better shot than most. But let's see if you've kept those skills sharpened."

Joseph followed his father over to the small wooden bench that served as a makeshift shooting station. A scoped rifle, a classic .308 bolt-action, lay ready, along with earmuffs and a box of ammunition. Michael passed the earmuffs to Joseph, who slipped them on, the world muffling in an instant.

They spent the next ten minutes trading shots at various distances, the thunderous cracks of the rifle carrying across the fields. Joseph felt a rush of adrenaline, the old sense of bonding with his father tugging at his heart. He never truly loved shooting—he'd done it because it was an avenue to spend time with the man he so admired. Still, muscle memory kicked in; bullet after bullet slammed into steel targets with resounding clangs.

When Joseph finally lowered the rifle and set it on safe, he glanced over at Michael. His father wore a faint, proud smile.

"Well, you haven't lost your touch," Michael admitted, stepping up and examining the targets through binoculars. "Tight grouping at three hundred yards. That's impressive."

"Luck, mostly," Joseph said, grinning. "I've had a lot on my mind, so maybe I was aiming all that stress at the target."

Michael chuckled. "Stress is part of life, son. Sometimes it helps your focus, sometimes it doesn't. But you shot well—better than me, if I'm being honest."

For a second, Joseph just gaped, touched by the admission. "You sure? You're always the one who taught me you have to be steady under pressure."

"Yep, and you just proved me right," Michael said. Then his expression shifted, drifting into the thoughtful. "Now that we've settled that, I'd like to hear the story of how you met Salma... one more time."

Joseph frowned, setting the rifle down gently. "Dad, you know that story like the back of your hand."

Michael's voice softened. "I know, but humor an old man. It's important to me. I love hearing it, especially from you."

Realizing how serious his father was, Joseph nodded, an indulgent smile forming. He took a seat on the old bench, and Michael sat next to him. A chill breeze rustled the grass.

"All right," Joseph began, staring across the moonlit field. "It was in Antakya. I felt so homesick—being away from you, Mom, the States. It was the first time I'd been out of the country for longer than a few weeks, and I had no clue what I was doing with all that Byzantine archaeological work. I was just this grad student rummaging around dusty ruins, focusing on the region's old churches and relics. You remember how often we'd talk on the phone. The calls were so expensive."

Michael nodded, his eyes flicking with memory. "Your mother nearly had a heart attack when the phone bill arrived."

Joseph smiled. "She insisted I go to Mass if I missed home. 'If you want to feel at home, you gotta go to church,' she'd say. I wasn't all that devout, but I did it anyway. I walked into this centuries-old Catholic church, heard the chanting and the bells, smelled the incense—and I'll tell you, Dad, I felt something shift. I still can't pinpoint it. Anyway, once Mass ended, I stepped out into the courtyard... and there she was. Salma."

He paused, recalling the image of her leaning against a stone column, lit by the golden Turkish sun. "She had this grace about her, a kindness in her eyes—but also a confidence that set her apart from everyone else. I first assumed her brother Aziz was actually her boyfriend, so I pretty much clammed up. But then I noticed they behaved more like siblings—bickering and laughing at the same time."

Michael grinned. "I can imagine the relief on your face when you realized he was her brother."

"Oh yeah," Joseph said, chuckling. "But I was still awkward, and she was... well, she was obviously out of my league. She came up to me, made small talk—about the weather, about the liturgy. I couldn't believe it; she was flirting, and I felt a million miles behind. Then we bonded over faith history—Chaldean Catholic heritage, the region's tie to early Christianity, all that. Eventually, I invited her to a weekday Mass, and she invited me to her family's place for dinner. Let me tell you, Dad, Middle Eastern hospitality is no joke. They brought out dish after dish... the best Mediterranean food of my life. I felt so welcomed, so seen. Her parents just embraced me like I was a long-lost cousin. And Aziz? He became like a brother to me from day one." Joseph continued, his voice carrying a mix of nostalgia and warmth. "Growing up half Lebanese and half American, I always felt like I was straddling two worlds. But being with Salma's family, it was like I finally found the missing piece of myself. It was the first time I truly felt fully alive, fully accepted."

Michael listened intently, noticing the light in his son's eyes. "You felt like you belonged," he said softly.

"Exactly," Joseph replied, nodding. "In their home, I wasn't just seen as an American. I was understood in a way that connected deeply to my Middle Eastern roots, to Mom's heritage. They got me, you know? It was enlightening, like discovering a part of me that had been waiting to be acknowledged."

Michael smiled, feeling a sense of pride and understanding for his son's journey.

Michael folded his arms over his chest, listening intently. "Go on."

Joseph swallowed, remembering the moment of epiphany. "There was a Mass one day—a small liturgy. During the consecration, when the priest lifted the host and said, 'This is my body,' something in me cracked wide open. All the knowledge you and Mom taught me over the years about God, everything I learned academically—it ceased to be an abstract concept. Suddenly, it was real, right there in my heart - that was not just a piece of bread. It was the body of Jesus given for me! At that exact moment, I heard this voice inside me say, 'As Jesus gave Himself for you completely on the cross, you are to give yourself completely to Salma.'"

Michael listened, face unmoving except for the flicker of understanding in his eyes.

Joseph's voice dropped. "When I glanced over, Salma was staring right back at me, tears in her eyes. After Mass ended, neither of us moved—there was this hush, like the hush we have here now. I finally asked her if she heard something in her heart during the consecration. She nodded, and we both knew we'd heard the same call."

A breeze swept past them. For a moment, the only sound was the rustle of leaves.

Joseph shifted. "Long story short, a few weeks later, I took her up to ancient St. Peter's Church carved into the side of the mountain—technically a pilgrimage site, not a functioning parish. Still, some American group was celebrating Mass there. After they left, we stayed behind to pray, alone in that ancient stone sanctuary. That's where I got down on one knee. I recalled to her how just as Jesus built his Church upon Peter the rock, I told her I brought her here because God has called us to be together forever and I want our marriage to be built upon the same faith that Jesus saw in Peter. With tears in her eyes, she said yes. We sat right outside that ancient Church overlooking Antioch till morning, marveling that this city was where Christians were first called 'Christians,' and the place where I truly encountered Christ—and my future wife."

Joseph paused, looking at his father. To his surprise, tears glistened on Michael's cheeks. The old man quickly dashed them away with the back of his hand.

"Dad," Joseph said softly, "you okay?"

"A wife," Michael murmured, voice thick, "is the greatest gift God can give a man. Son, your job, your career, your money—they're nothing compared to your wife. Cherish her. Take care of her every day of your life."

Joseph's heart gave a jolt of alarm. He rarely saw his father cry—if ever. "Dad, is everything all right?"

Michael took a shaky breath, then placed a hand on Joseph's shoulder. "I got some news this morning. Stage 4 cancer." He said it plainly, as if stating the weather. "Doctors say four to six months, maybe. I'm not telling your mother, not yet."

Joseph felt as if the rifle's recoil slammed into his chest. "What... Dad, no... this can't be real. There has to be a treatment plan." He reached for Michael's hand, voice shaking. "We'll fight this. There must be—"

Michael shook his head, eyes brimming but resolute. "They offered aggressive treatment, chemo, surgery. The doctors said it might buy a bit of time, but the side effects would be brutal. I'd lose my strength. I'd be in pain, maybe bed-bound. I decided to decline it, to trust whatever time God grants. I want to live what's left of my life on my feet, doing what I love, not in a hospital."

Joseph pressed his palms to his face, exhaling a ragged breath. Tears stung at the corners of his eyes. "Mom will kill you, Dad. You know that. She'll find out."

"Maybe, but not now," Michael said gravely. "I want these last months to be good ones. Please, Joseph, respect my wishes. Don't tell her. She'll have me running from specialist to specialist, and I don't want that."

Joseph hesitated, searching his father's gaze. The request felt impossible to honor. But he saw the steel in dad's eyes—the quiet acceptance, the certainty that he was doing what he needed to do.

"All right," Joseph said at last, voice quavering. "I promise." He pulled his father into a fierce hug, burying his face in the worn flannel of the older man's shirt. Michael's hand came up, patting Joseph's back gently.

They stayed like that for a long moment, father and son locked in an embrace. Joseph tried to speak, but words lodged in his throat. Then, quietly, Michael cleared his throat and leaned back.

"That's not the only thing," Joseph managed, wiping at his eyes. "I had a meeting with Father Ryan at Notre Dame. The Late Antiquities Department is being eliminated. My position is... essentially gone. I have a job interview tomorrow, but I don't know what's next."

Michael's brow furrowed. "That's not right. You have built up that department since you came and Notre Dame never axes growing programs. But if they're dead set on it... well, then. You might need a Plan B." He lifted his chin. "There's got to be something going on with the board. I've got a few old friends, a few connections. Even in retirement, I'm not without influence."

Joseph released a shaky sigh, nodding. "Just... keep it between us, please. Salma doesn't know either. I don't want to add more stress."

Michael's lips tightened. "All right, if that's what you need. But don't wait too long, son."

They exchanged solemn nods. Then, as though obeying some silent cue, both men pulled themselves together, blinking away tears. In an uncanny act of synchronicity, they straightened their shoulders and stepped away from the shooting bench.

"We should probably get inside," Joseph murmured. "Mom's going to wonder where we are."

"Yep," Michael said, drawing in a bracing breath. "Let's go, soldier."

Together, they walked toward the house, leaving the targets and the looming darkness of the backyard behind. As they opened the back door, they found Joelle and Salma busy setting the long dining table. The clattering of plates and silverware was a cheerful domestic sound, and the warm glow of the overhead chandelier contrasted starkly with the sober revelations in the yard.

Joelle, noticing their entrance, set down a bowl of tabbouleh with gusto. "Took you boys long enough. Everything okay out there?"

Without missing a beat, Joseph walked straight to his mother and wrapped her in a hug, one so tight she stiffened in surprise. "Thank you for everything, Mom," he whispered. "I'm so grateful for you."

Joelle blinked, then patted his shoulder. "What's gotten into you? Did you hurt yourself out there?"

He pulled back, forcing a small smile. "I'm fine. Just... wanted to remind you how important you are."

Michael followed suit, giving Joelle a quick, affectionate kiss on the cheek, though he avoided her searching gaze. Salma, sensing some shift in the atmosphere, cast Joseph a questioning look. He answered it with a tender, grateful squeeze of her hand. Her eyes shimmered with concern, but she said nothing.

They settled around the table. Steam rose from platters of roasted lamb, kibbeh, and grilled vegetables and tabbouleh. The kitchen smelled of garlic, lemon, and parsley, a bouquet that brought instant comfort to Joseph's senses. As everyone filled their plates, Joelle peppered the conversation with excited talk about Salma's upcoming doctor's appointment.

"Now, tomorrow's the day, yes?" Joelle said, voice practically vibrating with anticipation. "I have a good feeling about this, I really do."

Salma, ever modest, gave a small shrug. "It's just a routine checkup. But... we'll see."

Joelle pressed on, undeterred by Salma's reluctance. "You never know when good news will come. I've been storming heaven with my prayers."

Michael busied himself slicing lamb but cast Joseph a quick side glance, as if to say: We'll keep our secrets for now. Salma directed her gaze to her father-in-law. "So, Dad, how was your day?"

Michael calmly swallowed his bite. "Oh, you know. Daily Mass, breakfast with Father Kevin, a quick visit to the doctor for a routine checkup—nothing to report," he added pointedly, looking straight at Joseph.

Joseph nodded, swallowing the complicated emotions that threatened to roil in his stomach. "Same here," he said. "Just another day."

They conversed lightly through dinner, skirting around any topics that might betray the truths father and son had exchanged. Joseph nodded, feigned interest in the local parish events his mother discussed, and chipped in a joke or two about the bishop's homilies. Even as the words flowed, a current of tension hummed beneath the surface, recognized only by the two men. But Joelle and Salma seemed unaware, or at least they let it pass without comment.

Eventually, the plates were cleared, leftovers packed, and the warm sense of routine replaced the earlier solemn hush. When it was time to leave, Joseph and Salma took their coats from the foyer, promising to be back the next weekend. Joelle gave her daughter-in-law another big hug, whispering a final prayer for her. Michael embraced Salma as well, but his eyes lingered on Joseph, an understanding silently exchanged.

Outside, the night air carried the faint smell of damp leaves. The couple climbed into their car, shutting the doors softly, as if not to break the fragile bubble of peace that had formed. Joseph turned the key, and the engine sputtered to life. Silence settled between them while they navigated the winding drive leading back to the main road. Finally, Salma broke it, her voice quivering.

"I'm sorry," she said, tears suddenly pooling. "I tried to keep it together all night, but your mom's excitement about tomorrow—it gets to me." She took a trembling breath. "Fourteen years of marriage, Joseph. Fourteen. And we still don't have a child to call our own."

Joseph's heart clenched at her raw sadness. He reached across the console, lacing his fingers with hers. "Salma," he said softly. "Look at me."

She turned, eyes shining under the faint glow of the dashboard lights.

"You remember what we both heard at Mass in Antakya? 'This is my body, given for you.'" He paused, his voice thick with emotion. "That's the promise I made to you at the altar. No matter what happens—children or no children—that doesn't change."

Salma's tears fell freely now. Her lips parted, but words failed her. Joseph pulled the car onto the shoulder of the road. He put it in park, turned on the hazard lights, and swiveled to face her completely.

He brushed a tear from her cheek. "I love you. Unconditionally. If we're never blessed with children, my vow to God still holds. My love for you holds and it grows every day. I am completely fulfilled by you with or without children."

She let out a soft sob, pressing her forehead against his. "Joseph, I don't want to let you down."

"You won't." He cupped her chin. "You never have."

For a moment, neither spoke. The night was silent, save for the hum of the engine and the soft clicking of the hazard lights. Salma exhaled shakily, then nodded, determination kindling in her eyes. "We'll keep hoping, keep praying. But no matter what, I'm grateful for you."

Joseph kissed her gently, then eased the car back onto the road. They drove the rest of the way in a reflective hush, each lost in swirling thoughts of heartbreak, of precious family dinners, of uncertain futures. But overshadowing it all was a love that had carried them this far—and would carry them through whatever else was coming.

By the time they reached home, the house was silent and dark. They stepped inside, flicked on just a small lamp in the hallway, and wordlessly slipped off their shoes. Salma turned off the overhead light in the living room, casting them into gentle darkness again. She squeezed Joseph's hand one last time before heading upstairs. He followed, heart pounding with the magnitude of all that had transpired.

In the hush of their bedroom, Salma slid under the covers, eyes still wet, but calmer. Joseph lay beside her, curling an arm around her waist. He felt her breathe against him, matching his own slow rhythm. The future was uncertain—Michael's secret illness, Joseph's threatened career, and the continuing ache of childlessness—but at least for tonight, they held one another, anchored by that persistent, unwavering vow: This is my body, given for you.

And as the darkness of night settled around them, Joseph prayed silently, not just for answers, but for the courage to endure—

trusting that somewhere, in the midst of heartbreak and hope, God was at work, weaving a plan far bigger than he could imagine.

SIX

The Offer and the Grab

J oseph woke to a dim stripe of sunlight crossing the bed, the telltale sign that dawn had arrived. Salma lay beside him with her back turned, and for a moment, he thought she might still be asleep. He leaned closer, intending a gentle kiss on her shoulder. She shifted, yawned softly, then twisted around to face him.

"Morning," she murmured, voice husky with sleep.

"Morning," he answered. "Busy day?"

She nodded. "The big appointment, then errands—bank, post office, some groceries, and hopefully back in time to answer emails before lunch."

Joseph tucked a strand of hair behind her ear. "I hope everything's smooth."

He paused briefly, taking stock of her tired eyes. Part of him wanted to linger and reassure her they'd find a path through everything, but the clock read half past seven, and Salma had to leave within minutes.

"Love you," she said softly, then swung her legs over the edge of the bed and headed for the shower.

Joseph dressed in a plain button-down and jeans, grabbed a quick coffee in the kitchen, and kissed her goodbye by the front door. Their morning routine felt truncated, the conversation almost perfunctory. He told himself he needed to minimize the drama and not tell her about the meeting—she had enough on her plate.

Once Salma was gone, the house felt hollow. Joseph wandered back into the kitchen, rinsing his coffee cup before sorting through a small stack of unopened mail. Most were flyers or credit card offers, but one envelope from the mortgage company caught his eye. He slit it open, scanning the lines:

"Due to your updated escrow analysis, your monthly mortgage payment will increase to..."

His jaw tightened. The tax adjustment would add a few hundred dollars per month, money they could scarcely spare now that the Late Antiquities Department was shutting down—and with it, his job.

"Perfect timing," he muttered, tossing the paper on the counter. He felt a surge of anxiety. He was supposed to be the provider. He stared at the letter, the figure seeming to taunt him from the page. He stuffed it into a drawer labeled FINANCIALS, trying to put it out of his mind. Dwelling on it wouldn't help; he had to get ready for the meeting with Dr. Lavrov.

The morning sun glinted off the windshield as he maneuvered down quiet suburban streets. Though the bright rays suggested a pleasant day, an undercurrent of anxiety tailed him. His father's grim prognosis weighed on him like a lead vest; the entire situation with Notre Dame's board chafed at his sense of loyalty. He flicked on the radio for a distraction, but his mind replayed yesterday's conversation with Father Ryan about the department closing. He still felt a hollow betrayal.

Yet he couldn't fully suppress a spark of curiosity over this meeting with Dr. Lavrov. His published articles on Pope Gregory the Great's historical and political influence on the Eastern Church had intrigued Joseph. Lavrov had challenged the typical West-centric view by presenting evidence of Gregory's letters actively shaping Orthodox liturgy and monastic practices. Perhaps this conversation was an opportunity, not just an interruption.

He reached the campus by 9:35, parking near the Basilica of the Sacred Heart. Stepping out, he inhaled the crisp late-winter air. Overhead, the sky was a striking blue, the golden dome shining in the sunlight. He followed a winding path toward the Grotto of Our Lady of Lourdes. Students passed him in twos and threes, some sipping coffee, others chatting about exams. Everything hummed with normalcy, while Joseph carried the weight of imminent decisions.

Soon, the Grotto's rocky facade and statue of Mary came into view. A handful of people knelt or sat on benches, heads bowed in prayer. Nearby, a small knot of students in hoodies and jeans lit cigarettes. He always found it striking: devout prayer a mere few paces from casual disregard. Across the walkway, others strode past without giving the site a second glance. The entire spectrum of faith and apathy, packed into a single campus landmark.

Joseph checked his watch: 9:47. He leaned against a low stone railing near the Grotto entrance, scanning the clusters of visitors. Five minutes later, he heard a clear, confident voice behind him.

"Dr. Scanlon, I presume?"

He turned to see a tall man approaching in a black peacoat. He stood well over six feet and carried his fifty-something years with a polished composure. The suit jacket beneath his coat fit with crisp precision across his shoulders, and the dark vest accentuated his long, lean frame. Trimmed with exacting care, his refined facial hair—somewhere between a closely clipped beard and a sophisticated goatee—showed subtle flecks of silver. A square jawline and sharp cheekbones gave him a cultivated authority, while the measured scrutiny of his gray eyes suggested a man accustomed to respect without ever raising his voice.

"Yes," Joseph said, offering his hand. "Dr. Lavrov?"

"That's me. Thank you for meeting me here. I appreciate your punctuality."

"How was your trip from Chicago?" Joseph asked.

Dr. Lavrov dipped his head in a small nod. "Uneventful, which is how I like my drives."

He glanced around before continuing, "There are many prominent Russian Orthodox leaders in this region, and I take the opportunity to connect with colleagues whenever I visit. The Orthodox presence here has grown in recent years, and maintaining strong ties within our academic and religious circles is essential for the work we do. My center has partnerships with several theologians who have deep historical expertise in Eastern Christianity, and I try to ensure our research aligns with their contributions. You have a lovely campus and it's not far from Chicago. I chose the Grotto because it seemed like the spiritual heart of Notre Dame."

Joseph glanced back at the candles flickering. "It is. Many people think Notre Dame is entirely Irish in origin, but in truth, the Holy Cross priests who founded it were French. That explains this Lourdes-inspired Grotto."

Lavrov looked around with faint amusement. "Popular myth often ignores the French dimension." He gestured forward. "Shall we walk? I'd like to find a less crowded spot to talk."

They began along a path skirting a small reflecting pool. Joseph slipped his hands in his jacket pockets. "So, Father Ryan said you had a proposition related to Russian Orthodox studies. He hinted it might dovetail with my own research."

Lavrov's lips curved in a thoughtful smile. "I've long admired your work on the Keys of St. Peter. Your dissertation was particularly bold, suggesting the physical keys were real, not just a metaphor. You also addressed their supposed miraculous power."

Joseph inhaled sharply. "I realize it's controversial. Most academic circles dismiss relic traditions as mythology, but the evidence in Gregory's letters was too explicit to ignore. There were testimonies of healing linked to contact with these keys."

Lavrov brushed aside a strand of hair blown by the wind. "Controversy is usually where truth hides, Dr. Scanlon. You have no idea

60

how refreshing it is to speak to another scholar who won't dismiss those historical accounts outright."

They reached a gentle bend by the lake. A couple of ducks glided over the water's surface. Joseph felt momentarily relieved to be away from campus hustle.

Lavrov slowed his pace and turned toward Joseph. "Tell me, Dr. Scanlon, do you really believe the Keys of St. Peter are real?"

Joseph hesitated for a moment, adjusting his glasses as he considered his words. "Well, that depends on how one interprets Pope Gregory's writings. There are a few options. First, Jesus physically gave Peter keys as a sign of authority. Second, you could argue there were no actual keys at all, that the reference is purely metaphorical—symbolizing spiritual power given to Peter and his successors. Then, there's a third theory that suggests keys were placed upon Peter's body at his burial, as a visible token of his role within the early Church."

Lavrov let out a sharp exhale, waving a hand impatiently. "Yes, yes, I know all of this. I have read your dissertation at least twenty times. I am not asking what scholars think—I am asking what you believe."

Joseph pursed his lips, feeling the weight of the question. Finally, he spoke with quiet conviction. "I believe there are real keys. The details of how Peter received them may be lost to time, but I have no doubt they existed, and I believe they contain power."

Lavrov's eyes narrowed with interest. Joseph continued, his voice gaining intensity. "I have studied Pope Gregory the Great more than any other historical figure. He was not a man prone to superstition or embellishment. He was one of the most pragmatic leaders of his era, a man of faith, yes, but also a man of reason. When he told Bishop Anastasius that the keys possessed miraculous power, he meant it. He was not speaking in metaphor."

Joseph sighed, his tone turning wistful. "Yet despite all my research, despite the postdoctoral excavations I worked on, I never found anything that could prove or disprove their location. And when the Persians took Antioch in 613, any remaining trace of them was likely lost forever. We may never truly know what became of them."

Their walk brought them near the Basilica of the Sacred Heart, the golden dome shimmering in the afternoon light. Lavrov glanced at the towering structure before turning back to Joseph, his expression unreadable. "Perhaps we will know soon enough."

Lavrov paused, opened his briefcase, and drew out a tablet. "Thank you for answering my questions. I needed to know whether you are a true believer. Yes, we will get to the proposition but first I have something to show you." Lavrov opened an image on the tablet: a fragment of parchment, lines of ancient Latin script. He tapped the screen. "Let me know what you make of this text."

Joseph hunched over the image of the parchment. He translated under his breath, slowly and methodically:

To His Excellency Bonosus,

Amidst the relentless siege by the Persian forces, we find ourselves unable to escape the confines of our city. In these dire times, I have taken it upon myself to safeguard the sacred Keys of Peter from the clutches of these invaders. It is imperative that they remain hidden and out of their reach. Anticipating our likely exile, I have devised a means by which only a devout follower of Christ may recover them.

Simple instructions have been left within the hallowed cathedral, in the hope that one day Rome may dispatch someone worthy and righteous to reclaim these treasures of the Church and restore them to the rightful successor of Peter. I earnestly pray that your valiant defense of our city renders this precaution unnecessary.

With faith and hope,

Patriarch Anastasius

Joseph looked up, goosebumps along his arms. "Where did you find this?"

Lavrov's eyes flicked toward the Golden Dome. "It appears Notre Dame isn't the only place with a Golden Dome. My Center has been quietly funding a dig in Antakya—ancient Antioch for the last nine months. You mentioned in your writings that Gregory sent the Keys to Bishop Anastasius at the Church of the Golden Dome, which was later lost. My team has reason to believe we've located that very site."

Joseph's eyes gleamed with excitement as he continued, "You see, everything lines up perfectly now. Bonosus was indeed the governor of Antioch during the time when the Church of the Golden

Dome was said to have been constructed. Historical records mention his ambitious projects to enhance the city's prestige, but there was always a gap in the documentation—a missing piece that eluded historians for centuries." I've spent years on Antioch's history and even participated in excavations there. We never found the Church of the Golden Dome. I never dreamed someone would actually find it.

Lavrov responded, "In the aftermath of the recent earthquake in Hatay, our local contacts reported the partial collapse of structures along the Orontes River, revealing major archaeological layers unavailable prior to the earthquake." Our first dig discovered a massive golden dome in the ruins along the banks of the Orontes River. Most of it had been hidden or collapsed under centuries of mud, made worse by the recent earthquake."

Joseph's mind whirled. "But how? Isn't the Turkish government extremely protective about foreign-led archaeological digs?"

A flicker of amusement crossed Lavrov's face. "We have a very wealthy donor—a devout Russian oligarch—who, shall we say, knows the right avenues. Money and influence open doors, even in complicated jurisdictions."

Joseph swallowed, exhaling. "I'm stunned. If you found the Church of the Golden Dome, that's huge. Historic. I—"

"Exactly," Lavrov cut in. "And we need you. We have countless fragments turning up—Latin, Greek, Syriac. Our AI translations are laughable, especially with marginal notes or old script forms. Our AI translations fail miserably at archaic forms. What you were able to translate in 30 seconds took our team almost 3 days to get correct. We need a true scholar on-site, someone who also believes in the significance of relics. There's also reference to instructions that will guide us to the keys. We need someone who knows the period better than anyone else to guide us through the process. Time is crucial."

He produced an envelope from his briefcase. "The contract. In short: two hundred fifty thousand dollars upfront upon your departure. Upon success—meaning upon discovery of the Keys of St. Peter—an additional one-point-five million USD paid to you."

Joseph's knees felt weak. "That's... I can't even process that amount."

Lavrov nodded. "We understand it's an unconventional proposal, but you'd be crucial to our success. We can't rely on poorly trained translators or technology that fails. And we suspect time is short. Once word spreads, access might be blocked, or the site could be compromised."

Joseph's jaw clenched. Part of him was thrilled at the chance to chase the relics he'd studied his entire academic life. Another part screamed: My father's sick; I can't leave him.

Lavrov read his hesitation. "I understand you have personal concerns. But we have a short window. Politics, local tensions, the nature of relic-hunting—none will wait for us. I must have your decision now. I've arranged clearance for immediate travel tomorrow morning if you agree."

Joseph's thoughts spiraled: the mortgage statement, the lost job, his father's diagnosis. He also envisioned his father urging him not to waste his life.

Finally, he said, "I... I can't just drop everything. I still have commitments to my students, the University..." He trailed off, uncertain how much to divulge.

Lavrov lowered his voice. "Look here." He handed Joseph another paper: a letter signed by Notre Dame's Board of Directors. It confirmed a $75,000 severance for Joseph, plus arrangements for his students to finish out the term with other professors if Joseph took the position with Lavrov. He skimmed the page, stunned. "So, they're basically pushing me out, giving me money to leave quietly?"

Lavrov's tone softened. "It's an opportunity, Dr. Scanlon. You've poured years into your field, only to see your department defunded. Now you can continue your research on the biggest stage possible, with resources at your disposal. I understand the personal toll. But I'm afraid our flight is set for tomorrow morning. That's the latest we can delay. If you join us, you'd need to be on that plane."

Joseph felt his mouth go dry. They'd set this up behind his back? Father Ryan must have known.

"Your personal concerns are real. So are the realities that face our work in Antakya. If you want to do this, you must do it now. The flight leaves tomorrow at 8:30 a.m."

Joseph's immediate instinct was to call Salma. He stepped aside, phone in hand, but it went straight to voicemail. She was probably in the middle of her appointment.

He closed his eyes, remembering what his mother had told him: Leave what you can't control in God's hands. Right now, the future of his father's illness or their fertility was beyond his immediate power. This job offer—this was in his control.

As they continued their discussion, Joseph cleared his throat, aiming for a casual tone. "My wife, Salma, is actually from Antakya. Her family has deep roots there. If I take this position, we'd like to stay together during the visit. We have relatives who could host us, or we could arrange accommodations nearby." He watched Lavrov's expression carefully, but the professor merely offered a measured nod before clasping his hands together.

"I understand your desire to keep your family close, Dr. Scanlon, but I'm afraid that won't be possible," Lavrov said, his voice calm but firm. "The excavation site is highly sensitive, and security is our top priority. We have a secured compound adjacent to the dig where all team members are required to stay. This isn't just for your safety but for the integrity of the work. You know how it is with all of the Islamic extremism in the area. We cannot afford to allow our team to go out and about without proper security. The best I can offer is to arrange supervised visits with your family during approved times."

Joseph exhaled, glancing away briefly. He didn't like the idea of being separated from Salma for an extended period, especially with everything happening in their personal lives. But the offer on the table—the research, the money, the chance to be part of something historic—was too significant to let slip over logistics. Finally, he gave a reluctant nod. "Alright. If that's the best we can do, I'll make it work."

Joseph inhaled deeply, exhaling a final swirl of doubt. "I'll do it," he said, surprising even himself.

Lavrov's face lit with triumph. "Wonderful. Sign here."

Joseph scribbled his name on the contracts. Lavrov pulled out an airline ticket. "First-class. I'll see you on the plane."

They clasped hands in a swift, solemn handshake. "We'll do great work together, Dr. Scanlon," Lavrov said, voice humming with excitement.

They parted near the Basilica. Lavrov strode off toward the main building, while Joseph made for the Basilica parking lot, mind awash with adrenaline. The campus itself looked the same—students zipping around on bikes, clusters of friends chattering by the library—but Joseph felt as if his entire life had been flipped inside out.

"I can't believe I just did that," he muttered, patting his jacket pocket to confirm the contract copies and first-class ticket were truly there.

He descended a short flight of steps leading into the lot, scanning rows of cars for his old sedan. But as he turned a corner, an imposing black SUV shot forward from behind a parked van.

Tires squealed. Before Joseph could react, two men in dark tactical clothing sprang from the vehicle, one yanking open the rear door, the other grabbing Joseph's arms in a viselike grip.

"Hey!" Joseph shouted, terror lancing through his voice. He tried to twist free, but they were too strong. The second man jammed a forearm across Joseph's chest, half choking him.

A wave of raw panic surged through Joseph. This can't be real—this is campus, broad daylight—someone help me—

But in the deserted slice of the parking lot, no one was near enough or paying attention. The men shoved him inside the SUV; the door slammed shut. Joseph felt the vehicle lurch forward at high speed. His breath came in ragged gasps.

"Keep quiet," growled one of the armed men in thickly accented English, pressing a pistol to Joseph's ribcage. The other man swiftly zip-tied Joseph's wrists and put a large blindfold over him.

Joseph's heart hammered. He forced himself to think. What is going on? What have I just gotten myself into? The thoughts tangled in panic, and he realized he had zero control.

As the SUV screeched toward the exit, Joseph's mind flashed to Salma—God, please keep her safe—and to his father, who had only just told him about the cancer. Joseph had chosen to leave for Turkey tomorrow...but now, everything was upended in an instant of violence.

Outside the tinted windows, the shining dome of Notre Dame disappeared from sight, replaced by blurred roads. Joseph's life was about to change far more abruptly than even he'd anticipated.

All he could do was close his eyes, pray for a miracle, and hope that his decision to chase the Keys of St. Peter hadn't already led him straight into the jaws of peril.

SEVEN

The CIA

Joseph blinked hard as the blindfold was yanked from his face, his pupils constricting against the sudden flood of light. He sat in a steel chair, the weight of it anchored to the floor, in a windowless, soundproof room. A single table stood between him and the man sitting across from him—a polished professional in a tailored navy suit, his tie crisp, his shoes military-shined.

"Dr. Scanlon, I'm terribly sorry about all this," the man said, hands raised in mock surrender. "I know, I know—this isn't how a civilized society operates. But we needed to have this conversation somewhere secure, without distractions."

Joseph worked his jaw, flexing his sore wrists where the zip ties had cut into them. He exhaled sharply. "Who the hell are you?"

The man leaned forward, his expression one of practiced sincerity. "My name is Agent Mark DeLuca, with the CIA. These gentlemen here—" he gestured behind Joseph to where three men stood like sentinels "—are Special Agents from the FBI's Chicago Field

Office. Before you say anything, you haven't done anything wrong. Yet."

Joseph frowned. "Yet?"

DeLuca smiled, the type of grin a man gives when he knows something the other one doesn't. "We've been tracking Dr. Alexei Lavrov for quite some time, and as of an hour ago, we caught him on camera exchanging some very interesting documents. You were involved in signing documents with him. We need to know— what was in them? This could be an issue of national security."

Joseph hesitated. His mind raced through everything he had signed with Lavrov's group. Joseph knew all too well that the CIA had broad latitude and authority to engage in all kinds of force, and that understanding sent a chill down his spine. Then something clicked: the federal government couldn't force him to talk, not without due process.

"Am I under arrest? Can I please see an attorney" he asked, voice firm.

One of the FBI agents exhaled in frustration. "I knew this guy was too smart to be intimidated."

DeLuca sighed, waving a hand in the air as though swatting away the irritation. "No, Dr. Scanlon, you are not under arrest. And no, you don't need a lawyer—unless you really want one. I'd advise against that."

Joseph leaned back, crossing his arms. "Then I'm free to go."

DeLuca nodded. "Technically, yes. But before you storm out of here, I am able to offer you a classified account of who Dr. Lavrov is and to give you full disclosure of who you are doing business with."

Joseph leaned forward. " Yes, I am only familiar with his academic work. If there's anything else going on with this guy, please let me know."

DeLuca started to go through some items in his briefcase. "Now, the information I have to share with you about Dr. Lavrov is highly classified. In order for me to do so, you need to sign an NDA."

Joseph stared at him. "And if I don't?"

DeLuca shrugged. "Then you're free to leave, but you'll be given a very, very strong warning to stay away from Lavrov and his organization."

Another agent placed the document in front of him, a pen sliding across the table. Joseph skimmed it. The language was clear—and dangerous. If he broke the agreement, even by mentioning it to his wife, the CIA had the right to imprison him indefinitely. Joseph swallowed hard, recalling whispered tales of those who had dared to breach such agreements, only to vanish into the shadows of forgotten cells. At the same time, he needed to know what he was getting into with Lavrov. He inhaled sharply, hesitating for just a moment before signing.

DeLuca smiled, sliding a laptop from his briefcase. He clicked through a few folders before spinning it around. On the screen was a dossier of Dr. Alexei Lavrov. Agent DeLuca leaned back in his chair, watching Joseph's eyes scan the screen. "Dr. Scanlon, I need you to understand the broader context here. The world is shifting, alliances are changing, and so are the methods of warfare. As you know, the United States has officially withdrawn from NATO, stepping back from any formal commitments to intervene directly in the ongoing conflict between Russia and the Eastern European NATO nations."

Joseph's eyebrows furrowed, processing the implications. "So, what does that mean for us?"

DeLuca's expression hardened, his gaze locking onto Joseph's. "While we're not on the front lines, we've adopted a policy of indirect support for our allies in Eastern Europe. This includes leveraging our intelligence services to stifle and oppose Russia's advances. It's a complex and delicate operation, one where every piece of information matters, every connection is scrutinized."

He paused, allowing the weight of his words to settle in. "Dr. Lavrov, unfortunately, is a key player in Russia's strategic moves. He's not just an academic; he's an operative, deeply embedded in their network."

The room fell silent, the weight of DeLuca's proposition hanging heavily in the air. Joseph knew he was at a crossroads, his next move carrying significant consequences not only for himself but potentially for international relations.

"Lavrov," DeLuca began, "obtained his PhD in Orthodox Studies from St. Petersburg Theological Academy. Spent years in academia, became one of the most respected leaders in the Russian Orthodox faith and then—boom—out of nowhere, founded the

Center for Russian Orthodox Studies. Overnight, his net worth skyrocketed. Private jet, luxury properties, unlimited funding. And that's when he popped up on our radar."

Joseph's brow furrowed. "How?"

DeLuca swiped to another image. A grainy surveillance photo showed Lavrov shaking hands with a cold-eyed man in a Russian military uniform.

"This," DeLuca continued, "is Sergei Mikhailov, one of the most trusted advisors of President Igor Volkov. He is the Director of Russia's elite FSB - you know, the Russian Federal Security Service. He has the two most important jobs in Volkov's government — oversee Volkov's personal security to ensure no one assassinates him and to secure medical treatments to keep him alive.

The CIA holds a strong theory that Lavrov's Center for Russian Orthodox Studies is nothing more than a well-funded front for the FSB. The agency believes the Russian government is secretly bankrolling it, using it as a shell corporation to conduct state-sponsored operations under the guise of religious and academic work. And who better to lead such an operation than one of the most respected Orthodox scholars in Russia? Lavrov gives the center legitimacy on the world stage while advancing the Kremlin's interests.

Joseph felt the pieces snapping together. His initial meeting with Lavrov had felt off, but he couldn't quite put his finger on why. Now, everything made sense. The limitless funding, the extensive resources, the unusual control over his travel and lodging—it was all about keeping him contained and under surveillance. Lavrov wasn't just an academic. He was an operative, whether knowingly or not.

DeLuca nodded as he saw the realization dawn on Joseph's face. "We know this organization is a front for the FSB. What we don't know is what their exact objective is."

DeLuca paused to let this sink in with Joseph and continued. "Now, Volkov's health is a state secret, but we've received intelligence that he's suffering from Muckle-Wells Syndrome, a rare autoinflammatory disease that causes recurrent fevers, joint pain, hearing loss, and eventual organ failure. The condition can initially be treated with Biologic drugs like anakinra or canakinumab to help control the inflammation, but over time, the body becomes immune to the treatment, and the inflammation starts to take its toll again. Although there is no way to know, the reports we have indicate that the process of organ failure may be just around the corner."

Joseph's mouth went dry.

"Traditional treatments have failed," DeLuca went on, "and Lavrov's been seen traveling to Syria, Turkey and now America. We suspect he's after some cure he believes will save and extend Volkov's life."

Joseph spoke up. "He's after the lost Keys of St. Peter."

DeLuca squinted, leaning forward. "I'm sorry—he's after what?"

Joseph took a deep breath, steadying himself. "The Keys of St. Peter. Most people assume they're just a metaphor. You know, Jesus giving Peter spiritual authority in the Bible. Historically, theologians have understood that passage as symbolic. But my research suggests something else."

DeLuca looked confused, his brows knitting together. Joseph studied him for a moment before asking, "Are you a Christian, Agent DeLuca?"

DeLuca leaned back slightly, considering the question. "I wasn't raised Christian, no. But I have the utmost respect for the impact of Judeo-Christian values on America. I have my own beliefs, and at the end of the day, I think what really matters is just being a good person."

Joseph nodded, filing that response away, then continued. He reached down, pulling a well-worn Bible from his briefcase. He flipped to the passage, running his fingers along the text before reading aloud. "In Matthew 16, Jesus declares to St. Peter: 'I say to you, you are Peter and upon This Rock I will build my church. The Gates of Hell shall not prevail against it. I give you the keys of the kingdom of heaven. Whatever you bind on earth shall be bound in heaven; whatever you loose on earth shall be loosed in heaven.' Now, historically, scholars have believed this was Jesus granting Peter and his successors spiritual authority. But in the sixth century, Pope Gregory the Great wrote a series of letters—letters I just taught on yesterday that indicate the keys weren't just metaphorical. They were physical.""

DeLuca's brow furrowed. "You're saying these keys actually existed?"

Joseph nodded. "More than that—they were believed to have miraculous properties. Healing properties. Gregory sent them from Rome to Antioch, likely to protect them from the invasions at the end of the 6th century. That's the last recorded mention of them before they vanished. Twenty years later, there was no trace."

DeLuca leaned back, rubbing his chin. "And you think Lavrov is trying to recover them?"

Joseph exhaled. "I don't think—I know. I've spent time in archaeological digs in Antakya, the last known location of the keys. It's where I met my wife, where her family still lives and where my faith became real. If Lavrov is after them, he must believe they still exist. And if Russia is involved and bankrolling the excavation, then they must think those healing powers are real—and that they could be used to save Volkov."

DeLuca's expression darkened. "You're telling me the Russians believe these Keys are real? That they think they have supernatural healing powers?"

Joseph nodded. "That's exactly what I'm telling you."

DeLuca let out a slow breath, rubbing his temples. "And you were about to go to Antakya to find them for him?"

Joseph pulled out the contract and plane ticket. DeLuca looked it over. As he did Joseph continued, "The money was too good to be true. No historical society has that kind of funding. There is no way I'm going to be aiding Russia in this matter. I need to cancel this trip. Thank you for..." At that moment, DeLuca interrupted him. "Canceling your trip isn't an option."

Joseph stiffened. "What do you mean?"

DeLuca leaned in. "This is a golden opportunity. We need someone on the inside. We need you."

Joseph blinked. "Are you asking me to become a spy?"

DeLuca smiled. "Not a spy. A confidential informant. Your job will be to record everything that happens and simply provide us with intel. We will take care of the rest."

Joseph hesitated, his mind reeling. "How would I even communicate with you, to begin with?"

DeLuca waved a hand. "The FSB will be monitoring everything—your phone, your cell data, your internet, even casual conversations."

He looked back up at DeLuca. "That actually explains something. When I was discussing the job, I requested to stay with my wife's family in Antakya. Her brother Aziz has been one of my closest friends. It would have been the easiest and most natural option. Lavrov denied it outright. Instead, he set strict conditions—supervised visits only. No overnights. At the time, I thought it was just safety related, but now? Now I realize they are deliberately limiting my movement. They don't want me talking freely to anyone outside their circle." That kind of control made no sense for a standard academic excavation, but it made perfect sense if Lavrov was hiding something.

DeLuca inquired, "What is the full name and year of his birth?" "Aziz Haddad, 1982 I believe" the professor answered. DeLuca put the info into his computer and after 2 minutes, he pulled up a photo of Aziz. "Is this your brother in law?" he asked.

Joseph nodded, "You guys are the real deal. How do you have his info?"

"I don't just have his info. I have a confidential informant solution." He pulled up another screen, showing a profile of Aziz. "Aziz Haddad. Your wife's brother. Former Chaldean militia fighter."

Joseph leaned in, scanning the profile of Aziz on the screen. His mind reeled at the thought of involving his brother-in-law, but the logic was there. If Aziz had already earned the trust of the CIA, he could serve as a reliable conduit for information.

His mind drifted back to the late 2010s when Aziz had abruptly left Turkey. Joseph had always assumed he was visiting extended family, but any time he asked about that period, Aziz had been evasive, brushing off questions with vague answers. At the time, Joseph hadn't pressed, figuring it was personal. But now, seeing his name in a CIA database with a history of fighting against ISIS, everything clicked into place. Aziz hadn't just disappeared—he had been in Iraq, actively resisting one of the deadliest terror organizations in modern history. It all made sense now.

DeLuca's dark eyes gleamed with interest. "That's how we'll do it. Aziz is already in our system as a trusted contact. He's fought alongside Western forces against ISIS, and we know where his loyalties lie. If Lavrov is restricting your movement, Aziz is exactly the opening we need. We'll coordinate with our team in the region to make sure Aziz knows the protocol. You'll pass intel to him during those supervised visits, and he'll relay it to us. It's old-fashioned, but it's the safest way."

"And how exactly do you propose I do that without raising suspicion?" Joseph asked.

DeLuca folded his hands on the table. "We'll establish coded methods. A phrase, an object, an action—something innocuous that won't set off any alarms but will signal to us that you have intel. Aziz will know what to do. He's worked with us before, and he's got the experience to pull this off without drawing attention."

Joseph exhaled slowly, the weight of this assignment settling over him. He wasn't just agreeing to gather information—he was agreeing to infiltrate a high-stakes Russian operation with the very real possibility that, if caught, he'd be left with no way out.

Joseph exhaled, feeling the weight of the decision. His hands gripped the armrests of his chair, doubt creeping into his mind. "I need to be honest here—I'm not sure I can do this," he admitted, shaking his head. "This isn't what I signed up for. I'm a professor, not a spy. I don't have the training, and I sure as hell don't have the stomach for this kind of work. I need to back out."

DeLuca's expression didn't change, but there was a subtle shift in his demeanor—less recruiter, more negotiator. "Look, I get it. You're not a field agent, and no one expects you to be. But you're already in this, whether you like it or not. Lavrov has you marked. If you walk away now, you think he'll just let that slide? He's already gone to great lengths to keep you isolated in Antakya, away from your in-laws. That kind of control isn't for nothing. If you back out, there's a chance he sees you as a liability—and liabilities in his world have a way of disappearing."

DeLuca let a moment of silence settle between them before he spoke again. "Let me ask you something, Joseph—do you actually believe the Keys of St. Peter are real?"

Joseph hesitated, then nodded. "Yes. I do."

DeLuca leaned forward. "Do you believe they have supernatural healing power?"

Joseph swallowed hard. It was one thing to study relics as a historian, to analyze theological claims with scholarly detachment. But in his heart, deep down, he knew the answer. He had spent years chasing the history of the Keys, and the evidence all pointed to something more than mere legend. Finally, he exhaled and gave a single, firm nod. "Yes. I believe that, too."

DeLuca studied him for a beat, then sat back with a knowing expression. "Then you know what's at stake."

Without another word, he pulled his laptop closer and tapped a few keys. The screen shifted to a news webpage, a glaring headline catching Joseph's eye: NATO Casualties Mount as Eastern European Frontlines Crumble. Beneath it, a list of figures—another 3,000 dead this week alone. A casualty tracker ran in real-time, showing the growing death toll of Eastern European NATO troops. DeLuca turned the screen slightly, letting the brutal reality settle in.

"This isn't stopping," DeLuca said grimly. "Russia's aggression is only escalating, and with the U.S. sitting this one out, Europe is hemorrhaging soldiers. They're outmatched, outgunned, and out-maneuvered. Their only hope is if Volkov is removed from the equation. If he dies, there's a chance for de-escalation. But if those keys work—if Lavrov finds them and they heal him—we're looking at another three decades of Volkov in the Kremlin. If he doesn't get them, then it looks like Volkov's time on earth is coming to an end. Our sources tell us that in the event that Volkov dies, General Morozov is the most likely candidate to replace him and would de-escalate all wars in Europe. Think about it, Joseph. You could help stop that."

Joseph's chest tightened. He thought of his father, his wife, the students he was leaving behind. But he also thought of the greater fight—of faith, of history, of justice.

He nodded, the conviction settling in his gut. "I'll do it."

DeLuca nodded approvingly and reached into his briefcase, pulling out a thin folder. "Good. Then let's make it official." He slid the folder across the table. "This is your contract as a confidential informant for the CIA. It outlines your role, protections, and compensation. You'll be paid for your work, of course—hazard pay included. Sign it, and we move forward."

Joseph hesitated for only a moment before picking up the pen. His name scrawled across the dotted line, sealing his agreement.

DeLuca then pulled a small slip of paper from his pocket and placed it in front of Joseph. "This is a confidential emergency number. Memorize it. Do not write it down. If you ever find your-self in immediate danger, use it. The right people will answer."

Joseph stared at the numbers, repeating them in his head. He'd never been the kind of man to involve himself in this world, yet here he was, about to step into a shadow war between nations.

"One more thing," DeLuca continued, voice firm. "Journal all of your activities. Every detail—who you meet, where you go, what Lavrov discusses with you. Keep it hidden. When you meet Aziz during your first supervised visit, you leave the journal with him. Our people will handle the rest."

Joseph exhaled sharply, knowing what was coming next.

"You also cannot tell your wife. Or her family. No one. As far as they're concerned, nothing about this conversation, about your arrangement with us, ever happened. If you break this agreement, even to Salma, the consequences will be severe."

Joseph clenched his jaw. He had never kept anything from Salma. The very thought of deceiving her gnawed at him. But he had al-ready signed the non-disclosure agreement—he knew what breaking it meant. A life in prison, or worse.

He looked down at the paper in front of him, then back at DeLuca. His stomach twisted, but he nodded. "Understood."

DeLuca studied him for a moment before finally giving a satisfied nod. "Good man."

After the meeting ended, Joseph was escorted out of the building and into the parking lot where he found they had towed his car. The sun was beginning to dip below the horizon, casting a golden hue over the city skyline. His hands tightened around the steering wheel as he started the car, the weight of his decision pressing down on him. Every turn of the road felt surreal, like he was watching himself from the outside.

By the time he pulled into his driveway, the late afternoon light was fading. He sat in the car for a moment, staring at the front door. Inside, Salma was waiting for him, expecting an ordinary evening. But nothing about his life would be ordinary anymore. In the course of one day, he was hired by a Russian shell company posing as an academic non-profit organization, kidnapped by the CIA and recruited to be a confidential informant to spy on the Russians. Just when he thought nothing bigger could happen, he would soon realize how poor of an assumption that would be.

EIGHT

The Second Greatest Day

J oseph turned the key in the front lock and let the door swing open, stepping inside. The house lay quiet except for the distant hum of the refrigerator and the faint ticking of the old clock on the living-room wall. He slipped off his shoes, shrugged his jacket onto the coat rack, and then paused, listening for any sign of his wife. It struck him that it felt too quiet. That was when he saw her—Salma—leaning at the entrance, arms folded, eyes bright. It wasn't a harsh, impatient stance; it was more like she could hardly wait to speak but was trying very hard not to blurt something out too soon.

"Hey," Joseph said. The corner of his mouth lifted in a tentative half-smile as he set down his briefcase. "You're back early."

She let out a shaky laugh, unfolding her arms and stepping close. "I was waiting for you," she said softly, fingers drumming nervously on her forearm. "I wanted to be here first thing when you came in."

Immediately, Joseph's senses jolted with concern. "Everything okay? You look... excited, but serious."

Her eyes gleamed in the warm lamplight. "You won't believe it," she said, voice dancing between tears and exhilaration, "but this is the second greatest day of my life."

He blinked, apprehension coiling in his stomach. "The second greatest?" He took her hands gently. "Why second? And what's going on?"

"That's exactly what you asked me on the greatest day," she whispered. "Remember, you proposed outside St. Peter's overlooking Antakya. That was the happiest day of my life—until now."

Joseph squeezed her hands. "You're scaring me," he said with a shaky smile. "Spit it out, woman. I can't take the suspense."

She inhaled, tears welling in her eyes. "Joseph," she said, voice quivering. "I'm pregnant. The doctor confirmed it today—I'm about six weeks along. I've been feeling a little off for weeks, but I chalked it up to stress. They ran tests at the clinic, and the lab results came back positive. I'm pregnant."

For several seconds, Joseph stood silent, mind spinning. He saw her lips move, registering the words, but he needed a moment to let them sink into his heart. Pregnant. Pregnant. He felt a wave of emotion so enormous it squeezed the air from his lungs. Then it smashed through all his composure—tears sprang to his eyes, and he stumbled forward, enfolding her in a trembling embrace. A ragged sob tore from his throat.

She gasped at the intensity of his reaction. "Joseph! Baby—are you... are you happy?" Her hands came up around his back, supporting him as he pressed his face into her hair.

"Happy," he echoed, but the word was drowned by half-choked sobs. They were tears of joy, yes—but also tears built from weeks of hidden dread, from too many secrets swirling in the pit of his stomach, from the heartbreak of seeing his father's test results, from the stress of losing his own job, signing an agreement with a Russian shell company and becoming a CIA informant with his life on the line. He'd battled all these emotions on separate fronts, but hearing the word "pregnant" turned the floodgates wide open.

Still holding her tight, he struggled to breathe through the tears. "I can't—I can't believe it," he managed, voice breaking. "Fourteen years of heartbreak, all those prayers. And now—" He paused to catch his breath, shoulders shaking. "I'm so sorry I'm a mess."

"It's okay," she murmured, face pressed into his shoulder. "You're scaring me a little, though. Are you sure this is just joy?"

He loosened his hold, stepping back to look her in the eye. "I'm so happy," he said, voice trembling. "But I'm also—there's so much going on. With Notre Dame... with life... with everything. I've been carrying all of it, and now the relief is too big to contain."

She looked puzzled. "What do you mean 'with Notre Dame'? You told me you had a meeting, but you didn't say anything else. Is something wrong at work?"

Joseph tried to steady himself, inhaling sharply. "I was called in yesterday at 3:00 p.m. to meet with the president of the University, Father Ryan, and he informed me that the Notre Dame board of directors has just decided to eliminate the late Antiquities program."

Her mouth fell open. "Wait, what? They're shutting down your entire department? Is that even possible?"

"Apparently," Joseph said bitterly. "Father Ryan told me. He tried to fight it, but he lost. He was also unable to share with me any details due to the confidentiality of the board. So, I'm out of a job unless I find something else. And it gets more stressful... I found something else, actually."

She stared at him. "Something else? That's—when did this happen? What else have you been dealing with, Joseph?"

He exhaled slowly. "I know. It's a lot. Let's sit, okay? My legs are about to give out."

Together, they moved to the couch. He slipped his arm around her waist, but before he could speak, she pressed him gently. "So, the department's closing. That means you lose your tenure? Your research funds? Everything you built at Notre Dame?"

He nodded. "Yes. However, Notre Dame takes care of its own. The Anonymous board member who oversaw and led the elimination of the program took it upon himself to set up an interview for me. The interview happened this morning on campus."

"All right," she said, calmer now. "So, what's the new opportunity?"

Joseph leaned back against the couch. "The Center for Russian Orthodox Studies, led by Dr. Alexei Lavrov. I've read his work and he is the most respected orthodox scholar in the East. He has offered me a position—to be a consultant on a team to do archaeological digs in Antakya."

She turned fully toward him, eyes widening. "Antakya? My home?"

He nodded with a tentative smile, remembering the old church in the mountains where he proposed to her. "Exactly. They found new evidence that points to the location of the old Church of the Golden Dome. You know, from my research—where Pope Gregory supposedly sent the real Keys of St. Peter at the end of the sixth century."

She caught her breath. "Wait, so you might actually uncover the lost Keys you've spent your entire career studying?"

He nodded, a spark of excitement chasing away some gloom. "Yes. That's the dream, anyway. It's not a sure thing, but they uncovered partial inscriptions—Latin fragments referencing the Keys. They want me onsite as a lead consultant to advise the excavation. It's a rare, once-in-a-lifetime chance." Even though the news was fantastic, Joseph was still depressed.

She let out a soft whistle. "Wow. why aren't you excited?"

"Well... I already signed the offer" he said. "The offer was time-sensitive and required an immediate decision. I tried calling you, but your phone went straight to voicemail. Lavrov was only in town that day, and if I hesitated, the opportunity would be gone."

Salma's mouth parted, eyes flashing. "Wait, you signed already? Joseph, how could you—?"

He raised both hands. "Salma, I tried calling you. I must've dialed five times."

Her hand flew to her phone, sitting on the counter. "I turned it off for the tests, the scans, bloodwork—they don't let you have phones in some of those labs. There was no way I could pick up."

A tension-laden pause stretched between them. "That's what must've happened," Joseph whispered. "I'm sorry. I know this is... so unfair. But you should know, the offer was only valid in that moment. Lavrov was about to walk away."

Her lips trembled. "Why would an offer be that time-sensitive? That alone sounds suspicious. They needed you so badly that you had to decide on the spot?"

He nodded. "I don't know all of the details but apparently the dig and the funding are all time sensitive and they are running out of time. I know a few other Scholars who could potentially do what I do and even though he didn't say anything, I think I assumed to myself that he would have gone to another candidate. "

Salma's face paled further. She squeezed her eyes shut. "So... you really did this without me? I can't believe you!"

Joseph looked her in the eyes, "Salma, the contract guarantees me two hundred fifty thousand dollars that hits our checking account tomorrow morning when I am on the flight. In the event that we find the keys, we get an additional 1 million. The logic is that if they're found, it'll be a major historical event. They want to lock me into that success." He paused. "I know it sounds outlandish. But if it works out, it'll secure us for a long, long time, especially with a baby on the way. We can give this child every opportunity we never had."

Salma exhaled, rubbing her temples. "This is... a lot. More than I expected." She looked at him, her voice quiet but firm. "What happens next? What are the next steps?"

Joseph swallowed, the weight of it all pressing on him. "Tomorrow, 8:30 AM. We fly from Chicago O'Hare." He ran a hand through his hair. "

She blinked away tears. "Well," she murmured, "I have something else to tell you that might complicate all this. My pregnancy, according to the doctor, is labeled extremely high-risk." A wry laugh slipped out. "Of course, after all these years, it couldn't be easy."

He stiffened, dread gnawing at the edges of his joy. "High-risk? Why? Are you okay?"

"For now, yes," she answered. "But my doctor said I'll need extensive monitoring and progesterone treatments in Chicago. And that means I can't be traveling overseas. The doctor flat-out warned me that the effects of high-altitude air travel could potentially trigger blood clots. She advised me to stay local, near a major hospital with specialized OB units."

He frowned, a swirl of guilt and relief tangling in his gut. "That means you... you can't come to Turkey with me."

She nodded. "Right. Under normal circumstances, I would jump at the chance to see my parents, to have them by my side. But that's not in the cards. If I want to keep this baby safe, I have to follow the doctor's orders." Her eyes searched his. "You look almost relieved. Why?"

He exhaled, dropping his gaze. "I guess... I won't lie. I've got misgivings about you being close to that site, especially if some of these people funding it are unscrupulous. And the region itself—still dealing with quake aftershocks, social unrest, everything. The truth is, I've been roped into some high-level stuff. I didn't want you in harm's way."

"Joseph." She gripped his hand. "What exactly does 'roped in' mean?"

He paused, words churning in his chest. "Let's say I have reason to watch my back," he replied carefully. "And now that I realize I'm going to be a father, the gravity of that risk is... bigger than ever." He forced a small grin, trying to dispel the gloom. "But hey, good news is, your parents will be in Antakya. So at least I'll have friendly faces there. Maybe they can visit me in supervised sessions or meet me around the city. It's not perfect, but it's something."

She frowned, frustration etched in the furrow of her brow. "What is that about? Why can't you just stay with my parents? It's not like they're foreign spies. This is ridiculous."

He shrugged, a helpless gesture. "That's exactly what I said. Lavrov requires tight operational security, limited external contact. I—there's more to it, but I can't get into all the details. I had to sign some forms. There's a secrecy clause about certain aspects."

She stared at him, suspicion forming in her expression. "Joseph, you said yourself there's a wealthy Russian pulling the strings. This is borderline shady. Don't you sense that? Why would an archaeological dig require this level of control?"

He hesitated, trying to keep his face neutral. He thought about the fact that he was, in fact, a confidential informant for the CIA, and that none of this was purely academic. "It's a specialized environment," he said carefully, hating how vague he sounded. "International tensions. Unrest in the region. Artifacts worth millions if found. That combination spooks them. They're trying to minimize risk."

She studied him for a long second, then looked away. "I suppose there's a certain logic to it, but I don't like it. Lavrov might be a respected scholar, but who's pulling the strings?"

Joseph felt his stomach clench. He forced a calm nod. "It's a fair question. But I can't poke around right now. Not if I want to keep my job, and not if I want to sign on for that bonus. I know it's not ideal."

She made a frustrated noise and crossed her arms, staring at the dark TV screen. "What else aren't you telling me?" she asked quietly.

His chest tightened. For an instant, he nearly told her about the CIA side. He wanted to come clean about the side arrangement. But that would be one secret too many. He'd already broken trust once this evening. At least, he thought, letting her remain ignorant might keep her safer.

"There are certain conditions," he said aloud. "Like I said, the employer agreement with Lavrov is very tight. I've told you the gist, though. The main point is, I'll be away for a while. Possibly months at a time."

She pinched the bridge of her nose. "And I'm pregnant," she whispered. "I just found out I'm pregnant, and now you're telling me you'll be gone on short notice. This is what we both prayed for—look at me, I'm shaking." She held out a hand, indeed trembling. "Can't we slow down?"

Joseph felt the tension rising again. "That's how it felt from my side too. The severance documents were connected to this offer. If I took the offer for new employment, we got an extra seventy-five thousand and all my end of the term teaching responsibilities will be covered. I took this offer, hoping I could at least salvage something while I still had the chance."

She massaged her temple. "I understand. I do. I guess I'm just... rattled."

He nodded, his throat tight. "We both are."

She stared at the floor for a long moment, then lifted her head. "And we're going to have a baby. In just over half a year, our world flips upside down. Are we sure we should... you know, do this now? Maybe there's another option if you talk to Father Ryan or the board again?"

"Too late," Joseph said gently. "I signed. I accepted. There isn't an out, not without losing everything. The terms are set in stone."

"Okay," she said quietly, exhaling. Then she forced a small smile, blinking back the tears. "But we have a child," she repeated, voice wavering with fragile joy. "We've dreamed of this for so long, prayed so hard. We can't let the negativity overshadow our miracle. Right?"

He cupped her cheek. "Right. You're carrying our baby, our dream. Nothing can take that from us."

She nuzzled her face into his palm, letting the silence speak for a moment. Then her expression softened. "I'm sorry I lashed out. I'm still in shock from the test results, and I'm upset that you got cornered. But... at the same time, I trust God has a plan."

He nodded gratefully. "I know you do. Thank you for saying that."

She sniffled, wiping her eyes. "And I guess you have an early flight to prepare for?"

Joseph's eyebrows rose. "Yeah, I have to be at O'Hare very early tomorrow morning. Lavrov insisted. The flight goes to Istanbul first, then on to Hatay province. So, I have a bunch of packing to do. I was going to wait to tell Mom and Dad tomorrow, but with everything so hectic, maybe you could fill them in?"

She nodded. "Of course. That was always your mom's dream, to hear that we're expecting. Now we can finally share it. I'll call her or maybe even drive over in the afternoon if I can manage it. She's going to freak out with joy." A tiny laugh escaped her. "And I imagine your dad will too, in that stoic, quiet way of his."

Joseph tried to smile, but a flicker of sadness and worry passed across his face when he thought of his father's diagnosis. She noticed at once.

"Hey," she said softly. "You sure nothing else is bothering you?"

He forced a brighter expression, deciding to honor his dad's request and not tell anyone yet. "I'm good. Just tired. And overwhelmed. Let's... let's talk about the baby. I want to celebrate this moment."

She gave him a half-hearted grin and nodded. "Let's do that." She slipped closer, nestling her head against his shoulder. "Tell me what you see in your mind when you think of our child. Humor me."

He exhaled, letting the warmth of anticipation flood him. "All right. Well... first, I imagine a little hand wrapped around my finger, you know? The baby in a hospital bassinet, and I'm just standing there in awe. I can see you in that white postpartum gown, exhausted but smiling. I keep kissing the top of the baby's head, not believing it's real."

Her face brightened, tears shining in her eyes. "And then?"

"I see us bringing the baby home," he continued. "Mom and Dad waiting at the door, your folks Zooming from overseas or hopefully calling all day. Balloons, you know, silly 'Welcome Baby' banners. I see a million pictures pinned to the fridge, every snap more adorable than the last. I see that look in your eyes like you're the happiest woman alive."

She squeezed his arm, nodding vigorously. "Yes. I see that too. And I see you carrying our child into Mass for the first time—like we always talked about, how we'd pass on the faith. I see you holding the baby near the baptismal font. I see us asking Henry to be the godfather and having the baptism at the basilica right on campus. That might be a dream, but I'd love it."

Joseph stared at the ceiling, feeling the edges of a tear slip down the side of his face. "I see it. Maybe the baby will wail through the entire ceremony, but we won't care. It'll be proof of life, a celebration of everything we hoped for."

She sniffed, smiling through tears. "I also imagine introducing the baby to its cousins—my brother Aziz's kids. And my parents—oh, they'll spoil the little one to death. They'll run around the yard in Antakya, playing games I played as a child. It'll be perfect."

A soft laugh rose in Joseph's chest. "And at the same time, our child will have a foot in American culture too, probably wearing a little Notre Dame onesie, or a Chicago Cubs hat. I can't wait to see that."

They both laughed gently, hugging closer. The flickering lamplight cast them in a golden glow, as if capturing them in the stillness of a treasured memory. After a minute of silence, she placed a hand on her belly.

"You and me, we've prayed so long for this," she said, voice hushed. "I used to wonder if it would ever happen. But if it's happening now—maybe it's the best timing. God's timing."

He kissed her temple, letting the moment linger. "Yeah. God's timing," he echoed.

She looked him in the eye. "That's enough for me. And I trust God to guide you, even if I don't see the whole picture. I'll support you from here, no matter how long you're away."

He swallowed, an ache forming in his chest. "Thank you. That means the world to me. You asked how long I'll be gone? It's... indefinite. Could be a few weeks or even months if the dig proves tough. I can't make promises."

She forced a smile. "We'll be fine. Just promise you'll keep me updated daily, if the situation allows."

"I will." He paused, wiping a hand across his mouth. She shook her head, grinning. "And you know Aziz will keep his eye on you. He won't let you slack off!"

Joseph chuckled. "He's my personal drill sergeant. But yeah, I'm really looking forward to seeing them again. I'm sure your dad's going to talk my ear off about local politics, and your mom will try to feed me until I explode. Just like old times."

She rested her head on his shoulder. "With my family and God's protection, I'm sure you'll come back safe. I trust you and I trust God. I know things can be complicated over there, but you'll find a way."

A gentle pause followed. Then she exhaled and stood. "All right. Enough with the tears and daydreaming. If your flight is at eight-thirty, you need to be out of the house no later than five, factoring in traffic to Chicago. That means you should start packing tonight."

He let out a soft groan. This was all happening so fast. "Yeah, you're right. I was going to do a quick job in the morning, but that's probably not wise. And we need to let Dad and Mom know about... everything. Are you sure you can handle telling them I'm leaving? And about the baby?"

She planted her hands on her hips, adopting a mock-stern expression. "Joseph, your mother has been waiting for this news for fourteen years. She'll be over the moon to help. And your dad— well, you know how he is, but I'm sure he'll step up. That said, yes, I can handle it. You go do your packing. I'll call them and see if they can meet me tomorrow. If not, I'll do it over the phone."

He nodded, rising to his feet. "You're incredible," he murmured, cupping her cheek in his palm. "Thank you."

She smiled, eyes shimmering with a mixture of excitement and worry. "Go. Pack. I'll be here."

Joseph slipped away, heading down the hall to the bedroom. He flicked on the overhead light, flinching at the sudden brightness. He dragged his old suitcase from the closet and popped it open onto the bed. He realized with a hollow pang that he had no idea how long he'd be gone—should he pack for scorching Middle Eastern summers, or mild winters, or both?

"Lord," he muttered under his breath, tossing shirts into the case. "This is insane."

The gravity of everything weighed on him. He was leaving behind his newly pregnant wife—something he never dreamed he'd do. But they needed money, and this chance had fallen into his lap. It was an opportunity as rare as starlight at noon. And then there was the side arrangement with the CIA. He never asked for that, but they dangled just enough hints that he could do some good, pass along any suspicious details of Russian involvement.

His phone buzzed on the nightstand, drawing him from his thoughts. He picked it up to see a text from Father Ryan:

Heard the news, Joseph. My prayers are with you, Joseph. Go get those lost keys! Bon voyage. Let me know if you need anything from the ND side. Go discover the truth.

Joseph stared at the screen for a moment. Then he typed back a quick acknowledgment.

Thanks, Father.

He set the phone aside, continuing to fold his clothes. He rummaged for a few theology and archaeology reference books, then placed them carefully among his rolled shirts. This was so different from typical research travel. Not just academic field notes and cameras, but also documents to satisfy the Russians, an entire covert angle he hated thinking about. He tried to focus on the immediate tasks: clothes, toiletries, passport, tablet, chargers.

Time slipped by. After about half an hour, he heard a light knock on the door frame. Turning, he spotted Salma leaning there.

"Everything all right?" he asked.

She nodded, stepping into the room. "Your parents were already asleep, apparently, but I left a voicemail. Dad's phone must be off. Your mom's, too. I'll talk to them first thing in the morning. I might drive over if I can—depends on how I feel."

He set aside a final pair of pants, hurrying to her side. "Nausea?" He pressed a palm to her forehead. "Do you need something?"

She laughed softly. "I'm okay. The doctor gave me some medication for it. Just typical first-trimester stuff—though I'm nearly halfway through it already, ironically. That's how I didn't realize earlier. I thought it was just hormonal imbalance."

He winced sympathetically. "I'm sorry you're going through it alone."

She leaned her head against his chest. "I'm not alone. You're here right now. And that's enough for tonight."

He wrapped his arms around her, inhaling the subtle floral scent of her shampoo. A moment later, she eased away. "Finish your packing," she said, voice gentle but firm. "We'll face tomorrow head-on."

He nodded. "Right," he said, returning to his methodical folds, though his mind still buzzed.

Eventually, the suitcase was nearly full. He zipped it shut, then double-checked his passport in his messenger bag. Inside a zippered compartment, he wrote down the phone number that agent DeLuca gave him next to the journal he would use to get intel to the CIA. Already, the knowledge weighed heavily on him. But now, the threat took a different shape. With a baby on the way, everything was more precarious.

Just as he was about to set the bag aside, Salma walked into the room, carrying something behind her back. With a small, knowing smile, she pulled out two large gold-painted keys and held them up. "I was thinking... maybe you should take these with you. For motivation and good luck."

Joseph stared at them, his chest tightening at the sight. The keys—his keys. As a gift for his successful PhD defense, his father, Michael, had gone to a friend at Notre Dame's IDEA Center and commissioned them to design and 3D-print a set of large keys modeled after the ones depicted in Perugino's famous painting _Christ Giving the Keys of the Kingdom_ to St. Peter in the Sistine Chapel. His father had them printed with tungsten to make them nice and heavy. He painted in a rich gold finish and mounted on a custom display, a tribute to years of research and dedication. They had been a symbol of his work, a centerpiece in his study—until now.

He let out a small chuckle, shaking his head. "I don't know, Salma. I barely have enough room as it is. Plus, they're kind of big."

She arched an eyebrow, stepping closer. "I know how visual you are. Having them with you, seeing them, touching them—it'll keep you focused. Keep you motivated. You're going to find the real ones, Joseph. I believe that."

He hesitated for a moment, then exhaled, relenting. She was right—he had always been a visual thinker, drawn to tangible representations of his work. And if there was even the slightest chance that these replica keys could serve as a reminder of his purpose, then maybe he should take them.

"All right," he said, taking them from her hands. "They're not metallic, so they won't set off any detectors. I'll put them in my carry-on." He used his old excavating backpack as his carry on and threw it in the outside pocket.

A satisfied smile played on Salma's lips as he carefully tucked them into his backpack. "Good," she murmured. "Now, you'll always have something to remind you why you're doing this."

He stashed the keys and journal, forcing the tension out of his shoulders. The baby. The baby was the priority. He closed his eyes briefly, bracing himself. The next weeks or months would test him like never before—emotionally, spiritually, perhaps even physically. But turning back wasn't an option.

At last, he carried the suitcase to the door. "All done," he announced.

She gave a nod of approval, folding her arms. "Do you need me to set an alarm?"

He let out a dry chuckle. "I'll set my phone for three thirty a.m. That should give me time to shower and hit the road."

She hesitated, then approached him once more. "Joseph... I just realized we never actually celebrated. Yes, we cried, we argued, we planned. But we didn't truly celebrate."

His mouth curved into a tender smile. "You're right. This calls for some kind of toast. Though we have limited options."

They both headed to the kitchen. He rummaged in the fridge, withdrew a bottle of sparkling cider leftover from some holiday months ago. He cracked it open with a small pop, then poured it into two mismatched glasses. The sweet scent of apples rose, and the fizz hissed lightly.

"To us," he said, lifting his glass, "and to the child we never thought we'd have."

She raised hers, eyes shiny again. "To you, stepping into the unknown. To me, staying home. To us, bridging the distance."

They sipped, the cool cider refreshing on his tongue. Afterward, they set their glasses down, and she took his hand, guiding him gently to the couch once more. They curled up beneath a throw blanket, the hush of the late hour thick around them.

"I'm sorry," he said quietly, after a spell of silence. "For everything."

"You don't have to apologize again," she responded, leaning her head against his. "I understand the pressure you were under. It's not ideal, but it's life."

He nodded, swallowing the knot of guilt still lodged in his throat. "I just want to be the provider you deserve, especially now that you're carrying our child."

She turned, pressing a small kiss to his cheek. "You are. And if you're worried about how you feel on the inside, let's remember that faith doesn't depend on feelings. It's more than that—it's commitment, trust. God is bigger than our fear or doubt."

Her words aligned eerily with the swirl of emotions inside him. He couldn't have phrased it better. He let out a long breath. "You're right. Sometimes, I feel so weak. But thanks for reminding me that faith is more than a momentary emotion."

She didn't reply, but her hand found his, warm and certain. He rested his chin against her hair, letting the seconds tick by. Both of them needed rest—he had a pre-dawn wake-up call, and she was newly pregnant and exhausted.

At length, she whispered, "We should sleep. We'll face tomorrow— together, even though you'll be leaving."

He nodded, heart heavy but oddly calmed. "I'll do everything I can to get back here the moment I'm able. You and the baby are my priority. I promise."

She gave a slight smile and pulled him to his feet. They turned off the lights, leaving the house dark except for the gentle glow of a hallway lamp. Retreating to the bedroom, they dressed for bed quietly, mindful of each other's presence. Sliding under the covers together felt like stepping into a fragile bubble of peace.

As Joseph flicked off the bedside lamp, he let out a weary sigh. He'd promised her confidence and hope. Outwardly, he'd shown excitement, resolve, and unwavering faith. Inside, he battled a swirl of anxiety—his father's illness hidden, the job's secrecy, the potential dangers of working under Russian oversight, the possibility that the CIA's involvement could blow up in his face at any time. He wasn't sure he could live up to everyone's expectations.

But as he closed his eyes, feeling the comforting warmth of his wife's body beside him, he reminded himself of what she had just said. Faith didn't require him to have a certain feeling. It only required trust in the God who led them this far. That trust, he reflected, would have to sustain him through the flight, through the excavation, through however many months he spent under Lavrov's watchful eye, separated from the woman carrying his child.

He prayed silently for a moment, then eased closer to her, inhaling the faint scent of her shampoo. They had their baby, after all. That was worth every risk. And so, despite the swirl of emotions, Joseph drifted to sleep clinging to hope, remembering that what he felt in his gut was not the deciding factor. He repeated the words in his mind like a mantra:

Faith is not a feeling.

NINE

Among Strangers and Soldiers

J oseph's flight from Chicago to Istanbul had been booked with little fanfare, but the moment he stepped into the first-class cabin, he realized that life had radically changed in just a handful of days. The seats were wide and soft, upholstered in dark leather that gently enveloped him. A flight attendant appeared with a menu and a linen napkin draped over her arm. He thanked her in a polite, almost subdued tone. It still felt surreal—only a week ago he had been lecturing on the Pope Gregory letters in a Notre Dame classroom. Now, he was rocketing toward the Middle East on the dime of a Russian-funded expedition.

He glanced down at his phone, tapping it once to check for new messages, but his gaze lingered on the banking app. Sure enough, the promised sum of two hundred fifty thousand U.S. dollars had cleared into his account this morning. It was set up as a "consultancy advance." The deposit made everything feel final, no turning back. His father's grim diagnosis, the abrupt loss of the Late Antiquity Department, and a swirl of personal guilt over leaving home so fast—none of that had truly sunk in yet. But the money was real.

He fiddled with the phone, half hoping to see a text from Salma, but knowing she was likely at her own doctor's appointment. She had insisted he go—had prayed him out the door, in fact—and though he'd put on a brave smile, a piece of him felt torn away leaving her. His mind bounced between worry over her condition and the memory of his father's exhausted eyes, overshadowed by a secret that would soon become impossible to hide. Joseph forced himself to breathe deeply. There was a job to do, and for the sake of that job, a wealthy patron had just placed a small fortune in Joseph's lap. He closed his eyes and let the purring of the jet engines lull him into a half sleep, praying that somehow all of this turmoil might be worth it.

A few hours later, Joseph woke to the flight attendant gently touching his shoulder. Dinner service was about to begin. The meal was extravagant—filet mignon, fresh salad with balsamic drizzle, and real silverware instead of plastic. The pampering was welcome, though it couldn't fully erase the tension coiled in his gut. Still, he managed a polite conversation with his seat neighbor, a Turkish businessman wearing a sharp suit, who occasionally asked if Joseph was traveling for leisure or work.

"Work," Joseph said simply, trying not to divulge too many details. "Archaeological research in Hatay Province."

The businessman's eyebrows rose with curiosity, but Joseph let the conversation dissolve quickly, feigning tiredness. He sipped a final glass of water, stuffed his headphones in, and tried to let the hum of the cabin carry him away from his anxieties.

—

The layover in Istanbul's new airport was a blur of crowds, foreign announcements echoing overhead, and lines at passport control. As a first-class passenger, Joseph at least enjoyed a faster security check and a plush lounge to wait out the next flight. The lounge had floor-to-ceiling windows overlooking the tarmac, from which he watched planes roll in under the glow of floodlights. He recognized the livery of the next flight: a Turkish carrier bound for Hatay. In an hour, they'd board.

He used the time to check messages. The deposit was still there in his account, leaving him a little numb. Emails from colleagues trickled in, many of them oblivious to the fiasco at Notre Dame. A short text from Henry Briggs read, "Safe travels, Joe. Keep me posted. F.R. says hi." Joseph typed a quick thanks and stared at the phone, half expecting a call from his father. That never came. He reasoned Dad might still be out on the property, or maybe resting. He flicked the phone to airplane mode when the boarding call sounded.

—

The flight from Istanbul to Hatay was shorter, under two hours, but it felt more claustrophobic—this was a smaller plane, fewer frills, narrower aisles. At least the seat next to Joseph was empty. He used the time to read over a few reference documents Dr. Lavrov had emailed, describing how the 2023 earthquakes had revealed previously unreachable layers beneath Antakya's older quarters. The reading was dense, but Joseph's adrenaline spiked as he came across repeated references to "a golden dome," "a scriptorum," and "fragments of late sixth-century parchment." It was everything he had ever dreamed of verifying. Even half-verified, the rumors had been enough to uproot him from Indiana and deposit him here in Turkey.

His chest tightened. What if they really do have the Church of the Golden Dome? He tried to squash the swirl of excitement. If it was real, then he might be standing at a threshold that changed the entire understanding of early Church relics. And if it was real... he might also be stepping into the crosshairs of those who wanted to exploit or control those relics for reasons he could only guess at.

—

Stepping off the plane in Hatay, Joseph felt a rush of hot air slap him in the face. The region might have been battered by an earthquake a year ago, but the climate had lost none of its warmth. The airport was modest, a single terminal with large windows that overlooked the runways. Joseph navigated the brief line at passport control, nodding politely at the uniformed officer who stamped his passport without a word.

He wandered to the baggage carousel, praying his suitcase and equipment trunk had made the journey. To his relief, everything arrived intact. As he adjusted the straps on his carry-on, he surveyed the arrivals area. Families congregated around the exit, holding signs or hugging loved ones. Joseph felt a pang of longing for home. He spotted a man—tall, broad across the shoulders, wearing a leather jacket despite the heat—holding a small sign that read "Dr. Scanlon" in uneven black letters.

"That's me," Joseph muttered under his breath, heading over.

Up close, the man looked to be about thirty, but he carried himself with a discipline and bearing of someone older. He had a clean-shaven head, piercing gray eyes, and a jaw that suggested he'd taken (and maybe dealt) a few punches in his life. Definitely ex-military, Joseph concluded. Or maybe not even ex. The name on his sign was spelled in heavy block letters: SCANLON.

Joseph extended his hand. "Hello, I'm Joseph."

The man blinked once, stiffly returning the handshake with a grip like a vise. "I am Oleg. I pick you up." He fumbled a bit, his English clearly forced. "Welcome... to Turkey."

"Thank you," Joseph said, hoisting his carry-on. "Good to be here."

"Good," Oleg replied curtly. Then he reached for Joseph's suitcase. "You follow me, yes? Car this way."

Joseph allowed Oleg to grab the large case, noticing the man handle it as though it weighed nothing. Outside, the midday sun glared over a parking lot that looked half empty. Oleg led him to a squat, dusty SUV with tinted windows. The back was crammed with some gear—evidently Oleg had come prepared. With Joseph's luggage secured, Oleg slid into the driver's seat, fired up the engine, and blasted the air conditioning.

As they pulled out of the airport, Oleg glanced at Joseph in the rearview mirror. "Flight okay?"

"It was good," Joseph replied. "Long, but no problems."

Oleg nodded. "Long flight. Money good, though?" He ventured a half-smile, which Joseph realized was meant to be some form of friendly small talk.

Joseph tried to mask his discomfort at the question. "Yes, the arrangement is generous."

Oleg focused on the road ahead. "Lavrov, he say job important. Big job. Church of Golden Dome. Very old."

"That's what I hear. Dr. Lavrov said you found some old fragments in the scriptorum?"

"Yes, yes," Oleg said. He slowed to avoid a small cluster of goats crossing the roadside. "I was not there one year ago. But I come soon after. Earthquake broke ground, made big rubble. Our people, they look for, how you say… a new place to search. Then they find walls made of stones with old cross carving."

"The walls of a church?" Joseph prompted.

""Yes. People in the city call it the 'Golden Dome Church' from ancient times. It suffered significant collapse, but some parts remain. The roof fallen, yet the archway still stands. Inside, behind large stones, we discovered scriptorium. There are books and parchments, all covered in dust." Oleg shrugged, keeping his eyes on the road. "I'm security coordinator, so I ensure all protocols are followed. I no read the texts, but we did see some old writing. The team mentioned it's from Pope… Gregor… Gregorius?"

"Gregory," Joseph corrected, leaning forward with excitement. "Gregory the Great?"

"Da, Great Gregory." Oleg gave a short laugh. "Good for you maybe, for me just old paper. They also find small fragment, talk about 'Keys of Peter.' Boss man very excited. Boss man is Dr. Lavrov, yes?"

Joseph nodded. "Yes, that's him. So, you all have been here for about a year?"

"Team set up last year. They build many tents at first, then buy old motel near Orontes River. Now we have base. We keep site secure." Oleg glanced Joseph's way. "Many... how you say... watchers. Government officials, maybe other men who want to steal artifact."

Joseph's heart thumped. "Steal them?"

"Anything valuable, they try to steal. Art, relic, old things to sell. So, we have security detail."

Joseph let that sink in. The short drive from the airport into Hatay Province took them down a winding, potholed road. The land was scarred in places, with collapsed buildings occasionally visible in the distance—grim reminders of the massive quake that had shaken the region. Occasionally, Joseph saw partially demolished structures, tarps draped across gaps, and piles of broken masonry. Oleg navigated around them like an obstacle course.

"All stable now?" Joseph asked, eyeing a shaky edifice that looked on the verge of sliding into the road.

Oleg shrugged. "Stable enough. But local government is slow to fix. Our sponsor has money, so we hire local workers to help. They like us some days, not so much other days."

Joseph frowned. "Why wouldn't they like you?"

"Because we go to old sites. They want to help rebuild city. They think we care more about old stones than living people." He gave a slight shrug. "Maybe they are right, maybe not. Is complicated."

Joseph sighed. He could see how tension would arise if an archaeological dig overshadowed urgent humanitarian rebuilding. "Well, hopefully we can show them the value in preserving their heritage."

Oleg merely grunted in acknowledgment.

They drove on for another half hour, weaving between damaged roads until they reached a small cluster of buildings near a wide bend in the Orontes River. The water looked muddied, the banks lined with patchwork tents and half-demolished homes. Towering overhead were the remains of a battered motel sign, once neon but now a battered husk. The structure beneath it showed layers of fresh plaster. A few SUVs and trucks were parked around.

"Is compound," Oleg said, pointing. "We fix old motel. All dig staff live here."

Joseph swallowed. It wasn't much to look at—peeling paint, boarded-up windows on the second floor. But there were signs of new construction: recent cinder blocks, a modest chain-link fence. It was midday, the sun at its peak, and the dusty air carried the smell of cooking oil and grilled meats. His stomach rumbled in spite of his nerves.

Oleg killed the engine. "We go inside, meet, rest. Come."

Joseph followed him around the side of the building, where a makeshift courtyard had been fenced off. A small canopy provided shade over a half dozen picnic tables. A generator hummed nearby, cables snaking into the motel's ground floor. An open doorway led into what looked like an improvised cafeteria. Inside, Joseph found a group of about ten men and women seated around two large tables, talking and eating. Their voices—mostly Russian—lowered as they spotted him.

Oleg clapped Joseph's shoulder. "This is Dr. Joseph Scanlon. He new man from America." Some turned in their chairs, a few nodded, and at least one or two scowled.

A muscular guy in a sweat-stained T-shirt stood up first. He had a shaved head, with dark stubble across his jaw. Despite the casual clothes, Joseph could see the posture of someone who had spent serious time in uniform. He extended his hand with a wide grin. "Hey, buddy! Dimitri Sokolov, Field Director. We call me Dima. You're Joseph, right?"

Joseph shook the man's hand, feeling the calluses. "Pleasure to meet you, Dima."

Dima's grin was full of mischief. "So... you big professor from Notre Dame. Means you must be genius or CIA spy. We see which one, yes?" He laughed loudly, prompting a chuckle from a few others.

Joseph tried to laugh it off. "Well, hopefully neither is a problem" Joseph responded with quick sarcasm that masked his interior fear at their joke.

Dima waved a hand. "Is joke. We have good sense of humor, you will see." He turned to the group. "Everyone, pay attention! This is Dr. Scanlon, the man Lavrov told us about. He read old texts better than we read cheap Russian newspaper. Treat him good, or we send you back to donkey duty."

A wiry man with a neatly trimmed mustache raised an eyebrow. He had the sharp, angular features of someone perpetually unimpressed. "Artem Moroz, Site Supervisor," he introduced himself flatly. "We have a timeline to respect, so I hope you can perform quickly." His voice was clipped, betraying impatience. "I am ex-VDV. I do not like to wait. I was trained in archaeology at Lomonosov Moscow State University, so I understand the importance of precision and speed in our work."

Joseph nodded, not entirely sure how to respond. "I'll do my best."

Artem gave a tiny nod of acceptance. "Good."

A broad-shouldered man, slightly overweight with a jovial stature and a drooping eyelid stood next, giving Joseph a casual salute. "Grigory Ivanov—'Grisha'—Surveyor and GIS specialist. I do maps." He spoke with a comedic sparkle in his voice. "If you need to find bathroom, I can pinpoint coordinates to two decimal places." That earned a small round of laughter from a few of the people at the table. "I was in engineering corps for Russian Army. Now, I make advanced topographic surveys."

Joseph cracked a smile. "I appreciate that. Good to meet you."

Next, a man in a dusty button-down shirt raised his hand. His face carried gentle lines, and a gold wedding band glinted on his finger. There was a fatherly and integrity-filled look about him, suggesting wisdom and trustworthiness. "Ivan Petrenko, Finds Specialist. I trained in archaeology at Lomonosov Moscow State University. I used to be with the 76th Guards Air Assault Division. Now I specialize in cataloging artifacts. Father of three. Wish I was home with them, but here we are." He smiled, clearly homesick. "I classify everything: coins, bones, fragments, you name it."

"Three kids—that must keep you busy," Joseph said politely.

"It does, my friend. So, get it right," he teased, "so we can all go home sooner."

Another figure rose. She was tall, maybe mid-thirties, wearing jeans and an oversized T-shirt. She had long, chestnut hair cascading down her back, and her striking green eyes were framed by a pair of sleek, black-rimmed glasses. "Elena Ivanova , geoarchaeologist." She spoke with precise diction, no nonsense. "I analyze soil, sediment. The site's formation." She cleared her throat. "I trained in archaeology at Lomonosov Moscow State University, which has a renowned program. I am thorough, so expect many questions from me."

Joseph nodded. "I'll do my best to answer them."

A petite woman with dark hair, streaks of silver at her temples, offered him a coy smile. Her almond-shaped eyes, a deep shade of hazel, seemed to sparkle with a mischievous glint. She wore a fitted tan outfit that accentuated her slender frame, the fabric shimmering softly under the light. "Natalia Markova, conservator. I went to University with Elena and we are great friends. I'm the one who tries to keep these precious artifacts from crumbling into dust once they're exposed to air and I'm responsible for unifying the parchment fragments." She took a moment to run a hand through her hair. "The men might joke, but my job is essential." She gave Joseph an appraising look. "I'll be sure to call you if I... need an extra pair of hands." Natalia grinned at Elena, who mumbled something back in Russian, her tone playful but indecipherable to Joseph. The exchange left him unsure if Natalia's earlier remarks were flirtatious or simply part of a friendly jest between the two women. Joseph, unsure if that was flirtation or just an inside joke with Elena, responded with a polite "Glad to help."

Lastly, Dima gestured to three people sitting with trays of half-eaten lunches in front of them. "Here are the field archaeologists: Yakov, Sasha, and Zoya." Each gave a quick greeting. Yakov, a medium-built man with alert eyes, said he'd done a stint with the Russian peacekeepers in the Caucasus. Sasha and Zoya, both women in their late twenties. They nodded politely, then returned to sipping their drinks. Their approach to Joseph seemed guarded, as though they were still deciding what to make of him. They were responsible for the discovery process.

"Now you see our wonderful family," Dima declared dramatically, with a wave of his arms. "Most of us have some background in the military, but we are archaeologists at heart. Or mercenaries for old stones, who can say?" He shrugged theatrically. "We do serious work here, yes?"

A smattering of chuckles rose, but Joseph sensed an undercurrent of tension. He was clearly the outsider—the American. And in the midst of the current geopolitical climate, that might not always be comfortable.

One of the men in the back, wearing a black T-shirt, piped up with a grin, "CIA, KGB, FSB, NSA—who can keep track, right?" The rest roared with laughter, all eyes on Joseph. He forced a grin and chuckled along, trying to show he wasn't rattled.

"Relax, guys," Dima said, raising his palms. "He is our new friend. He help us read old books so we can finish mission. Less suspicion, more cooperation, da?"

"Da," came a few half-hearted replies, before everyone returned to their food. Oleg guided Joseph to a seat at one of the tables, then promptly wandered off, presumably to rejoin the security detail.

Dima, noticing Joseph's unease as he staired at Oleg's table, leaned in closer and spoke in a low voice, "Those guys you're looking at? They're all security contractors. Tough as nails. They served on Russian military bases in Syria before taking on this gig. Not the kind of men you want to mess with."

Joseph nodded, counting 10 of them in total and trying to mask his apprehension. "Do they speak any English?"

Dima shook his head. "Not a word. They stick to Russian. Oleg is the only one of them who speaks English and it is not so good. But trust me, you don't need to understand their language to know you should steer clear. Just keep your head down and let them do their job."

Dima clapped him on the shoulder again. "You hungry, yes? We have cafeteria. Food is not so good, but better than field rations. Go get plate, then we find your room."

Joseph nodded and collected a bowl of lentil soup, some bread, and a bottle of water. He realized he was ravenous, the day's travels and the swirling adrenaline leaving him starved. He sat down, forced some small talk with a few team members about how hot it was here compared to Indiana. The language barrier was an issue—some spoke passable English, others only a few words. The conversation was halting, punctuated by translations from the bilingual ones. Still, Joseph tried to remain friendly, gleaning bits of each person's story. Slowly, the tension eased to a tolerable level.

After lunch, Dima took Joseph around the back of the building, pushing open a door that led to a dim hallway. The place definitely still resembled the old motel it once was: chipped tiles on the floor, cheap veneer doors. Now, however, Joseph noticed a row of cots and crates stacked with equipment along one wall.

"We store gear here," Dima explained, pointing to the crates. "In the bigger rooms, we have labs for cleaning artifacts. Watch your step—some leaks in the pipes. Also, watch for scorpions." He winked in that mischievous way again.

Joseph forced a chuckle. "Good to know."

They climbed a narrow staircase to the second level, passing a few closed doors from which Joseph heard the hum of air conditioning units. Dima stopped at the third door on the left and pushed it open, revealing a small room with a single bed, a metal desk, and a battered wardrobe. A ceiling fan spun lazily overhead.

"Is not five-star, but better than a tent, no?" Dima asked with a grin.

Joseph placed his carry-on on the bed, looking around. "Yes, definitely. I appreciate it."

"We have Wi-Fi for the team," Dima continued, stepping inside. "Cell data is worthless here, too many outages, or government blackouts. But we have satellite link. Not super fast, but you can message and do your important research. Password is 'VolkovEmpire.'" He wiggled his eyebrows. "They set it. Some inside joke about President Volkov wanting to be world leader or something. I don't think so, just a strong nationalist."

Joseph stiffened. "Right. Thank you."

Dima raised his palms theatrically. "No problem. Just do not download big American movies. We have limited bandwidth." Then he leaned closer, his tone dropping conspiratorially. "Also, do not expect privacy. The system is run by... special men. Probably FSB watchers. So, if you talk to family, keep it... normal. Understand?"

"I understand," Joseph murmured. He had already suspected as much.

Dima nodded. "One more thing. You mention you want to see family in city?"

"Yes, my in-laws live in Antakya," Joseph said, stepping over his duffel. "Well, they're not exactly in the city center right now—they moved after the quake. But they're close."

"Lavrov told me you want to visit them. I have security instructions: no one leaves compound alone. You will have an escort. For your safety. That okay with you?"

Joseph nodded calmly. "Yes, that's fine. I promised Dr. Lavrov I wouldn't roam around unguarded. Just want to see them, maybe tomorrow, if that's possible."

Dima's eyes narrowed. "You sure they are who they say they are? You American, they are Middle Eastern. I need to be sure no... extremist ties?"

Joseph inhaled slowly, controlling his frustration. "I'm actually half-Lebanese with dual US and Lebanese citizenship. My in-laws are devout Catholics—Chaldean Rite. My father-in-law runs a restaurant that is frequented by Christians and stays close to his faith. They've been in this area for generations. No extremist connections, no hidden agendas. They hate violence."

Dima studied him for a moment, then gave a shrug. "Okay. We check all carefully. If they are truly normal, you can see them tomorrow after day's work. You will take one security man, maybe two. We do not want trouble. What is the man's name?"

"Namir Haddad. Thank you," Joseph replied, forcing a polite smile. "I appreciate it."

"Yes, yes, I will run a check on him" Dima said, taking a step back. "You are probably very tired, da? Best to rest. We have real briefing tomorrow morning, 0700. Do not be late." He winked again. "Welcome aboard, Joseph."

With that, Dima turned and left, the door clicking shut behind him. Joseph sank onto the bed, the springs squeaking. Sweat clung to his skin, and the single ceiling fan offered only limited relief. Exhaustion hit him like a wave. He rummaged in his pocket for his phone, turned on the Wi-Fi, and connected using the password—VolkovEmpire. He half chuckled to himself at the irony of the code. After a few seconds, a tiny icon showed he had a stable, albeit weak, connection.

He opened a messaging app, typed a short text to Salma:

Joseph (7:22 PM):

Hey sweetheart, I'm here safely. The place is rough, but I have a room and Wi-Fi. How are you holding up? How's the baby? I'm about to collapse with jet lag, but I love you and miss you already.

He hit send, watching the little status indicator swirl. Finally, it showed delivered. A minute later, his phone buzzed.

Salma (7:24 PM):

Praise God, you made it. Doctor says everything looks stable. I'm still very early in the pregnancy, so please keep praying. I'm praying for you, that you'll make big discoveries and stay safe. I love you. Rest, my love.

Joseph felt a deep ache in his chest. It was the first time she'd so openly used the word "pregnancy" with him since his departure. The thought brought relief and fear in equal measure—there was so much at stake, both physically and emotionally. He typed a quick reply:

Joseph (7:25 PM):

So happy to hear that. I'll do my best here. Rest well, darling. Love you always.

He thumbed the phone off, setting it aside. For a moment, he let himself imagine a future—her belly growing, his father possibly still alive to meet their child, this entire dig concluded. It was a dream scenario, but the reality of it felt far away. Right now, he was a stranger in a compound full of ex-military Russians, searching for relics that could rewrite history. And he was tethered to them by more than intellectual interest: the quarter-million dollars in his account guaranteed he'd see this job through.

He lay back, the pillow stiff and lumpy, the overhead fan spinning in slow circles. A swirl of unanswered questions tugged at him. How far would these people go to find the Keys? He had seen their suspicious eyes, heard the jokes about the CIA. He had no illusions about this being a straightforward academic expedition. Yet, for better or worse, he was in.

He shut his eyes. Exhaustion crowded out his anxiety, and within seconds, he sank into oblivion.

Tomorrow, the real work—and the real uncertainties—would begin.

TEN

Fragments and Introductions

Joseph woke well before dawn, long before any of his colleagues stirred. The abrupt time difference had knotted his sleep schedule, and at 4:00 a.m. sharp he was wide awake in his cramped quarters. He lay still for a minute, blinking at the ceiling, recalling the swirl of events from the previous day: his first briefing with Dima, the flurry of artifact fragments, the hidden tensions he sensed throughout this makeshift headquarters. The building he occupied had once been an old roadside motel—an austere two-level block of stained stucco walls and flickering neon. Now, hastily repurposed, it served as their central base of operations for the dig in Antakya. The hallway doors remained the same cheap plywood, but the second-floor corridor was lined with weathered plastic crates labeled "Fragile," "Samples," and "Parchment." Power cords and extension cables draped from the old ceiling fixtures, transforming what had once been an unremarkable motel into a hive of clandestine archaeology—and perhaps something more.

He had three hours until his next scheduled briefing with Dima, the earnest Russian colleague overseeing daily operations. Joseph rose quietly, careful not to disturb the occupant of the room next door—he thought it might be the nighttime security guard, a burly man who came and went with minimal conversation. In the corner of his own small room, a single fluorescent lamp sputtered into life. Books were stacked on the little rickety desk. It still amazed him how few of his references had been digitized: the deeper he dove into Late Antiquity, the more reliant he was on old tomes with fragile spines, margin notes by long-deceased scholars, and archaic footnotes scrawled in Latin or Greek. He wondered if modern research—AI programs, digitization—could ever truly capture the richness of these physical relics of knowledge.

He lit the desk lamp fully and rested a few volumes in front of him. One was a compendium of Pope Gregory's epistles, the other a bilingual edition of early Syriac Christian documents. As he flipped through, he caught himself reflecting on the corridor outside: he recalled stepping over dusty tarps, noticing the faint odor of cleaning chemicals from the housekeeping closet. He hadn't even seen a formal security station, but he felt eyes on him every time he passed that main hallway camera. The situation was unusual for a standard archaeological mission—too many uniformed men, too many hush-hush conversations in Russian. He suspected the FSB might be quietly monitoring them all, especially any foreigner. Even with Lavrov's academic veneer, there was an undercurrent of tension that hung in the motel's dim corridors.

Joseph tried to read a few paragraphs of ancient commentary on the "Claves Petri" references but found his concentration drifting. His laptop pinged with an incoming email. He frowned—who would be writing him at this hour? Opening it, he saw it was from his father: Michael Scanlon.

Joseph, hope you're safe and well. I had coffee this afternoon (your morning) with an old friend on the Notre Dame board. I'm not naming names, but we started talking about what's been happening with the Late Antiquities Department. Son, something's off. He says the decision to dissolve the department was sudden and came from pressure up top. I plan to look deeper—never liked seeing good men railroaded. Let me know you're okay, and if there's anything I can do.

Love you.

—Dad

Joseph swallowed, anxiety curling in his stomach. If his father was sniffing around the board, that might draw unwanted attention. And if the FSB or other intelligence types were indeed tracking communications, it could place his father at risk. Joseph quickly typed a reply:

Dad, I appreciate your concern more than I can say, but please—don't investigate. I'm right where I'm supposed to be. All's fine here. Call it an odd assignment, but it's my job for now. Focus on your own health and well-being, okay?

Love you.

—Joseph

He paused, reading his own words, trying to make them sound calm and confident. With a final click, he sent his reply, hoping it would arrive without any digital interference.

He snapped his laptop shut with a sigh and rubbed at his forehead. Four-thirty in the morning. Still far too early to disturb anyone else, but ironically, it might be just the right time to call home. In South Bend, it would be evening. Perhaps he could catch Salma before she went to bed. He pulled out his phone, found the best corner for a halfway-decent signal, and dialed. After three rings, she answered.

"Joseph?" Her voice was thick, as if she'd been dozing on the sofa.

"Hey," he said gently. "Hope I'm not interrupting anything important."

"No, not at all." He heard the rustle of blankets, imagined her curled in their living room. "I was just reading some paperwork. The last day of the workweek ended a couple of hours ago, so I'm enjoying my quiet time."

He grinned, pressing the phone closer to his ear. "So... any updates from the doctor?"

A pause. Then came her soft exhale. "Still good news. The baby's stable, no complications so far."

Joseph closed his eyes, relief and longing colliding in his chest. "I miss you. I want to be there holding your hand, hearing every detail from the doctor in person."

"I miss you, too. But we agreed, right? This job came at the strangest time, but it might be divine providence. We can pay our mortgage; we can keep afloat... and who knows—maybe you'll find the lost Keys of Peter after all." She tried for a note of encouragement, though her voice wavered slightly.

He chuckled softly. "Wouldn't that be something? Keep praying for me. I feel like the walls have ears here."

"Always," she whispered. "I love you."

"I love you more," he said, heart brimming with gratitude. "Get some rest, and if you need me—"

"I'll call," she finished. "Stay safe, Joseph."

They hung up. For a moment, he simply held the phone against his forehead, eyes shut, offering a silent prayer for his wife, their unborn child, and all the unknowns looming around them.

By 6:30 a.m., he was in the building's makeshift cafeteria—really just the converted motel lounge. The space had been stripped of most motel furniture; tables were lined up in rows, with a few battered chairs scattered around. The coffee machine was manned by a local Turkish cook wearing a stained apron, who flashed Joseph a welcoming grin as he approached.

"Merhaba," Joseph said, remembering some basic Turkish.

The cook nodded, ladling thick, aromatic coffee into a small cup. Joseph drank deeply, savoring the bitter edge. He recognized it as a strong Turkish brew—a far cry from the drip coffee in South Bend.

Midway through his drink, a familiar figure appeared in the doorway—Dima. Tall, broad-chested, with a neatly trimmed beard, he wore a casual jacket and slacks. He saw Joseph and approached with a genial smile.

"Early riser, I see," Dima said in accented English.

"Jet lag, mostly," Joseph replied. "Good morning."

Dima motioned for Joseph to follow him toward a quieter corner. "I'm glad I caught you before we start the day. We'll share a proper breakfast in a minute, but I wanted to talk first."

Joseph studied him curiously. "Is something wrong?"

"No, not at all." Dima's laugh was surprisingly warm. "But I want to prepare you for your new workspace... and your new collaborator."

Joseph's brow furrowed. "You mean Natalia?"

Dima nodded. "Yes. Natalia is brilliant. Seriously, she's one of the best we've got at classifying and reconstructing textual fragments. But she's also, shall we say, unpredictable. Some days, she's lost in the text, barely speaking. Other days, she can be extremely forward, asking personal questions or making personal remarks. She does have a temper, but rarely shows it unless she feels cornered."

"I can handle that," Joseph said with a shrug. "Honestly, I've worked with all types of academics." As he recalled their brief introduction, Joseph couldn't help but notice Natalia's striking presence. Her beauty was undeniable, the kind that could easily turn heads and leave a lasting impression. She carried herself with a confidence that seemed to magnify her allure, the kind of woman who could intimidate men with just a glance. But Joseph had learned long ago not to let appearances throw him off balance. He gained the ability to look beyond captivating exteriors and regard others for their virtue and character.

"Of course," Dima continued. "I just don't want you caught off-guard if she says something strange. She might test you. She also asked about you after your initial introduction. Maybe your interest in Gregory's letters intrigued her. Or maybe she's excited to offload some of her workload."

Joseph tried to hide his discomfort. "Right. Well, I'm looking forward to collaborating. I won't be thrown."

"Good," Dima said. Then he lowered his voice. "She's married, by the way. I'm not implying anything—just letting you know. She keeps to herself, but sometimes new arrivals see her ring and wonder where her husband is. He visits occasionally. They're quite private. If you have any confusion about her comments or gestures, don't overthink it."

Joseph nodded, a flicker of relief. "Got it."

They chatted casually over the food, sharing small jokes and observations about local culture. Dima seemed genuinely passionate about the project, even if Joseph suspected he reported to other superiors. After they finished, Dima led Joseph up a different staircase than the one Joseph had used. This flight was narrower, leading them to a wide landing on the second floor: the old motel conference room. A sign reading "Authorized Personnel Only" was pinned crookedly to the door.

"This used to be where they hosted big gatherings," Dima explained as he fumbled with a key. "Now we've turned it into a combined lab and office space."

The door swung open, revealing a wide area partitioned by tall shelving units. Tables were strewn with scanning equipment, bright desk lamps, and carefully labeled plastic bins. Computers hummed in every corner. A few large boards stood against walls, pinned with plastic-sleeved parchment fragments and photographs. Joseph quickly counted at least half a dozen people milling about, though it felt eerily quiet—everyone worked in near silence or spoke in hushed undertones.

Dima guided him past two large worktables. "Over there is where Ivan and Elena do the cleaning and conservation. They remove debris, examine the parchment fibers, rehydrate if needed. Then they photograph everything in high-res, sometimes using ultraviolet or infrared to catch hidden text. Natalia's domain is right here." He pointed to a cluster of desks backed by a tall whiteboard covered in pinned translations, sticky notes, and scrawled references in three different languages.

Natalia was seated at a station with three enormous monitors forming a semicircle around her. She looked up when they approached, her gray eyes cool and focused. "Hello," she said, polite but distant. She wore a simple black sweater, sleeves rolled to her elbows, exposing slender forearms. A few strands of dark hair had escaped her ponytail, framing her face in a slightly disheveled way that contrasted with her otherwise professional bearing.

"Natalia," Dima said with a cordial nod. "I'm bringing Joseph up to speed on the process. He'll be working closely with you on identification, classification, and—"

"Physical reconstruction," she interrupted, tapping one of her screens. "We have dozens of fragments that might piece together into a single letter or document. The AI helps match fiber patterns, stains, and letter shapes, but someone has to interpret them."

Joseph sensed a slight tension in her posture. Their previous, brief meeting had felt odd—he recalled a stray remark from her that left him uneasy to say the least. Clearing his throat, he said, "I look forward to cooperating. Dima's told me you're the best at this."

Natalia's lips twitched, not quite a smile. "He flatters me." Then her tone softened. "But I do appreciate having another academic around. It helps."

For a moment, they stood there, the hum of the computers filling the void. Finally, Natalia motioned to two adjacent chairs behind the monitors. "We might as well start. Sit."

He settled into the seat next to her. The desk was cluttered with printouts, sticky notes, and partial translations. He glanced around. "So, how's everything organized?"

She tilted the center monitor so he could see. "I feed scanned images into an AI tool that tries to match patterns: corners, tears, water damage. It also analyzes letter shapes or partial words across Latin, Greek, and Syriac scripts. The program proposes probable fits, but I have to confirm each one. Half the time, it's off by a fraction of a millimeter, and we have to rely on paleographic clues to confirm alignment."

Joseph nodded, impressed. "So, you're bridging the mechanical and the human approach."

"Exactly." She angled in her chair to face him. "Look, I'm sure you've read all about the systematic steps—cleaning, conservation, photography, digitization, classification. I've been leading the identification and reconstruction tasks until now. But with so many new fragments turning up every day, we need extra brainpower. That's where you come in."

Her voice was clipped, businesslike. Yet she was giving him her full attention, as though weighing his capabilities. He glanced around. "Dima said we'll be sharing a workspace?"

She nodded. "Yes. There's an empty desk next to mine. We'll be here for hours on end, matching fragments, cross-checking references in those big medieval volumes you lug around." She paused, then her tone shifted. "In my experience, that many late antiquity tomes usually indicates strong convictions—either religious or purely historical."

"Why not both?" Joseph offered with a small smile.

She tapped a pen on the desk. "Fair enough."

He remembered Dima's aside and decided to approach the topic gently. "So, I recall at our last meeting, you said something about how we were bound to work together or something like that. I, um, hope I didn't misread your meaning."

She lifted a brow. "I say a lot of things. Don't take me too seriously." Then she cleared her throat. "I'm married, so it's not as though... well, anyway, my husband came for a quick visit last month, but mostly we each do our own thing. He's busy with his work and Moscow is far away." Natalia's husband, Maxim, was a striking man with sharp features and deep-set blue eyes that seemed to hold a world of their own. Joseph tried to read her expression, which was mild but guarded. "You seem happy?"

Natalia's voice warmed slightly. "Yes, I am. He's supportive, in his own way. We just—" She hesitated, eyes flicking away. "We each have big ambitions, which can mean we're rarely in the same place for long." Then she gave a quick, bright laugh. "But it works. Truly." Maxim was deeply immersed in his pursuit of academic accolades, often presenting at international conferences and publishing papers that earned him respect in his field. Despite his professional successes, the growing tension between them was palpable. Natalia often felt like a mere spectator in her husband's life, their conversations increasingly limited to logistical exchanges. The distance, both physical and emotional, had become a chasm, leaving her to navigate her own path while he remained consumed by his ambitions.

Joseph recognized a practiced note in her tone, as though she'd repeated that line more than once. A flash of sympathy rose in him. "That must be tough. Kids ever factor into that picture?"

Her face stilled. "No," she said simply. She didn't clarify whether it was by choice or circumstance. "What about you? You're younger than I expected. Mid-thirties? Married?"

"Late thirties," Joseph corrected with a friendly smile. "Married for fourteen years. We had a long struggle with infertility—didn't think it would ever happen. Then, out of the blue, just before I left for this trip, we found out she's pregnant."

Natalia's eyes widened. "That's... quite a miracle."

"I think so." Joseph felt a surge of warmth. "I can hardly express how grateful I am. But I'm missing all the little moments. My wife just told me the doctor wants her to avoid flying, so I have no idea when I'll see her in person."

For a heartbeat, Natalia seemed almost distressed, her gaze slipping away. "I see," she said softly, then immediately pivoted. "Well, congratulations. I hope everything goes smoothly." She cleared her throat. "Anyway, we should focus on these fragments, yes?"

He noted her discomfort and let the subject drop. "Sure, let's see what you've got."

She gestured to the screens, pulling up a specific set of digital scans. "This cluster forms the partial letter that convinced Dr. Lavrov to bring you out here—that references the mention of *Claves Petri*. We managed to piece it together from about sixteen separate scraps. What do you make of this letter from Bishop Anastasius?"

"You see," he began, "Pope Gregory, in a moment of foresight, likely sent the Claves Petri—the Keys of Peter—to Bishop Anastasius at the end of the 6th century. This was during the Lombard invasion of Rome. The best theory is that he did this to preserve them in a safer location, and Antioch, under the protection of the

Byzantine Empire, seemed ideal. It was already a repository of sacred relics like the True Cross and the Holy Lance."

He paused, glancing at her to ensure she was following. "But then, history took a cruel turn. In 611, the Persians attacked Antioch, and by 613, the city was sacked. Khosrow II, the Persian emperor, was relentless in his quest to seize the most significant religious and historical artifacts."

"And this letter from Bishop Anastasius?" she prompted, leaning in closer.

"The letter suggests that Anastasius realized the keys couldn't be smuggled out during the siege. So, he likely devised a plan to hide them within the city. He must have gone to great lengths during those two harrowing years to ensure they were concealed, leaving behind clues that only true Christians could decipher and not the Persian Zoroastrians."

Natalia's eyes lit up with recognition. "That makes so much sense. The field archaeologists are constantly unearthing pieces that seem cryptic at first, but now... it fits. These aren't just random artifacts; they're part of a larger puzzle left by Anastasius."

"Exactly," he nodded, excitement creeping into his voice. "These fragments are more than relics; they're a map, a testament to the bishop's dedication to protect the sacred keys. And with each piece you find, we're getting closer to uncovering his hidden trail."

Natalia nodded. "The bishop was taken captive, presumably. We found these references in the margins that suggest he was scrambling to hide the relics."

Joseph tapped the screen. "Right. He'd have had nearly two years to do it before the final sack. So, the question is, where? The letter hints Anastasius left clues 'for the faithful who come after him.' He obviously believed the Keys were more than a symbol."

"It lines up with these other fragments I've been translating," Natalia said. "Some are more cryptic—snatches of liturgical phrases or secret instructions, maybe. The field archaeologists keep sending me updates from the Golden Dome site. They're turning up new shards each day."

Joseph felt his pulse quicken. "That's extraordinary. If he had two years, he could have buried them, hidden them in a sealed chamber, or anywhere in the city which was under siege for two years."

Joseph exhaled, excitement sparking. "So, it's not just a matter of rummaging around in the ruins. We have textual clues that might lead us to the actual resting place of the Keys. This is starting to feel like we're on the cusp of something huge."

Her eyes met his, and for a fleeting moment, there was an unspoken charge between them—a shared passion for uncovering the truth. Then she reached out in her excitement, lightly touching Joseph's forearm. "Exactly," she said, almost breathless. "We're unraveling a centuries-old puzzle in real time. My data is finally making sense!"

The contact was brief, but Joseph felt it, a faint friction in the air. Natalia must have realized it too, for she withdrew her hand abruptly, clearing her throat. "Anyway," she said briskly, "I have a wall over here where I'm mapping out partial translations, printing out each snippet. Let me show you."

They stood and walked to a partition near the back, a tall cork-board plastered with small pinned-up documents. Joseph noticed short lines in Latin, Greek, and Syriac scrawled beneath each pinned fragment—Natalia's working translations, color-coded.

"This is incredible," Joseph breathed. Then he let out a soft laugh, an almost boyish glee washing over him. "I feel like a freshman at Notre Dame all over again, discovering the vastness of knowledge for the first time."

Natalia regarded him for a moment, her expression inscrutable. Then, unexpectedly, she smiled. "I like your enthusiasm, Joseph. It's good to see genuine passion in a place like this."

He was about to respond when the door opened and Dima reappeared. "Hey, how are we doing? By the way, Joseph, I almost forgot: we're scheduled to visit the Golden Dome site in an hour. Thought you'd want to see it in person."

Joseph's eyes lit up. "Absolutely. That's exactly what I was hoping."

Natalia nodded, her earlier reserve melting a fraction. "We can gather a few relevant notes, then head out together. If we're lucky, they'll have uncovered new segments overnight."

"All right, let's not waste any time," Dima said, gesturing for them to follow him. "Dress light, though—it's already getting hot out there."

Joseph and Natalia shared a glance, then stepped away from the corkboard. He felt a surge of anticipation, as though stepping onto sacred ground. The promise of seeing the Golden Dome—a site lost for centuries—stirred him like few academic pursuits ever had.

They gathered their materials, stashing printouts in folders. Natalia carefully powered down her monitors. Side by side, they exited the makeshift conference room and wound down the stairs. The corridor below was busier now, local laborers and serious-faced men in plain clothes brushing past. Joseph spotted sidearms on a few belts, the tension in the air more pronounced.

Outside, the morning sun bleached the motel's cracked parking lot. They cut through a side gate, stepping onto a dusty street that paralleled the Orontes River. Buildings flanked them on either side—some half collapsed from last year's quake, others propped up with scaffolding. People bustled about, a few with donkey carts or pushcarts piled with produce. A pungent mix of spices and diesel hung in the muggy air.

Natalia shielded her eyes from the glare. "This reminds me of my first real dig, years ago in western Syria," she murmured. "So much chaos, yet so much history beneath every footstep."

Joseph nodded, the battered cityscape reminding him of the times he and his wife had visited the region. He inhaled deeply, letting the swirl of aromas and languages ground him in the present.

She gave him a small, almost conspiratorial smile. "Then let's go see what awaits us."

And, with that, they walked on together, the old motel shrinking behind them as they ventured to the site.

ELEVEN

Under the Shaken Dome

Joseph Scanlon shielded his eyes from the midday glare as he stepped out of the dark SUV. In front of him loomed a jumble of towering cranes, backhoes, and stacks of concrete barriers—a makeshift fortress of machinery. Rows of high steel fencing ringed the excavation perimeter, and tight-lipped guards armed with rifles stood at the gates. He could see their watchful gazes even behind tinted sunglasses. Whatever work was going on behind those fences, it was closely protected from prying eyes.

"Strict security," Joseph murmured. A brisk wind caught the hem of his jacket, flapping it against his legs.

"No one in or out without clearance," replied Dima, a man with a taut, controlled energy, dressed all in black and wearing a badge that bore the emblem of the Center for Russian Orthodox Studies. "We can't risk the local looters, or even worse, local media," he added dryly. "Shall we go?"

Joseph nodded. They bypassed two more guards stationed near a row of portable floodlights, then entered a temporary corridor made of galvanized steel panels. Taut tarps covered the top, forming a tunnel that blocked any external line of sight. Somewhere beyond the tarps, heavy machinery thrummed a steady bass note.

"We've made fresh progress, so I'll show you everything. But first, you need a helmet." He handed Joseph a white hard hat. Dima wore an orange one himself. "Watch your step. The quake left the ground uneven."

A little further on, the corridor opened onto a wide, newly excavated bowl in the earth. Joseph's breath caught at the scale of it: the entire area had collapsed into a sunken pit, revealing the curved top of a golden dome. In places, dusty earth and rubble still clung to the dome's flanks, but enough had been painstakingly cleared that brilliant metal glimmered in the sunlight.

"This is part of the reason we're all here," Dima said, voice reverent. "We're now certain this dome is the legendary 'Church of the Golden Dome'—the one you spoke about in your dissertation. The earthquake last year cracked open layers of old building foundations. We've spent months carefully removing debris to get where we are."

Joseph took it all in—massive scaffolding bracing sections of the dome, huge hydraulic supports preventing more collapse. Volunteers and field archaeologists in fluorescent vests threaded among the beams, shining flashlights into dark crevices. It looked like a modern city had grown atop an ancient church, and only this violent shaking had forced the two worlds to meet.

"Let's head inside," Dima said, guiding Joseph toward a temporary steel staircase that descended around the dome's curve. "Just watch your footing. We have partial scaffolds to stabilize the dome from within."

They made their way down. At the bottom, a wide opening gaped, the edges jagged where centuries of stone had crumbled. Flood-lights cast overlapping cones of brightness on interior columns, walls, and dust-laden air. The temperature dropped noticeably—cool, almost damp.

"We started from the top—quite literally—then cut an entry through the collapsed vault," Dima explained. "Beneath the dome, an entire subterranean structure survived. Let's go."

They entered a broad corridor that sloped downward. The illumi-nation revealed mosaic floors underfoot, intricate patterns of bright reds, gold, and azure squares. Joseph gasped at their con-dition. Only a few chips were missing, as if the centuries had passed them by.

"Remarkable, aren't they?" Dima knelt to run a careful hand over the mosaic. "We have sections that read in Greek: references to 'Ἰησοῦς Χριστός'—Jesus Christ—and mentions of the Virgin Mary and Saint Peter. A few fragments from older Latin inscriptions, too."

Joseph exhaled in wonder. "The details are stunning," he said softly. "It matches references in Evagrius Scholasticus—he wrote about a richly decorated floor in this church. He was a 6th-cen-tury historian from the region, one of the best eyewitnesses to Antioch's grandeur before the Persian invasion."

Dima straightened, curiosity piqued. "Evagrius Scholasticus? Not a name I've heard from the team yet."

Joseph smiled, pushing up his glasses. "He documented local churches in detail. According to him, the Church of the Golden Dome had elaborate mosaics praising Peter as 'the holder of the Keys.' Evagrius also said the building's design featured a large rectangular sanctuary with rooms branching off for teaching and scriptural storage. I see we're heading that way now."

Indeed, the corridor opened onto a main sanctuary—a long rectangular space, its boundaries still marked by fragments of stone columns that had once upheld the walls. Most upper walls had collapsed, leaving only waist-high ruins and scattered arches. Yet the rectangular footprint was clear, and at the far end stood a raised platform with a partially intact altar.

"Altar," Joseph breathed, stepping forward. There were faint scriptural inscriptions on the remaining stone edges—he spotted stylized crosses, short lines of Greek that looked like biblical verses. "This must be the altar they used during Mass."

Natalia had arrived with Joseph but stopped to chat with other members of the team. She finally caught up with Dima and Joseph and arrived with a cautious smile. Her work boots were coated in dust. "We've dated this altar to the early 3rd century, though it might incorporate older materials," she said. "A miraculous find, truly. And the walls—while most have collapsed, their foundations confirm the building's scale."

Joseph let his fingertips hover over the altar's broken edge, reading a portion of text: "ἐγένετο δὲ... In English, maybe from the Book of Acts... 'And it came to pass...' Something referencing apostolic authority, I'm sure."

"Let's continue," urged Dima. He led Joseph deeper into the labyrinth. Another passage branched off to the left—a smaller corridor with multiple adjacent rooms. Most were caved in except for two. The first was an arched chamber with benches and narrow shelves.

"Scriptorum archive," said Dima, shining his flashlight across wooden remnants and stone niches in the walls. "At least, that's our guess based on parchment containers we found. This is where we've discovered the majority of the fragments."

Three field archaeologists stood among piles of earthenware shards, carefully cataloging them. One of them, a tall man in a dusty vest, waved Joseph over. "Dr. Scanlon, welcome. We've extracted around two dozen sealed jars here. Inside, we found parchments in Greek and some in Syriac. We think a handful might be in Latin."

"Sealed jars," Joseph repeated, glancing at the thick ceramic pieces. They were plain, utilitarian shapes—nothing ornate. "Humble indeed. If the bishop or the scribes wanted to preserve messages from invaders or looters, hiding them in everyday pottery would have been clever. You wouldn't expect anything precious inside these dull containers."

"We're still analyzing," the archaeologist said, "but the dryness of the sealed jars did wonders for preservation. Also, there's evidence of scorching along the outer surfaces—maybe a fire at some point?"

Dima nodded. "Yes, we suspect the Persians burned parts of the church. The walls show blackened stone. A huge conflagration likely consumed the upper levels, but these lower vaults were somewhat protected. The quake centuries later sealed it all."

Joseph bent down, picking up a shard with charred edges. "It's exactly what the historical record described: the Persians set fire to the city, scorching its houses of worship." He replaced the shard gingerly. "And now you've found documentary fragments referencing the Keys. That's extraordinary."

Natalia added. "Yes, we have partial lines about the Keys in one scrap. We suspect there's more. We're still piecing together the texts. If there's a hidden chamber or special reliquary niche, we haven't found it yet."

Joseph took a moment to let that sink in. "Well... you could keep digging forever around random corners, but let me share a hunch." He stepped back, clearing a space among the half-crumbled shelves. "Bishop Anastasius was cunning. If the fragment Dr. Lavrov showed me is authentic, it implies the Keys would only be found by faithful Christians—people who can interpret whatever coded guidance is left behind. My guess is that somewhere in these archived parchments is a clue—a guide. He wouldn't leave the Keys out in the open. He'd rely on cryptic references or hidden instructions to preserve them from the wrong hands."

One of the archaeologists frowned. "You think we're wasting effort on the site's side rooms, searching for a secret vault?"

Joseph nodded sympathetically. "For now, yes. Focus on retrieving, translating, and deciphering every parchment you find. That's our best shot. The letter I read suggests the location of the Keys was documented."

Dima exhaled in relief, almost as if Joseph's instruction gave him clarity. "All right. We'll shift the team's priority to systematically scanning all archival finds. Natalia, can you coordinate that?"

"Certainly." She offered Joseph a grateful nod. "Thank you."

They wound their way back to the main sanctuary. Joseph paused, gazing up at the half-exposed underside of the dome overhead. The gilded interior had been blackened in patches by centuries of neglect and quakes, yet it still held a majesty that made his heart clench.

"Joseph," Dima said, resting a hand on his shoulder, "I need to check on something up top. We can ascend together—unless you'd like to stay?"

Joseph shook his head. "Go ahead. I'll be right behind you." He gave a respectful half-smile to the other Russians. "You all can head up, too. I just need a moment here."

They parted quietly, leaving Joseph in the stillness of that underground sanctuary. A hush settled over ancient stones that had once echoed with the chanting of monks, with the whispered prayers of countless believers. He closed his eyes, letting the weight of centuries wash over him. He recalled Evagrius's descriptions of local worshippers, huddled in this space even during times of war—an unbroken line of faith linking them all.

Bowing his head, Joseph whispered aloud, the words wavering in the thick air. "Lord, you led me here. You know the secrets Bishop Anastasius left behind. Please grant me wisdom, guide my steps

148

to find the Keys—and keep them from being exploited for evil. Let me do justice to the faith of those who once worshiped here."

A profound sense of calm filled him. He opened his eyes, offered one final glance at the mosaic floors that had survived cataclysm and centuries of darkness, then turned to ascend the scaffold steps.

Above ground, the sunlight felt almost harsh after the cool dimness below. The construction barriers were still in place, the guards still posted, but the day seemed brighter than when Joseph first arrived. Dima stood by a row of cargo trucks, talking into his phone. Spotting Joseph, he ended the call.

"Everything all right down there?" Dima asked.

Joseph let out a slow breath. "Yes. All right, and yet... more mysteries to uncover than I can count."

Dima nodded. "That's the nature of this place. Now, there's one more item. We received word you'd like to visit your wife's relatives on the far side of Antakya?"

Joseph perked up, a rush of gratitude warming him. "Yes, if possible. With the tension in the region, I wasn't sure if it'd be permitted."

"Well, your request is approved," Dima said with a small grin. "Oleg will escort and supervise you per our security protocols. He's waiting just outside the main gate."

"Thank you, Dima." Joseph meant it. After everything, he ached to see some family who might comfort him—and perhaps share knowledge about Antioch's old traditions.

Dima clapped him lightly on the back. "Safe travels, Professor. We'll keep working on the parchments."

Joseph turned to see a tall Oleg standing by a black SUV near the exit. He gave Joseph a polite nod, opening the passenger door in silent invitation.

With one final backward glance at the fortress of fences and humming machinery, Joseph walked off toward Oleg, mind whirling with newly discovered wonders and half-formed hopes. This land had once cradled Christian worship in its prime. Now, in the wake of an earthquake, it might yield the ultimate relic—and Joseph prayed he would be the faithful steward that history, and perhaps God Himself, required.

TWELVE

Antakya Homecoming

Joseph Scanlon stood on the cracked sidewalk in the late afternoon sun blazed overhead, shimmering in the dusty air waiting for Oleg. Only a week had passed since he'd accepted Dr. Lavrov's offer to come here—under the auspices of academic research—yet the city already felt like home again. Time had changed the place in ways he could scarcely believe. He glanced at his phone, checking messages from Father Ryan, from Henry Briggs, and from Salma. Each text carried traces of his old life back in Indiana, yet the uncertainty and danger of this new assignment had quickly become his reality.

Oleg, the broad-shouldered security contractor strode up to Joseph with a glower. Dressed in a black t-shirt stretched taut across his muscled torso, Oleg looked every part the ex-military type. He tipped his chin in a brusque greeting, offering none of the typical Middle Eastern pleasantries Joseph might have expected from local staff.

"Mr. Scanlon," Oleg said, pronouncing Joseph's last name with a heavy accent. "You come. We drive now."

Joseph offered a polite nod, ignoring the man's flat tone. "Yes, I need a ride into the old city district."

Oleg simply gestured to a dusty, dark SUV parked along the curb. The two men approached in silence. The door gave a tortured squeak as Joseph pulled it open and slid inside. Almost immediately, an oppressive wave of heat—trapped within the car—welcomed him, but he dared not complain.

Without a word, Oleg started the engine and jounced down the uneven street. Buildings of concrete and stone, many sporting patches of recent quake damage, lined their route. The SUV navigated around rubble piles, impromptu construction, and detours set by local authorities struggling to repair crumbled infrastructure. Joseph took in the sight of scaffolding leaning at precarious angles; painted signs in Arabic and Turkish flapped in the warm breeze.

After a few minutes, Oleg spoke in halting English. "You live in America, yes? Notre Dame professor."

Joseph forced a cordial smile. "That's right. A professor of history. My specialty is Late Antiquity."

They jolted over a deep pothole. Oleg tapped the steering wheel with blunt fingers. "Why you come here? Not safe, this city. Especially not safe now." He paused, his tone half-accusatory. "Volkov's war. The West makes big threats. I read the news. American interference. So...why you come?"

Joseph heard the hostility creeping into Oleg's voice. Beneath it, he detected real curiosity, or perhaps suspicion. Joseph resolved to remain neutral. "I believe I'm here because Dr. Lavrov needed an expert on the time period. The excavation site is a once-in-a-lifetime find. This city has layers of history—Roman, Byzantine, Ottoman. That matters more to me than current politics."

Oleg pursed his lips, unimpressed. "Politics always matter."

Joseph tried to keep his breathing calm. "I don't deny that. But I'm not here to debate the conflict in Eastern Europe. I'm just here to focus on the archaeological work."

They lapsed into silence. As they entered the winding streets of downtown Antakya, the SUV slowed to a crawl. This was a district Joseph recalled vividly from his postdoctoral days: narrow roads flanked by vendors hawking roasted nuts, steaming kebabs, and saffron-laced sweets. Faded flags hung from tangled wires overhead, occasionally fluttering whenever a breeze passed through.

Suddenly, Oleg cleared his throat. "So...your father is from America, yes? I read file. He is...old?"

Joseph's pulse skipped. *He read my file?* "Yes, my father is American," he replied carefully. "And yes, he's older. Retired."

Oleg shot a sidelong glance. "And your mother from Lebanon. She left during civil war. Moved to America. Catholic, right?"

Joseph gripped his seatbelt. There was no reason for Oleg to pry into these details. "Yes, that's correct. I'm from a mixed background."

Oleg's eyes narrowed. "Means you used to war. Lebanon had war, yes?"

Joseph exhaled slowly, maintaining composure. "I'm not sure what you're implying. My mother escaped war. I never saw it myself."

They lurched forward again, weaving around a donkey cart piled high with pomegranates. Oleg let out a dismissive grunt and fixed Joseph with an oddly penetrating look. "You Americans always lie about not wanting war. Then you secretly fund weapons, punish Russia. People die. So, I ask: do you support your government's stance on President Volkov's rightful claim to restore Russian borders?"

Joseph felt heat rise in his chest. This was no idle conversation. Still, he forced a measured tone. "I'm a historian, not a policy-maker."

"You have no opinion?" Oleg persisted.

Joseph swallowed, intentionally evasive. "I think centuries of conflict in Eastern Europe have created complicated fault lines. I wish it could be resolved peacefully."

"Mmm." Oleg said nothing more for a moment. They turned onto a narrower lane, where the roads seemed older, flanked by arched doorways and stone facades. "Well," Oleg continued, voice thick with cynicism, "I see. Peace, sure. But in the end, you side with your country."

Joseph forced a disarming smile. "A person can't help his home-land. But that doesn't mean we can't appreciate another perspec-tive."

Oleg pressed his lips into a thin line. "We see." He slowed the ve-hicle beside a squat home with a carved wooden door. The archi-tecture was distinct: a classic Levantine style with ornate shutters and swirling metal latticework. Joseph recognized it immediately.

He leaned forward, heart pounding. The Haddad family home—his in-laws.

Oleg killed the engine. "You have two hours. That is the limit. I will wait in car." His gaze pinned Joseph to the seat. "Understand? Two hours. Not one minute more."

Joseph gently exhaled. "Yes, of course. Thank you for bringing me."

He reached for the door handle, but Oleg added, "If you are late, I come in and get you. And that will not be nice. Clear?"

His tone bristled with intimidation. Joseph met his stare calmly. "Crystal clear." He pushed the door open, stepping onto the sun-baked curb. As he shut it, Oleg rolled the window down just enough to keep an eye on him. For a moment, Joseph thought to ask if Oleg wanted some water or coffee—simple hospitality—but the look on the Russian's face silenced that impulse. Instead, Jo-seph walked up the short flight of steps toward the Haddad home, shoulders tense with relief at finally being free from that tense conversation.

The heavy door swung open the instant Joseph knocked. Standing there was Miryam Haddad, her smile like sunrise, arms already outstretched. She was shorter than Joseph remembered, or perhaps he had just gotten used to taller American acquaintances. Her hair, once fully black, was now shot through with silver strands, styled in a neat bun. Her face lit up with childlike delight.

"Yōsif!" she cried, using the Arabic version of his name. "You are here at last. Alhamdulillah!"

Before he could speak, she pulled him into a tight embrace. He felt the gentle brush of her cheek against his, inhaled the comforting scents of rosewater and fresh cardamom. This was more than politeness; it was genuine maternal affection.

Joseph stepped inside, every sense alive with familiarity. The interior was exactly as he recalled: warm, earth-toned walls, embroidered cushions scattered about, subtle religious icons perched on shelves. In the corner, a large cross with Chaldean script hung beside a photograph of Pope Francis visiting Iraq. The smell of spiced lamb and simmering tomato sauce drifted in from the kitchen, confirming that dinner was already underway.

Standing further inside the living room, waiting almost shyly, was Namir Haddad, the father. Tall and lean, with a dignified mustache, Namir was the opposite of shy—except when tears threatened. Joseph remembered he'd always had a paternal softness for all his children. Namir had run an import-export business for decades, shipping goods between Turkey and Chaldean Iraq. He prided himself on connections across half a dozen countries and an unshakeable faith that God provides.

Stepping forward, Namir greeted Joseph. "Habibi! It has been too long." He clasped Joseph's shoulders, then drew him into a firm hug. "You must come inside, sit, rest. You are family."

Joseph let out a laugh, a tension-venting sound. "Shukran, Uncle," he said respectfully, though Namir was technically his father-in-law. The older man insisted Joseph use the affectionate term. "It's wonderful to see you both."

No sooner had Joseph stepped deeper into the living room than the youngest Haddad sibling bounded in—Celina, just 22, with curly dark hair cut shoulder-length. She squealed, threw her arms around Joseph, and gave him rapid-fire kisses on both cheeks. Her black eyes sparkled with excitement.

"Welcome back, my oh-so-famous brother-in-law!" she teased, her lightly accented English bouncing with energy. "You look thinner—are you not eating enough in America?"

"But you are in Antakya now, and I intend to feed you so much you won't walk straight."

Miryam beckoned them all into the living room. "Sit, please. Namir, bring Joseph something to drink. Fresh lemonade with mint, yes?"

Joseph's heart filled with warmth. He realized in that moment how very deeply he had missed the Haddads. The swirl of conversation, the touch of their embraces—this was the Middle Eastern hospitality that always made him feel fully alive. In their presence, the complicated tensions outside faded; inside these walls, he was simply family. No suspicious watchers, no departmental closures, no war headlines—just the unconditional acceptance of people who once welcomed him as a son before he'd even proposed to their daughter.

"They chatted in a mix of English, Arabic, and the local Turkish dialect. Miryam eagerly asked for updates on Salma's pregnancy progress. Joseph beamed with a gentle smile, "We have wonderful news. Salma is pregnant, but it's a high-risk situation, so we're being extra cautious."

"Nonsense," Miryam said, tossing a hand. "Your mother Joelle is praying too fiercely. Everything will be fine. Saint Charbel is unstoppable."

Namir nodded vigorously. "We love Saint Charbel. The Lebanese Maronite tradition is so strong. Let's not forget your mother prayed for me last year when I was ill, and look at me now—healthy as a lion!"

Joseph felt a wave of gratitude wash over him as he sipped the fresh lemonade. The tangy sweetness danced on his tongue, so reminiscent of the early days when he'd first visited this house. Then, Celina peppered him with questions. "How is life at the university? Are you still the big professor? Are your students driving you crazy?"

He swallowed, stalling for a moment before answering. "Oh, well...some changes, which brings me here..." and gave them a summary of the offer and the goal to find the keys of Peter.

As laughter flowed, Joseph felt the suffocating tension from Oleg's interrogation drain away. Here, he could breathe in acceptance and affection. This was the magic of the Haddads—reminding him that no matter the politics or strife outside, love and family endured.

Suddenly, a flurry of voices erupted outside, and the door burst open. Aziz Haddad, eldest son, entered like a triumphant soldier returning from a victory. In many ways, that was exactly who he was: he had fought real battles, displayed real heroism. A tall man in his mid-forties, Aziz possessed an arresting presence—finely sculpted features, an aura of confidence in every stride, and a thick, well-groomed beard that framed a dazzling smile. He wore a casual white shirt with the top two buttons undone, revealing a small cross around his neck. He moved with the brash ease of someone who knew he was beloved.

"Ya Mama! Ya Baba!" he called, dropping a bag by the door and rushing to envelop his mother in a massive hug. Miryam fussed over him, kissing his cheeks, patting his broad shoulders as if to confirm he was real. Namir stood next, gripping Aziz's arm, then pulling him into a fatherly bearhug. Celina hopped in place, squealing, "Aziz, you big brute, you smell like the outside!"

He turned to her, mock-offended. "It's the cologne of the righteous, sister!"

Amid their laughter, Aziz's gaze settled on Joseph. For a split second, his eyes flashed with both joy and something else—knowledge of secrets that overshadowed their reunion. Still, a delayed wide smile broke out, and he extended his arms. "Joseph, my brother. Too long."

Joseph embraced him. Aziz pounded him on the back, then stepped away, scanning Joseph's face. "You look...older," Aziz teased. "But maybe more handsome, no?"

Joseph responded in kind. "Impossible—Aziz, you're always the best-looking man in the room. Anyone standing next to you looks pale by comparison."

Aziz grinned at the well-worn banter. The entire family dissolved into chatter, competing with each other to ask Aziz about his travels. Eventually, they turned the topic to Joseph and his wife.

Aziz, in a jesting mood, turned to Joseph. "You do realize I'm counting on you to take perfect care of my sister, yes? You're the only man on Earth whose well-being I hold second to hers. If she's not a hundred percent happy, we will have a conversation...a short one."

Joseph smirked. "Your sister would kill me herself before letting you have the pleasure. I think I'm safe, though: I treat her like the queen she is."

Aziz laughed heartily, grabbing Joseph's shoulder. "That's the spirit." His eyes sparkled with camaraderie, but Joseph noticed the flicker of tension behind that brightness. They both understood the real reason Joseph was here—and that it wasn't purely academic.

The conversation drifted on, with teasing, jokes, and familial banter. Eventually, Aziz took Joseph aside. "Come, we need best friend time," he announced, raising his voice so their parents heard. "We'll go up to the roof. Mama, we'll steal him for just a moment, I promise."

Miryam flapped her hand as if to shoo them. "Go, go, but come back soon. Dinner is nearly ready."

They ascended a narrow flight of stairs to the flat rooftop terrace. The vantage point revealed Antakya's skyline—a jumble of low-slung buildings, satellite dishes, and minarets punctuating the horizon. The swirling evening sky bled from gold to pink, the air thick with the scent of roasted peppers and spiced meats drifting from neighboring homes. A pair of battered plastic chairs stood by the waist-high parapet, and Aziz sank into one, letting out a heavy sigh.

Joseph joined him, the tension from hours of subterfuge knitting back into his shoulders. They exchanged a look—one that communicated relief at being able to speak freely.

"Crazy, isn't it?" Aziz said first, voice low. "I never thought I'd see the day where *you* become the infiltration guy. My quiet scholar brother-in-law turned...covert operative. God has a sense of humor."

Joseph shook his head. "I hardly know how I got here myself. It started with Father Ryan giving me the news that my department was shutting down. Next thing I know, Dr. Lavrov is offering me a contract to help decode ancient texts—only I soon discover he's tied to some powerful Russian FSB leader, and the CIA tapped me because I'm the only one who can move freely between them and Western intelligence." He paused, inhaling the twilight air. "I'm not trained for espionage. This is insane."

Aziz studied him quietly. "My friend, I've seen enough to know that normal life can vanish overnight. Look at me: I left here to reconnect with our relatives in Mosul—just in time for ISIS to overrun the region. I ended up joining a Chaldean militia. The CIA gave us arms, training, intelligence. We fought to take back our towns. I never thought I'd do that. But sometimes, you step into the role that's needed. No one else can do it."

Joseph nodded, recalling how the family had whispered of Aziz's role as a crack sniper but never pressed him for details. Aziz had returned from war a changed man—more confident in his faith, yet burdened by unspoken stories.

Leaning forward in his chair, Aziz pointed a finger at Joseph. "But you—what intel do you have for me to pass back to the CIA?"

Joseph slid a folded slip of paper from his pocket. "This is the first batch. It lists the excavation's progress, the coordinates of each new dig site, the extent of the structures we've uncovered, and the presence of certain private security contractors—likely FSB agents from Russia." He handed the paper to Aziz, who opened it, scanning quickly.

Aziz whistled under his breath. "You're thorough. This is good. I'll pass it to the contact the CIA assigned me. They're here, in the city, though not openly. They give me a place, a time, we meet. Simple as that."

Joseph gazed at the sprawl of Antakya. "I don't know how often I can visit. Lavrov's team monitors me all day at the site. I'm only here now because I asked if I could see my in-laws. And even then,

I have an escort—some guy named Oleg. He's parked outside, counting the minutes."

"Oleg?" Aziz repeated. "Have you told him about this side trip to the roof?"

Joseph shook his head. "No. He's not friendly—keeps asking about my stance on Russia's war. He's suspicious of me."

Aziz's mouth pressed into a grim line. "He's probably not just a mercenary. If he's the only English-speaking guard, that's an easy way for them to keep an eye on you. Watch your back."

Joseph nodded. "He told me I only have two hours to stay. Also said he'd drag me out if I'm late. Not exactly a warm vibe."

Aziz rose, stepping to the parapet. He peered over, scanning the street below. "Is that his car? The black SUV?"

Joseph joined him at the edge, pointing to the vehicle. It sat near a flickering street lamp. But as the men looked closer, they saw the driver's seat empty.

Aziz tensed. "He's not in the car."

A spike of alarm ran through Joseph. "He could be outside, pacing around, or making a phone call. Or...he could have come closer."

Aziz clenched his jaw. "We should end our meeting soon. The last thing we need is for him to eavesdrop on this conversation."

They stepped back, slipping into the shadows behind the rooftop's small half-wall. Aziz folded the paper with the intel and slid it into his jacket pocket. "No one else knows you're passing information?"

"No," Joseph said. "I told no one, not even Salma. Safer this way."

Aziz exhaled. "Good. Let's keep it that way. We'll keep our communications subtle. Whenever you get a chance to see my parents again, I'll show up—just 'coincidentally'—and we'll find a private moment." He clamped a hand on Joseph's shoulder. "We can do this, brother. Watch yourself, though. These FSB guys don't play around."

Joseph gave a tense nod. "Don't worry. I'm not eager to be a martyr."

Aziz's expression gentled. "You are a man of faith, but also of logic. I trust your instincts." Then, with a determined sigh, he forced a casual smile. "Now, let's go downstairs. Mama's cooking can't wait, and I won't let those stuffed grape leaves get cold."

Joseph mustered a grin. "Agreed." They clasped hands in silent understanding, then headed down the narrow stairs.

The rest of the evening swept Joseph into the warm tide of Haddad hospitality. Miryam had outdone herself: plates of spiced rice with lamb, tangy tomato-cucumber salad garnished with mint, and an array of mezze—hummus, baba ganoush, dolma—covered the low table in the living room. Celina hovered around him, piling more food onto his plate despite his halfhearted protests, and Namir poured sweet tea into little glass cups. They all laughed when Joseph recounted silly anecdotes of the first time he tried

Middle Eastern coffee, nearly choking on the grounds, a decade ago.

At intervals, Joseph's mind drifted to Oleg, to the possibility of being overheard or monitored. But the Haddads' genuine kindness, the enveloping love in their eyes and voices, created a bright shield around him. For a couple of hours, Joseph let himself bask in nostalgia, delighting in each morsel of food and each spirited conversation. He only grew uneasy when he checked his watch and realized his two-hour window was nearly up.

At last, Joseph stood, brushing nonexistent crumbs off his pants. "I need to go. My...escort is waiting."

A flurry of farewells ensued. Miryam insisted he take a bag of leftover food. Namir embraced Joseph with fatherly affection, kissing his forehead. Celina squeezed him so hard he gasped for breath. Finally, Aziz gave him a playful punch to the arm, then enveloped him in an embrace. "We'll see you soon, inshallah," Aziz said quietly. They locked eyes, each acknowledging the secret they now shared.

Joseph stepped outside to find Oleg leaning against the SUV, arms folded, features inscrutable in the glow of a single streetlight. His posture radiated impatience. Without a word, Joseph climbed into the passenger seat. Oleg got in, started the engine, and jerked the car away from the curb. Not a single question was asked; not a single courtesy was offered. Joseph snuck a glance at Oleg's profile—stone-faced, lips pressed together in a thin line. Clearly, something had made him even colder than before.

The drive back to the gated compound where Joseph was lodging was marked by tense silence. Gone were the earlier attempts at conversation about politics or Joseph's family. Now, Oleg offered only a single glare at a red light, as if conveying that Joseph's time was strictly policed. Joseph kept his eyes on the passing streets, forcing himself to remain calm and think through the next steps: he would pass on more details to Aziz as the dig progressed, remain watchful for hints of Russian infiltration, and continue his official duties under Lavrov.

At last, they arrived at the compound's gates—grey cement walls topped with razor wire. Oleg stopped, showed an ID card to the guard, and the gate rolled aside. Once inside, Joseph stepped out. Oleg slammed the SUV door and drove off without a backward glance.

Tension knotted Joseph's shoulders. He fished out his phone, tapping a quick text to his father: *All good here, Dad. Safe so far. How are you feeling?* A wave of sorrow accompanied that query. He knew Michael's days were numbered, but the older man insisted on living them unbound by pity.

Next, Joseph sent a note to Salma: *Just left your parents. They're as loving as ever—and so excited for us. I love you.* He lingered on the words, wishing he could do more to ease her struggle with loneliness and all the silent worries that dogged them.

He turned toward the small guesthouse assigned to him within the compound. Around him, the sky was fully dark, the stars winking. A lone guard patrolled with a rifle slung over his shoulder. Joseph quietly slipped into his quarters, locked the door, and leaned against it. Exhaustion finally settled in. The day had been emotional in every sense—reuniting with family he cherished, forging a secret alliance with Aziz, and enduring Oleg's suspicion.

He flicked on a lamp, scanning the sparse furnishings: a narrow bed, a table with a lamp, a small closet. No pictures, no decorations. He set his bag of leftover food on the table and dimmed the light.

As he settled onto the bed, Joseph's mind churned with half-formed prayers, concerns, and joys. He pictured the Haddad household, still probably laughing, sipping sweet tea, talking about how wonderful it was to see him again. He prayed that no harm would come to them if the covert mission was uncovered. Then he thought of his father, hoping beyond hope that four-to-six months might stretch longer, that he might see Michael's face again in person.

Pulling the sheets over himself, Joseph recognized how drastically his life had changed. Yet a strange calmness underpinned his anxiety. He felt as though he was on the path he was meant to walk, however dangerous. He was doing what he could to protect the innocent, to uncover the truth about the Keys, and to preserve some measure of peace.

He whispered into the darkness, "Lord...protect us." Then he clicked off the lamp, letting sleep envelop him at last.

THIRTEEN

Veils of Earth and Heaven

The wind rustled low across the excavation site at Antakya, a persistent whisper among the newly erected tents and half-exposed foundations. Days became weeks, and weeks turned into months since Joseph Scanlon's first weeks in Turkey, yet each sunrise seemed only to reveal more fragments of the ancient puzzle. Through that time, Joseph and Natalia had become something of a legendary duo among the researchers and became real friends. Together, they were the backbone of the translation project: Joseph, with his unparalleled knowledge of Latin, Greek, and Syriac dialects, and Natalia, with her skill in harnessing the AI scanning and stitching technologies. As the months passed, their professional collaboration blossomed into a deep and enduring friendship. It began with small gestures—Joseph bringing Natalia her favorite coffee on long workdays, and Natalia surprising Joseph with rare texts she discovered in digital archives. Their camaraderie was filled with laughter and mutual respect, creating an atmosphere that was both playful and genuinely upbuilding.

Natalia, intrigued by Joseph's calm demeanor and the depth of his insights, began to ask more about his faith. She was curious about the personal encounters and beliefs that seemed to guide his life with such steadiness. Joseph, always patient and open, shared stories and teachings, not as a preacher, but as a friend sharing a part of his world. These discussions often led to lively debates and reflections, each learning from the other.

Their conversations took on a more personal tone when Natalia started inquiring about Joseph's relationship with Salma. She noticed the way his eyes lit up whenever he mentioned her name, and she found herself genuinely interested in the dynamics of their bond. Joseph spoke of Salma with warmth and admiration, sharing anecdotes that revealed the strength and tenderness of their relationship. Natalia's curiosity extended to Salma's pregnancy, a new chapter in Joseph's life that he was eager to embrace. She asked questions about their preparations, the emotions they were experiencing, and the hopes they held for their growing family. Joseph appreciated Natalia's genuine interest and found comfort in discussing these personal aspects of his life with someone who truly cared. Together, they not only advanced the translation project but also built a connection that was as profound as the texts they worked to preserve.

Each morning, they would arrive at their makeshift scriptorium—an improvised lab with strong LED lamps and the hum of scanning machines—and spend hours poring over scraps of parchment salvaged from sealed containers discovered in a hidden sub-chamber. Bit by bit, the scraps coalesced into entire documents.

It was exhausting work. Sometimes, they would gather a dozen slivers from the multiple containers and discover they formed only half a page of text. But there were triumphs, too, as they recovered entire pieces in surprisingly good condition: collections of Scripture passages, letters, and, most notably, writings attributed to St. Ignatius of Antioch. Joseph's pulse had quickened at the latter discovery. St. Ignatius—Apostolic Father and third Bishop of Antioch, believed to be a disciple of the Apostle John—was a crucial figure in early Church history. His epistles, composed while traveling under Roman guard toward his eventual martyrdom in Rome, had guided early Christians in Antioch and far beyond. His letters shaped theology about Christ's divinity, the structure of the Church, and the importance of unity under the bishop's leadership. If these newly discovered fragments were authentic, they might contain nuances of Ignatius's teachings never before known—an invaluable find for early Christian scholarship.

But it wasn't only these theological gems that filled Joseph's days. He was still in constant correspondence with his wife, Salma, whose pregnancy had proven agonizingly difficult. She spoke, in gentle but forthright language, about the daily morning sickness, her dizzy spells, and the doctor's warnings that this would be a delicate pregnancy. Yet the conversations also burned with devotion: she missed him fiercely, and each note ended with her own small prayer, a hand-drawn cross, and a swirl of hope. Joseph's heart ached for her. He tried to reassure her that he would return home soon, if only for a short break, but the dig demanded more and more from him.

The difference this time was that Joseph was not alone in the region. He continued to have dinner every week with the Haddad family, who had welcomed him into their home early in his stay. The family matriarch, Miryam, treated Joseph like a wandering son, always ladling extra helpings of spiced lamb onto his plate and scolding him affectionately if he seemed tired. Aziz continued to coordinate the CIA updates both ways. Aziz was proud to serve as a local liaison for the Agency, making sure that if anything suspicious occurred around the site or if political tensions flared, Joseph would be forewarned. In turn, Joseph passed along general updates about the project's progress, though he carefully guarded any truly sensitive details. Joseph himself had little patience for such politics, but he trusted Aziz, who had proven loyal and circumspect.

Despite the warm reception Joseph received from the Haddad family, not everyone in the region was as welcoming. Oleg and the security team still regarded Joseph with great suspicion, their eyes always following him with a watchful intensity. Oleg, in particular, continued to act distrustfully toward Joseph, as if expecting him to slip up at any moment. The team had even coined an internal joke about Joseph, saying he had the nerve to treat him like an undercover CIA agent, a quip that never failed to elicit a chuckle among them, a laugh that Joseph could never fully share in. Still, he couldn't help but feel the weight of their suspicion whenever he passed by, a constant reminder of the fine line he walked in this complex web of alliances and mistrust.

After the first couple of weeks, Dr. Alexei Lavrov returned to the dig. At first, he was as effusive and collaborative as Joseph remembered—making quiet jokes in his perfectly tailored suits, stepping delicately across the rubble as though mindful not to disturb the centuries-old dust. Yet, day by day, stress had begun to etch lines into Lavrov's otherwise composed features. His cordial greetings grew shorter. He barked orders at different team members. His eyes flashed with impatience when the scanning equipment lagged. Whispers spread through the camp: Dr. Lavrov was under siege by external pressures, perhaps by the very people funding this venture. Rumors abounded of phone calls in the dead of night where he pleaded in hushed Russian tones, or email threads swiftly closed whenever anyone approached. Joseph tried to remain detached from the gossip. Nonetheless, it was impossible to ignore the mounting tension.

By the seventh week, Joseph and Natalia were laboring in their shared office. Outside, the midday sun punished the white canvas, drenching the interior in bright, filtered light. Tables were scattered with parchment fragments in various states of reconstruction. The stale air smelled faintly of coffee, dust, and the occasional whiff of an old library—testament to the ancient documents they painstakingly pieced together.

Inside, Natalia tapped away at her laptop, running the specialized AI programs that scanned, stitched, and guessed at the missing words in the partial texts. The AI's strength was pattern recognition: it could match the fibers and edges of each scrap, even attempt to correct for water damage. But it couldn't interpret the words with the nuance Joseph brought; it easily confused older forms of script, especially in the more obscure ancient dialects.

At a side table, Joseph hunched forward in his chair, flipping between multiple references—an old Latin dictionary, a Greek lexicon, a 19th-century German commentary on script variations from the region, and a handful of bookmarked biblical verses. The conversation from the other tables drifted in and out. Now and then, a team member or a local field worker might pop in with a new fragment or ask about where to store certain artifacts. Typically, Natalia would answer so Joseph could remain deeply focused.

At last, he exhaled and leaned back. "Natalia," he called across the table. "I've got all the fragments for container G-14 lined up. Let's see if your AI can unify them into a single page."

She stood, brushing a stray lock of hair behind her ear. "Sure. Hand them over." She fed the scanned images into her software. Within moments, the system produced a single PDF with a carefully reconstructed page. Joseph zoomed in. His eyes danced back and forth, scanning for any anomalies. The text was, indeed, in ancient Syriac.

"Looks promising," Natalia said, leaning over his shoulder. "But you'll have to do the real reading."

Joseph carefully enlarged the top lines. They both noticed the heading at once. He started to sound it out, stumbling over the archaic ligatures. After a moment, he gave a short, amused snort. "Well, this is interesting: '*It is the glory of God to conceal something, and the glory of kings to search it out.*'"

Natalia's eyebrows rose. "Is that from Scripture? I don't recall the exact reference."

"It's close to a verse in Proverbs," Joseph answered. "Proverbs 25:2, to be exact. It's just introduced here as if it were a heading—

like a motto." He paused, letting the meaning sink in. "This is un-usual. Let me keep going."

Now that the text was stabilized, Joseph read slowly, translating out loud:

"To him who is faithful and true.

2 Timothy 1:14: Keep the good thing committed to thy trust by the Holy Spirit, who dwells in us.

Follow the wisdom and you will discover the authority that has been protected for you."

Joseph's breath caught. "Natalia, this is referencing biblical verses, but not in the standard Greek or Latin. It's in Syriac—and inter-estingly, the wording is identical to how the Latin Vulgate renders those passages." Natalia paused everything she was doing, grab the pen and paper and started dictating what he was writing. He cleared his throat and continued:

"Acts 5:15: Insomuch that they brought forth the sick into the streets, and laid them on beds and couches, that when Peter came, his shadow at the least might overshadow any of them, and they might be delivered from their infirmities."

The healing power of Peter has been fully imparted on to that which you seek.

Natalia clutched the edge of the table. "So, it's referencing the tra-dition that even Peter's shadow could heal the sick—and it says that power is on 'that which you seek'? Joseph, this must mean the Keys, right?"

Joseph nodded, feeling a surge of excitement that set his pulse thumping. "I've never seen such a direct statement before. This letter is basically claiming that the same healing power described in Acts 5:15 now resides in the physical object we believe to be the Keys of St. Peter." He turned the page carefully, scanning further lines.

> "*Matthew 12:43: And when an unclean spirit is gone out of a man he walketh through dry places seeking rest, and findeth none. 44 Then he saith: I will return into my house from whence I came out. And coming he findeth it empty, swept, and garnished. 45 Then he goeth, and taketh with him seven other spirits more wicked than himself, and they enter in and dwell there: and the last state of that man is made worse than the first.*
>
> *That which you seek is not yours. It is of the first of the Apostles and his successors. Be warned not to seek to use that which you seek outside proper authority.*"

Natalia let out a quiet whistle. "This is practically a cautionary note about demonic possession or evil spirits. 'Not to seek to use that which you seek outside proper authority...' That's oddly specific. Joseph, what do you think it means?"

Joseph leaned back, recalling the discussion from weeks earlier. "It reminds me of that story Gregory the Great recorded about the Lombard soldier who tried to steal the Keys. That soldier ended up stabbing himself in the throat, as if possessed." He shook his head. "They believed the Keys were so consecrated that misusing them invited demonic attack. Now, combining it with Matthew 12:43–45, it implies the relic is protected spiritually—and to attempt to wield its power without the authority of Peter's successor is to open yourself to malevolent forces."

"Wild," Natalia murmured, eyes wide. "But it's consistent with the earlier texts. This letter is basically a direct warning."

Joseph swallowed hard. "I don't think this would have been written unless someone had already tried to exploit the Keys improperly—maybe that Lombard soldier or others like him."

He flipped further and read the next lines:

"*Matthew 7:7: Ask, and it shall be given you: seek, and you shall find: knock, and it shall be opened to you.*

To His Church upon this altar you shall go."

"'...upon this altar you shall go'..." Joseph echoed.

Natalia's eyes lit up. "The altar! That has to mean the altar in the ruins we're excavating. The Church of the Golden Dome. It's literally telling us to look there."

Joseph frowned. "It's possible, but in the site plans, we've already uncovered a significant portion of the altar area. We found relic niches, but no sign of any hidden chamber or secret compartments. Let's keep reading."

He moved to the final lines:

"*Revelation 6:15: And the kings of the earth, and the princes, and tribunes, and the rich, and the strong, and every bondman, and every freeman, hid themselves in the caves and in the rocks of mountains.*

From this place, descend deep into the depths of the earth where you shall find that which you seek. Follow the signs of authority all the way down"

Natalia stared at him. "Deep into the earth beneath the altar," she said, pointing at the screen. "They might have constructed a crypt far deeper than we realized—maybe even below the known sub-levels. All the earlier collapses or natural disasters could have buried it further."

Joseph caught his breath, scanning the paragraph again to see if he'd missed any subtle hint. "It's definitely implying a hidden chamber. The letter tells them to go to the altar, then to descend from there. This aligns with the rumors that the Church was built over older sanctuaries. So, yes—if the Keys were indeed hidden to protect them from invaders, that's where they might be." He inhaled, excitement mingling with a deep sense of caution. "But it also contains warnings we need to investigate..."

Natalia pressed a button on her phone. "I need to get Dr. Lavrov. This might be the key—no pun intended—to everything."

"Wait, Natalia, I want to make sure we interpret all of it correctly," Joseph said, scanning the lines again. "We've gleaned a lot, but historical texts can be subtle. We can't just barge in—"

But Natalia was already stepping to the hallway. "Dr. Lavrov needs to see this!" She ducked outside, letting the door open, flooding the hallway with sunlight.

Joseph remained behind, rereading the lines in a swirl of half-belief, half-trepidation. Could it really be so literal? A chamber beneath the altar? He'd suspected that the Church might hide deeper levels, but direct textual proof was unprecedented. And that caution about demonic forces... a chill ran through him. He murmured a silent prayer for guidance.

Moments later, Natalia returned with Dr. Lavrov in tow. The man's forehead glistened with perspiration as if he'd jogged across the compound, but his eyes shone with intensity. "Joseph, Natalia—tell me you've found something conclusive," he said, voice unsteady with suppressed excitement.

"Let me read you the entire letter, start to finish," Joseph answered. He did so, his voice measured, occasionally pausing to elaborate on the biblical references. With every verse, Lavrov's tension melted into something more jubilant. By the time Joseph reached the final lines about descending into the depths of the earth, Lavrov let out a triumphant laugh.

"Thank God!" he exclaimed, and for once the lines of stress on his face vanished. "You realize what this means? The letter is explicit: 'To His Church upon this altar you shall go'—that's our church, the Golden Dome. Then, 'descend deep into the depths of the earth.' My dear Joseph, we must open up the area beneath the altar. I'll order new excavation teams to focus all efforts there. We'll break through any floor sections if we must. We'll find this chamber."

Natalia threw Joseph a glance as if to say, *Well, that's certainly a strong reaction.* "Dr. Lavrov," she said softly, "there might be structural concerns, especially if we don't have a comprehensive scan. The site is fragile. We don't want a collapse."

But Lavrov gripped the edge of the table, eyes gleaming. "I understand caution, but we can't wait. My benefactors"—he exhaled—"they've been threatening to pull funding if we don't produce results soon. This letter is proof we're on the brink of a monumental find. I can show them photographs of the text, your translations, and they'll keep the money flowing." He turned to Joseph and pressed a hand to the younger man's shoulder in a rare gesture of warmth. "Bringing you onto the team was the greatest decision of my life. You've just saved this entire operation, my friend."

Joseph forced a polite smile. "I'm glad we could help. But, Dr. Lavrov, we can't jump to the conclusion that the Keys are physically intact under there. The letter might also be symbolic, or referencing an older crypt—"

"It's crystal clear," Lavrov interrupted. "Peter's healing power. The letter specifically says the object holds that power. The final clue is about going beneath the altar. We start the dig tomorrow at first light."

Natalia and Joseph exchanged uneasy looks. "We still need to analyze the other fragments in container G-14," Joseph ventured. "There might be clarifications or instructions. We can glean how to access that sub-level without damaging what's inside or harming the site's stability."

Lavrov gave a brisk nod, though his posture was resolute, his jaw set. "Fine, do whatever analysis you want—*tonight*. But tomorrow, excavation starts, no delays. In fact..." He raised his voice so some interns could hear. "Everyone! Tomorrow, we begin a special excavation under the altar. We suspect a hidden crypt. Prepare the equipment, scanners, and structural reinforcement. Spread the word."

An excited murmur passed through the team, though a few looked anxious. Lavrov spun back to Joseph and Natalia. "In celebration, we'll host a party tonight. Food, drinks—vodka, the best of the motherland. A chance to unwind before we get to the real heart of the matter."

Natalia grinned. "You're serious about a celebration?"

"We've been working relentlessly," Lavrov said. "We deserve at least one evening of good cheer. Everyone on the team is invited. This dig is about to become world-famous. Now that we have our textual proof, I can't see how we fail." He turned to Joseph, eyes brimming with uncharacteristic enthusiasm. "We are close—so close—to finally finding the Lost Keys of St. Peter."

In the hush that followed, Joseph nodded slowly, remembering the warnings in the letter. "*That which you seek is not yours... be warned not to seek to use that which you seek outside proper authority.*" An unsettling mixture of excitement and caution settled over him. Joseph couldn't help but feel a thrill at the prospect of finally uncovering the truth that had eluded him for so long. As an undercover CIA confidential informant, this wasn't just another mission; it was a high-stakes game where one wrong move could have dire consequences. The weight of his role pressed heavily on him. He had to stay sharp, vigilant, and above all, cautious. The excitement of the chase was intoxicating, but he couldn't afford to let it cloud his judgment. With a deep breath, Joseph steeled himself, ready to navigate the dangerous waters ahead. Indeed, they might be on the verge of unveiling a centuries-old secret. But at what cost?

Lavrov patted Joseph's shoulder. "Tonight at sundown, the courtyard of the base camp. It's time to celebrate."

With that, the director swept out of the conference room. The hum of the workday resumed, but a current of fresh energy buzzed through every corner. The rumor was out: tomorrow they would dig under the altar, and the elusive relic might finally reveal itself.

Natalia sank into her chair, letting out a long breath. "Did you see how excited he was? I've never seen him that... affectionate."

Joseph nodded, pressing his lips together. "He's been under enormous pressure. This is the first tangible piece of evidence that justifies the entire project. I can't blame him for wanting to seize the moment." Natalia leaned back in her chair, a playful smile dancing on her lips. "Well, Joseph, I suppose this calls for a little celebration, don't you think? Maybe a toast to our success and to seizing the moment?"

Joseph chuckled, raising an imaginary glass. "To us, then. For all the late nights and endless cups of coffee."

"To us," Natalia echoed, her eyes sparkling as they met his. "And to the thrill of finally seeing it all come together. You know, I always knew you had it in you."

He shook his head, a modest grin spreading across his face. "I couldn't have done it without you, Natalia. Your insights were invaluable."

She leaned in slightly, her voice dropping to a conspiratorial whisper. "Well, I guess that makes us quite the team, doesn't it? Maybe we should make this a regular thing—celebrating our little victories."

Joseph's eyes lingered on hers for a moment longer than necessary, a hint of curiosity flickering in his expression. "I'd like that. A lot."

Natalia laughed softly, a gentle, teasing lilt to her tone. "Good. Then it's settled. We'll toast to every success, big or small. And who knows, maybe one day we'll have something even bigger to celebrate."

He nodded, a warmth spreading in his chest. "Here's to that day, then."

They sat in comfortable silence for a moment, the air between them charged with excitement. Natalia's gaze lingered on Joseph's face, a subtle, unreadable emotion in her eyes before she looked away..

Natalia lowered her voice. "You looked worried."

"I am," Joseph admitted. "I just don't want us to rush in blindly. That letter was as much a warning as it was a map. We need to proceed with care—both historically and spiritually."

She folded her arms. "In other words, you're worried about crossing lines that the text specifically says we shouldn't cross?"

Joseph gave a half-smile. "That, and also the physical safety. If the letter's correct, it's basically saying the Keys are truly powerful. If we have no regard for their rightful authority, we could be repeating that Lombard soldier's mistake."

Natalia reached over and gently placed a hand on his shoulder. "Let's be honest: do you think there's real danger? Spiritual or otherwise?"

He paused, looking at the half-finished translations on the table. "Yes," he said quietly, surprising even himself with how certain he felt. "I do."

They sat in silence for a moment, the tension crackling like static in the air. Through the room's thin wall, they could hear the happy chatter of other workers, the clang of metal tools, a small cheer from someone who must have heard about the new discovery.

Natalia continued, "Tomorrow's another day. But maybe we can glean a little more from the rest of these fragments tonight—so we go in with open eyes."

Joseph released a breath he hadn't realized he was holding. "Yes. Let's do that."

They shared a determined look. Even if the entire camp was gearing up for a triumphant excavation, Joseph vowed he wouldn't step forward blindly. The letter's admonitions echoed in his mind: *'That which you seek is not yours... Follow the wisdom and discover the authority... The healing power of Peter has been fully imparted...'* The longer he studied these lines, the more he sensed that the real challenge might not be the mechanical act of unearthing the crypt, but rather respecting the cosmic story behind it—a narrative of faith, authority, healing, and possibly real spiritual peril.

FOURTEEN

Bonds and Boundaries

Joseph pressed the phone to his ear, stepping out onto the small balcony just beyond his cramped second-floor quarters. The afternoon sun dipped low over the battered rooftops of Antakya, gilding them in a soft, copper glow. The air still held the warmth of midday, but a faint, cooler breeze was rising from the Orontes River. He wanted somewhere quiet—somewhere away from the bustle of the newly energized excavation—so he could speak freely with his wife.

The phone rang once, twice, three times. Joseph found himself irrationally anxious, as if her not answering would snip the last thread that tethered him to his life in the States. On the fourth ring, the line clicked, and a small rustle sounded.

"Joseph?" came Salma's gentle voice. She sounded a little winded, as though she had rushed to grab the call.

He closed his eyes, letting out a breath he hadn't realized he'd held. "Yes, it's me. You doing okay? I hope I didn't catch you at a bad moment."

"Never," she said, the warmth in her tone a balm to his frayed nerves. "I was just resting on the couch. Mornings make me so nauseous; it's easier if I lie down in the afternoon. How are you? I've been praying you'd call soon."

Joseph leaned against the balcony's railing, staring at the pastel skyline. "I'm good. Actually, I'm better than good—I'm excited. We had a major breakthrough at the site." He told her about the deeper corridor they had cleared that morning and the new fragments Natalia had painstakingly reassembled. "It looks like we're even closer to figuring out how Bishop Anastasius hid the Keys of Peter. It's...incredible. I can't fully describe it. Natalia and I spent hours matching textual references to put the letter together."

Salma's gasp made him smile. "Joseph, that's wonderful. Honestly, you sound the happiest you've been in a while."

He acknowledged that, a small laugh escaping. "I am. I mean, it's still nerve-wracking—there's a lot of watchful eyes around here—but academically, it's thrilling. And Natalia's been a great collaborator." As soon as the words left his mouth, he recalled the time Salma gently expressed concern about him working so closely with an attractive colleague.

He heard a tiny pause on the line. "Right... Natalia," she murmured. "You've mentioned her before. I'm glad you have good teamwork, but don't forget boundaries, okay?" Her tone was caring, not jealous or accusatory, but Joseph felt the need to reassure her.

"Of course," he said promptly. "Listen, I always talk about you—constantly, actually. She asks about the pregnancy and everything. She's not just curious about the relics; she's asked me dozens of questions about you, about our marriage, about life in the U.S. She's—she's just got her own marriage and we are just in the exact same boat doing our best to finish this mission and get back to our spouses."

A breath passed through the line. Then Salma's voice came softer. "I trust you, Joseph. I really do. You've always been transparent. And if you're telling me she's respectful, then I won't make an issue of it. Just... promise to remember what we've prayed about. It's easy to forget the lines when you're under stress."

He nodded to himself. "I know. Thank you. And I do remember. You matter most—always."

"Good." She hesitated. "So, do you want to hear about my day? My OB checkup went okay, but the doctor wants me to come in for more frequent visits. There's a new medication they might put me on to stabilize the pregnancy hormones. It's complicated, but basically, they want to be ultra-cautious."

Joseph's heart sank a bit at not being there to hold her hand through these decisions. "Tell me everything," he urged. "I'll listen. Promise."

She launched into a careful explanation of what the doctor had said—her hormone levels, the possibility of bed rest in a month or two, the worry about preterm labor. Joseph tried to picture it all: the sterile exam rooms, the bright overhead lights, the fetal heartbeat monitor that had so often been silent in previous years. Now, at last, they had a child's faint rhythm. He yearned to be there.

"Remember," he said when she finished, "you're not alone. Mom's there, the Holy Cross fathers are close if you need spiritual support. And as soon as I can, I'll come back to check in."

"I know, love," she replied gently. "The baby and I are praying for you. Keep safe. Don't do anything reckless."

He swallowed, the irony of her last sentence twisting his gut, given how deeply embroiled he was in espionage. "I'll be careful," he managed.

"All right, I should lie down again," she said. "Just hearing your voice helps me so much. Call me soon, yes?"

"As soon as I can," he promised.

They exchanged a final goodbye, and the call ended with a muted click. Joseph lingered on the balcony, phone in hand, staring at the rust-red minarets in the distance. For a moment, he allowed himself to imagine the child's future—to imagine a time when they'd be together as a family, perhaps exploring these same streets in safer days.

A beep from his laptop on the small desk inside startled him from his reverie. He had left the laptop open and connected to the compound's Wi-Fi. Setting the phone aside, Joseph stepped back in, closing the balcony door behind him. A wave of stifling heat lingered in the cramped room, so he flicked on the old overhead fan. The new email's subject line flashed: RE: Updates. The sender: Michael Scanlon—his father.

Joseph's pulse quickened. He'd asked his father to let the matter of Notre Dame's Late Antiquities Department die, but it seemed Michael had done the opposite. Quickly, he sat at the desk, the old metal chair squeaking, and clicked on the email.

From: Michael Scanlon
To: Joseph Scanlon
Subject: RE: Updates

Joseph,

I know you told me to let sleeping dogs lie regarding the board's decision to close the Late Antiquities program, but curiosity got the better of me. I can't stand to see your life's work snuffed out without an explanation. I met up with a friend on the board—an older fellow named Gerald Norris. Gerald and I go way back; we collaborated on a philanthropic project decades ago. He claims the official line is "financial redirection," but he let slip that someone else on the board, a certain Marvin Kozlov, might have been the driving force.

Gerald confided that Kozlov has suspicious connections to a Russian multinational corporation—something about a large "donation" that preceded the board's final vote on your department. Gerald's words, not mine, but it sure smells like bribery to me. So, I asked around a bit more, and the rumor is that the Russian government or one of its major business arms bribed Kozlov to push for the closure. I know this sounds outlandish, but given everything that's happening globally, I wouldn't be surprised if there's more to the story. Possibly they wanted you out of Notre Dame, so you'd be forced somewhere else...

Listen, I'm no detective, but I can't let this rest. If the Russians are behind the board's decision, that means they're interfering not just in your career, but in the university's integrity. You know me, son— I've only got so much time left, and I refuse to spend it ignoring this. I'll keep poking around, see what else I can learn. Don't worry about me. God is in charge of my days, not some disease.

Write me when you can, but do whatever you need to stay safe. Let me handle the board business.

I love you, son.

Dad

Joseph read it twice, each line plunging him deeper into alarm. Marvin Kozlov? A bribe from a Russian multinational to effectively sabotage Joseph's department? So that was how Lavrov's group had swooped in at precisely the right moment to offer him a contract. The revelation sent a shiver down his spine. He looked warily at the small Wi-Fi router blinking in the corner. If the FSB was indeed monitoring traffic—and they almost certainly were—then reading this email might look suspicious. That alone could cause trouble for him and, worse, for his father.

He felt his mouth go dry. The fear of the Russians scouring his father's trail was overshadowed by another fear: that Michael, with only a few months left, wouldn't relent in his search for truth. What if they discovered Michael's meddling? Joseph's heart hammered at the thought of the dangers that might pose.

But to ignore his father's email or to scold him would be an insult; it was too big a piece of news, and Michael was set on it. Joseph's mind raced—he needed to craft a neutral reply that would not tip off watchers. Hands hovering over the keyboard, he typed:

From: Joseph Scanlon
To: Michael Scanlon
Subject: RE: Updates

Dad, Thank you for the update. I appreciate your support. Things are fine here, no need to worry about me—great team, amazing progress. They treat me well. I'm sure everything will work out in the end. I trust your judgment in looking into whatever is going on back home. Just please be safe, okay?

Love you,

Joseph

He read it over, hoping it sounded benign. Great team, amazing progress—standard compliments that might appease any Russian intelligence reading over his shoulder. He hit send, heart beating fast, and closed his laptop. The fan overhead did little to dispel the flush of adrenaline that crept over him.

Moments later, a sharp knock came at his door. Joseph jumped, half expecting Oleg's glaring face. But when he opened it, he found Dima there, wearing a broad grin.

"Joseph!" Dima spread his arms in a welcoming gesture, that usual spark of mischief in his eyes. "You forgot the time, my friend? Everyone's in the old compound lobby already, waiting for you and Natalia. We're celebrating the breakthroughs from today."

Joseph forced a smile, working to compose himself. "Ah! Sorry, lost track. I'll be right down."

Dima didn't immediately move. He peered at Joseph's unsettled features. "Everything okay?"

Joseph nodded a bit too quickly. "Yeah, yeah, all good. Just a bit tired. Let's go celebrate."

"All right, come on then," Dima said. He pivoted and led Joseph through the hallway to a steep set of stairs descending to the ground floor. As they walked, Joseph tried to wipe worry from his expression, forcibly shifting his mind from his father's revelations to the present. The last thing he needed was Dima or anyone else suspecting that he'd just discovered a possible Russian infiltration in the Notre Dame board.

At the bottom of the stairs, the motel lobby stood in a glaring contrast to the gloom outside. String lights had been hung from the low ceilings, and a cluster of battered couches was pushed to the edges, opening space in the center. A long folding table stood flush against the wall, covered in trays of Russian fare—blini with red caviar, bowls of shchi cabbage soup kept warm by small burners, plates of salat olivier (the classic potato salad), and a teetering tray of pirozhki pastries. Several bottles of vodka gleamed among plastic cups. Joseph picked up the distinct scents of dill, sour cream, and caramelized onions, drifting along with the underlying note of stale cigarette smoke that lingered from whomever had used the motel previously.

A raucous cheer went up as soon as Joseph stepped inside. "Hey, the hero arrives!" someone yelled in Russian. Applause rippled around the room, accompanied by broad smiles. Joseph caught sight of Elena Volkova the geoarchaeologist raising a half-empty glass, her cheeks already pink from alcohol. Next to her, the field archaeologists Yakov, Sasha, and Zoya stood in a loose trio, each with shots in hand, laughing at some shared joke. Artem Moroz and Grigory ('Grisha') Morozov hovered near the food table, piling pastries on plates. Oleg lurked by the doorway, arms crossed, but even he had a plastic cup in one hand. Joseph found himself unsurprised that Oleg was glued to the perimeter, likely more interested in security oversight than a party.

Only Ivan was absent. Joseph scanned the room and realized Ivan was missing from the group. He was about to ask about him when Dima, weaving among the others, beckoned him forward.

"Welcome, Joseph!" Dima bellowed, clearly wanting everyone's attention. "We're here to celebrate the extraordinary progress made by our textual team—Joseph, Natalia, and the rest of us mere mortals who assisted them." That garnered a wave of laughter. "We're getting so close to deciphering that old bishop's secret. Tonight, let's have good food, good drink, and good fellowship."

A cheer rose, though Joseph noticed a few half-lidded, watchful eyes. The entire group had a certain tension beneath the camaraderie—as if everyone was determined to enjoy themselves, to forget the daily weight of suspicion, to drown out the war that overshadowed them. Joseph recognized the dynamic: a forced jollity that sometimes surfaces among soldiers in uncertain times.

He made his way around the room, returning warm greetings. Natalia stood near a corner by a cheap plastic table that displayed a large samovar for tea. She gave him a small but genuine smile, though a flicker of something unsettled lingered behind her eyes. He returned her smile, intending to speak with her soon. For now, Dima tugged him away, pressing a shot glass into his hand.

"Come, come, a Russian toast!" Dima crowed. The group gathered, and Sasha poured clear vodka into each glass with surprising speed. Joseph looked down at the liquor. He rarely drank more than a single glass of wine or beer. Vodka was a different domain. "Ah, I'll pass," he said quietly to Dima.

Dima's eyebrows shot up. "No, no, we celebrate properly," he said in mock gravity, though behind it was a real cultural expectation. "You do at least one shot. Look, even Oleg is doing one."

Joseph sighed, noticing how everyone—except Natalia, who was still by the samovar—clutched a glass. The last thing Joseph wanted was to offend. "All right. Just one."

Dima grinned. "Perfect." He lifted his own glass. "To progress, to knowledge, and to the discovery we chase! Hurrah!"

A thunderous "Hurrah!" followed. Joseph tossed back the shot. An immediate burn scorched his throat, tears springing to his eyes, but he forced a cough-laugh. The group exhaled in satisfaction, slapping each other's shoulders.

"Another?" someone asked. He shook his head, raising a palm in polite refusal. The clamor of voices resumed, and he drifted away.

Before he reached Natalia, Grisha grabbed Joseph by the sleeve. "So, my friend," Grisha said in English, his accent thick. "When we are finished here, do you have big plans? You found relic, you go back to America a rich man?"

Joseph's chest felt warm from the vodka. "Maybe. But mostly I want to be with my wife and the baby coming."

Grisha nodded. "Yes, yes. Family first. I have a boy, six years old. Hard to be away. But we all do what we must."

Dima approached then, hooking an arm around Joseph's shoulders in a comradely fashion. "Speaking of returning home, Joseph, what do you do when your name is in the history books for recovering the famed Keys of Peter?"

Joseph tried to ease into the camaraderie. "I guess I'll publish all the academic papers I can, maybe teach a special course. But mostly, I'll want a quiet life. We've spent so long wanting a child. I can't wait to be around for every moment."

Dima grinned broadly, his eyes twinkling with mischief and warmth. He released Joseph and turned to the rest of the group, raising his voice to gather their attention. "Everyone, gather 'round! It's time for another toast!" he announced, reaching for a bottle of vodka that gleamed under the dim lights. With practiced ease, Dima began filling each glass to the brim, the clear liquid shimmering as it caught the light. "To Joseph and the future scholar or adventurer in the making!" he declared, lifting his own glass high. The group erupted in cheers, their glasses clinking together in a harmonious chorus. Joseph, feeling the warmth of the moment and the camaraderie of his friends, raised his glass as well, a broad smile stretching across his face. As he took a hearty sip, the vodka burned a fiery path down his throat, and he felt a pleasant, buzzing warmth spread through his limbs. He laughed, the alcohol loosening his usual reserve, and joined in the lively chatter, the joy of the moment mingling with the anticipation of the future.

"Mm, fatherhood," Dima teased. "You'll find that's a job bigger than any excavation. If you need tips, you know I have two little devils running around back in Volgograd." He chuckled. "But truly, if all goes well, we'll remember these months forever. We'll have stories for our grandchildren. We'll laugh about the time the scaffolding collapsed, or the day you nearly fell into that hidden pit." He leaned in, eyes shining. "It's good to see you let your guard down for once, Joseph. Drink more, enjoy yourself. Tonight is about friendship, not just artifacts."

As Dima excused himself to greet others, Joseph rubbed the back of his neck, feeling a bit guilty for half-enjoying the festivities while carrying so many secrets. Then he noticed Natalia was alone at one of the battered sofas, her posture hunched, her arms crossed tightly. She stared at the floor, ignoring the swirl of merriment. Joseph approached her quietly, weaving around a couple who were dancing in a tipsy sway to Russian ballads playing from a portable speaker.

He plopped down on the sofa next to her. "Hey," he said softly. "I've been meaning to say thanks—for everything you did with those fragments. This celebration is mostly about you, you know." Her eyes flicked to his, a ghost of a smile crossing her lips before vanishing.

"Don't shortchange yourself, Joseph," she answered. "You're the one who recognized that mention of Anastasius's coded references. If you hadn't made the link to his earlier letters, I'd still be puzzling over random scraps."

He shrugged. "It's a team effort." He studied her face. "You doing okay?"

Natalia tried to maintain her composure, but the strain was evident in the way her fingers fidgeted with the hem of her sleeve, twisting and untwisting the fabric. Her eyes were glassy, as if she were holding back a tide of emotions. She took a deep breath, her shoulders rising and falling as she attempted to steady herself. But a slight tremor in her voice betrayed her when she finally spoke. "It's just... a lot, you know?" She glanced away, blinking rapidly, as if to keep tears at bay.

"I just tried to call my husband, Nikolai. I wanted to tell him how close we are to unraveling the Keys. Thought he'd be thrilled, but..." She gave a derisive huff. "He ended up... basically mocking me. Accusing me of bragging. Saying I only ever do these digs to be in the limelight. It got ugly."

A pang of empathy struck Joseph. "I'm sorry. That must hurt. Does he not support your work?"

Her eyes flicked down. "He used to be proud of it, I think, but now it's like...he gets jealous if I accomplish something. He complains I'm never home, that I'm putting my career first. Yet ironically, he's the one who said we should hold off on kids because he didn't want them interfering with his own ambitions. Now he says I'm 'overshadowing' him." She balled her fists. "I don't know. Maybe we never really had a proper foundation. Maybe it was just... physical attraction, success, excitement, you know? We were the star couple at the university. People said we were unstoppable. But that hype doesn't last forever. What do you do when the spark is gone?"

Joseph recalled his wife's words, about boundaries and the reason behind a marriage. "I'm definitely no relationship expert," he began gently. "But from experience—marriage can't be built on things that shift when circumstances change, like fame or success. For me and Salma... if it was about money, or excitement, or even fertility, we would've quit a decade ago. Our foundation's deeper. Our faith, our vow, the sense that we're meant for each other's well-being. When you have that... changing events don't break you."

Natalia stared at the threads of a small tear in the sofa's arm. "I guess that was never us," she said bitterly. "We never prayed about anything, we never considered moral or spiritual aspects. It was just... that rush of being two brilliant young academics who looked good on paper. Now, I see it's empty."

He reached out tentatively, letting his hand rest on her forearm in a supportive gesture. "I can't tell you what to do. But maybe you two need an honest talk. Figure out if there's something more to hold you together, or if it's time to rebuild your foundation from scratch."

She sniffed, blinking away tears. "Yeah... maybe you're right." The party's music rose around them, an incongruous bounce of melody undercutting her sadness. She gave him a watery half-smile. "Thank you, Joseph. I appreciate your kindness."

He nodded, about to respond, when the lobby door banged open. Everyone turned, the music abruptly dropping in volume. Ivan Petrenko, the find specialist and father of three, stumbled in, face contorted with a grief so raw it was terrifying. His chest heaved as though he'd sprinted a mile. The entire room fell silent, confusion rippling among the partygoers.

"Moy syn!" Ivan croaked, voice strangled. "My son—my Dmitri...he's dead." His eyes, wild with despair, darted among them. People stood in shock, setting down drinks, stepping closer as though to help.

In a heartbeat, Joseph was on his feet, dread hitting his stomach. Others pressed in too: Dima, Sasha, Grisha. Ivan's words tumbled out in half-sobs. "He was drafted—eight months ago, Dmitri turned eighteen, they forced him in the army. Volkov's war in Poland... I just found out he was... he was killed in Warsaw today. We lost hundreds today, they say." His voice choked. "My boy was barely an adult."

The party atmosphere shattered. The upbeat music still played from the portable speaker, but no one was dancing. The entire room froze in shock. Ivan threw his head back, tears carving lines down his cheeks. "Proklyat Volkov! Curse that man—he sends our sons to die for his empire! He lies about glory while our children pay the price. He's a murderer!"

Joseph's heart hammered. The anguish in Ivan's voice was unstoppable. He felt a wave of sorrow for the man whose whole life had just collapsed. The mention of Volkov's name brought immediate tension. Sure enough, Oleg and two other security contractors stepped forward, their expressions grim. They advanced on Ivan, who continued screaming at the top of his lungs, cursing Volkov, cursing the war, cursing the monstrous ambition that robbed him of his son.

Oleg's voice was surprisingly calm. "Ivan," he said, "let's not do this here." He signaled his men, and they each took one of Ivan's arms. Ivan jerked away, trying to free himself, but they were too strong.

"No—get off me! Don't you see what Volkov does? This is who you serve!" he shouted. "Are we not men with families? We obey, we dig, we smile—and our children die in his wars. Proklyat—damn all of this!"

Joseph wanted to intervene, to comfort Ivan, to do something. But the contractors pinned Ivan's arms behind him, forcibly steering him toward the exit. Oleg opened the door, and in seconds they were outside. The door slammed shut, muffling Ivan's wails. The music kept playing in the uneasy hush, echoing around the stunned group.

Dima approached the door, looked out the window, then turned to the silent crowd. He lifted his palms in a pacifying gesture. "Easy, everyone," he said, though his voice trembled. "Ivan is... he just heard devastating news. Let's not jump to conclusions."

But the tension was uncontainable. A low murmur broke out. Sasha, frowning deeply, muttered, "Why is Volkov not on the battlefield himself, if this war is so necessary?" Zoya, eyes wet, whispered, "Dmitri was just a boy. If they force our youth to fight, it's—it's madness." Another voice hissed, "Russia needs victory. We must defend our motherland's borders." More murmurs, arguments half-formed. The crowd was unraveling, grief and anger welling up in bursts of condemnation or just numb shock.

Joseph felt Natalia clasp his arm. She seemed unsteady, face pale. "Dear God," she whispered. "I knew it was bad, but... he lost his son. Eighteen? That's so young."

At that moment, the door opened again. This time, Dr. Alexei Lavrov stepped in. Joseph noticed an unusual solemnity in Lavrov's bearing. He surveyed the room, clearly sensing the chaos. "What happened?" he asked, voice firm. Someone told him, in rushed Russian. Lavrov set his jaw. He flicked off the still-playing portable speaker with a snap of a button. An oppressive silence followed.

Lavrov drew himself up, arms raised as though to gather them in. "My friends, I know this is a heavy blow. Let us not blame each other here, in this place of celebration. Our hearts go out to Ivan. We pray for his son's soul."

A low murmur of agreement. Some eyes reflected raw fear. Lavrov pressed on, "Remember, we are here for a sacred mission. Whatever happens beyond these walls—whatever wars or tragedies—our calling is to preserve the faith, the heritage of our Orthodox tradition. We must keep our heads, continue this work, and trust God to bring good out of evil. Yes?"

A mixture of nods and uncertain looks rippled across the group. Slowly, the raw tension eased to a subdued heaviness. Lavrov gestured for them to set down their drinks. "Let's not let grief or anger tear us apart. We will find a way to help Ivan, to be with him in mourning. But for now, let us keep our eyes on the reason we are here. We have the chance to restore something holy to the Church, to all believers."

Some responded with subdued agreement. Others stared at the floor. Sensing the moment, Lavrov spoke softly again, "Pray for Ivan and Dmitri. Pray for Russia, for all who suffer. And let's press on with our mission tomorrow. That is the best we can do."

A hush followed. One by one, they drifted to the exit or to their rooms, no one mentioning the celebration or the half-eaten food. Joseph found himself standing in the middle of the deserted lobby soon, Natalia at his side, the last vestiges of the party's color and music still lingering in scattered balloons and leftover plates.

He exhaled deeply, hearing distant sobs from somewhere outside, followed by hushed voices of the security men. He prayed silently for Ivan, for Dmitri's soul. The heartbreak was a sharp reminder of the unstoppable violence roiling beyond these dusty streets.

Dima returned from the door, glancing around. "All right, folks," he said in a near-whisper. "We've had enough for tonight. Let's get some rest. We'll regroup in the morning." He met Joseph's eyes, giving a slight nod. Joseph returned it. There was nothing more to say, the horrors of war speaking far louder than any denial or toast.

Natalia gently touched Joseph's shoulder, her voice trembling. "I'll see you tomorrow, yes?"

He nodded. "Yes. And Natalia—take care. Really."

She bowed her head. "I will." She slipped away, stepping into the corridor. One by one, the Russians left, until Joseph was alone. Quietly, he grabbed a stray plastic cup from the table, disposing of it in an overstuffed trash bin. He saw the half-empty vodka bottles, the trays of congealing blini. They seemed obscene in the aftermath of such news.

Finally, Joseph walked out, footsteps echoing on the battered tile floor. He ascended the stairs to his cramped room, each step heavy with the knowledge that any illusions of normalcy had died tonight. War had intruded directly into their group. The tension, the fear, the heartbreak—these threatened the team's morale, their loyalty, even their willingness to keep searching for the Keys. And all the while, Joseph's father dug deeper into conspiracies at Notre Dame, and Joseph himself faced the risk of a powerful Russian state that would not hesitate to crush them all if it served Volkov's aims.

Shoulders slumped, he reached his door, stepped inside, and turned the lock. Sinking onto the edge of the bed, he thought of Salma—her pregnancy, the precarious life forming inside her. He closed his eyes, recalling her advice to keep boundaries, to rely on faith. But events were spiraling beyond his control. A father had lost his son this very day on a battlefield hundreds of miles north.

Joseph's own father was fading from cancer, determined to keep stirring the pot. And they were racing to uncover the Keys of Saint Peter, a relic that might—if the legends were true—grant unimaginable power to those who possessed them.

With trembling hands, Joseph clasped them together, bowing his head in an earnest, voiceless prayer. For Ivan's shattered heart, for Natalia's fracturing marriage, for the Russians' illusions of victory, for every grieving family, and for his own father who refused to sit idle. He prayed for mercy, for guidance—some sign that all this sacrifice and heartbreak wouldn't be in vain.

Outside, the night whispered across the quake-ravaged city, while inside the compound, what remained of the day's celebration lay in sad remains. Tomorrow would come with new challenges, new revelations. For now, Joseph could only cling to faith—and hope.

FIFTEEN

A Convergence of Paths

Morning broke over the makeshift compound with a surprising flurry of activity, even more so than usual. It was barely past six-thirty when Joseph Scanlon stepped out of his cramped room and headed toward the cafeteria. He'd slept fitfully—his mind churning with half-formed plans, concerns about the dig's safety, and the knowledge that Dr. Lavrov wanted them all assembled first thing. Even from a distance, he could hear the low hum of voices and the clank of metal trays echoing in the hallway. There was a sense of urgency in the air, as if the entire crew knew the day would bring something pivotal.

As Joseph entered the cafeteria—a long, refurbished space that had once been a motel lounge—he noticed it was packed. People stood shoulder to shoulder at one end, their attention riveted to a mounted television broadcasting a Russian news channel. Dima was near the front, seated at one of the plastic tables, watching intently alongside Yakov, Sasha, Grigory, and several others. Even the usually jovial Natalia was silent, arms folded, eyes locked on the screen.

Joseph grabbed a mug of coffee from the service counter, weaving around a few men in dusty boots and drab T-shirts, then joined Dima. The news anchor on TV—a stern-faced woman in a crisp black blazer—was speaking rapidly in Russian over footage of rolling tanks, lines of soldiers, and a color-coded map highlighting Eastern Europe. The banner running beneath her declared, in Cyrillic letters Joseph could barely parse, something about "significant advances in Poland."

Dima glanced up at Joseph. "Morning, Professor," he said, voice subdued. "We're watching updates. Seems our forces made big gains in Poland overnight."

The word "our" reminded Joseph just how many Russian ex-military personnel surrounded him. He gave a small nod and sat beside Dima. "I can see that. Everyone looks so serious."

Dima gestured at the television where they were replaying a short clip of President Igor Volkov from a speech weeks ago. "They keep showing old footage," he explained. "He was supposed to give a new address today, but it got canceled again. Second time this month."

From Joseph's other side, Grigory—Grisha, as some called him—leaned forward. "My brother-in-law works for the Ministry of Defense," Grigory said in low, urgent tones. "He told me last night that the rumors about the president's health are growing louder. They've been masking it from the public, but each time he's scheduled to appear, something happens."

Yakov scoffed, folding his arms. He was a wiry man with thick eyebrows and perpetual skepticism. "That's all hearsay. The official line says President Volkov is tending to 'personal matters.' I see no reason to disbelieve it. He's a busy man leading a war. Sometimes schedules change."

Grigory set his jaw. "There is nothing more personal than your own health. Mark my words, Volkov is not well." He shot Yakov a meaningful look. "You don't have to be a conspiracy theorist to see it."

In the corner, Sasha—a petite woman who handled some surveying tasks—crossed her arms over her chest. "If he's sick," she said bluntly, "let it be his time to leave the earth. War would probably wind down if Volkov is gone."

A hush fell at her words. Dima's eyes flickered nervously. "Sasha!" he barked. "Don't discuss such matters here, especially not with an American CIA agent in our midst." He cast Joseph a wry grin, eyes flashing with mock alarm.

A ripple of laughter spread through the crew. Joseph caught the joke and grinned, lifting both hands in feigned surrender. "You heard the man. As a CIA agent, I'm obligated to meet with my handler this afternoon and repeat everything you say about President Volkov." Another round of laughter followed. Even Natalia cracked a faint smirk. But in the corner, Oleg stood stoically, arms folded, his gaze locked on Joseph with no mirth in his eyes. The silence from Oleg was enough to chill any sense of levity.

Joseph tried to ignore Oleg's stare, turning back to Dima. "By the way, I wanted to talk to you about the altar area in the Golden Dome excavation. We need extra bracing around that collapsed northern column. The structural scans were concerning. One slip and we risk losing a big chunk of the arch."

Dima's expression softened as practical matters took precedence. "Yes, you did mention that. I'll bring it to Dr. Lavrov's attention. It's definitely a priority. We can't have the dome caving in before we uncover whatever's underneath."

Joseph exhaled, relieved. "Thank you. I just don't want us racing into the altar substructure too fast."

Dima set his coffee mug down. "It's on my to-do list. Let's see if we can finalize that plan by midday."

Almost on cue, an electric hush blanketed the cafeteria. Everyone turned as Dr. Alexei Lavrov entered through the main doors. Tall and impeccably dressed in a slate-gray suit jacket—despite the dusty setting—Lavrov radiated tension and purpose. His face bore deep lines of fatigue that Joseph hadn't noticed before. He paused at the threshold, scanning the crowd until he found Dima.

"You," Lavrov said simply, beckoning. Without waiting, he crossed to a private corner and motioned for Dima to join him.

With an apologetic shrug, Dima excused himself from Joseph's side. The pair then sat at an empty table, speaking in rapid Russian. Joseph couldn't catch many words, but from their body language—Dima's hands up in an almost pleading gesture, Lavrov's jaw set in determination—he deduced something was going on with the timetable. Possibly the same "rushed" feeling that had hovered over the compound since dawn.

Joseph sipped his lukewarm coffee, mind drifting. He realized with a start that he hadn't updated Agent DeLuca or the CIA on the most recent parchment fragments Natalia and he had deciphered. A sense of urgency prickled at him. If any fresh developments pointed to the Keys, he needed to pass that on. Time was ticking, and the Russians certainly wouldn't let him stroll around the city unsupervised.

He looked back at Lavrov and Dima. Now Lavrov's voice rose, echoing across the cafeteria in harsh, clipped Russian. Joseph couldn't make out every word, but "seychas!"—"now!"—rang clearly, followed by an abrupt final remark. Lavrov stood, pivoted on his heel, and strode out. Dima watched him go, face taut with worry. Slowly, Dima returned to Joseph, slumping into the seat Lavrov had vacated.

"That didn't look pleasant," Joseph murmured.

Dima released a slow breath. "Lavrov is insisting the deeper excavation around the altar happens today. I tried to caution him—like you said, we need a few more days to secure that arch. But he won't hear it."

Joseph's stomach flipped. "Today? That's a major risk to the structure."

"I know," Dima said, rubbing the bridge of his nose. "But he's adamant. I'm not sure why. He says it's urgent, no time to wait." He exhaled. "I'll do my best to at least put some basic supports in place, but we'll have no official engineer on site. It's not ideal."

Joseph frowned. "We can't just ignore safety concerns because he's impatient."

Dima nodded. "I told him that, but he shut me down. Something about 'an important milestone' and how we can't afford further delays." He paused, looking at Joseph with a touch of sympathy. "We'll manage. In the meantime, you had mentioned needing to see your in-laws?"

It took Joseph a second to shift gears. "Oh—yes. I do. I'm sorry I didn't bring it up earlier. I was hoping to do that this morning, if it doesn't interfere with the excavation schedule. Realistically, I'm not needed until we interpret anything new. There's not much text for me to examine yet."

Dima considered, tapping the table in thought. "You've earned it. We appreciate everything you've done so far. The situation's tense, but you can go for a couple hours. Oleg's busy, though; maybe I can spare someone else." He cast a glance around, quickly spotting another security man—a tall, unsmiling figure with short-cropped dark hair. "Yes, that's Vitaly. He'll drive you."

Joseph exhaled relief. "Thank you."

Dima waved it off. "No problem. Just don't vanish for too long. We might need you to translate or confirm anything uncovered."

Joseph nodded fervently. "Understood. I'll be back soon."

Dima pulled out his phone. "Message your family. They can't wait to see you, right?"

Quickly, Joseph typed out a note to his father-in-law, Namir: *Salam, Baba. Any chance I can drop by soon? I have a free morning.*

Within moments, a reply lit up the screen: *Ahlan wa sahlan, Yōsif! Come now, we are always ready. I'll tell Aziz.*

Joseph felt a spark of excitement and anxiety. Good—Aziz was the real reason he needed to go. He'd pass along the new intel about the letter's location clues to the CIA, ensuring that no crucial update was missed. For all the talk of a structural rush, there was also a possibility they might indeed find the Keys soon if the dig pressed on. The U.S. needed to know.

Dima nudged him. "That was quick."

"Namir's always quick with a welcome," Joseph said wryly.

"Vitaly doesn't speak English," Dima warned. "But he knows the city well, and he's less prickly than Oleg. Should be fine. Go talk to him—I'll handle the paperwork."

Joseph stood, feeling the coffee roil in his stomach. *This is it*, he thought. *A chance to slip more intel to Aziz.* If the Russian team ever found out he was actually CIA, they would never forgive him. Oh the irony. He quietly left the cafeteria. Outside, Vitaly was standing near a black SUV, arms crossed, exhaling in the sweltering sun. Dima joined them briefly to confirm the instructions. Vitaly gave a curt nod, opened the passenger door for Joseph, and soon they were on their way.

They navigated the busy roads of Antakya, where reconstruction and daily life collided in a chaotic dance. Buildings still showed cracks from the previous year's earthquakes, and some roads were half-blocked by scaffolding. At last, they turned into the Haddad family's neighborhood—narrow lanes, carved wooden doors, and the distinctive odor of simmering spices drifting from open windows.

The SUV rumbled to a stop in front of Namir's home. Vitaly glanced at Joseph and pointed firmly to his watch, indicating a time limit. Joseph gave a thumbs-up and a polite smile, then stepped out into the thick morning heat.

The door swung open almost as soon as he knocked. Miryam stood there, vibrant as ever, her face lit with joy. "Yōsif, welcome!" she proclaimed, pulling him into a warm embrace. "It's been too long—two weeks? We were worried they locked you in that camp forever."

He laughed, letting her motherly affection calm his nerves. "I missed you all."

Namir appeared next, a tall, lean man with a ready grin. "My son," he said in Arabic, clasping Joseph's hand. "Come, we have fresh tea. Miryam made lemon pastries, too."

They ushered Joseph into the living room, which always radiated a comfortable timelessness: plush cushions, patterned rugs, icons of saints on the walls, and the aroma of fresh cardamom. Joseph felt tension melt away with each second in this familial sanctuary. He quickly explained how he only had a short window—maybe an hour at best—before returning to the dig.

Miryam patted his arm. "Then we won't waste a moment. Tea is ready, and you must at least sample the pastries."

They sat in a circle of soft couches, the conversation flowing easily. Talk of local events, the city's slow post-quake recovery, news of relatives. Miryam asked for updates on Salma's pregnancy. Joseph recounted that everything remained stable but high-risk. Namir prayed aloud for a healthy child, crossing himself in the Chaldean style. Joseph silently thanked God for in-laws who prayed so fervently.

Partway through the conversation, the front door clicked open again. Joseph heard a familiar booming voice in the hall. "Mama, you said my coffee—Ah! We have a visitor!"

Aziz stepped in, hair slightly ruffled, face gleaming with friendly mischief. He wore a casual collared shirt and carried the confident air that always preceded some good-natured teasing.

"Aziz!" Joseph exclaimed, rising. They embraced, and the warmth in Aziz's eyes spoke volumes. "I see your timing remains impeccable."

Aziz laughed. "Mama texted me: 'Joseph is here, hurry if you want pastries!' I sped over like a hungry wolf."

True to form, Aziz launched into jokes, praising Miryam's cooking in exaggerated fashion, telling Namir he looked younger every day, and calling Joseph his "favorite American troublemaker." All four of them bantered and chuckled for ten minutes. Then, once they'd had their fill of small talk, Aziz gave a meaningful glance to Joseph.

"Excuse me, family," Aziz said, adopting a mock solemn expression. "I must borrow Joseph for a moment. Important business on the roof, you know."

Namir waved them off. "Go, go. Don't be too long. We want to feed him more!"

Aziz led Joseph through the narrow corridor and up the winding stairs to the rooftop terrace, where a few battered chairs overlooked the city. The morning sun was higher now, casting short shadows across the mosaic of rooftops. A gentle breeze carried hints of spiced cooking from countless neighboring homes. They closed the door behind them, ensuring privacy.

They approached their usual spot near the low parapet, each leaning a hip against it. For a moment, they surveyed the city in companionable silence. Joseph felt that familiar pang of gratitude that Aziz was on his side.

Aziz cleared his throat, turning to Joseph. "I can see from your face you've got news. Let's hear it."

Joseph nodded. "Yes. But you said you had something to share first?"

Aziz smiled politely. "Let's do yours first, habibi. You're the one on the front line of this dig."

Joseph inhaled slowly, steadying himself. "All right. In short: we discovered a big breakthrough and oblique clues written in ancient Syriac that would be confusing to a Persian but clear to a faithful and intelligent Christian pointing in the direction to the keys."

Aziz raised a brow. "So they really might be close to finding it?"

Joseph shrugged. "Possibly. The first theory is that the keys are below the altar of the Church although it's not clear to me that is the case. Regardless, Dr. Lavrov is forcing a big push *today*, which escalates everything. He seems to be under a lot of stress and pressure to demonstrate results."

Aziz let out a low whistle. "So if they break through, the Keys might be uncovered soon. That's huge."

Joseph nodded, chewing his lip. "Exactly. And that's why I needed to see you. The Americans need to know about this sudden shift. If the Russians find the Keys—assuming they exist and hold any healing property—they'd likely rush them straight to Volkov."

Aziz's face darkened. "Yeah, that would be catastrophic. The man is fueling an entire war. If he's saved, there is no deescalation in sight." He paused, scanning the city below. "I'll relay your intel. But that's not all. There's a message for you: DeLuca wants an in-person meeting. Face-to-face, with no middlemen."

Joseph felt his pulse quicken. "When and how? You know the Russians never let me out of their sight."

"Right. And that's the big problem," Aziz said, folding his arms. "We can't risk DeLuca coming here. My parents might be put in danger, and your watchers would notice instantly." He shook his head.

"We need a plan. Some neutral location in the city, a place where you can slip away from your escort for a few minutes."

"Like the Old Town marketplace," Joseph ventured. "Crowded streets, small alleyways."

Aziz grinned. "Exactly. The next time you schedule a 'family visit,' request that it be an outing to the bazaar. We'll say Mama wants something special—maybe fabrics for baby clothes, or spices. The Russian guard will tag along, but in the busy side streets, we can lose him briefly. Ten minutes, that's all we'd need. DeLuca can slip in, talk to you, slip out, and you can meet the guard at the next corner."

Joseph felt a mix of excitement and dread. "It's risky. If they catch me ditching the guard, I'll be in serious trouble. And so might you."

Aziz shrugged. "Here's another idea. I know Father Jaddou has confessions in two days at St. Luke's downtown at noon. I can arrange to get DeLuca into the guest confessional, which is hardly ever used. You can have your 'face-to-face' meeting there." Joseph chuckled, "I've always felt uncomfortable with face-to-face confessions." Then he added, "Lavrov is a man of faith; he'll understand my need to go to a Roman Catholic confession." They agreed to the plan.

Joseph let out a tense breath. "All right. Two days, old town, St. Luke's. A quick vanish and reappear. We just have to hope the Keys aren't found before then. If Lavrov is pressing the excavation, this could move fast."

Aziz placed a hand on Joseph's shoulder. "We do our best. Meanwhile, pray that if the Keys are truly hidden, they'll stay hidden a bit longer—at least until you can coordinate with DeLuca. "Joseph hesitated for a moment, then leaned in closer to Aziz, lowering his voice. "There's one more thing I need from you, Aziz. Something crucial." Aziz nodded, his expression attentive and serious. "I signed a non-disclosure agreement with the CIA. It prevents me from sharing any details of my mission with them and any information about the Russians' purposes with the FSB." He paused, gauging Aziz's reaction. "But you never signed an NDA, right?"

Aziz shook his head, a small smirk forming. "No, I never did. Makes sense, though. They couldn't enforce one here in Turkey even if they wanted to."

"Exactly," Joseph said, relieved. "I need you to call my father, Michael. Tell him everything—he needs to know. Tell him that he needs to contact Father Ryan at Notre Dame and to use his connections to get word of everything happening here to the Vatican. Tell him also to be prepared to help, and to be careful not to mention anything in emails or phone calls to me, since I'm being monitored." Joseph's eyes held a plea, a silent request for trust and action.

Aziz's grin widened. "Consider it done, habibi. I'll talk to him. You know I've worked with the CIA, but I never trust them? Never. I've got your back, habibi. We'll make sure your father is ready for whatever comes." The two men exchanged a firm handshake, sealing the pact of trust and shared purpose.

Joseph nodded, suddenly craving the simplicity of his old scholarly life. "InshAllah," he said, adopting the Arabic expression for "God willing."

Aziz smiled, then gestured for Joseph to bow his head. "Let's pray together."

They both lowered their heads as Aziz spoke quietly in Arabic, something akin to a blessing or invocation: "*Ya Rabb, guide us in these dangerous times. Protect Joseph from harm, grant peace to our lands, and let truth prevail over greed. Keep the wicked from the Keys, and let your will be done.*"

Joseph felt a warm reassurance in his chest as Aziz's words flowed. He whispered an "Amen" in English at the end, touched by the sincerity of his brother-in-law's faith.

When they returned downstairs, Namir and Miryam greeted them with inquisitive smiles, but asked no prying questions—trusting that if it were urgent, they'd be told. Joseph tried to appear relaxed, exchanging more small talk and accepting one last pastry for the road. The hour was nearly up, and he knew Vitaly wouldn't be patient.

At the door, Miryam fussed, pressing a small container of sweets into Joseph's hands. "Take these for your ride back. Share them with your friends, or just enjoy them all yourself."

Namir embraced him, whispering, "Come back soon, inshallah. May God protect you."

Aziz gave him a final grin, nodding slightly in confirmation of their plan.

Joseph stepped out into the bright midday sun. Sure enough, Vitaly stood by the SUV, arms folded. He opened the door with a silent stare. Joseph climbed in, tucking Miryam's pastries carefully by his feet. As the engine roared to life, he looked back, seeing Namir and Miryam waving from the doorway. Aziz lingered behind them, that same determined spark in his eyes.

The vehicle rumbled off through the winding streets, heading toward the Golden Dome excavation site. Joseph replayed the entire conversation in his head: the promise of an in-person meet with DeLuca, the danger of losing a guard in a busy marketplace, the new intelligence about the altar vault. So many converging paths, all swirling around those ancient Keys of St. Peter.

He gazed through the window at the city sliding by: battered, beautiful, full of secrets. It struck him that the fate of nations, perhaps even the fate of a war, might hinge on relics hidden beneath the cracked dome of a church that once stood tall in the centuries after Christ. And now Joseph—an academic who'd never spied on anyone in his life—was caught at the center of it.

As the SUV wove through traffic, a fleeting sense of calm enveloped him. If the plan worked, he'd soon provide crucial intel to the CIA. At least that was something. But he couldn't shake the feeling that time was speeding toward a climax. Whether for good or ill, the next steps would be decisive—and Joseph prayed he'd be on the right side of the keys that might open heaven…or unleash more earthly chaos than ever.

With that sobering reflection, he settled into the seat, bracing himself for whatever waited at the excavation. Dr. Lavrov wanted to push ahead *today*, risking structural collapse just to reach that hidden altar vault. Joseph clenched his jaw, clutching the pastry tin tighter. One thing was certain: the calm of morning was already giving way to the storm of midday, and soon, every side's designs on the Keys would be thrown into sharper, more perilous focus.

SIXTEEN

A Cracked Foundation

Joseph arrived at the dig site, winding through a maze of temporary barriers as the Turkish sun beat down with unforgiving intensity. The stale dust along the road clung to his boots, marking each step he took toward the towering framework of scaffolding and heavy equipment. Armed guards— grim-faced Russian contractors—stood at the checkpoint. Their eyes, ever-watchful, betrayed neither welcome nor warmth. This morning, even the usual cursory nod was replaced by lingering stares. The atmosphere felt heavier than usual.

At the final checkpoint, a broad-shouldered guard with a severe brow patted down Joseph's excavation back pack. The man said nothing, only gave a curt wave to signal that Joseph was free to proceed. Joseph offered a polite smile, though it was wasted on the man's stony exterior. He trudged forward, heart thrumming with residual tension from the security gauntlet.

Beyond the barricade awaited the newly expanded excavation camp, humming with activity. A line of men and women in neon vests hurried to and fro, transferring crates of archaeological instruments, portable generators, and sealed plastic tubs for storing fragile finds. At the center of it all, overshadowing the rest of the camp, stood the battered dome of the ancient basilica. The quake that revealed its hidden structure had also left it precariously perched amidst layers of half-collapsed rubble. Crews had reinforced it with steel supports, some of which Joseph recognized from his previous visits. But today, he saw more equipment than before: tri-pods to run ground-penetrating radar, motorized lifts, extension cords snaking across the stone floors.

Joseph paused, letting the swirl of busyness wash over him. He inhaled slowly, recalling that he was here under more than scholarly pretenses. With a subtle shake of his head, he forced himself to focus on the job at hand: the centuries-old puzzle that might reveal or disprove the very existence of the Keys of St. Peter.

He descended below the collapsed archway, where Dima was waiting. Dima wore his typical black field uniform, though the dust caking its edges and the sweat darkening the collar told Joseph he'd been at this for hours already. The man's square jaw tensed when he spotted Joseph.

"You're on time," Dima greeted, wiping his brow with a gloved hand. "Good. We can use you today."

Joseph nodded, scanning the array of equipment that cluttered the once-pristine approach to the church interior. "More equipment than usual, isn't it?"

Dima exhaled. "Yes. Dr. Lavrov arrived earlier this morning with a caravan of new devices—ultrasound sensors, drilling rigs, specialized cameras. He says we need to step up our efforts around the altar."

Joseph frowned. "The altar..." Last time Joseph had seen it, that small raised platform—charred by centuries of fires and half-buried in quake debris—was still partially intact. He remembered the reverence he'd felt down there, seeing the mosaic floors and the battered remains of that holy place.

"Come on," Dima said, starting toward the narrow passage leading inside. "You won't like what you find."

Joseph followed him into the dim corridor where electric lanterns cast overlapping circles of cold white light across the collapsed stone. The deeper they ventured, the more claustrophobic it felt. A swirl of dust motes hovered in the air. Halfway along, they reached a broad opening. Joseph blinked, adjusting to the scene in front of him.

An entire crew was assembled around the sanctuary—eight or nine workers in olive-green jumpsuits, hauling large spotlights, drill bits, and crowbars. At the heart of this commotion, near the once-majestic altar, stood Dr. Alexei Lavrov. Tall and imposing, he wore pressed khaki trousers and a crisp shirt, as though unbothered by either the heat or the dust. Behind him, an array of scanning equipment beeped steadily. The battered altar itself...was largely gone. Someone had taken hammers and crowbars to it, leaving only a ragged foundation. Chunks of sacred stone lay in uneven piles.

"What...?" Joseph breathed, stopping short. He felt as though the wind had been knocked from him. "They broke it apart?"

Dima's lips formed a tight line. "Lavrov ordered it first thing this morning. He insisted the Keys might be hidden inside. Apparently, the old structure 'had to be compromised' in the name of thoroughness."

Anger and a surge of dismay churned inside Joseph's gut. He forced himself to steady his voice as he approached. "Dr. Lavrov."

Lavrov turned, eyes bright with a fervor that verged on impatience. "Ah, Professor Scanlon. You finally join us." He gestured dismissively at the altar fragments. "We're making progress. We had to remove this centuries-old obstacle to ensure nothing was hidden within."

"Obstacle?" Joseph echoed, voice taut. "This was a consecrated altar, a piece of history, potentially older than the 6th century. You've practically destroyed it."

A flicker of annoyance crossed Lavrov's face. "Don't be dramatic," he snapped. "We documented every inch. The scanning suggested a cavity could exist inside the lower portion. We had to be sure we weren't missing a chamber for the relics."

Joseph swallowed his protest. It took every ounce of restraint not to challenge him in front of the entire crew. He glanced at Natalia, who stood off to the side, crossing her arms. She caught Joseph's eye, her expression pained, but said nothing.

Nearby, an old portable generator hummed, cables trailing like serpents across the broken mosaic floors. Lavrov had set up an array of scanning devices—portable ultrasound units, used to detect hidden voids or passageways. Several laptops perched on a collapsible table, each manned by a Russian technician monitoring readouts. The hum of electronics mingled with the clang of steel tools striking stone.

"If the Keys were placed in an altar reliquary," Lavrov was saying, addressing a cluster of archaeologists, "then we must do what it takes. The stone can be reconstructed later, but if those relics lie within, we cannot lose time."

Dima stepped forward. "I still say we need additional structural stabilization. Look around—these walls haven't been fully braced since we tore out a portion of that column last week. If we keep drilling into the foundation—"

Lavrov waved a dismissive hand. "We have enough bracing. Focus on the task: I want every inch scanned and tested. We can't let fear of an earthquake or a little structural fragility stop us."

Joseph noticed the clenched muscle at Dima's jawline. "Very well," Dima said stiffly. "We'll keep going, but I caution you that ignoring safety protocols could—"

"Ignoring them?" Lavrov barked. "I see everything well supported. If you want more scaffolds, by all means, fetch them. But do not slow me down." He turned away, effectively ending the discussion.

Dima seethed in silence, then beckoned Joseph and Natalia aside. "This entire push is reckless," he muttered, voice low so only they could hear. "But I have to follow instructions or they'll replace me. Keep your eyes open."

Joseph nodded gravely, noticing how Natalia's gaze never left the battered stones. She looked as though she might weep for the altar's destruction. He gave her a gentle tap on the shoulder. "We can salvage the fragments later and see if they can be pieced back into something resembling the original. Let's not lose hope."

She swallowed, whispering, "So much history, lost in a single morning."

An hour dragged by. Crew members chipped away at the shattered foundation, while others directed scanning beams into the newly exposed rubble. Lavrov hovered, scowling at monitors, barking for updates every few minutes: "Any sign of a hollow compartment? Any unusual metallic readings?" He kept glancing at his watch, muttering about "wasted time."

Dima paced near the columns, conferring quietly with a few other team leads Artem Moroz, the site supervisor, and Grisha, the GIS specialist. All three exchanged concerned looks. Joseph overheard the words "unstable," "shifted beams," "stress cracks forming around the edges."

A shrill beep cut through the subterranean hush. One of the Russian techs called Lavrov over, pointing to a laptop. "We're picking up some irregularities in the sub-floor, about two meters down. Possibly empty pockets or air channels from quake damage."

Lavrov's eyes lit with impatience. "Then what are you waiting for? Drill there."

Moments later, the mechanical roar of a power drill filled the chamber. Joseph felt the floor beneath him tremble. Stone dust poured from overhead as if the very dome above them resented this intrusion. Crack. A deep rumble, low at first, shuddered through the sanctuary. Joseph's eyes snapped upward. Tiny shards of mortar pattered onto the mosaic floor.

Dima rushed forward, raising his voice to compete with the drilling noise. "Shut that off! Everyone, hold—!"

Too late. A jagged fissure snaked up the nearest wall. Joseph heard a low groan from overhead. Then a chunk of the corner arch gave way, tumbling down in a cloud of debris. Someone screamed. The men operating the drill scrambled to dodge falling rubble. A large block crashed onto the mosaic at the edge of the site, sending shards flying.

"Back! Everyone, back!" Dima hollered, pushing workers away from the epicenter. A swirl of dust enveloped them, stinging Joseph's eyes and throat.

A thunderous crack echoed. The entire left side of the arch collapsed in a slow-motion crumble, revealing a mouth-like cavity in the wall. Stones rained down. With a burst of adrenaline, Joseph grabbed Natalia's arm, yanking her backward as a volley of smaller rubble clattered around them. The dust thickened, and the generator lights flickered momentarily.

Amid the chaos, Joseph glimpsed three of the Russian workers pinned under lumps of falling debris. One wore a name patch reading "Igor," while another seemed to be a younger man Joseph recognized as Pavel. They cried out in pain. A woman wearing a bright pink bandana—probably Zoya, one of the archaeologists—was struck on the arm. She screamed, dropping to her knees. Several others rushed to help them.

"Get them out, hurry!" Dima roared, voice breaking. Instantly, Joseph, Natalia, and a few others sprinted forward. Joseph heaved rocks off Igor's torso, ignoring the searing ache in his arms. Igor's face was pale, streaked with dirt, but he was breathing. Nearby, two security men pulled debris off Pavel's legs. Zoya clutched her limp arm, biting back whimpers as Natalia helped her stand.

The swirl of dust eventually settled enough for them to see. Dima called for a retreat. "Up the stairs—move them to open air! Now!" He signaled an emergency call on the radio.

A frantic chain of events followed. In less than ten minutes, emergency personnel from the local municipality arrived with stretchers, oxygen masks, and first-aid kits. The injured were hauled up and guided out of the corridor. Joseph coughed, watery-eyed, as he helped push a stretcher bearing Igor.

When the last of the wounded were evacuated, Joseph joined Dima, Natalia, and a handful of shell-shocked workers at the surface level. A wave of hot daylight slammed them, a stark contrast to the darkness below. The paramedics hustled the injured into waiting ambulances. Several onlookers—other dig team members, a few anxious security guards—milled around, all speaking in hushed tones.

Dr. Lavrov appeared from behind a cluster of crates, his expression thunderous. His usually pristine attire was caked in dust. "Where the devil are they taking those men?"

"To the nearest hospital," Dima answered, clearly exasperated but trying to remain civil. "Igor took a heavy blow to the chest. Pavel might have a fractured leg. Zoya's arm is definitely broken."

Lavrov grimaced as if injured himself by the inconvenience. "Fine. Let the local medics handle it quickly. They're not the only workers we have."

Joseph stared at him in disbelief. "That's your only reaction? We nearly lost people today—because you insisted on drilling without more reinforcement."

Lavrov's nostrils flared, but he said nothing. Instead, he jerked his head toward the battered access tunnel. "We need to see if anything was revealed by that partial collapse. If there's a newly exposed cavity, we must explore it. We can't wait for them to bring in more bracing."

Dima pinched the bridge of his nose. "We just had an accident," he insisted. "The structure is compromised. No one should go back in until we set up stable scaffolding and run fresh structural checks."

Lavrov advanced on him, voice dropping to a cold hiss. "Your job is to secure the site so we can continue. You have two hours. If you can't do it, I'll bring in my own people from St. Petersburg, men who aren't timid."

A muscle twitched in Dima's jaw, but he gave a quick, sharp nod. "Very well. Two hours." He pivoted, leaving to bark orders at a group of waiting laborers.

A tense hush fell. With surprising efficiency, the uninjured members of the crew set up new supports, hammered braces into place, and tested the tunnel's stability. Joseph and Natalia hovered on the periphery, sharing dismayed glances at Lavrov's relentless pace. Even so, they found themselves drawn back underground after the new scaffolding was half-installed. Dr. Lavrov demanded it. "We must confirm once and for all if anything is hidden below the altar," he repeated.

So, once again, they descended into the sanctuary. This time, Joseph's heart pounded with unease at every groan or settling of debris overhead. Dust clung to every surface. Broken columns lay askew where they'd fallen. The place no longer felt like a sacred space—just a gutted ruin.

For a full two hours, they combed the site. Lavrov ordered scanning of each newly exposed pocket, hoping some narrow crack might yield a metal reading or an ancient casket. Technicians set up beeping handheld detectors, while archaeologists rummaged through loose stone. Natalia photographed areas that might show inscriptions. Joseph knelt, checking for hidden compartments in the rubble, though his gut told him it was fruitless. The Keys, if hidden by Bishop Anastasius, were unlikely to be stashed in such an obvious place. Joseph had read enough of the bishop's marginal notes to suspect the real hiding spot was deeper, or more cleverly concealed.

At intervals, Lavrov stalked from one corner to the next, scanning readouts on the instruments, muttering to himself in Russian. Each minute that passed seemed to darken his mood. By the end of two hours, the scanners had found nothing. Not a single relic, no glimmer of gold keys, nor a sealed box in the foundation. Even the caretaker's notebooks—if any had been left behind—were lost in the wreckage.

Finally, with the team exhausted and the site precarious, Lavrov let the scanning operation wind down. "Shut it off," he snapped at one of the techs, who quickly cut power to the last active device. Lavrov's gaze roved the circle of onlookers—Joseph, Natalia, Dima, and about five other staff members.

"Well?" Lavrov demanded, his voice echoing in the hush. "Do we see anything? Any clue at all from these worthless scans?"

Artem Moroz, the site supervisor, cleared his throat. "No, sir. The readings are negative for any void large enough to hold relics. Just debris."

Lavrov scowled, turning sharply to Joseph. "You told me the altar was a prime candidate. All your historical talk about relic-chambers under the sanctuary. You said there was a chance."

Joseph stiffened, cheeks flushing. "I said it was a possibility, based on the newly discovered letter we found. I haven't had enough time to cross-reference everything. You insisted on rushing."

"Rushing?" Lavrov's voice rose. "We've been at this for months! We bring you here, pay you a fortune, and you produce nothing but theories. Now we face collapsed walls, injuries, wasted resources. Where are these legendary Keys?"

Joseph felt his temper surge. He took a step forward, ignoring the anxious flicker in Natalia's eyes. "This fiasco—smashing the altar, drilling into unsafe walls—was your decision. You refused Dima's request for additional stabilization. You demanded we push forward without a thorough read of the latest parchment fragments."

"Watch your tone," Lavrov growled.

"No," Joseph retorted, voice shaking with pent-up frustration. "I'm here to do my job, but you won't give me the time or the caution required. You wanted instant results, ignoring safety. Now, three people are in the hospital, the altar is destroyed, and we're no closer to finding the relics. This fiasco is yours to own."

A tense silence gripped the chamber. Dima, clearing his throat, moved to Joseph's side. "He's right. We all wanted to search the site thoroughly, but your impatience caused the hazards."

Lavrov's fury flared. He spat something vicious in Russian Joseph only caught the word for "insubordinate" and maybe "useless." Then, in English, he snarled, "You dare blame me? I have superiors waiting for updates. If I do not show progress, they'll replace us all."

Dima's eyes narrowed. "And do you think that justifies risking more accidents?"

Lavrov jabbed a finger at him. "I'm warning you, Dmitri Sokolov. Solve these operational issues or face termination. As for you," he turned on Joseph, "I brought you here to interpret the letters, so interpret them. Don't hide behind your precious caution."

With that, he spun on his heel and stormed toward the exit, shouting over his shoulder, "I expect results—soon." His footsteps thundered away, followed by a few of his personal security men who scampered to keep up.

The makeshift excavation team stood in stunned silence. In the flicker of lamp light, Joseph could see the slump of shoulders, the weariness etched on dust-caked faces. Finally, Dima inhaled, voice subdued. "Enough. Everyone, go back to your quarters. We'll do another structural check in the morning. Pray for Igor, Pavel, and Zoya." He looked to Joseph and Natalia. "I'll open any resources you need to study the documents. Just figure out where we should search next, or how to prove we're not digging in vain."

Joseph's anger receded, replaced by a tight pang of guilt. He despised Lavrov's methods, but that didn't make him immune to the knowledge that people could lose their jobs—potentially their lives—if this hunt continued fruitless. "Thank you, Dima," he said quietly. "We'll re-check the parchments, the old charts, any marginal notes. We might've missed a coded reference about where to look."

Dima's eyes held a flicker of respect as he nodded. "Yes, do that. I need something solid to placate Lavrov next time he shows his face." A grim smile tugged at his lips. "Now get out of here before the rest of the ceiling decides to drop on us."

Joseph and Natalia gathered their personal bags and carefully picked their way out of the half-collapsed sanctuary, mindful of each shifting stone. The generator lights flickered behind them, casting eerie dancing shadows on the rubble-strewn path. A swirl of stale air rushed at them as they climbed the ramp to the surface.

Emerging into the night sky was like a small rebirth, an exhalation of fear. The day's final glow had long since faded, replaced by a canopy of stars. The site was quieter now that half the workforce had dispersed—only a few roving guards stood watch, exchanging terse words in Russian or Turkish. The hush felt unnatural after so much clamor.

They walked side by side, passing the deserted check-in station where earlier commotion still lingered in battered crates and half-unraveled hoses. Natalia rubbed her temples, voice laced with sorrow. "I can't believe we destroyed that altar for nothing."

Joseph sighed, hoisting the strap of his messenger bag higher on his shoulder. "I know. The parishioners who worshiped there centuries ago... I can't help thinking we've shown them such little respect."

Natalia's mouth turned downward, grief etched on her features. "I studied conservation to preserve relics, not to smash them. Now we're complicit."

He laid a gentle hand on her shoulder. "We'll do what we can to repair the damage. Reconstructing the altar is possible, at least partially. But first, we need to figure out where the real hiding place might be. Otherwise, Lavrov will keep pushing for more recklessness."

She nodded, though her shoulders remained tense. "Let's go back to the lab, cross-reference every marginal note. I have a few of the older scans we haven't fully deciphered."

Joseph attempted a reassuring smile. "Yes. Let's dig deeper into the documents—the real place to search."

They reached the compound's perimeter fence, beyond which waited the makeshift dormitory building. The bright floodlights stationed at corners made it impossible to see beyond the fence's glare, though Joseph knew well that the city extended just a few blocks away, with families trying to rebuild their lives after the quake. He thought of the Haddads, of Aziz and his clandestine tasks. A flicker of guilt danced in his chest: so many secrets, so many agendas swirling here.

He inhaled the cool night breeze, letting it clear his head. There was no undoing the damage in the sanctuary, nor the injuries from earlier. But he still had a duty—to ensure that if the Keys of St. Peter truly existed, they wouldn't become tools of oppression. For that, he needed to keep up the facade, keep decoding, keep balancing on the tightrope of espionage and archaeology.

He mulled over the day's events: the violence done to the altar, the near-fatal collapse, the furious accusations. The bright possibility of discovering an ancient treasure had become overshadowed by power struggles and reckless ambition. He glanced up at the sky. Stars blinked indifferently, as though unmoved by human triumphs or tragedies.

"Lord," Joseph whispered, voice husky in the darkness, "show me how to do what's right."

Then he turned on his heel and headed inside, stepping deeper into a labyrinth of competing loyalties, haunted ruins, and the faint hope that the secrets of Bishop Anastasius might still guide him to the truth—and keep these relics from unworthy hands.

SEVENTEEN

The Church on the Rock

J oseph awoke with a strangled gasp. In the dim glow of the lone bulb overhead, he registered his harsh, ragged breathing before anything else. His heart pounded as if he'd been running a race—fleeing some threat in his dreams. For an instant, the images clung to him: piles of debris collapsing onto screaming figures, Natalia's face half-hidden behind swirling dust, Oleg's scowl, Dima yelling for reinforcements...

He shut his eyes, exhaling slowly. It was morning, though not yet light enough to define the battered walls of his little motel room. The ceiling fan whirred with a soft, uneven hum. In the dream, he had carried the weight of the fallen beams on his back like Atlas, feeling responsible for every bruise on his team, for every chunk of collapsing rubble. Rationally, he knew the events that had caused partial cave-ins yesterday were not his fault—he was only a scholar, not the site safety supervisor. But the guilt still gnawed at him.

He rolled onto his side, reaching for his phone on the cracked nightstand. The clock read 6:12 a.m. Already, his mind was swirling with what needed to be done: more translating, more cross-checking fragments, more covert communication with Aziz and, indirectly, the CIA. And on top of it all, the emptiness he felt at being without Salma's physical presence. It almost hurt to breathe.

He tapped in her number, listening to the buzz of the dial tone. She picked up on the second ring.

"Joseph?" came her familiar voice, thick with grogginess.

"Hey, sweetheart," he said softly, trying to steady his breath. "Hope I'm not calling too early."

She let out a little sigh. "No, it's fine. I was sort of awake anyway. I can never get comfortable. My back is killing me—this pregnancy is definitely... different than I ever imagined. I'm thrilled, but my body is protesting."

He felt a pang of regret that he wasn't there to help. "I wish I could give you a back rub right now," he murmured. "I hate you going through all of this alone."

A soft laugh sounded through the phone. "Thanks, Joe. So, how's your day shaping up? Still busy?"

He paused, fighting the urge to immediately confide how undone he felt. Last night's nightmares still gripped him. But an internal wall shot up: if he confessed that he was sleepless and anxious, she'd worry about him—and stress was the last thing she needed.

"I'm okay," he lied, voice more curt than he intended. "Just the usual. You know... deciphering manuscripts, dealing with tight security. The air is dusty, so it's... well, the typical dig stuff."

Her tone sharpened with concern. "Joseph, you don't sound like yourself."

He forced a chuckle that fell flat. "I'm fine, love. Probably just a bit of exhaustion from the day before."

"No, I can hear it in your voice. It's more than that. Is something wrong?"

His throat constricted. The images of last night's dream flickered again—dust choking the corridors, beams cracking. "No, Salma, nothing's wrong," he said, all too quickly. "I—I'm sorry, I can't talk long. I have to meet Natalia for breakfast and get started. We've got a backlog of texts to decode."

"Wait, Joe—"

"I love you," he cut in, shutting his eyes tightly. "Don't worry about me, okay? I'll call again soon."

She made a faint sound of protest, but expressed her love and they ended the call. Heart pounding, he slumped back against the pillow, consumed by guilt.

"I'm sorry," he whispered to the empty room, as if Salma could still hear.

He pushed himself up a few minutes later, washed his face in the tiny sink, and dressed in khaki pants and a clean button-down, ignoring the swirl of unease in his stomach. By the time he stepped out into the second-floor corridor, the late summer sun had begun turning the cracked windows a hazy gold.

In the makeshift cafeteria on the ground floor, he found Natalia at a battered wood table, two cups of strong Turkish coffee already steaming. A small spread of olives, cheese, sliced tomatoes, and fresh bread adorned a metal tray. She looked up, giving him a subdued smile.

"You're early," she noted, stirring sugar into her coffee.

"I didn't sleep well," Joseph admitted. He slid onto the folding chair opposite her. "Thanks for setting this up."

She shrugged, pushing a plate toward him. "I was hungry, and I guessed you'd want a proper breakfast. Helps fight stress."

He tried for a grateful grin. "Yeah... I appreciate it."

They ate in relative silence for a moment, the pungent coffee reviving Joseph's senses. Outside, trucks rattled by, ferrying building supplies to the continuing excavation.

"So," Natalia ventured, setting down her cup. "After yesterday, it's obvious the site is... precarious. But we can't stop."

Joseph pressed the heel of his hand against his forehead. "We suspect it's all from Bishop Anastasius, right? Hiding the Keys. The translation references all these scriptural passages. Some we recognized right away, some are cryptic. The writing is... clearly intended to show enough for a Christian but confusing enough for a Persian."

Joseph nodded slowly, swallowing a piece of bread. "I keep feeling the pressure of time, Natalia."

She sipped her coffee, eyes flicking across his face. "I'm not blind. I see all the armed men. I know they're not typical site security. But we can't do much except keep going, right?"

Joseph and Natalia finished their breakfast and headed to their conference scriptorum. Natalia went right to work examining parchment scraps on her computer looking for potential clues.

He flipped open his notebook, where he'd carefully copied the translated text that led them to excavate the altar. He read:

"'It is the glory of God to conceal something, and the glory of kings to search it out.' Proverbs 25:2

'To him who is faithful and true,

"2 Timothy 1:14: Keep the good thing committed to thy trust by the Holy Spirit, who dwells in us."

Follow the wisdom and you will discover the authority that has been protected for you.'

'Acts 5:15: Insomuch that they brought forth the sick into the streets, and laid them on beds and couches, that when Peter came, his shadow at the least might overshadow any of them, and they might be delivered from their infirmities.'

The healing power of Peter has been fully imparted on to that which you seek.

'Matthew 12:43: And when an unclean spirit is gone out of a man he walketh through dry places seeking rest, and findeth none. 44 Then he saith: I will return into my house from whence I came out. And coming he findeth it empty, swept, and garnished. 45 Then he goeth, and taketh with him seven other spirits more wicked than himself, and they enter in and dwell there: and the last state of that man is made worse than the first.

That which you seek is not yours. It is of the first of the Apostles and his successors. Be warned not to seek to use that which you seek outside proper authority.'

'Matthew 7:7: Ask, and it shall be given you: seek, and you shall find: knock, and it shall be opened to you.

To His Church upon this altar you shall go.'

'Revelation 6:15: And the kings of the earth, and the princes, and tribunes, and the rich, and the strong, and every bondman, and every freeman, hid themselves in the caves and in the rocks of mountains.

From this place, descend deep into the depths of the earth where you shall find that which you seek. Follow the signs of authority all the way down'

Joseph sat in the dimly lit study, surrounded by stacks of books and scrolls. The air was thick with the scent of aged paper and ink. He flipped open his notebook, intending to start his review from the beginning of his translation. Yet, his eyes were irresistibly drawn to the main verse that had led them to the altar, the crux of their current quest: "To His Church upon this altar you shall go." His Church? Who's Church is he referring to?"

With a sense of urgency, he decided to first focus on this line. As he went through the ancient Syriac text, tracing each character with his finger as he read, every word was as it should be, each phrase matching his previous translation, until he reached the word "altar." The word used on the reconstructed parchment was "shu'a'" (ܟܐܥ).

Joseph paused, his brow furrowing in concentration. Part of the challenge of translating ancient languages lay in the necessity of context to provide definition. Here, context was scarce, and the text seemed deliberately cryptic. He reached for his concordance, flipping through the pages until he found the entry for "shu'a'" (ܟܐܥ).

His training had always led him to interpret this word as "altar," especially in religious texts where altars were commonly fashioned from rock and stone. But the concordance offered another possibility—simply "rock." Joseph considered this. In a religious context, "shu'a'" often meant altar, but in its most basic form, it was just rock.

He read through the passage again, this time substituting "rock" for "altar": "To His Church upon this rock you shall go." The implications of this simple substitution were profound. What if they had been misled by a single word, chasing altars when they should have been seeking a rock?

The realization hit him like a revelation. If "rock" was the correct translation, it aligned with the foundational scripture of the Church itself—Peter being the rock upon which the Church was built. The Phrase "To His Church" refers to Peter's Church. Joseph's heart raced as connections formed in his mind, paths of thought branching out like a vast, intricate web.

He leaned back in his chair, staring at the ceiling, the weight of discovery settling over him. This was more than just a linguistic puzzle. It was a clue that could alter the course of their search, perhaps even the understanding of their entire mission.

He called Natalia over. He pointed to the scribbled note in Syriac. "This part about 'To His Church upon this altar you shall go.' The ancient Syriac uses the word *shu'a'* (ܩܘܿܥ). Typically, we translate that as 'altar.' But context is ambiguous, maybe deliberately so. Because in older Syriac usage, *shu'a'* can also mean 'rock.' Altar... rock... in Christian tradition, they merge in meaning sometimes."

Natalia's brow furrowed. "So... you suspect it means 'rock' in this instance?"

"Yes. The text might truly read: 'To His Church upon this rock you shall go.' That's reminiscent of Matthew 16:18—'And so I say to you,

you are Peter, and upon this rock I will build my church.' Peter is the rock."

Natalia's eyes widened. "Wait, wait. You're telling me the letter instructs the seekers to go to a Church of St. Peter—quite literally built on or in a rock?"

A small smile lit Joseph's face, the first genuine gleam of hope he'd felt all day. "That's exactly what I think. And I happen to know such a place: The Church of St. Peter carved into the side of Mount Starius, right on the east end of the city. One of the earliest Christian worship sites in the world. I proposed to Salma there, actually."

She blinked, impressed. "So it's real, not just a lost ruin?"

"Oh, it's very real. It's only used by pilgrims now. Officially, it's a historical site and not an active parish church. It's partly a cave. Tourists pay a small fee to get in."

Natalia nodded, excitement stirring in her expression. "So maybe that's our next lead—because the text says we must 'descend into the depths' from that place. If Bishop Anastasius hid the Keys, he might've chosen a site connected to Peter's name."

"Exactly," Joseph said. "We need to see if there's an underground passage or crypt beneath that cave church. The text mentions 'Follow the signs of authority all the way down.' We must find it."

Natalia leaned back in her chair. "We need to tell Dima. He'll coordinate with Lavrov."

Joseph agreed. "I'll do that."

Joseph raced down the hall and spotted Dima's familiar form in the doorway. The squat man wore cargo pants and a dark T-shirt, scanning the cafeteria with hawklike focus.

Joseph waved him over. "Dima! You're just in time."

Dima ambled closer. "Morning, folks. You look like you have big news."

Joseph nodded, launching into an abbreviated recap of the translation twist. Natalia chimed in, explaining the potential double meaning of *shu'a'*. They concluded with the revelation that the Church of St. Peter might be the next site.

"That's... interesting," Dima said, eyes gleaming. "And it's right here, near the city?"

Joseph nodded. "Just outside, on the slopes of Mount Starius. If the bishop's instructions are accurate, that's where we should look."

Dima rubbed his chin. "Then let's not waste time. We have vehicles. I can get an SUV. Let me just phone in a quick request for you to join me."

He pulled out his phone, stepping aside to make the call. Natalia murmured to Joseph, "Stay safe, okay? And keep me posted if you find anything. I'll dig deeper into the other fragments."

Joseph nodded, shouldering his bag. "I will. Thanks for your help this morning."

A moment later, Dima finished his call and motioned for Joseph to follow him. They traversed the dusty courtyard outside the motel, bypassing two uniformed guards. Within minutes, they were in a dark SUV, driving east across the city.

They navigated winding roads past half-collapsed buildings and ongoing reconstruction. The day blazed bright overhead, but a faint haze of smog blurred the horizon. On the eastern edge of Antakya, the slopes of Mount Starius began to rise, overshadowing the city like a silent sentinel.

Dima parked at a small makeshift lot near the base of the mountain. "We'll have to climb on foot. I see a sign there for the Church of St. Peter, so we're in the right spot."

They climbed stone steps that zigzagged up the mountainside. After a steep ascent of a few hundred feet, they arrived at a broad stone courtyard that overlooked the entire city. Joseph paused, momentarily breathless—not just from the climb but from memories flooding him.

"This courtyard," he said softly, gesturing. "It's a place of reflection. After I proposed to Salma, we sat on that bench for hours, gazing at the lights of Antakya below."

Dima nodded, scanning the surroundings with a soldier's precision. "Beautiful."

The courtyard itself felt like a sanctuary between the outer world and the solemn interior of the rock-hewn church. Its walls of ancient stone gave a sense of protection, sheltering them from the bustle below. A large stone basin stood near the center, rumored to be an early Christian baptismal font. It bore centuries of weathering, each scratch perhaps a story.

"People say it predates the Crusades," Joseph said in hushed awe.

Further left, a raised platform offered a vantage over the courtyard. Joseph eyed the stone bench, half-lost in memory. "That's where I actually asked Salma to marry me," he admitted.

Dima gave a polite nod. "I see why you love this place. The air, the view..."

A statue of St. Peter stood near the entrance of the church—a modest marble figure holding keys, a symbol of his primacy and the very reason they came. Olive trees and green vines grew in cracks along the rocky mountain face, adding life to the otherwise somber gray-brown stone. The Orontes River sparkled in the distance, weaving through the city.

Near one corner of the courtyard, a cluster of stone outcroppings looked like they might have once been watchpoints or monastic overlooks. Joseph recalled seeing them during the earlier trips with Salma. Now they stood quiet and slightly crumbling, vestiges of a time when pilgrims and guardians might have watched over the city.

After taking in the view, the two men approached a small kiosk, where a caretaker collected a nominal fee from tourists. Indeed, a few visitors milled about, mostly local families or foreign back-packers, all drawn by the historical grandeur of this sacred place.

Entering the stone passage, they stepped inside the Church of St. Peter. Immediately, the ambiance shifted—cool, damp air, faint echoes, and the hush of reverence. The inside resembled a cave-chapel, carved directly into Mount Starius. Rough stone walls, flecked with faint traces of old frescoes, seemed to whisper memories of nearly two millennia of worshipers. Artificial lights revealed an arched ceiling overhead.

"This is it," Joseph breathed. "Tradition says St. Peter himself preached here, forming one of the earliest Christian communities."

They advanced toward a small raised altar at the far end, though 'altar' was a generous term for the slab of ancient stone. A battered stone chair to the right might have been used by bishops centuries ago. On the left, older baptismal niches huddled in the dimness. Joseph approached them, heart hammering with the realization that they might be treading on the cusp of an enormous discovery.

He and Dima circled behind the sanctuary to find a fenced-off area. A flimsy chain and a simple sign in Turkish indicated this part was closed to the public.

Dima glanced around. No guard in sight; the caretaker was nowhere near. "Better to ask forgiveness than permission," he muttered with a wry grin.

They quietly unhooked the chain and slipped behind it. Beyond a narrow corridor, the passage opened into a small sacristy-like room. Boxes of cleaning supplies, stacked chairs, and random maintenance tools crowded the space, as if some caretaker used it for storage.

But what drew their attention was a darker recess at the far end. Three cave-like openings yawned in the stone. Each was tall enough for a person to slip through.

Joseph's pulse thudded as they approached, shining their phone flashlights on the wall above each entrance. Carvings emerged from the shadows. Over the left tunnel—a dove. Over the center—Chi-Rho, the ancient symbol of Christ. And over the right tunnel—two small crossed keys.

"Keys," Dima whispered. "The sign of authority!"

Joseph stared in awe. "This has to be the next step. Anastasius must have known about these tunnels. Maybe they used these caverns in the earliest centuries. And the one with the keys... it's almost too perfect."

They snapped pictures with their phones, the beams of light illuminating old chisel marks. Possibly Byzantine-era carvings, or maybe older. Joseph couldn't say for sure yet.

Dima gripped Joseph's shoulder. "I think we found our lead, my friend."

Joseph exhaled a shaky breath. "Yes." A grin spread across his face, relief and triumph blended in one. "If Anastasius wanted to hide the Keys of Peter, what better route than a secret tunnel in the Church of St. Peter itself? It's almost too obvious!"

They both laughed softly, excitement easing the tension that had weighed on them for days.

"Let's not push our luck," Dima said, lowering his phone. "We've got enough photos for now, and it's getting late. Let's report back to Lavrov."

Joseph nodded. "Right. We'll need permission to do any real excavation here. Religious site. The government, local religious authorities... it's a bureaucratic minefield."

They carefully retraced their steps, reattaching the chain behind them. Slipping into the main chapel, they drew only a few curious glances from the handful of tourists.

On the drive back, Dima texted the tunnel photos to Lavrov and placed a call through the SUV's Bluetooth system. Joseph listened as Dima summarized the find. The line crackled, and Lavrov's measured voice came through.

"So," Lavrov said coolly, "you have indeed found a carved symbol of keys at the Church of St. Peter. That's... promising."

Dima turned the wheel, navigating traffic. "Yes, very. It aligns exactly with Joseph's translation. We believe the Keys might lie somewhere beneath that rock church."

A pause. Then Lavrov replied, "We'll have to proceed carefully. A place like that requires official permits. We can't simply drill or dig. We need cooperation from the Turkish Ministry of Culture and local Christian authorities. I'll make inquiries first thing tomorrow. For now, do nothing rash. Understood?"

Joseph leaned forward. "Understood, sir."

Lavrov did not congratulate them. He simply said, "Fine. I will be in touch," and ended the call.

Dima exhaled, glancing at Joseph. "That was... anticlimactic."

Joseph shrugged. "He's probably treading carefully. The last thing he wants is an international incident over a holy site. Meanwhile, we have to keep quiet."

They continued in silence, each pondering the magnitude of the discovery.

Night had fallen by the time they reached the motel compound. Joseph parted ways with Dima in the main corridor. Climbing the stairs, he headed straight for the second-floor conference room, where Natalia usually worked late scanning fragments. Sure enough, he found her hunched over a table with a magnifier.

She looked up, tension melting into relief. "You're back! Did you find something?"

Joseph grinned broadly, recounting the entire excursion to the Church of St. Peter: the courtyard, the hidden area behind the sanctuary, and especially the three tunnels.

"That's incredible," Natalia breathed. She stood so quickly her chair almost tipped. "This means we've validated the second half of Anastasius's letter—this concept of going deeper beneath the rock and following the signs of authority."

Joseph nodded. "Yes. If we can get official clearance, I suspect we'll discover the final resting place of the Keys. Honestly, if we succeed, we might be closing out our time here soon. The entire dig at the Golden Dome was a stepping stone to this."

Natalia clasped her hands together, momentarily excited. But Joseph caught a flicker in her eyes—something akin to sadness.

"That's wonderful," she said, then faltered. "I can't wait for all this to... to end. We'll get to go home. Back to normal."

But her lips parted uncertainly, as if the words weren't fully honest. Joseph sensed a hesitance, a tension in the way she folded her arms across her chest. Her posture suggested she might not truly want everything to end. Perhaps she relished their closeness, the sense of shared purpose they'd developed.

He cleared his throat, ignoring the odd tingle in his stomach. "Well... we're not done yet. There's the final stage. We still have a lot of partial lines to translate. Once the actual excavation starts at the church, we'll probably need every clue from the bishop's cryptic instructions."

She forced a bright smile. "Right. More late nights at the desk, then."

He offered a short laugh. "Yes... guess so. But for now, I'm beat. I'm going to crash. We can pick up tomorrow."

They shared a lingering look. Something unspoken pulsed in the air—an undercurrent of closeness that he refused to acknowledge. Then she nodded and eased back into her chair, returning to her scanning as though nothing had happened.

Joseph slipped away to his room, mind swirling. Once inside, he set down his bag and grabbed his phone. He typed a quick text to Salma:

Joseph (9:48 PM):

Hey love, I'm sorry about earlier. It's been a crazy day, but I have great news. We found something huge at the Church of St. Peter—a hidden set of tunnels. We believe it's the next step to finding the Keys. I'm excited, and I wish I could share all the details in person. I miss you so much. I hope you're feeling better. Love you always.

He waited for a moment. No reply. Likely she was asleep; the time difference made it late morning for her, but she'd said she was tired. He texted a second message:

Joseph (9:50 PM):

Get some rest. We'll talk tomorrow, okay? I love you.

He set the phone aside, sighed, and flicked off the overhead light. Darkness swept in, the fan overhead continuing its steady hum. The day's triumph battered at his fatigue, wanting him to stay awake and plan for the next steps, but exhaustion won out. He lay back, eyes fluttering shut.

Despite the swirl of success—finally having a solid lead about the Keys—an unease coiled in his chest: Salma's frustration, the looming threat of the Russians, his father's illness, his CIA entanglement. He said a silent prayer, begging for guidance, for strength, for some measure of peace.

Eventually, the hum of the fan merged with his slow, rhythmic breaths, and Joseph drifted into a dreamless sleep, lulled by the promise that the Church on the Rock might soon reveal the keys to everything he'd sought since the day he first believed that relics, indeed, carried the living pulse of faith.

EIGHTEEN

A Day of Confessions

Morning light dappled the walls of the makeshift compound, a mosaic of sun and shadow filtering through the high mesh fencing. Joseph Scanlon stepped out of his cramped room into the open-air courtyard, where a faint breeze stirred the branches of a lone pomegranate tree. The sky was clear and blue, and the dusty ground radiated warmth that promised a scorching afternoon.

He was still a bit surprised Dima had agreed so readily to let him leave the compound. Typically, every step outside required meticulous scheduling. But Dima, who orchestrated logistics for this excavation team, seemed in a reasonably good mood—likely because Dr. Lavrov was spending his day on video calls with superiors in Moscow and trying to secure new excavation permits from the Turkish Directorate of Cultural Heritage and Museums. With the leader thus occupied, the staff had scattered to handle gear checks, pack crates, and ready themselves for deeper excavation once the government's approval arrived.

Joseph and Natalia, meanwhile, had been granted the morning off. That alone felt like a luxury after so many relentless days. The plan was for Joseph to head out with Oleg later in the morning, bound for St. Luke's in the old part of Antakya to make his long-overdue confession.

Still nursing a mild sense of relief, Joseph wandered toward a square table near the center of the courtyard, ready to enjoy another beautiful morning in Antakya. A battered umbrella cast partial shade over its surface as he sat down, inhaling the fragrant air that was tinged with the scent of blooming jasmine. His gaze drifted across the courtyard, and he was pleasantly surprised to see Natalia approaching.

She looked absolutely breathtaking, her transformation a dazzling departure from her usual casual work attire. Her makeup was flawlessly applied, accentuating her striking features, and she adorned a sophisticated dress that shimmered and danced with the light at every step. The sight of her left Joseph momentarily breathless, as if the air had been stolen from the room, and he found himself captivated by the allure of the woman approaching him—so different from the Natalia he had seen every day since his arrival.

"Good morning, Professor," she said brightly, setting down a small tray with two steaming cups of coffee. She offered him a seat beside her, an inviting smile playing on her lips.

"Wow, Natalia, you look... amazing! What is the occasion" Joseph remarked with friendly humor. "Let me guess—Maxim's coming into town?"

Natalia laughed, a sound that danced through the courtyard. "No way," she replied, shaking her head. "Elena and I have plans to go out for dinner and do some shopping in town. We need to feel like real women again. We've already arranged for a security escort for the outing."

Joseph chuckled, appreciating her candor. "Well, you certainly look ready to turn some heads," he said. The air between them was light and easy, leaving him to wonder if this change was just for today or if there was more to it.

Joseph cracked a smile. "Thank you. Never turn down coffee."

They both sat, the morning hush punctuated by the distant rumble of a generator and the occasional shout from workers hefting equipment at the far end of the compound.

For a moment, they savored the fresh brew. Joseph inhaled its aroma, letting the tension in his shoulders ease. "We don't often get quiet like this," he remarked, swirling the coffee in his paper cup. "Feels almost like a normal day."

Natalia tilted her head, letting out a light, contented sigh. "I'll take any normal day we can get. So, no frantic requests from Lavrov this morning—how does that feel?"

He made a gentle, playful show of checking his phone. "Feels suspicious, to be honest. I keep expecting someone to burst in, waving a new fragment that needs immediate decoding."

Natalia laughed, then her voice grew animated. "But speaking of fragments—what we accomplished yesterday in re-analyzing the parchment was so exciting!"

A little shiver of excitement rippled through Joseph. He set his coffee down. "Yeah, and more importantly our find has restored the hope that was all but lost after the collapse."

Natalia nodded. "And we're the ones who found it, Joseph. We should let ourselves be proud. So, to success." She raised her cup in a mock toast, eyes twinkling.

He clinked cups gently with her. "To success indeed."

For a short while, they chatted about the mosaic floors they'd uncovered, the intricately carved pillars, and how the quake's devastation ironically revealed the hidden layers beneath Antakya. Their voices danced through the courtyard, mingling with the hum of the compound. At that moment, Joseph realized that win his time. If this dig was up, he would genuinely Miss the friendship and company of Natalia. In the midst of all the chaos, they truly brought out the best in one another.

Eventually, Natalia's curiosity shifted. "So, do you have any updates on your wife's pregnancy?"

Joseph's expression softened at the mention. "Not really. Yesterday she had a full day of doctor's appointments, so we never got to talk. I left her some messages, but she was probably in and out of scans. I'll try again tonight."

Natalia tilted her head in concern. "That must be hard, being away for something so important."

"It is," he admitted, a note of longing entering his voice. "But we both felt this was a calling. Also, the money from this job—especially if we actually find the Keys—could change our future. Still, I hate missing those little day-by-day details of her pregnancy."

She took a careful sip of coffee. "Well, at least we have a break this morning. We could do something fun before I go out for dinner— let's go explore the bazaar or maybe just walk around. Clear our heads."

Joseph smiled, though he seemed a bit preoccupied. "I'd actually love that. But..." He paused, exhaling. "I haven't been to confession in the longest time, and I finally got permission to head into town this afternoon. I really need it."

Natalia's brows rose. A teasing light danced in her eyes, but she also seemed genuinely puzzled. "No way! You are practically the purest person I know. There's no way you need to go to confession!"

Joseph gave a self-deprecating chuckle. "I don't think you know me well enough. Are you saying that you don't have sin issues?"

Her gaze flicked down, and for a heartbeat she looked genuinely uncertain how to respond. At last, she lifted her shoulders in a shrug. "Of course no one is perfect, but I don't see how telling God you're sorry through a priest is actually going to change anything—especially since God accepts you just where you are."

He nodded, respecting her perspective. "It's true that God loves us right where we are," he said evenly, "but He loves us too much to leave us where we are. He wants to draw us closer to Him into his life of love."

Natalia pondered that, pressing her lips together in a thoughtful pout. Joseph recognized she wasn't mocking, but simply voicing her genuine skepticism about confession. He drummed his fingers on the table, considering how best to explain.

"I used to wonder about it too," he began. "But let me tell you a story. Early on in my marriage, I was so sure I was right about something—some issue with finances, if I recall correctly. My wife and I had a huge disagreement. I refused to back down because I was convinced I was in the right. But the reality was, it was just my pride. We went weeks barely talking. Our house felt cold even though we shared meals and routines."

Natalia's expression grew sympathetic. "You two always looked so perfect."

He gave a rueful smile. "Trust me, no marriage is perfect. Eventually, I realized I was being stubborn. I swallowed my pride, admitted I was wrong, and asked for her forgiveness. She saw my sincerity. It was like flipping a switch. In the span of a single conversation, all that love and joy came rushing back."

He paused, letting the memory wash over him. "That's the thing—just because she still accepted me before I apologized didn't mean our relationship was fine. There was a deficit of love, a strain. And it wouldn't have gone away if I'd never owned up to my side. Confession with God works the same way."

Natalia tapped her cup, nodding slowly as if a piece of a puzzle had just clicked into place. "I never thought of confession like this."

A quiet overcame them again. She looked off toward the compound gates, her dark eyes troubled. "I wish my husband would be more like that in our relationship. He hasn't even called or texted me in a week."

Joseph's tone turned gentle. "Have you tried calling or texting him?"

A flicker of defiance crossed her face. "No, but I still want to blame him."

He gave a measured sigh. "The process of forgiveness has to start with one person. If you want more in your marriage, maybe you should be the one to start the process with him."

That statement clearly stirred something raw in her. She set her cup down with an unsteady hand. For a second, Joseph feared she might lash out. Instead, her eyes filled with tears. "I honestly do not know what I want in my marriage," she whispered, shoulders trembling.

Natalia took a shaky breath, trying to steady herself as the tears threatened to spill over. She clasped her hands tightly in her lap, her fingers twisting nervously. "It's just... I feel so invisible sometimes, like I'm not even part of his world anymore," she admitted, her voice breaking slightly. "We used to share everything, talk for hours about our dreams, our fears. Now it's like we're strangers living under the same roof."

Joseph, moved by her vulnerability, slid closer. Gently, he wrapped an arm around her in a supportive gesture. She let out a choked sob, leaning her forehead against his collarbone.

Natalia sighed, wiping her eyes with the back of her hand. "No, it's not. I just... I want to feel loved again. I want to feel like I matter to him, like I'm more than just a fixture in his life."

"You deserve to feel that way," Joseph encouraged. A minute passed in hushed heartbreak. The courtyard felt oddly intimate, as though the rest of the compound had drifted away. Natalia continued, "I feel like I made a mistake with Maxim and I would be lying if I didn't think about leaving him for someone else." Joseph was silent... just trying to listen and support her in her sorrow. Finally, Natalia's breath caught, she lifted her head up from his shoulder with tears glistening and looked at him in the eyes with the question. "Have you ever doubted your marriage, Joseph?"

He swallowed. Memories flickered—years of childlessness, arguments, cultural differences. Yet always, the abiding sense of being bound to Salma in love. He tried to shape an answer, but before he could respond, the courtyard's air snapped taut with tension.

Oleg barged in, heavy boots scuffing the ground. He wore a smug look that sent chills down Joseph's spine. "Apologies if I'm interrupting," he drawled with mock sweetness, "but I have to break up your affair."

Natalia jerked upright, flushing with shock and anger. She spat something in Russian, voice crackling with outrage, while Joseph raised his hands in a peacekeeping gesture.

"She was sharing something painful," Joseph tried to explain quickly, mind still racing from Oleg's insinuation.

Oleg snorted, crossing his arms over a broad chest. "Relax, I'm not going to tell your spouses. Not my problem if you two want a cozy chat. If I had a chance with Natalia, I'd probably do the same thing." He twisted his mouth into a leer. "No wonder you have to go to confession."

That last remark sparked fury in Natalia's eyes. She lunged, arm swinging in an impulsive attempt to slap Oleg's face. He dodged, seizing her wrist with a practiced grip. His reflexes were as swift as they were intimidating.

For a frozen instant, he held her there, both of them breathing hard. Then he released her with a pointed sneer. Natalia staggered back, tears fueling her rage. "You... pig!" she spat in Russian, stepping away as though she couldn't bear being near him.

His voice turned cold. "Try that again, and you'll regret it."

Joseph moved to place himself between them, arms spread protectively, though he suspected Oleg could break him in half if he chose to. "Look," Joseph said, swallowing the dryness in his throat, "Natalia was upset about personal matters. Your timing... it's—"

Oleg flashed a humorless grin. "Save it, professor. I'm not your priest. I couldn't care less about your personal drama." His expression hardened. "Now get to the SUV. We're leaving. After-lunch trip, right? You want confession, you'll get it. Maybe your last supervised trip if we're lucky."

He pivoted on a heel, heading back the way he'd come. Joseph turned to Natalia, who still looked stricken, tears smudging the corners of her eyes. He wished he could do something more, but Oleg's near-violent display had rattled them both.

"I'm sorry," Joseph whispered to her, feeling that any further comfort might only invite more scandalous accusations.

She looked at him, watery eyes reflecting her confusion and pain, and gave a half-nod of acknowledgment. She brushed at her cheeks, drawing a shaky breath.

Summoning what calm he could, Joseph grabbed his small satchel from a nearby chair. He wanted to say something else—some reassurance that she wasn't alone, that her marriage and life could find better days. But the words caught in his throat. Oleg's heavy footsteps echoed as he stomped away, presumably to start the car.

Joseph shot Natalia one last apologetic glance, then turned to follow Oleg. He hated leaving her in such a state, but he had no choice. The guard was waiting, and any further confrontation might blow up into a public scandal that could cost them both.

Within minutes, Joseph found himself stepping into the dusty black SUV. Oleg, behind the wheel, gave Joseph a sardonic look as he slammed the passenger door shut. "Buckle up."

NINETEEN

The Signal

A humid breeze drifted in through the open window of Oleg's SUV, carrying with it the mingled scents of grilled meat, car exhaust, and a faint undertone of sea brine. Joseph Scanlon was strapped into the front passenger seat, tension running through his spine as he stared out at the buzzing metropolis around them. They had set out from the compound on the outskirts of Antakya, navigating a route that led them first through the city's newer districts before turning toward the ancient heart of town.

The modern district displayed an unexpected liveliness even under the hot sun. Wide avenues bustled with pedestrians dressed in everything from sleek Western-style suits to more traditional robes. Shiny storefronts and café terraces lined the sidewalks, each flaunting bright advertisements. Men and women idled at umbrella-shaded tables, sipping small cups of strong Turkish coffee or savoring sweet tea in slender glasses. Vibrant displays in boutique windows announced seasonal sales; neon signs flickered above kebab shops and electronics stores. Every so often, a battered building showed the lingering damage from last year's quake, its bricks braced by scaffolding while the city's unstoppable life pressed on around it.

Joseph caught glimpses of contemporary apartment blocks that rose high above the older, single-story structures, forming a curious tapestry of old and new. The fresh, glass-and-steel facades glinted in the midday light, standing guard over smaller historic corners that had stood for centuries. Antakya's identity seemed to thrive in its coexistence of modern ambitions and ancient heritage, a city constantly rewriting itself but never erasing its past.

Inside the SUV, Oleg cut the steering wheel sharply around a cluster of parked scooters, his expression set in his habitual scowl. He wore dark glasses and a black t-shirt that stretched over his powerful torso. Words between them had been minimal ever since they departed. From time to time, Joseph sensed the man's curious, almost challenging sideways glances, as if testing for a reaction.

"Is busy today," Oleg remarked at last, eyes flicking toward a line of cars honking at a traffic light ahead. A donkey cart stacked high with crates of peaches was blocking part of the intersection. The donkey seemed unbothered by the horns, but the driver of the car behind it was leaning out of his window, shouting an agitated string of Turkish phrases.

"It always is," Joseph said mildly. He took in the swirl of city life around them. "Antakya never sits still."

Oleg offered no reply. Instead, he revved the engine and maneuvered around the donkey cart, ignoring the scandalized shout of the cart's owner. They proceeded down a broad boulevard where palm trees lined the median, their leaves clattering in the hot wind. New commercial blocks with glossy signs declared the presence of global clothing brands, an array of bank offices, and a sprawling shopping mall. Even Joseph, who had visited Antakya many times, felt a surge of surprise at how thoroughly modern some pockets had become.

Gradually, though, the SUV left behind the wide, contemporary roads and turned onto narrower, timeworn streets. The drift of modern sleekness gave way to older neighborhoods, the architecture shifting to smaller family-owned shops, cozy cafés with wrought-iron chairs, and corner grocers whose produce spilled onto the sidewalk. The hum of conversation in multiple languages—Turkish, Arabic, Armenian, a bit of French—rose to Joseph's ears when they stopped briefly behind a cluster of pedestrians crossing the street.

"This is still the new city, but with older corners," Joseph remarked, almost to himself. "When we reach the real old quarter, you'll see the roads change again."

"Fine," Oleg grunted.

They turned at a low roundabout, passing a modest park where children chased each other around a fountain. Moments later, they veered onto a one-way street that was distinctly older in feel. The asphalt thinned, turning patchy. The sidewalk's curbstones showed their age, chipped and worn. And then they arrived at the threshold of the historic district—a simple, unassuming intersection where wide roads narrowed into a network of cobblestone alleys.

The atmosphere changed in an instant. The older quarter greeted them with winding, uneven lanes flanked by stone buildings. Terracotta roof tiles glowed in the midday sun, while balconies of intricately carved wood jutted above the streets, sometimes so close that they nearly touched their counterparts across the alley. Here, the city's heartbeat felt deeper, echoing with layers of centuries past.

Oleg slowed to a crawl, forced to negotiate the SUV around sharp corners and abrupt inclines. Noise from the modern district fell away behind them, replaced by a pleasant murmur of local life. Voices echoed in the tight alleyways, drifting from open windows or from hidden courtyards where neighbors chatted across partition walls. Joseph glimpsed some of these courtyards through carved wooden gates—lush pockets of greenery featuring lemon or orange trees, shaded by lattices, reminiscent of a more tranquil era.

They passed a small plaque indicating Uzun Çarşı Caddesi, the old market district. It was a place Joseph knew well. The narrow street opened into a wide corridor of shops and stalls—spices arranged in vivid pyramids of red pepper flakes, turmeric, saffron; displays of pomegranates, figs, and bright oranges. Vendors stood behind their tables, beckoning passersby with calls in Turkish or Arabic, boasting the finest goods. The hum of haggling, laughter, and distant music from a radio completed a tapestry of urban life.

Women in brightly colored headscarves leaned over displays of handwoven textiles, while a group of teenage boys gathered around a vendor selling secondhand electronics. The air smelled of ground coffee, toasted sesame seeds, and a thousand other subtle aromas. Joseph ached to linger. He remembered strolling here with his wife, searching for a spice blend her mother had recommended, then stopping for sweet kunefe at a local café.

But the SUV pressed on, creeping through the throng. Oleg tapped the horn lightly to alert the crowd. A swirl of pedestrians parted grudgingly, many tossing annoyed glances at the large vehicle intruding on their footpath. The old bazaar was better suited for carts and foot traffic than modern SUVs.

They emerged from the thick of the bazaar to find themselves alongside a small square dominated by the Habib'i Neccar Mosque. Its elegant minaret rose gracefully against the brilliant sky. Even from the car, Joseph sensed the quiet dignity of the site—one of Anatolia's oldest mosques, steeped in centuries of devotion. A modest courtyard extended before it, where worshippers entered and left with serene expressions. Stone arches gave the courtyard a timeless shape, while a fountain in the center offered water for ablutions. The hush there contrasted with the nearby commotion, underscoring the spiritual calm that sacred places always exuded in this city.

Oleg cast a fleeting glance in its direction, his jaw set. "This part is... old," he muttered.

"Historic," Joseph corrected gently. "It's a mosaic of cultures—look, just up that hill are old Christian houses, some with hidden chapels. And we're about to see more."

They turned onto another lane, narrower still, where tall, antique houses pressed close on either side. Their sun-bleached walls were accented by red-tiled roofs, painted shutters, and delicate wrought-iron balconies that had survived countless quakes. Many featured interior courtyards—a hallmark of Antakya's architecture—where families once gathered in the evenings for conversation and respite from the heat. Some houses boasted small open gates, revealing glimpses of stone-paved yards adorned with trailing vines or potted flowers. Others were locked behind wooden doors set with hammered copper studs, their secrets firmly shuttered.

A final turn brought them into a tranquil side street where the hustle died away to a calm hush. At its end stood St. Luke Catholic Church, nestled amidst high-walled houses like a guardian of faith in this labyrinthine quarter. Joseph felt a rush of memories: attending a weekday Mass here as a lonely graduate student, the swirl of incense blending with candlelight.

St. Luke's exterior was unpretentious but stately, the stone walls weathered by centuries of wind, sun, and more than one quake. Tendrils of ivy crept along the edges, lending a gentle, living touch to the aged facade. A small bell tower reached toward the sky, its silhouette sharp against the brilliant Mediterranean sun. There was no grand spire or lavish decoration—only the quiet confidence of a place that had endured.

Oleg pulled the SUV to a stop along a stone curb. Instead of waiting inside, he immediately killed the engine and slid out, scanning the surroundings. Joseph's heart sank a little. He had hoped the man would remain behind, but Oleg's cautious nature trumped convenience. Quickly, Joseph climbed out, shutting the door behind him. The air was thick with midday warmth, but an undercurrent of coolness from the old stones teased at his skin.

He took a step toward the church, noticing how the wooden doors—aged to a silvery hue—stood slightly ajar, as though inviting him in. The family he had come to see was nowhere in sight. In fact, the courtyard was nearly empty, except for a handful of people trickling out, presumably after morning devotions.

"I come with you," Oleg said, voice low. "Better I keep eye on you. Is not safe alone." His stare made it clear he simply didn't trust Joseph to slip away or meet some unknown contact.

Joseph offered a neutral nod, schooling his expression. "Sure. Let's go in."

The doors creaked softly as Joseph pushed them open, stepping into the dim interior. Immediately, the temperature dropped. A sense of peace settled around them like a benediction. Soft candlelight glowed along the walls, illuminating faded frescoes depicting biblical scenes. The hush of centuries hung in the vaulted ceiling, as though every whispered prayer had left behind an echo.

Rows of pews stretched forward, polished by innumerable hands and knees over the ages. A faint aroma of incense clung to the air—a blend of frankincense and myrrh, sweet and woody. High above the altar was a large painting of St. Luke, born in Antioch himself, his eyes solemn, pen poised as though capturing the Gospel's truths. Sunlight filtering through stained-glass windows scattered shards of colored light across the stone floor, a radiant mosaic of ruby, sapphire, and gold. Even Oleg paused, hesitating on the threshold.

Nearby, a handful of parishioners knelt in silence. On the left side, Joseph noticed small confessional booths. A wooden sign indicated that confessions would be heard at noon. Two or three people waited quietly in line, heads bowed in reflection.

Joseph took a step forward, intending to slip into a pew to pray. But Oleg's presence, tall and watchful behind him, felt stifling. The big man crossed himself in a perfunctory manner—perhaps out of old Orthodox habit—then moved to the back pew. He sat, arms folded, scanning the church with narrowed eyes, as though expecting danger behind every statue.

Joseph inhaled slowly. The hush amplified the creak of his footsteps on the old wooden floor. The confessional line was short. A small lamp above the confessional door turned green, signifying it was open for the next penitent. Joseph joined the line, thankful for a chance at partial anonymity.

He couldn't be sure if Oleg recognized the confessional queue for what it was. The Russian had chosen a vantage point near the entrance, presumably so Joseph couldn't slip out through any side exit. Joseph glanced back once, meeting Oleg's suspicious gaze. He offered a weak smile and turned forward again. One by one, the line advanced until the woman ahead of him disappeared into the booth.

"Just a few minutes," Joseph told himself. The interior hush made him mindful of each breath, each rustle of clothing. He silently prayed that the next occupant of the confessional would indeed be the "visiting priest" he was told to expect—someone arranged, presumably, by the CIA. But what if it wasn't? He had no real guarantee. The idea of speaking code words to an actual confessor was terrifying, not to mention sacrilegious.

When it was his turn, suddenly the green light for the visiting priests confessional turned green. Without hesitation, Joseph slipped inside.

Inside, the confessional was lit only by a dim overhead bulb. The old wooden partition offered a choice: remain behind the grated screen or walk around the divider for a face-to-face confession. A sign in Turkish and English indicated the priest's willingness for either. Joseph took a trembling breath and moved around the screen.

Seated there, dressed in simple Turkish garb, was Agent Mark DeLuca. Aziz and Fr. Jaddoe made it happen! Had Joseph not known him, he might have taken the man for a local Capuchin or a traveling priest. He wore a loose-fitting black robe typical of visiting clergy, a linen stole embroidered with subtle motifs, and a short keffiyeh-like scarf to help him blend in with the region's style. His hair was trimmed close, his normally clean-shaven face graced by a few days' worth of stubble, as if he'd wanted to appear older and more devout. Only his eyes gave him away—sharp, assessing, brimming with urgency.

DeLuca smiled in recognition, though he kept his voice low. "Bless you, my son," he said quietly, forcing a faintly priestly intonation that sounded almost convincing. Then he dropped the act. "Joseph, it's good to see you. God, I've been waiting. I wasn't sure you'd make it."

Joseph settled onto the wooden kneeler. "Agent DeLuca, you blend in well," he whispered, fighting to keep his voice steady. "But time is short. Oleg's out there—he insisted on coming inside."

DeLuca's expression flickered with concern. "He's the big shaved-headed fellow? He's high-level FSB. We have him on record. Nasty piece of work." Then he regained composure, leaning in. "First—thank you for the intel you got to us through Aziz. Our people are very grateful."

Joseph exhaled, a rush of relief. The tension in his shoulders eased a fraction. "So you received the details I've been sending on the sites and security measures?"

"Yes." DeLuca nodded. "It's confirmed what we suspected: these men are all ex-Spetsnaz or have FSB ties. Not your typical museum-guard types. We also picked up chatter that President Volkov's health is in a tailspin. He's canceled his upcoming public appearances, yet continues to direct the war in Eastern Europe from behind the scenes. He have good reason to believe that he is likely experiencing early organ failure"

"That tracks," Joseph whispered. "Lavrov's been unhinged with pressure. Every day, he demands results. Our progress is the only thing that matters to him, and he's making questionable decisions to hurry the dig forward. Something's changed in the last week or so. He must know Volkov is running out of time."

DeLuca pursed his lips. "That leads me to item number two: your infiltration has climbed the chain of command. The President of the United States himself is aware. And, well...he's directed every available resource into making sure the Russians do not get their hands on these so-called miracle Keys."

Joseph's stomach twisted. "But I heard he's not a particularly religious man."

DeLuca offered a wry smile. "He's not, but the intel about these keys suggests a real threat. If they're as potent as the historical record implies, giving the Russians the chance to heal their leader and keep him in power indefinitely is unacceptable. The White House is taking no chances."

Joseph rubbed his brow, letting that sink in. "So what's the plan?"

"That's where you come in, Joseph," DeLuca said, leaning closer. "I have been given full operational responsibility but my plan depends on your updates—the who, where, and when. I need the earliest warning possible."

Joseph began summarizing in hushed tones. He explained their greatest recent breakthrough: "The evidence we found at the Golden Dome dig provided instruction that the keys lie within the ancient cave church of St. Peter, on the mountainside just north of town. Known historically as the Grotto of St. Peter. There's a sealed-off passage behind the sanctuary that local tradition says connects to deeper caverns. There are signs carved into the rock that confirm the instructions. Today Lavrov is pushing local authorities for excavation permission. We suspect the relic is hidden there, just like the letters of Anastasius suggested."

DeLuca's eyes lit with interest. "So you're close?" "I believe so, although I don't know how many layers remain," Joseph replied. "Will you be on the discovery team with Lavrov?" he continued? "Yes, if—when—they find the Keys, I'll likely be there. My language and historical skills are essential for verifying authenticity on the spot."

"That lines up with what we expected," DeLuca said. He pulled a small tablet from beneath his vestments, tapping the screen. Up came a satellite image of the slopes near the old St. Peter's Church. "We're working off GPS coordinates. The parking area is down here, about a quarter mile from the site. Joseph, how far is that on foot?"

Joseph traced a route with his fingertip. "Far enough that it's a good climb. There's a single narrow path leading up to the entrance. Vehicles can't get too close. It'll be easy for the Russians to post guards or set up vantage points."

DeLuca nodded grimly. "We have two strategies. Option One: if you can discreetly secure the Keys before Lavrov's men do and slip out, that'd be ideal. Option Two: if you can't, we'll come in with a helicopter strike team from our US Incirlik Air Base. It's about a thirty-minute flight, so we can respond fast once we know the relic is in play." He paused, meeting Joseph's gaze. "We'll need a signal from you the moment the Keys are found. Understood?"

Joseph swallowed. "Yes, but how do I send that signal? Underground caves can kill reception."

"Exactly," DeLuca whispered. "That's why we have this." He reached into a small satchel and withdrew a rectangular device, about the size of a deck of cards, matte plastic with no visible antenna. "A VLF transmitter—very low frequency. It'll punch a signal up through hundreds of feet of rock. Our listening station on the outskirts can pick it up from miles away."

Joseph turned it over in his hands, noticing it weighed almost nothing. "No metal?"

"Correct. It's polymer-based. Shouldn't set off typical detectors. Put it in your bag or pocket. Hold this button for three seconds, a red light will activate and it'll broadcast a unique signal that alerts us you've found the Keys and need air support."

Joseph exhaled. "All right. I'll keep it on me. They do random checks, but they mostly look for standard contraband or metal. I can definitely hide this."

DeLuca gave a tight nod. "And then we mobilize. We'll have Delta Force troops on standby, loaded onto a helo. They'll land near the site, neutralize the Russian threat, and extract the relic."

"How do I avoid getting caught in the crossfire?" Joseph asked in a hushed voice, anxiety curling in his chest.

DeLuca responded. "Our hope is that our show of superior firepower will force Russians to surrender before a shot is fired. But we understand that given the desperation of the situation that likely will not happen." DeLuca reached into his robe again and produced a small plastic crucifix on a thin cord. "Wear this around your neck. It contains a low-power RFID beacon. Our guys will have augmented reality overlays identifying your exact position. They'll know to protect you, keep you out of the line of fire."

Joseph gingerly accepted the item. He held it to the faint candle-light, noticing its unremarkable design—exactly the point. "So that's how you'll know I'm friendly."

Joseph slipped the crucifix over his head. It felt surreal—holy icon meets covert tracking device.

"There's more," DeLuca added quietly. "We can't rely solely on the helicopter. Some of the terrain might be tricky for an immediate dust-off. So I've contracted your brother-in-law Aziz to assemble a small ground team of local ex-Chaldean fighters. They'll be close to the site in local vehicles, blending in. If something goes wrong, they'll step in. Once you are secured, they will transport you to our CIA safehouse and we will debrief there."

Joseph's tension loosened at the mention of Aziz. "Thank you. Aziz and his men know the region intimately. They're good people."

"They proved themselves against ISIS. We're lucky to have them," DeLuca said. Then his gaze turned serious. "One final measure, in case you need it."

From another hidden pocket, DeLuca drew out a slender eight-inch blade. It was black, with a sheen that was definitely not metal. "Carbon fiber," he explained. "Ultralight, nonmetallic. You can pass it through a metal detector. It's strong enough for self-de-fense. I pray you won't need it, but if these Russians try to take the Keys...we can't let them leave with them."

Joseph stared at the blade, his stomach clenching with revulsion. The notion of stabbing anyone was anathema to him—he was a historian, a teacher. Yet he forced himself to accept it. "I—I understand," he stammered.

"It's thin. Slip it into your excavation pack. They'll never suspect. Only use it if you must." DeLuca's dark eyes flickered with empathy at Joseph's distress. "I absolve you of any future sins," he joked softly, a wry twist of lips.

A hollow laugh escaped Joseph. "Amen," he murmured, tucking the blade between the pages of his old traveling Bible. The incongruity felt almost sacrilegious. But necessity was necessity.

"How soon do you think the dig will break into the cave system?" DeLuca asked.

Joseph's forehead creased. "Hard to say—could be days, weeks, or we might discover the entire lead is worthless. But from the artifacts and texts we've decoded, I strongly suspect we're close."

DeLuca nodded. "Then we'll stay on high alert. The moment you confirm that final passage is open and you're heading in, keep the transmitter on you."

Joseph's pulse fluttered. "All right. I'm on board."

From outside the confessional, footsteps echoed. A shuffle of people, quiet coughs, and the soft murmur of devout prayer. Joseph realized his time was running short. "Oleg is probably suspecting me already," he whispered.

DeLuca's expression darkened. "He's a dangerous man. We have a file on him. I can't stress enough—don't provoke him unless you have to."

Joseph rose from the kneeler. "I'll watch my step."

In a careful hush, DeLuca and Joseph exchanged a final glance of understanding. Then, as though concluding a legitimate confession, Joseph bowed his head, crossing himself, and stepped away. The small confessional door creaked open.

The church's interior hadn't changed, still tranquil and bathed in flickering light, but Joseph felt Oleg's presence like a smoldering brand. Sure enough, the tall Russian stood by the last pew, arms folded. The moment Joseph emerged, Oleg's eyes narrowed.

"So," Oleg said in English. "You told all your sins? Must have been long confession." His voice dripped suspicion.

Joseph exhaled, forcing a casual shrug. "Best to be thorough." He started walking up the aisle, heading for the exit. "Let's go."

Oleg's mouth twisted. "Is that so? Maybe I confess. I have many sins...like lying, harming men." He sneered. "Shall I see if priest handle me?"

Joseph paused near the door, turning to meet the Russian's gaze. Without warning, Oleg stepped past him, stomping toward the visiting priest confessional. Immediately, an elderly Turkish woman waiting in line snapped something sharply at Oleg in her language, pointing out the queue. Her tone was scolding, insisting he respect the order. Oleg barked a harsh retort in Russian, clearly not intending to wait. Then he waved a dismissive hand and wheeled around, giving up.

"Waste of time," he growled. "Let's go."

Joseph suppressed a wry grin at the old woman's bravery. He quickly followed Oleg outside. The sun assaulted them again, so bright after the church's dim interior. Oleg's posture was tense as he stomped across the short courtyard to the SUV. A group of local children stared at the imposing Russian, giggling nervously.

Inside the vehicle, the engine sputtered to life. Oleg immediately jerked the steering wheel, pulling away from the curb with a squeal of tires that made onlookers jump. Joseph tightened his seat belt, holding onto the door handle as they veered around a corner.

They retraced their route, weaving back through the old quarter's snaking alleys. Passing once more through Uzun Çarşı Caddesi, Joseph noticed the sun had shifted; many stalls were closing for the midday lull, while café tables filled with families seeking a late lunch. He glimpsed the distinct silhouette of Habib'i Neccar Mosque's minaret one last time, standing over the city with quiet grace.

As they made their way onto the dusty road leading back to the compound, Joseph tried to stifle the gnawing dread. In his mind, he saw the flickering candlelight of St. Luke's, remembered DeLuca's urgent whispers, felt the plastic crucifix pressed against his chest. He pictured the day the call would come: a half-buried cave, a handful of Russians armed to the teeth, a set of golden keys rumored to hold miracles in their metal. And behind them, invisible but powerful, the helicopter from Incirlik, his brother-in-law's militia in battered trucks, a swirl of unstoppable confrontation.

Oleg braked hard, the SUV lurching to a halt before the compound gates. Guards slid them open. Joseph squared his shoulders, bracing for the next chapter of this labyrinthine mission. For now, he was returning with a heavy burden of secrets and alliances. Sooner or later, all those secrets would unravel in the echoing darkness of an ancient cave—and Joseph prayed he would be equal to the task when the time came.

TWENTY

Between Faith and Fear

Joseph returned to the compound at dusk, stepping through the modest iron gate that separated the outside world from the makeshift headquarters. A pair of security guards offered curt nods but did not speak. Their rifles slung over their shoulders like silent warnings. It was a routine that had grown familiar but not comforting—this uneasy hush seemed to mirror the tension Joseph felt in his own mind. He navigated the dim hallway, past stacks of equipment and rolled-up tarps, and found himself drawn to the glow of the cafeteria at the end of the corridor. Music and low chatter drifted out, oddly cheerful amid the dull neon lights overhead. Tonight, it crackled with fresh energy. Dima, clad in his usual black jacket, saw Joseph first and beckoned him over with a wide grin that contrasted with the lines of worry embedded on his face.

"Good to see you back in one piece, Professor," Dima said, leaning in close to be heard above the chatter. "Have a seat. I've got news."

Joseph let his excavation pack slip off his shoulder, resting it by a chair. "News? Let me guess—something about the permit?"

Dima's grin stretched even wider. "You won't believe this—Lavrov somehow convinced the Turkish authorities to give us the green light. It's official: we can start excavation at the Church of St. Peter." He gave a short laugh. "I'd say I'm impressed, but let's be realistic. Our dear doctor always finds ways when official channels fail."

Joseph's brows lifted in genuine surprise. "Already? These kinds of permits usually take weeks of approval. What changed?"

Dima shrugged, offering an ironic tilt of his head. "Hmm, you know how these things go. Perhaps the officials discovered new admiration for our mission, or maybe, just maybe"—his lips quirked slyly—"someone around here provided a little 'motivation' in the form of... generosity." He cleared his throat dramatically, then winked. "Nothing is proven. But we Russians, we have a gift for courtesy, you understand?"

An unexpected laugh escaped Joseph, mild and cautious. Dima's indirect hint at a bribe was both comedic and unsettling. "If that's the case," Joseph said, "then Lavrov really is unstoppable."

"Apparently so," Dima replied, glancing around to make sure no one else was listening too closely. "But don't get carried away. We got the permit under specific conditions. The Turkish government wants us to keep the noise down—no heavy machinery, no massive drilling rigs. Low impact tools only." He ran a hand through his short hair, exhaling. "And that could slow us down considerably."

Joseph nodded. "Better slow and safe than not at all, I guess."

Dima tossed him a half-smile. "Wise words. Are you hungry? There's quite a spread tonight, courtesy of Lavrov's celebratory mood."

Before Joseph could answer, footsteps sounded behind them. In walked Dr. Alexei Lavrov, impeccably dressed as always, steel-gray hair combed neatly. A hush fell over the few scattered conversations as he crossed the room with deliberate steps. He halted a short distance away, giving Joseph a courteous—though not warm—nod.

"Joseph," Lavrov said, his tone measured. "I trust you had a productive confession experience earlier?"

Joseph felt the weight of the question, though it was delivered with the politeness of a formal greeting. He cleared his throat. "Yes, it was... clarifying. Thank you for asking."

Lavrov nodded once, then inhaled as though pushing aside personal curiosity. Joseph stepped forward, forcing a friendly smile. "I also want to congratulate you on securing the permit. Dima just filled me in. That was incredibly fast—"

"You can thank me when we find the Keys," Lavrov interjected, dismissing the compliment. He held Joseph's gaze for a moment too long. "Until then, it's premature to celebrate."

Joseph's lips parted in surprise at the abruptness. But he managed to keep his composure, recalling the enormous political and financial pressures on Lavrov's shoulders. "Understood," he said softly, then ventured, "Dr. Lavrov... is everything all right? You've seemed a bit on edge these past two weeks. Not quite yourself."

Lavrov's mouth twitched in what might have been a smile, though it fell short of warmth. "I'm eager to finish our work, that's all. My family waits in Moscow. Perhaps you could relate, yes?" He raised a brow. "You also have a family to return to—your pregnant wife. I wonder why you're not more...driven."

Joseph pressed his lips together, a swirl of conflicting emotions rising in his chest. He could hardly explain the moral or spiritual burdens that made him slow, cautious. He opted for silence, which Lavrov took for acquiescence. With a dismissive hand, the Russian turned to gather a plate from the corner buffet.

Joseph, summoning his voice again, asked, "So, Dr. Lavrov, how soon before we start searching the caves? The last I heard, your team was still assessing the passages."

Lavrov set down his plate, turning back. "They're already there. I dispatched the remainder of the excavation team this afternoon to examine the main tunnel, the one with the inscription of the Keys above the entrance. A preliminary pass, if you will." He exhaled. "We launch the real discovery process at first light tomorrow." Then, as though to lighten the tone, he tossed Joseph a faint grin. "I'll need you front and center. You are, after all, the man with the knowledge. You ready to become a millionaire?"

Joseph tried to mirror the grin. "Absolutely," he said, though his conviction faltered. The truth was, the money no longer meant what it once did. But Lavrov clearly didn't sense Joseph's misgivings. Instead, the Russian nodded approvingly.

"Good. Then get some rest, all of you," Lavrov announced, raising his voice so that the half-dozen staffers in the cafeteria could hear. "We have a long day tomorrow. But first—" He waved an arm toward the tables. "We celebrate with the best Turkish food I could find. Let me describe it for you."

Heads turned, some out of curiosity, others out of genuine hunger. Lavrov began to list each dish with a flourish, switching briefly into well-pronounced Turkish for emphasis:

- Iskender Kebap: Thin-sliced lamb layered over pita, soaked in tangy tomato sauce and melted butter, topped with thick yogurt.

- Lahmacun: Crispy flatbreads spread with minced meat, tomatoes, onions, and herbs, rolled up with fresh parsley and lemon juice.

- Dolma: Grape leaves stuffed with a mixture of rice, ground meat, and spices, simmered in a tangy broth.

- Mercimek Çorbası: A velvety red lentil soup drizzled with chili-infused oil.

- Baklava: Layers of flaky pastry filled with crushed pistachios, drenched in sweet syrup.

He named off more—feta-stuffed peppers, grilled eggplant, and even a pile of simit bread rings dusted with sesame. Though his voice was cool, he spoke of the food with reverence, as if paying tribute to centuries of cultural heritage.

"Enjoy," Lavrov finished simply, placing a small helping of each dish onto his plate. "Tomorrow, we work. Tonight, we dine." With that, he retreated to a corner to eat alone, posture rigid, mind likely far from the dinner.

Joseph followed suit, gingerly placing kebap and dolma on his tray. The smell was enticing, but his appetite felt half-dead with tension. At a round table, he slid into a seat beside Dima, and a couple of the local Turkish workers joined them. Conversation sprang up in halting English, overshadowed by awkwardness. People asked about the day's events—nothing deep, just small talk about the scorching weather, the local elections, or the unpredictability of the Orontes River. Joseph responded politely but remained distant. His mind churned with tomorrow's mission: the uneasy partnership with Russians, the concealed truths about Lavrov, the CIA's stake in these relics.

He tried to savor a bite of the Iskender Kebap, which was succulent and tangy, but found himself chewing mechanically. The flavors felt muted against the swirl of complexities overshadowing everything. Dima, though usually brimming with humorous barbs, seemed equally subdued, offering only short remarks about the "amazing marinade" or how "Joseph must be too polite to ask for seconds." Their exchange lacked real warmth.

Not long afterward, Joseph pushed his plate away, half-full. The cafeteria noise had grown to a gentle hum of forks on plates, an occasional laugh, but Joseph felt like an outsider. With a forced smile, he excused himself, claiming fatigue, and carried his tray to the drop-off station. A few watchers—security men—eyed him from across the room. He gave them no sign of worry, just a small nod as he stepped out into the corridor.

His small second-floor room was a relief, a space where he could breathe unobserved. The overhead bulb buzzed faintly, casting a yellowish glow. Kicking off his shoes, Joseph settled onto the lumpy mattress. The day's weight pressed on him in waves. He recalled Lavrov's biting question: *Why are you not more driven to return to your pregnant wife?* The unspoken answer: because so much more was at stake. Because he was entangled in a clandestine war that not even Salma could suspect.

He picked up his phone and dialed. Her voice answered after the third ring, a warm hush that made him ache with longing.

"Joseph!" Salma said, sounding breathless. "I was hoping you'd call. How are you?"

He closed his eyes. "I'm... here. And hearing your voice helps."

A soft laugh. "I've had a wonderful day. Your mother joined me for a morning doctor's appointment—I just wanted her there for moral support. Everything looks good so far. I'm still early, but the doctor said things are progressing nicely." Her voice danced with excitement. "After that, we spent the afternoon looking at baby clothes online. She can't help herself; she wants me to pick everything in pastel colors." Salma laughed again, and Joseph pictured the radiant smile that must be lighting her face.

He smiled despite himself. "That's Mom—she prayed for this for years. I'm glad you two had some time together."

"So am I," Salma agreed. "Enough about me. Any news from your end? Please tell me something exciting. You sounded so mysterious last time."

Joseph shifted on the bed, glancing at the door as if it had ears. "We've found... the next step," he said carefully. "There's a hidden passage beneath the Church of St. Peter. Ancient inscriptions from Bishop Anastasius seem to point right to it. Tomorrow morning, we'll begin the deeper excavation. If all goes according to plan, we might confirm the Keys' location soon."

Her little gasp of delight stirred static on the line. "Really? So you might be done with your work soon! Joseph, that's incredible—you'll come home, and we can finally celebrate. The baby will have you here. Doesn't that feel amazing?"

He wanted to share her enthusiasm, to rejoice in a quick reunion, but the unresolved dangers clenched his gut. He pictured Oleg's suspicious glare, the FSB men who roamed the compound, and the discreet carbon-fiber knife tucked away in his excavation pack—the CIA's silent reminder that this was not merely academic archaeology. A sense of dread welled up, stealing the joy from Salma's sweet anticipation.

She sensed the pause and lowered her voice. "Joseph, are you okay? You're quiet. I know there's so much you can't tell me, but I also know you. I can hear the weight in your silence."

He exhaled shakily. "I'm... I'm just tired, Salma. Tired of the grind, I guess."

"I don't fully understand what's going on," she admitted gently. "But God does. He knows the details you can't share with me. Do you want me to pray with you?"

Joseph had braced himself for more questions, but her gentle offer touched him in a way no interrogation could. "That's exactly what I need," he said, his voice cracking.

Immediately, she began, her tone hushed but confident: "Heavenly Father, I lift up Joseph to You. Protect him, guide him, give him wisdom and courage for whatever tomorrow brings. We trust You with our lives and with the life of this child. We entrust Joseph to Your care. Saint Charbel, patron of miracles in this land, I entrust my husband to your intercession and care. In Jesus name I pray, Amen."

Tears pricked Joseph's eyes. He pressed a hand over his mouth to keep from weeping aloud. "Thank you," he managed.

A gentle silence passed between them. Finally, Salma murmured, "I love you, Joseph. And I can't wait for you to be home with me and our baby. Promise me you'll try to stay safe?"

"I promise," he whispered. "I love you. I love both of you."

They lingered on the line a moment longer, exchanging good-nights and well-wishes for the baby. When at last the call ended, Joseph sat on the bed in darkness, the phone still clenched in his hand. The overhead bulb flickered once, then steadied. In the hush, he could almost imagine the swirl of distant voices—Lavrov's impatience, Dima's half-jokes about bribes, Oleg's accusations of infidelity, and the unspoken presence of those who saw him as a spy. Yet piercing through all that was Salma's prayer: a small, bright flame in the gloom.

He rose wearily, setting his phone on the desk. Tomorrow, he'd enter a centuries-old cave in search of relics that might change world history—or be used as a tool in the intensifying conflict that had claimed so many lives in Eastern Europe. He didn't know if he'd be made a hero or a pawn. With a heavy sigh, Joseph flicked off the light and lay down, but before he could close his eyes, the vibration on his phone went off. It was a text message from Aziz. It had praying hands and said, "Don't forget to pray to your guardian angel tonight :-)." Joseph smiled and responded, "Thank you for the reminder, brother." Sleep eluded him for a long while. In the end, it was Salma's quiet prayer that replayed in his mind, lulling him into a restless slumber where faith and fear met in equal measure, and dawn promised to bring answers he might not be ready to face.

TWENTY-ONE

The Gates

Morning came earlier than usual, or so it felt. Joseph Scanlon awoke to the faint hum of the motel's make-shift generator, blinking groggily at the ceiling fan spinning in slow circles. He rolled onto his side, limbs heavy with fatigue, and checked the time on his phone: 4:52 a.m. Barely enough rest, but there'd be no more sleep. Lavrov had arranged for an early start, insisting that the entire team be on-site at the rock-hewn St. Peter's Church before sunrise. As Joseph swung his legs over the edge of the cot, he noticed the gray light filtering through the dusty window, revealing an overcast sky.

He couldn't help but think about the text message Aziz had sent him just before Joseph had collapsed into bed last night and gave thanks for the faith of his brother in law. Stifling a yawn, he grabbed a half-full water bottle from the small bedside table and took a swig. Antakya's dryness left him perpetually parched. While rummaging for a clean shirt, Joseph tried not to dwell on the swirl of uneasy details that had overshadowed last night's anxious dreams: the hush-hush phone calls, the angry scowls from the Russian security contingent, Oleg's unflinching suspicion, and, above all, Lavrov's mounting impatience to uncover the Keys of St. Peter. This morning would be crucial.

When he'd dressed—khaki pants, a simple cotton shirt, boots, and a light jacket—he checked once more for the must-have gear: his excavation backpack. It was the same weathered, olive-drab pack he had carried onto the plane when traveling to Antakya. Sliding open the front zipper, he confirmed it still contained the small transmitter disguised as a black flashlight. Tucked in the outside mesh pocket was his old Bible and folded into it was the slender carbon-fiber knife hidden in its pages. He made sure everything was secure.

At precisely 5:25 a.m., he shuffled into the motel's dingy lobby, where Dima—coffee in hand—was wrangling the rest of the archaeology crew. Sasha, Yakov, and Elena stood by the dusty front desk, wearing matching looks of groggy determination. Mortem was nowhere to be seen, but Joseph assumed he'd turn up soon. Morning rays, dimmed by thick gray clouds, spilled through the grimy windows. Outside, the gloom deepened, blanketing the parking lot in drab half-light.

"Early start," Joseph mumbled, nodding to Sasha. She gave him a bleary-eyed shrug.

Dima tapped his watch. "We have to load the gear. Then we drive in a caravan to the Church of St. Peter up on the mountainside. Everyone ready?"

Muttered yeses and nods ensued. Meanwhile, Elena huffed quietly, readjusting the straps of her own battered backpack. The tension in her posture said everything: none of them were exactly *eager* to continue rummaging around tunnels that might collapse at any moment. But they had their orders.

Mortem hurried in, wearing a thick fleece jacket. "I'm here, I'm here," he said breathlessly, the last to arrive. "Sorry—had trouble finding my spare flashlight."

Dima offered him a curt nod, evidently wanting to keep to schedule. "Let's go, folks. Grab everything. The trucks are waiting out back."

They stepped out into the parking lot, where a row of battered SUVs idled. The morning air lay thick with humidity, and the sky overhead churned with low gray clouds, threatening rain. Even at this early hour, security staff scurried about—stern-faced men in black jackets hoisting crates of gear and double-checking the vehicles. Joseph recognized Oleg's silhouette among them, giving clipped orders to a pair of equally imposing men.

Joseph cast a glance around, noticing who *wasn't* present. Natalia. He felt a slight pang. Over the last several weeks, she had been his steady partner in deciphering the centuries-old parchments, uncovering vital clues about relic storage and cryptic instructions left by early Church figures. She should be here for a day as important as this—unless something had changed.

He turned to Dima. "Natalia's not coming?"

Dima shook his head briskly. "Lavrov ordered her to stay back at the motel. After that fiasco with Ivan, he needs her to handle the work of securing and cataloging all the extra parchments and artifacts we found at the site for transport to Moscow." His voice dropped as if he sympathized. "I heard her complaining that it's an enormous job, especially with new discoveries from Saint Ignatius of Antioch. But Lavrov gave no choice."

Joseph felt a jolt of excitement hearing the name: Saint Ignatius of Antioch, among the earliest Church Fathers. Historically, his letters were crucial for understanding Church structure, theology, the importance of the Eucharist, and tradition. Although Joseph had not been able to translate the new Ignatius of Antioch letters, he did see that they covered the topics of prophecy and healing in the early Church, subjects that mainstream patristics had long overlooked.

He let out a slow breath, his eagerness overshadowed by the knowledge he had no time to study them. It was a quiet comfort. If Natalia was tasked with that, she'd do it thoroughly and preserve every detail, making sure no page was lost or smuggled away without record. Also, she would be outside the line of fire in case there was a confrontation. Still, Joseph frowned. "Ivan's meltdown left a gap, I guess," he said softly, recalling the day the Russian archaeologist had broken down in tears after his son died in the war. He'd been quickly dismissed.

"Yeah, the meltdown. Lavrov had no patience." Dima eyed Joseph meaningfully, though he said nothing more.

And with that, Joseph slung his pack over his shoulders.

By 5:50 a.m., the team had stowed their gear. Six archaeologists—Joseph, Dima, Elena, Mortem, Sasha, and Yakov—piled into two SUVs. Another two vehicles carried security forces. Clouds pressed low in the sky, as if sealing them inside this unsettled world of half-light. Joseph sat in the back seat of the second SUV, next to Mortem, who fiddled anxiously with the buckles on his backpack.

The drive took them out of the battered city center, up a winding road that threaded along the foot of the mountains. The faint rumble of shifting gears filled the cabin as the SUV climbed. Joseph gazed out the window at the slope: scrubby vegetation, scattered olive trees, and sharp outcroppings of stone. A watery sun tried to push through the overcast sky, but mostly the day remained muted, everything painted in grayscale.

Joseph couldn't escape the thought of Aziz's text: *Pray to your guardian angel.* Had his brother-in-law found new information about Lavrov's backers? Or did he just sense danger swirling around Joseph? However intended, it reminded Joseph that a greater hand might be at play. He offered a silent prayer for safety—for the entire team about to venture into dark, unknown tunnels. The stark reality: This was far more than a dusty academic search. People's lives were on the line.

As the caravan rounded a bend, St. Peter's Church came into view up the mountain: a stone façade carved into the mountainside, an ancient cave sanctuary where the first Pope celebrated early masses and now the location of his lost keys. A narrow lane led to a parking area. Beyond it, the famous flight of stone steps climbed to the church's main entrance, now flanked by newly posted signs in Turkish, Arabic, and English:

CHURCH CLOSED FOR ARCHAEOLOGICAL INVESTIGATION
KEEP OUT | TEHLİKE | خَطَر

Joseph's heart sank. This had once been an open pilgrimage site, beloved by local Christians. Now it was all barricaded behind security fences, overshadowed by men with rifles. The row of black-clad contractors, nine in total, stood at attention near a pop-up checkpoint. Oleg himself was there, scanning faces with narrowed eyes.

The moment the SUVs stopped, Oleg and his men fanned out. "Everyone out!" Oleg barked, gesturing for the archaeologists to line up near the steps. The contractors brandished metal detector wands. Joseph exchanged uneasy looks with Mortem as they took their places.

One by one, the wand beeped over pockets and belts. Tools were opened, rummaged through. Joseph's heart pounded. Would they question the carbon-fiber knife? Or the small transmitter disguised in his bag? He had carefully hidden it among flashlights and notepads—hopefully enough to pass any casual inspection.

Sure enough, a scowling guard hovered the detector around Joseph's torso. "Backpack," the man grunted in heavily accented English. Joseph held it open, letting the guard shuffle some of the items aside: notebook, flashlights, bandages, small spool of rope,, the Bible with its worn cover peeking out. The guard scowled, pulled it partially free.

The guard's suspicion lingered, but Oleg—standing behind him—gave a curt wave to let it pass. The guard let out a grunt, pushed the back pack that once served as his airplane carry on, and finished scanning.

"Go," he said, stepping aside.

Joseph exhaled. He stepped past the checkpoint, glancing around. The day's gloom felt heavier for these militarized men posted around a once-sacred threshold. The rest of the team cleared security similarly, carrying their battered kits of picks, brushes, measuring instruments. *Archaeology meets paramilitary might,* Joseph thought wryly.

Near the church entrance, three more guards stood behind a newly erected table with a battered sign-in log. Another layer of bureaucracy, Joseph guessed. He recognized one guard from the prior day at the Golden Dome site—this time the man was decked out in heavier gear, bulletproof vest included. *Why so many guns?* Joseph asked himself. But that question, he supposed, had an obvious answer. The deeper they dug, the more certain it became that the Russians expected confrontation or sabotage. Or maybe they simply wanted to deter curious locals. Either way, it chilled him.

They filed up the steep stone staircase. The air grew damper, cooler. In older times, the hillside's rough facade would offer a dramatic reveal of the historical cave church. Now it seemed overshadowed by scaffolds and tarps the Russians had installed. The once-inviting threshold was partly sealed by a chain-link gate. Oleg slid it aside to let them pass.

Inside, the church's stone walls soared overhead. Dim electric lanterns had been placed around the perimeter, illuminating centuries-old arches carved from living rock. A platform had been set up near the old altar area, supporting computers, a generator, and random stacks of excavation crates. The pews, if they'd ever existed in earlier centuries, were long gone; only the naturally formed seats hewn into the sides of the cave.

At the makeshift altar stood Dr. Alexei Lavrov, as if presiding over a solemn liturgy. He wore typical field gear: cargo pants, a heavy canvas jacket, sturdy boots. But he also had a certain regality about him, chin lifted, posture straight, eyes reflecting a resolute fervor. There was something preacher-like in his stance.

He raised both hands to beckon the arrivals. "My friends," he said, voice echoing softly in the stone space, "please, come closer. Let us have a briefing before we begin the day's work."

Joseph and the others took seats on crates or perched on boulders arranged near the altar. Ten minutes earlier, the group had been half asleep in the caravan, but the hush inside the ancient sanctuary sharpened every sense. Dima, Mortem, Sasha, Yakov, and Elena gathered in a tight ring. Oleg and his men were ringed around the perimeter, rifles slung, eyes alert.

Lavrov cleared his throat. "Today... is a very important day for the Russian people," he announced, turning so that his words carried across the church. Then he flicked a glance at Joseph. "Forgive me, Professor, but I shall first address my countrymen in our native tongue."

Joseph nodded his head politely, though he felt a twinge of worry. He wouldn't understand what Lavrov was about to say. A *direct appeal to the 'children of the motherland'?* That smacked of a political or even religious rally. The Russians around him straightened, as if anticipating something stirring.

Lavrov's tone shifted seamlessly to Russian. For nearly ten minutes, he spoke in broad, rhythmic cadences, something almost sermon-like in his delivery. Joseph picked up only stray words—"Volkov," "mother Russia," "legacy," "sacred." The archaeologists, most of them Russians, listened intently, many nodding at intervals. Sasha's eyes glistened with emotion. Mortem seemed enthralled. Even Oleg, standing at a distance, paused to absorb the speech. The power in Lavrov's voice was undeniable, filling the ancient cave with echoes of conviction.

Joseph found his gaze drifting to the half-buried altar behind Lavrov, then to the jagged corridor that led deeper into the subterranean chambers. The entire site was a testament to centuries of devotion—earliest Christians who had once worshiped in secrecy, forging their identity "upon this rock." They might never have imagined that, 1,400 years later, a group of Russians and an American professor would be here searching for the lost keys of St. Peter. Joseph wondered what those early believers would say of Lavrov's fervor. *Lord, let me not lose sight of the sacredness here,* he thought. *Let me not reduce it to just politics or relic-hunting.*

Finally, Lavrov halted. The hush stretched for a few breaths, the Russians wearing rapt expressions. Joseph glimpsed watery eyes among some. Then Lavrov switched to English:

"Professor Scanlon, dear colleagues, I apologize for speaking Russian first. But I needed to address the men who stand with me, who share the burden of our homeland. Today is crucial, and we shall succeed."

Joseph offered a tight smile. Sasha and Yakov were practically glowing from Lavrov's speech. Elena's posture seemed less enthusiastic—she looked mildly uneasy—but she said nothing.

Lavrov continued in English: "Last night, the men finished mapping the first one hundred feet of the main tunnel. You will recall the carved keys over the entrance. Well, once inside, the passage runs for about fifty feet before opening onto a large chamber. Beyond that, the system branches again to three more tunnels that we have yet to explore. It's an absolute labyrinth. Under normal conditions—best equipment, best team—mapping it might take months. But we do not have months."

His statement hung in the air. The short timeline, Joseph knew, was code for *Volkov's health crisis*. The others in the archaeology group stirred, some trading puzzled glances. But Joseph did not blink. He was well aware of the hidden agenda.

Lavrov cleared his throat. "Our approach, then, must be expedient while still being as safe as possible. We do not want more accidents. But we also cannot linger. This morning, the entire archaeology team—Dima, Joseph, Sasha, Yakov, Elena, Mortem—will head below with me. We'll do a thorough visual search for any sign referencing the 'authority bestowed upon Peter' or any phrase that might indicate a repository for the Keys. Mark every clue. We have set up rope lines, and we have safety equipment. These tunnels twist in ways we cannot predict. We must be very careful. Understood?"

Quiet murmurs of assent followed.

The corners of Lavrov's mouth tightened. "All right, that is all. Suit up, gather your packs, and be ready in five minutes. Oleg's men will remain at the checkpoint to ensure no unauthorized persons disrupt our operation. I will have a mining VLF radio transmitter that is linked to Oleg's walkie. If we need support, we can radio to him on the surface. Let us be about it."

With a curt nod, he waved them to retrieve their caving gear.

Everyone dispersed around the old sanctuary to rummage through crates of harnesses, helmets with mounted lamps, coil upon coil of rope, gloves, kneepads, and other spelunking essentials. Joseph slipped on a safety vest, double-checked his headlamp, then tested the batteries in his handheld flashlight. A nurse kit was strapped around his waist—standard in a scenario that might involve rock slides or cuts from jagged stone. He found a battered climbing harness that fit well enough around his hips. Next to him, Mortem fumbled with the straps of his own harness, cursing softly in Russian under his breath.

Yakov and Sasha, apparently more experienced, clipped their gear with confidence, tightening buckles without fuss. Elena meticulously inspected each piece, her eyes flicking from the harness stitching to the carabiners. Meanwhile, Dima, stoic as ever, quietly helped them ready, checking harness tension and handing out extra flashlights. The hiss and pop of the portable generator accompanied them.

Within minutes, they formed up at the entrance to a side corridor branching off from the main cave-church interior.

Lavrov arrived, hooking a carabiner to his belt. "All set," he said tersely, stepping forward to lead. The gloom beneath that carved symbol seemed to swallow them as they ventured in.

The air changed immediately past the threshold: cooler, slightly damp, with an odd hush that swallowed their footsteps. Their headlamps carved cones of yellowish light in the darkness, revealing a narrow stone corridor tall enough for them to walk single file. The floor sloped downward, rough underfoot. The entire place smelled of ancient dust and damp rock, reminiscent of catacombs Joseph had visited in Rome, but more claustrophobic.

They trudged carefully. After about fifty feet, the passage widened drastically, opening onto a large subterranean chamber. Lavrov flicked his headlamp left, then right, revealing a vaulted space that soared up beyond their beams' reach. Stalactites hung from the ceiling like jagged teeth. The floor was relatively flat, scattered with small boulders and crumbling debris. Some corners were lost to shadows.

"This is the chamber," Lavrov said, voice echoing. "It extends maybe fifty feet across, though we haven't precisely measured yet." He pointed to where the far walls vanished into blackness. "There are multiple exits, some of them we suspect lead deeper. Be mindful."

The team fanned out, stepping carefully over fallen slabs of stone. Every few steps, they paused to shine light along the walls. At one edge, Elena stooped to examine faint markings. Dima traced a large fissure in the floor, muttering about potential hazards. The

sense of being in an alien world under the mountain was profound. Joseph, using his small notepad, scribbled any sign or symbol they encountered.

Ominously, Oleg's men were not here with them. Joseph realized
the security detail was posted up top, presumably letting the archaeologists do the "grunt work." That left them alone with Lavrov
in these caverns. The silence, broken by dripping water and shifting boots, heightened the sense of tension.

Soon, they saw three distinct tunnel openings on the chamber's
far side:

- One was broad, easily wide enough for three people to walk
  abreast.

- The other two were narrow slits, barely enough for one person
  at a time.

Lavrov nodded at them. "We suspected more branches, but these
three are the largest. The rest are smaller cracks, impassable.
Sasha, Yakov, Elena—investigate these side passages. I'll remain
with Joseph, Mortem, and Dima in this main chamber a bit longer
to look for clues. Watch your step."

Nervous glances were exchanged, but Sasha set her jaw. Yakov
and Elena murmured agreements. Each group had rope, walkie-
talkies, and enough headlamps for the job. Sasha went toward the
wide tunnel on the left. Yakov took the narrower central path.
Elena moved to the narrow path on the right. They turned, each
calling a quick farewell, and disappeared into the blackness.

Joseph, left behind with Lavrov, Dima, and Mortem, resumed scanning the chamber. Flicking his beam along the floor, he saw centuries of layered dirt. The Russians must have barely begun clearing it, for lumps of tumbled rock and piles of loose rubble lay everywhere.

After perhaps ten minutes of searching in near silence, Mortem called out, "Something here!" His voice echoed eerily. Joseph and the others converged on him near the chamber's center, where Mortem was kneeling with his light focused on the ground. In the dust, faint but legible, were carved words in an ancient script.

Joseph squatted, brushing away debris. The inscription was in Latin, the letters weathered but decipherable. He read slowly, out loud:

"Enter ye in at the narrow gate: for wide is the gate, and broad is the way that leadeth to destruction, and many there are who go in thereat. How narrow is the gate, and strait is the way that leadeth to life: and few there are that find it!"

A chill prickled Joseph's skin. He recognized the biblical verse from Matthew 7:13–14. But apparently it had been deliberately placed here—perhaps a clue from the early custodians who'd hidden the Keys?

Mortem scratched his head. "What does it mean for us? Some moral lesson?"

Joseph rose, shining his light toward the three tunnels. "Could be. Look—two of them are narrow, one is wide. The text is basically cautioning that the broad path leads to destruction. The narrow path leads to life."

Dima's eyes widened. "Sasha is in the wide tunnel," he said, voice taut. "We told her to go there."

Instantly, Lavrov's face hardened. "We need to recall her—fast. She might be heading into a death trap." He spun on his heel. "Come on."

Dima bolted forward first, shouting, "Sasha! Sasha, come back!" Their footfalls thundered across the chamber. Joseph and Mortem hurried at their heels, adrenaline surging. The wide tunnel loomed like an open maw. They heard only the echoes of their own voices bouncing off the stone.

Then, from within that wide passage, came a deep rumble. Like distant thunder but dangerously close, it reverberated through the ground, sending tiny stones skittering. A moment later— **CRACK**—an avalanche of falling rock. Dust exploded outward. The entire corridor seemed to quake.

"Nyet!" Dima hollered. He lunged toward the tunnel entrance, arms out as if to physically hold back the collapse. Joseph, heart pounding, wrenched him back as a fresh wave of debris tumbled from above, choking the passage.

When the tremor subsided, they rushed in. Or tried to. The path was blocked by tons of rock, dust swirling like a suffocating fog. Joseph coughed, eyes watering. Through the gloom, he heard Dima's ragged breath.

Mortem stared at the blockade in horror. "She's… still in there," he said, voice barely above a whisper.

Lavrov pressed a hand against the newly formed wall of stone, face pale. "Sasha," he murmured, expression pained. Then he flicked a grim look at the floor near the entrance, where a snapped rope trailing into the rubble indicated that Sasha had once been anchored. "The rope's severed."

Dima bent to examine a cluster of bent rods half-buried under the broken stones. "Looks like a primitive tripwire system. She must have triggered it. Some kind of ancient sabotage system." He spat, rising abruptly. "They booby-trapped the wide path to keep intruders out."

Joseph, heart hammering, crouched at the rock pile and began pulling away chunks of debris by hand. Mortem joined him, face set in desperation. The dust coated their throats. The stones were large and heavy, requiring both hands to shift them even a few inches. After a minute or so, they'd made no real progress.

Lavrov's voice cut through, calm but steely. "Joseph, Mortem, hold." He lifted his walkie-talkie and barked into it: "Oleg, send three men down here with picks and shovels. We have a cave-in, possibly a casualty. Move quickly." Static crackled in response, then Oleg's terse acknowledgment.

Dima let out a shuddering breath, turning on Lavrov. Furious Russian words spilled from him, too rapid for Joseph to parse. Lavrov's posture stiffened. The conversation continued in heated Russian, tension thick as gunpowder. Lavrov's face flickered with an emotion Joseph had never seen in him: genuine anguish. Then, in an almost imperceptible beat, he forced it down, adopting the iron-willed composure of a man used to making tough calls.

Mortem, still kneeling by the rubble, gave Joseph a pleading look. "We can't just give up. She might still be alive."

Joseph nodded. "We have to keep trying." He seized another stone, ignoring the scrape of it biting into his palms. But the mass was enormous. The corridor must have collapsed for yards, with hundreds of pounds of debris. Even with help, rescue might take hours. If Sasha was pinned or worse…

Lavrov's footsteps crunched behind them. "We can't waste indefinite time. If she triggered a full collapse, I—" He paused, wincing. "We'll do what we can, but we must continue the mission as well. The clock is ticking."

Dima wheeled around, fists clenched, shouting more heated words in Russian. Joseph caught enough to sense Dima was calling Lavrov heartless. Another short, sharp exchange followed. Lavrov's voice lowered. He looked to Joseph, Mortem, then back at the pile. For an instant, heartbreak flickered across his face, as if torn between humanity and the mission. Then he steeled himself and pivoted on his heel.

"Men are on their way," he said with a forced calm. "They will attempt to clear the rubble. But we can't all stand here digging. Joseph, Dima, Mortem—come with me."

"No!" Dima snapped. "I won't leave Sasha."

"She's your friend; I understand," Lavrov said, voice unwavering. "But I am in command. We have obligations to fulfill. The security detail plus three volunteers can do more than we can. We must move on. It's an order."

Joseph's gut twisted. Mortem looked on the verge of defying him outright. But slowly, footsteps approached from the main chamber: three more security contractors arrived, armed with collapsible shovels and picks. They surveyed the ruin and set to work, grim-faced.

Dima lingered, sorrow etched on his features. Lavrov caught his gaze. "I'm sorry," he said softly, though the note of finality was chilling. Then, with that, he turned and headed back to the big cavern.

Mortem scrambled after Dima, who was kneeling by the collapsed corridor, voice cracking as he whispered a last entreaty for Sasha to answer. Silence. Joseph placed a trembling hand on Dima's shoulder, willing some measure of comfort. "They'll do their best," he managed, though he himself doubted it.

At length, Dima stood, eyes brimming with fury. "Fine," he breathed. "But if she dies…" His words trailed off, as if he couldn't voice the full threat. Then he stomped after Lavrov. Joseph and Mortem followed, hearts full of anxiety. The wide tunnel was effectively sealed, a shocking testament to the ancient cunning that guarded these passages.

As they stepped back into the main cavern, Joseph's thoughts spiraled. *Enter through the narrow gate*, the scripture had warned.

Sasha had done the opposite, walking unsuspectingly down that wide path to destruction. The weight of it all was immense.

Lavrov's footsteps echoed as he led them toward the center of that chamber again, where the biblical verse was carved. The Bishop had built a literal death trap behind the wide corridor. Joseph felt chilled to the bone, remembering the purpose behind it: *Preserve the Keys from the unrighteous.* A deep dread churned inside him. Even if they located the Keys, how many more traps lay waiting?

Dima trudged at the rear, face grim, not meeting anyone's gaze. Mortem hovered beside Joseph, as if seeking silent reassurance. And Lavrov, with a faint slump in his shoulders, radiated tension.

At the edge of the big chamber, Lavrov stopped. He gazed back at the collapsed corridor, where the security detail's muffled shouts echoed through the dust. Then he turned forward once again, forging ahead into the gloom.

"Come," he said in a hollow voice. "We have little choice but to proceed."

And so the next step of their harrowing search began, overshadowed by tragedy and the ancient warning carved into the stone beneath their feet.

TWENTY-TWO

A Bridge of Hope and Desolation

"We heard the rumble," Yakov said, his voice tight with concern. "What happened?"

Lavrov sighed heavily, the weight of regret evident in his eyes. "We found a clue that told us to avoid the broad way. But it was too late. Sasha... she triggered a trap."

Elena's eyes widened in horror. "A trap? Is she...?"

Lavrov shook his head, his voice somber. "The cave-in buried her. Three security contractors are on their way to dig her out, but we had to keep going."

Yakov ran a hand through his hair, his expression stricken. "We never should have sent you down those tunnels. The risks..."

"We had no choice," Lavrov interjected softly. "We needed answers."

The group fell into a heavy silence, the echoes of their shared fear and uncertainty filling the vast cavern around them.

"Byzantine engineers were incredibly skilled," Joseph said, breaking the heavy silence. "They had the potential to develop all sorts of traps and countermeasures. We must remember that this city endured a two-year siege. The bishop had ample time to work with city engineers to ensure that any wrong steps by the wrong people would leave them in great peril."

Dima, his voice sharp with frustration, chimed in. He began issuing directions to the team, his words clipped and authoritative. "We need to pause the exploration and bring in our ground-penetrating radar units. We need to start mapping out every meter of what we will cover from now on. We can't let this happen..."

Lavrov interjected gently, his tone calm despite the tension in the air. "Dima, our GPR tech is too large to get into these tunnels. And the process would take too long. We must continue the search."

Dima erupted in harsh Russian, his words a rapid-fire torrent of anger and defiance. Joseph, though unable to understand the specifics, could sense the intensity of Dima's emotions. He had the distinct impression that Dima was on the verge of resigning.

Lavrov, his face impassive, suddenly pulled out a pistol with a swift, unexpected movement. The sudden click of the safety being released echoed through the cavern, freezing everyone in place.

"What the hell, Lavrov?!" Joseph yelled, stepping back in shock and disbelief. "Is this really necessary?"

Dima's eyes widened, the fire of anger now tinged with something else—fear. But he stood his ground, meeting Lavrov's gaze with defiance.

Lavrov switched to English, his voice steady despite the gravity of the situation. "Everyone is needed to continue this expedition and I don't think we need to talk anymore about this." He gestured with the pistol, a silent but firm command.

He then attempted to regain control of the situation, his tone reasonable. "The only mistake made was not thoroughly investigating the large cavern before sending the three to check the tunnels."

Lavrov turned his attention to Yakov and Elena. "Give me a status check on your tunnels."

Yakov, his voice trembling slightly, spoke first. "My tunnel... it came to a dead end."

Elena piped up, her voice filled with a mix of fear and excitement. "My tunnel was indeed very narrow, but... but I saw fish carved into the side of the wall."

Lavrov frowned, his brow furrowed in confusion. "Fish? I don't understand how fish are signs of authority."

Joseph stepped forward, his voice filled with the weight of historical knowledge. ""From now on I will make you fishers of men." Peter was a fisherman." He paused, allowing the significance of the reference to sink in. "The fish symbol was called "ichthys" and important in the Byzantine empire. It goes all the way back to Peter as the leader and fisherman of Jesus's disciples."

Lavrov's eyes lit up with excitement. "Then we continue!" He turned and began to lead the way with renewed vigor.

Dima, however, remained defiant. He marched ahead of Lavrov, his posture rigid. "This is still my team," he declared, his voice laced with bitterness. "If anyone is going to be hurt in these mad circumstances, it will be me."

Lavrov tried to placate him, his tone conciliatory. "Dima, accidents happen. We need to keep our minds on the big picture. We are on the verge of the largest archaeological discovery since the Dead Sea Scrolls."

Dima responded in garbled Russian, his words lost in a mix of anger and frustration.

Lavrov, seemingly deciding to ignore Dima's outburst, reached for his radio. He spoke into the device in Russian, informing Oleg of the team's move into the next tunnel.

The team moved forward, their headlamps cutting through the oppressive darkness. They entered the narrow tunnel that Elena had explored, and it was indeed uncomfortably confining. The walls pressed in on either side, and the low ceiling forced them to hunch over. The air was thick and stagnant, and the silence was broken only by the sound of their own breathing and the scraping of their boots on the uneven floor. Yet, despite the discomfort, the tunnel was passable.

Midway through the tunnel, Joseph's eyes caught a series of Latin words etched into the wall. He stopped, his heart pounding with anticipation. Carefully, he traced the ancient letters with his finger.

"It's another scripture verse," he announced, his voice echoing in the confined space. He translated the inscription: "Hebrews 10:23: 'Let us hold fast the confession of our hope without wavering, for he is faithful that has promised.'"

The others gathered around him, their faces illuminated by the beams of their headlamps. "What does it mean, Joseph?" Elena asked, her voice filled with curiosity.

Joseph frowned, his brow furrowed in thought. "I have no idea," he admitted. "It's a powerful verse, but... I don't see any immediate connection to our situation."

The others shared their own interpretations, their voices hushed with reverence. Yakov believed it was a warning. Lavrov, ever pragmatic, simply stated that its meaning would likely become clear in time.

They continued onward, the weight of the verse hanging heavy in the air. The tunnel twisted and turned, each bend revealing more of its claustrophobic nature.

Suddenly, the narrow tunnel expanded dramatically into an awe-inspiring chasm, the change so abrupt it took their breath away. One moment, the pressing confines of the tunnel walls enveloped them; the next, they were standing on the precipice of a vast, gaping void. The air was cooler and carried an echo of the subterranean river far below, a whispering current hidden in shadow.

Their headlamps swept across the abyss, the light barely grazing the far side, highlighting jagged rock formations that seemed to stretch endlessly into the darkness. The walls of the chasm shimmered with veins of minerals, glinting like stars against the deep night of the rock. Below, the river's muted roar spoke of ancient secrets and relentless motion, a dark ribbon threading through the heart of the earth.

Suspended over this chasm was a bridge that defied time itself. Crafted from ancient timber, its weathered planks passed the test of time and communicated the excellence of their engineers. The bridge was anchored to towering natural pillars of stone, rising majestically from the depths like sentinels. Though its appearance was aged, the bridge exuded a quiet strength, its beams entwined with creeping tendrils of luminescent moss that cast an otherworldly glow from their headlamps, contrasting with the darkness below.

Standing on the rocky ledge where the tunnel ended, they were about 1.5 meters above the entrance to the bridge. To step onto it was to commit to the unknown, to trust in the bridge's resilience against the passage of time. The silence was profound, save for the distant rumble of the river, and the air was tinged with the scent of damp stone and ancient wood. It was a place where the very essence of adventure hung in the air, a gateway to mystery and wonder.

The distance across the chasm was significant, perhaps fifty meters. On the other side, the bridge ended at what appeared to be the entrance to another tunnel, carved into the wall of the chasm.

As they peered down at the bridge, Joseph noticed something etched boldly into the first plank. He knelt down to examine it more closely. It was a single word, carved in elegant Latin script: "SPES."

"It's Latin," Joseph said, his voice filled with a mixture of awe and trepidation. "It means 'hope.'"

A collective gasp filled the air. "Hope?" Elena whispered, her voice barely audible.

"I have no idea why the word 'hope' would be carved onto this bridge," Joseph admitted, his mind racing.

Mortem, ever the pragmatist, offered a suggestion. "Perhaps it is an encouragement," he said, his voice laced with a hint of optimism. "Perhaps it means we are close."

Lavrov, his voice filled with excitement, reached for his radio. He spoke rapidly in Russian, informing Oleg that they had made it safely across the chasm. Oleg responded in Russian, his voice crackling through the static.

Lavrov turned to the team, his expression serious. "We are not taking any chances here. We will exit the narrow tunnel onto the bridge one at a time. We will take a 200-meter rope, and one person will go ahead of the others with the rope and set up an anchor on the other side, from which everyone can securely cross."

Mortem stepped forward, his voice calm and confident. "I volunteer. I am most experienced person for job" he said in his best English possible.

Before Mortem jumped down onto the platform, Elena was by his side, assisting with his preparations. She deftly helped him knot the rope to his harness, her fingers moving with practiced precision. As they worked, they spoke softly in Russian, their conversation a blend of focus and camaraderie.

Elena asked Mortem if he was ready, her eyes meeting his with a steady assurance. Mortem confirmed that everything had been checked, giving his equipment a final inspection.

With a determined nod, Elena tied herself to Mortem's rope, ensuring that everything was secure. She indicated that she would take the end of the line.

She turned to Joseph, Yakov, and Lavrov. "Alright, you three, head down to the platform with Mortem," she instructed, nodding toward the descent. "Once you're on the platform, make sure to attach your carabiners."

With their plan set, Mortem leaped down onto the platform, knowing the other men were right behind him. Dima, Joseph, Yakov, and Lavrov followed, jumping down onto the platform as well.

As the collective weight of the five men pressed onto the platform, it descended gradually, creaking ominously as it did so. The platform was like a scale that had weight added to it, the rough wood groaning under the strain. The platform sank about half a meter, triggering a hidden mechanism that had lain dormant for centuries. Suddenly, a network of concealed pulleys sprang to life, their presence a well-kept secret until now. The Byzantine ropes, thick and ancient yet remarkably sturdy, began to slither through the wheels, which groaned and squeaked with the effort. The cacophony of sounds reverberated through the chasm, each squeal amplified by the cavernous space, creating an eerie symphony that danced off the rock walls.

From somewhere deep within the bowels of the mountain, upstream, a new sound emerged. It was the unsettling rumble of massive rocks shifting, a deep, growling noise that spoke of monumental forces at play. The air seemed to vibrate with the sheer power of it, rich with the scent of earth and damp stone.

In the shadows of the tunnel, Elena stood tense and alert, her eyes flicking between the platform and the darkness beyond. She was tethered to Mortem by a length of rope, the lifeline between them. The dim light cast flickering shadows across her determined face, illuminating the jagged walls around her in brief, ghostly flashes. Each new sound sent a shiver up her spine, the ancient machinery and the shifting earth a reminder of the perilous depths they had dared to enter.

An initial wave of panic washed over Mortem, Dima, Yakov and Joseph on the platform. Dima, his eyes wide with fear, tried to climb back up the wall of the chasm, but the surface was too slippery.

Lavrov, his voice booming with authority, yelled over the din. "Some kind of trap has been activated! We need to get across quickly!" In Russian, he commanded Mortem, "Run!"

Mortem, his face grim with determination, took off running across the bridge. Lavrov, Joseph, Yakov, and Dima followed at a more measured pace, their hearts pounding in their chests.

As Mortem made it halfway across the bridge, the sound of some-thing loud and massive came rushing toward them from upstream in the chasm. They pointed their headlamps in the direction of the sound. In the distance, they saw a giant tidal wave, its dark waters churning and frothing, rushing toward them with incredible speed.

Lavrov yelled at Mortem to hurry, his voice strained with urgency.

Suddenly, amidst the chaos, the scripture verse from the tunnel appeared in his mind: "Let us hold fast the confession of our hope without wavering..." The words played over and over, like a man-tra, each repetition bringing a sense of clarity amidst the panic. But then, like a bolt of lightning illuminating a dark sky, the con-nection became clear. Hope. It wasn't just an abstract concept; it was their lifeline. Joseph's eyes widened as he realized the signif-icance. The bridge they were running across wasn't merely a structure but a symbol and bastion of their hope for safety from the rushing water coming at them. The word "Hope" etched onto the bridge was that which they needed to hold fast to - literally.

His heart pounded in his chest, but now it was with a renewed sense of purpose. He skidded to a halt, the soles of his boots scraping against the gritty tunnel floor. He turned to face Dima and Lavrov, who were close behind, their faces etched with ur-gency and fear.

"Stop!" Joseph's voice was powerful, cutting through the noise of their frantic escape. "Hold fast to the bridge! It's the key!" He paused for a moment, letting the importance of his revelation settle in their minds. "The bridge is our hope, and we need to hold fast!"

Joseph's eyes locked onto theirs, conveying not just the urgency but the unwavering belief in his words. He could see the flicker of understanding ignite in their eyes, transforming confusion into determination. The bridge was more than their path forward; it was their anchor, and with every fiber of his being, Joseph knew they needed to grasp onto it with all their might.

Hearing Joseph from the tunnel, Elena yelled at Mortem, her voice echoing with desperation. "Mortem, stop! Grab the bridge!"

But Mortem continued to run, his eyes fixed on the tunnel entrance on the other side. "I can make it!" he yelled back. He was close. His voice filled with a desperate hope. The rush of water was almost upon them.

Joseph, Dima, Yakov, and Lavrov braced themselves, gripping the wooden planks of the bridge with all their might.

He was almost at the end of the bridge, the safety of the tunnel entrance just a few feet away. But then, with a deafening roar, the power of the wave hit Mortem like a wrecking ball. The force of the water was immense, and it swept him off the bridge and into the churning river below.

Elena witnessed the horrifying scene, her scream of agony echoing through the chasm. She looked down and saw the other men take a deep breath as the water washed over their heads.

Then, Elena realized with a chilling certainty that she was still connected to Mortem's rope. She frantically began to untie herself from the rope, her fingers fumbling with the knots. She worked with a desperate frenzy, her heart pounding in her chest. She was almost free, just a few more twists of the knot...

But it was too late. The force of Mortem's weight, combined with the power of the wave, violently pulled her. She was yanked off her feet and dragged into the water torrent, disappearing with a blood curdling scream into the churning chaos of the chasm.

After the initial force of the wave hit the men on the bridge, the level of the water eventually began to lessen, the water receding in a way that happens after the crest of a wave hits and diminishes. Dima, Joseph, Yakov and Lavrov after holding fast to their bridge of hope, gasping for air, popped their heads up above the water. They had just enough time to see Elena screaming as she was pulled down into the depths of the chasm. They yelled after her, their voices filled with despair.

The relentless river surged over the bridge, its current a powerful force of nature. Clinging tightly to the slick handrails, they navigated the treacherous crossing, each step a calculated move against the water's push. Upon reaching the opposite side, they encountered another platform, its wood worn smooth by time and elements.

As the combined weight of the four men settled onto it, the platform again started to sink like a scale, sinking gracefully about half a meter into the depths below. Like the first platform it was the trigger that set a hidden mechanism into motion. A complex network of pulleys sprang to life, their gears whirring with newfound purpose.

Upstream, the sound of monumental stones grinding into place reverberated through the air, a low rumble that crescendoed into a thunderous stop. Within mere moments, the once-turbulent water began to recede, its chaotic dance tamed as it returned to a gentle, placid flow. The transformation was swift and surreal, as if nature itself had bowed to the ancient engineering that commanded it. The river lay before them, serene and undisturbed, a testament to the ingenuity woven into the very fabric of this place.

Dima's face was twisted with grief as he began to mourn aloud. "I can't believe they're gone," he said, his voice choked with sorrow. "All of my teammates... lost."

Lavrov, however, seemed almost detached from Dima's pain. His eyes gleamed with a mix of awe and excitement. Turning to Joseph, "Can you believe what the Byzantine engineers accomplished?" he asked, almost to himself. "Their genius is astounding. Imagine creating a weighted fulcrum and pulley system to control the flow of an entire subterranean river!"

Dima looked at him, incredulous. "How can you think about that now?" he asked, his voice filled with disbelief.

Lavrov shrugged, his gaze still distant. "It's hard not to admire such ingenuity, even in the midst of tragedy," he replied.

"Only something of immense spiritual power could merit this level of safeguarding," he declared, his voice filled with conviction.

The four men climbed into the new tunnel. Right at the entrance, etched into the rock in ancient Latin, Joseph saw another inscription. He read it aloud, translating the words: "2 Timothy 4:7-8: 'I have fought the good fight, I have finished the race, I have kept the faith. Now there is in store for me the crown of righteousness, which the Lord, the righteous Judge, will award to me on that day.'"

Joseph stared at the inscription, his heart heavy with the weight of loss and the mystery of the ancient engineers. The words spoke of perseverance, of finishing the race, of keeping the faith. But what was the race they were running? What was the faith they were being asked to keep?

Lavrov, his voice filled with renewed determination, clapped Joseph on the shoulder. "We can't stop now," he declared, his eyes burning with a fierce intensity. "We are so close! The honor and memory of Mortem, Elena, and Sasha demand that we continue."

Dima, still in grief but convicted that they must honor their comrades, nodded in agreement. A spark of resolve flickered in his eyes.

Joseph, despite the turmoil in his heart, felt a surge of determination. He would not let the deaths of his companions be in vain. He would press on, driven by a mixture of grief, curiosity, and a growing sense of purpose. The Lost Keys of Saint Peter were within their grasp, and they would not be deterred.

TWENTY-THREE

A Test of Faith

The hush that fell was absolute, as if the cavern itself had paused to witness the four figures pressing on through its depths. Echoes of their last effort—tumbling rocks and scraping boots—still whispered along the ragged walls behind them. Joseph Scanlon, still catching his breath, glanced around at his companions: Yakov and Dima, whose sweat-dampened faces showed equal parts awe and tension, and Dr. Alexei Lavrov, whose sharp-eyed focus burned with an almost feverish light.

They had come this far together through endless corridors, down precipitous slopes, and past immersive Byzantine traps. The site itself had been battered by time and centuries of secrecy. Now they descended yet another modest tunnel, one that felt closer, narrower than those before, as if pressing them deeper into the earth's silent heart. The walls dripped with condensation, creating small rivulets that cut lines in the dust and left the stone glistening beneath their headlamps.

The group advanced carefully. Every five steps, a murmur passed among them. It was Lavrov's idea, carried out in reverential hush.

A string of Latin words, each one echoing with quiet force. Yakov would pause, read the single word faintly etched upon the wall in Latin, and then Joseph would translate in a low, clear voice:

"Upon...This...Rock...I Will Build...My Church."

The final word resonated, as though the corridor itself recognized the ancient phrase. Joseph felt a shiver run along his spine. The synergy of these words—quoting the Gospel verse from Matthew 16:18—was not lost on him. In the hush that followed, a crack appeared at the tunnel's terminus. As they approached and exited the tunnel their headlamps unveiled a spacious chamber.

They filed in slowly, stepping in and the air felt different—still, cold, and thick as if it had not been disturbed for centuries. Their beams swept across a wide stone floor, revealing the outlines of old murals flaking from curving walls. Golden flecks of mosaic glinted where the paint had worn thin. On the ceiling, cracks spiderwebbed, each one filled with ancient dust.

In the center of the cavern yawned a massive hole, perfectly round, about fifteen meters in diameter. The edges were rimmed with jagged stone, as if an underground well had collapsed in on itself. One by one, they approached carefully.

Joseph's pulse kicked up at the sight. "Be careful," he breathed. "That drop looks... profound."

Dima and Yakov shone their headlamps down, arms extended. Far below—perhaps fifty meters—sat something that caused the white beams to flicker in reflection. At first, Joseph thought it was just more rock, but as he peered closer, he saw it was carefully carved. A large engraving of keys, each about a meter in length, had been chiseled into the cavern floor. The shape glinted faintly, possibly inlaid with a metal that caught their lamplight.

Lavrov gave a low whistle of wonder. "Keys," he breathed, voice echoing. "We are on the right path, my friends. A sign—quite literal—of what may lie beneath."

Yakov swallowed audibly. "It must be at least a fifty-meter drop," he said, leaning carefully forward. "I can't see a direct walkway, just the hole. Looks like the entire floor gave way here."

Joseph shifted his light around the pit's interior, noticing squares carved into the limestone at regular intervals. "Hold on—look at the walls," he said, gesturing. "There are these rectangular indents, almost like handholds or footholds, spiraling downward. Possibly a means of climbing."

Dima frowned, moving to the edge to examine them. "They're spaced in a pattern, yes. But no guarantee they're stable. Could be centuries old, and with any shift in weight... it'd be a sheer hazard."

Lavrov agreed. "It's a precarious slope. We can't risk free-climbing something we've never tested." His gaze turned to Dima. "How many ropes do we have left?"

Dima wiped sweat from his brow. "Two, I believe." Lavrov set his jaw. "We'll have to rig a descent. The keys must be close. But we also can't all go. There may be more hidden dangers below."

Joseph felt the tension spike. The entire expedition had culminated in something beyond academic curiosity. Danger lurked in every shadow. And yet, the idea of turning back now seemed impossible—like spurning destiny.

Lavrov nodded decisively. "Dima, Yakov, you will control the ropes from up here. Joseph and I will go down. With care."

Joseph opened his mouth, feeling a jolt of alarm. Did he have a choice? Perhaps not. But to his own surprise, he realized he wanted to go. After all, everything he'd studied for years—letters from Pope Gregory, the Lombard tale, the scribes' attempts to hide the Claves Petri—pointed to these final steps. Yes, there was danger, but also an unshakable sense of calling.

"I'll do it," Joseph said simply. "Let's prepare."

Yakov and Dima exchanged glances. "We can anchor the lines to the stalagmites near the entrance," Dima suggested. "They look sturdy enough. Then we'll belay from here. We just have to be sure the rope length is enough to get you all the way down."

Joseph crouched to examine the spool of rope they'd carried. The brand was foreign, designed for industrial loads, but it looked strong enough. "We'll double-check the knots," he said, voice tight with adrenaline.

Lavrov was already shrugging off his backpack to retrieve a harness. Joseph and Lavrov each threaded loops around their waists and thighs, then they attached themselves to the ropes Dima prepared. The air seemed thick with unspoken tension, the hush broken only by the hiss of fabric, the clank of metal buckles.

At the pit's rim, they tested the lines, tugging to ensure the anchors held fast. The floor, pocked with cracks, still seemed capable of supporting them. Joseph tested his harness with a tentative lean; the rope tensed, then held. Satisfied, Dima nodded. Yakov, putting on gloves, looked at them grimly.

"Just keep a steady pace. We'll lower you as gently as we can. If you slip or the wall crumbles, we'll hold you, but... well, it's a long way down."

Lavrov's expression was resolute. "We know the risks."

Joseph slid carefully over the edge, letting the rope take his weight. Lavrov did the same a few feet to Joseph's right. The stone was shockingly cold against Joseph's outstretched fingers. Step by step, they walked themselves down, leaning back on the ropes. Dima and Yakov managed the belays, feeding line at a measured pace.

The first ten meters went smoothly, albeit with Joseph's heart hammering. Little shards of rock clattered downward at intervals, echoing faintly in the gaping space. The moist air smelled of earth and minerals. Joseph's breath sounded painfully loud inside his helmet.

Fifteen meters... twenty... The carving of keys at the bottom grew clearer. The lines that formed their bows and shafts appeared meticulously crafted, shimmering in the subdued glow of headlamps. Joseph wondered who had carved them, and how many centuries ago. Did they too feel this trembling sense of awe?

At about halfway, Joseph's foot slipped on a ledge of crumbling limestone. He gasped, fumbling for a better hold on the rope. Immediately, the line caught him. Yakov must have felt the tension above because Joseph heard a hiss as the rope feed halted. His heart thrummed.

"You all right?" Lavrov's voice echoed across the pit, taut with concern.

"I'm fine," Joseph managed, swallowing. "Just a loose rock."

They continued downward, each meter seeming to stretch time. Finally, after what felt like an eternity, Joseph's boots landed on firm ground. He exhaled a shaky breath. His headlamp revealed a circular stone platform at the bottom of the pit, about three or four meters across. Lavrov joined him moments later, each man unfastening the tension from their harness.

Dima's voice crackled from the distance. "We see your lights moving around. Are you stable?"

Lavrov pulled out his walkie-talkie. "Yes, we're down safely. There's another tunnel entrance here. We'll proceed."

"All right," came Dima's cautious reply. Joseph turned to examine the immediate surroundings. The massive engraving of keys spanned the floor. He crouched to trace its surface, noticing that the channels were at least an inch deep and appeared inlaid with something like copper or maybe a gold alloy. Faint lumps of mineral deposit had crusted around the lines, evidence of eons of underground seepage.

The sense of overshadowing presence was impossible to ignore. His mind briefly flicked to the CIA, to Oleg's suspicious presence, to the broader conflict they all tiptoed around. None of it mattered in this moment—only the sanctity of what lay before them. "But let's see what that tunnel leads to," he said.

Indeed, at the far side a dark archway beckoned, carved neatly into the rock. It rose perhaps two meters high, enough to walk through if they bent slightly. Lavrov pressed forward without hesitation, Joseph on his heels. Their footfalls echoed softly.

Just inside, the corridor angled downward at a gentle slope. The walls were set with small niches, each containing a burnt-out oil lamp or bits of unrecognizable debris. The rocky ground felt more finely worked here, almost like a laid stone floor, though battered by time. Their headlamps illuminated a swirl of dust motes, disturbed by their presence.

Lavrov lifted his walkie-talkie. "Oleg, come in."

A faint crackle answered, then Oleg's low voice: "Yes, I read you."

"We are at the base of the pit, proceeding through a descending tunnel. Seems stable so far. Will advise." Lavrov's tone was clipped, official.

"Understood. Keep eyes open. We have your lines secure."

Lavrov lowered the radio, glancing at Joseph. "We're so close, I feel it. Everything from the old letters, from Pope Gregory's epistles, from the labyrinth's layout, it all points here. Our journey is nearly done."

Joseph felt a ripple of anticipation. The environment pressed in with the presence of centuries. The stone whispered secrets in every crevice, secrets of hidden faith, of men who had died to protect what was cherished as holy. "Let's hope," Joseph said softly.

They advanced, each step echoing. The temperature dropped a bit further. Ahead, the corridor opened into a new cavern of lesser size—more like a chamber. And at its far end rose a massive circular stone, tall and imposing, reminiscent of ancient tomb seals Joseph had seen in church iconography or read about in historical texts.

Joseph paused, gesturing towards the massive circular stone with a sense of reverence. "Look at that," he said to Lavrov, his voice echoing softly in the dim chamber. "This sealing stone is a testament to ancient craftsmanship. It's designed with such precision—a near-perfect circle, fitting snugly into the circular recess. You can see how gravity and the stone's own weight create a formidable barrier. It's as if the earth itself is holding it in place."

He stepped closer, pointing to the groove etched around the opening's perimeter. "This groove acts like the wards of a lock, securing the stone firmly in its seat. It's ingenious, really, how the sheer mass of it naturally settles into position, making any attempt to move it a daunting challenge."

Joseph's gaze traveled to the edge of the stone, where a subtle pivot notch was evident. "And there, you see? A stone pivot point. It's designed for a fulcrum of specific size and weight, allowing a means to possibly shift this colossal seal when needed."

But before he could examine more of the seal, something else claimed his attention: to the left side of the seal on the wall stood an eight-foot cross, carved into the very stone. The top soared near the cavern ceiling. All around it, arranged in a breathtaking mosaic, were various Christian symbols. Each icon was fashioned with colored stone or glass tesserae: a Sacred Heart, the Chi Rho, a small child, the image of the Apostle Peter, the globe or "the world," a dove, the cross again, Mary, a lamb, the Ichthys (fish symbol), a chalice, and an angel. Each glowed faintly under the lights, as though centuries of darkness had done little to dull their vibrant hues.

Under every symbol, Joseph saw a round hole about ten inches in diameter. They were perfectly carved recesses, each blackened with time, presumably deep enough to hold an arm's length. Instantly, his stomach twisted with foreboding.

"That's... quite a puzzle," Lavrov muttered, stepping closer. "And look," he added with a quiet gasp.

In the faint glow, Joseph saw it: a skeleton sprawled partially on the floor, with its entire right arm jammed into one of the holes. The ancient bones wore the remnants of a tattered sleeve. Its skull lay turned toward them, jaw gaping in a silent scream. The rest of the body had collapsed in an awkward position, as though pinned or trapped. Dust coated it in a thick shroud, but the shape of the contorted bones was unmistakable.

Yakov's voice would have cracked with alarm, had he been there to see it. Joseph shuddered at the thought. Clearly, the poor soul had come here once, searching. He never left.

Lavrov exhaled slowly, kneeling near the remains but careful not to disturb them. "They weren't the first, it seems," he said in a hushed tone. "Dear God… must have gotten stuck, perhaps by some mechanical device triggered by the wrong choice. And then died here alone, in the dark."

Joseph's throat went dry. "A warning to us. Those letters from Anastasius hinted that only the faithful might pass. This must be the final test."

Lavrov walked slowly around the mosaic-laden cross, trailing a cautious fingertip over each symbol's brilliant tiles. "Look at this stone seal behind me," he said, gesturing with his flashlight at the colossal circular stone that appeared to block the next chamber. "Carved upon it is the Icon of Christ Pantocrator, see? Look at the top—the mosaic shape of His face, one hand raised in blessing, the other holding a book. Under the image of Christ, Joseph translated the Latin out loud: 'The key to access the key must be released when you identify the most important thing to me. Choose wisely.'"

Joseph pressed his lips together. "So… we must pick the one symbol among these that Jesus Himself would deem 'most important.' Then, presumably, we reach in and activate the release for that giant stone. If we choose incorrectly…" His gaze flitted to the skeleton's outstretched arm. "We face the same fate as him."

They circled each mosaic symbol in turn: The Chi Rho (marking His identity as the Messiah), the child ("Let the children come to me"), the Icon of the Apostle Peter (to whom He entrusted the keys), the world (God so loved the world), the dove (the Holy

336

Spirit), the cross (the center of the Christian faith's redemption), Mary (His mother), the lamb (Christ often depicted as the Lamb of God), the Ichthys (the fish symbol of Christ), the chalice (the Holy Eucharist), and an angel (messengers of God's will).

Each or any of them could be "the most important." Joseph felt lightheaded from the enormity of it. Generations of theological reflection had wrestled with what is "most important" to Christ. Could it be children? He cherished their innocence. The world? He died for it. The cross? The central sign of sacrifice. Peter? The rock on which He built the Church.

"It's maddening," Joseph said, shaking his head. "That skeleton apparently guessed wrong. He stuck his hand in the hole beneath the icon of Peter—" He pointed to the remains: the hole was set beneath the Icon of the Apostle Peter, ironically showing the man must have believed that was the correct choice.

Lavrov's face was taut. "A terrible end. It must have locked his arm instantly." He turned to Joseph. "Now is the moment, Professor. We stand at the final threshold. You know the Christians of this period better than anyone else. It is why we made the investment to bring you here. It's time for you to prove that we made the right choice." His voice was not cruel, but it held a certain gravity that gave Joseph a jolt: Lavrov was gently but unavoidably commanding him to risk his own arm.

Joseph swallowed, heart beating in his throat. "I... I can't be certain," he started. "Everything in Scripture points to so many essential truths—God's love for the world, the Holy Spirit's presence, the childlike faith He desires, the cross as the ultimate sacrifice. But He also gave the Keys to Peter." He rubbed his forehead, where sweat glistened. "Each symbol is so important."

Lavrov's expression softened, but urgency flickered in his eyes. "We cannot linger forever. Our mission depends on this. Now choose. Show me what your faith reveals. I stand behind you, Joseph."

With trembling breath, Joseph closed his eyes. The subtle hum of the chamber pressed in, as if the centuries were waiting. He offered a silent prayer, reaching deep into the simplest core of his heart. After a moment passed, Joseph's eyes were resolute.

Without hesitation—despite the hammering in his chest—Joseph crossed to the mosaic of Mary. The icon was rendered in a serene expression, her head draped in a deep-blue veil, arms parted as if in welcome. Below it yawned the dark hole. Joseph forced his breathing steady, remembering that skeleton in the corner. Then he extended his right arm and thrust it in.

The interior walls of the recess felt cool and rough. He slid his arm deeper, up to the elbow. The stone pressed around him, and for a heartbeat, fear seized him that it would lock. At the end, he felt something akin to a lever or protruding block. Summoning his courage, Joseph pressed firmly.

The block gave way with a scrape. He felt a smooth sliding motion, like a gear shifting. Then, with a rumble, the vertical beam of the eight-foot cross at the chamber's center seemed to pop forward from the wall revealing a large stone column. Joseph quickly withdrew his arm. The vertical stone beam of the cross was now offset by several inches, revealing that it was more than decorative. It was shaped like a stone column—indeed, a fulcrum.

A new hush descended. Lavrov's voice, full of admiration, broke the silence. "You did it! Joseph, that was brilliant."

Joseph sagged in relief, cradling his still-free arm. He turned to meet Lavrov's grin. "How did I know it was Mary?" With relief, Joseph said, "When I closed my eyes, I saw images swirling in my mind: the Cross, the child, the world. Then, in the darkness behind his eyelids, I rapidly saw a scene: Christ on the cross, gazing down. And there was Mary, His mother, standing with John. Jesus, in His last moments, ensuring her care, giving her to John, giving John to her. It was the final act of love at the end of His earthly life. If that was so dear to Him that He used precious breaths to secure it, how could anything overshadow that? How could anyone be more important than his mother?" He continued, "For Catholics, we always say we love Mary because Jesus loved her first, and best. She's the mother He chose, the mother He cared for to His dying breath. We believe Mary's significance is intimately bound with Christ's. Jesus loves her immeasurably. At that moment, I realized no other symbol could hold that same personal significance."

Lavrov placed a hand on Joseph's shoulder, his eyes shining with a certain reverence. "Your reflection humbles me, Joseph. I admire the conviction. Now, let's see if this fulcrum can unseal that massive stone door."

Joseph and Lavrov pressed hands against it, testing the weight. It was heavy, but balanced so it pivoted on a hidden axle near the base. Carefully, they lowered it horizontal, forming a sort of giant lever.

They maneuvered it across the room, every scrape echoing like thunder in the quiet. The mosaic cross's stone edges made a harsh sound sliding across the floor, sending pebbles rolling. Eventually, they positioned it at the stone pivot point of the circular seal. With a groan of stone on stone, they set the cross's base into the pivot.

"All right," Joseph said, pressing gloved palms to the rough surface. "When we apply force, the top end should nudge the seal out of its recess. But be ready. It might only move partially."

Lavrov gritted his teeth. "Yes, let's do it together."

They leaned in unison, applying steady pressure. The fulcrum pressed into the seal's edge. For a moment, the stone refused to budge, as though centuries of spiritual tension held it fast. Then it gave with a heart-stopping crack—dust puffed from the edges and the entire circle of stone shifted a few inches. A whoosh of stale air blasted out, swirling around them in a sudden gust that smelled of ancient must and secrets locked away.

Joseph coughed, eyes watering from the unexpected rush. They pressed harder, trying to widen the gap enough for a person to slip through. The stone ground loudly, shifting more about a full meter open, but after that point it refused to move. The sheer mass was too great, the geometry of the chamber limiting their leverage. When they let up even slightly, the seal slid back into place, sealing itself with a resounding thud.

Lavrov wiped his brow, panting. "We can open it partially, but not all the way. If we let go, it slams shut. That's... quite the design."

Joseph turned to him. "It means we can't both go through. One of us has to keep pressing the lever, while the other slips inside. That's the only way to hold the stone in position. It's too heavy for anything else."

A gleam of purpose danced in Lavrov's eyes. "Yes. Then so be it. Joseph, no one has more right than you to see what's beyond that seal. You discovered the correct symbol. You interpret the texts. You alone recognized Mary as the key. I will remain here, keep the stone from rolling back fully. You pass inside, retrieve the Keys if they're indeed there. Then come back."

Joseph's heart hammered. Part of him yearned for this moment— he had dreamed of it, studied it, prayed about it. Yet now, standing at the precipice, he felt a sudden dread. The swirling drama of CIA entanglements, of potential conflict with Russia, of personal revelations about sacred relics loomed large in his thoughts. He realized with sinking clarity that once he claimed the relic, the real fights would begin. Still, how could he refuse? This was his life's purpose. Or was it?

He swallowed. "I understand," he said quietly, mind flicking to his pregnant wife, to the father who might be living his last months. He could sense the unstoppable momentum that had brought him here.

Lavrov clasped his hand. "I trust you, Joseph," he said, his voice thick with resolve. "You'll handle them with reverence."

Joseph nodded, stepping up to the lever again. "On your count, we push. Once there's enough space for me to slip through, hold it steady. I'll be as quick as I can."

Lavrov moved to stand at the pivot, bracing his body. "Ready?" he asked.

Joseph set his feet, gripping the stone fulcrum. "Ready."

Together, they pulled. The stone seal shifted with a spine-tingling groan. Dust and grit rained down in an avalanche of motes. Slowly, the gap opened: half a foot, a full foot, two feet wide. Lavrov poured his weight onto the lever. The stone hung there, trembling with violent tension, as the seal opened enough for Joseph to slip into the chamber. Joseph's mind flooded with thoughts. His heart pounded with the finality of crossing from one life to another. He was stepping into the heart of a millennia-old secret, the culmination of everything Pope Gregory and Bishop Anastasius had struggled to protect. Even as excitement surged, he felt dread coil in his stomach. Because retrieving the Keys wouldn't just fulfill a dream, it would blow open the door to new dangers and moral quandaries. The relic's powers could tilt destinies, and the entire world might change if the wrong people laid hands on them.

In that moment, Joseph realized: he was living the exact moment he'd fantasized about in his academic pursuits. Instead of unbridled joy, he felt a solemn weight, as though the entire chamber pressed upon his shoulders. He'd give anything, ironically, not to be here now, if it meant his family were safe and the relics could remain untainted by worldly agendas. Yet there was no going back.

"Go!" Lavrov grunted, muscles corded, veins visible in his neck. At this word, Joseph leapt through the opening into the final chamber.

TWENTY-FOUR

The Encounter Between the Powers

Joseph stepped through the threshold into an air thick with incense and centuries of dust. A moment ago, the hush of anticipation had almost lulled him. Now, the hush turned ominous. The corridor behind him narrowed like the throat of a winding cave, gradually giving way to a space immeasurably more elaborate than anything he had seen in the prior chamber. Here, under the flickering half-light of his headlamp, he beheld a marvel of Byzantine craftsmanship, half-buried beneath centuries of rubble and newly revealed by their dangerous excavation.

For long moments he simply stood there, heart pounding, rooted to the stone floor. The sense of holiness and dread mingled together. Though half collapsed in areas, the chapel-like enclosure still shone with a regal, otherworldly grandeur. Pillars carved with braided vines rose from cracked bases to meet a half-dome overhead, the surfaces encrusted in flaking gold leaf. The walls exuded an age-old solemnity, as if they, too, had witnessed centuries of prayers whispered by quaking believers in a world beset by invasions and disasters.

Clusters of ancient candles—long burned to their stubs—lay scattered across the floor amid shards of once-pristine marble. Chiseled into the walls, faint icons of saints glimmered with bits of gold filigree, tarnished but still luminous in the feeble dancing glow that Joseph's lamp provided. Every whisper of movement seemed amplified; the acoustics of the place magnified the smallest shift of a foot or scraping of a bag. An atmosphere of haunting stillness pervaded, as though the hush had endured since the day the reliquary chamber was sealed, waiting for someone to stir it again.

He exhaled slowly, aware of the dust swirling through the beam of his headlamp. Beside him, Dr. Alexei Lavrov—still holding open the old seal—lifted his own lamp, which cast elongated, jittering shadows along the] columns. The flicker of illumination revealed mosaics underfoot, each a swirl of azure, gold, and carnelian depicting biblical scenes. But it was the object at the end of the room that drew Joseph's full attention now—a large, ornate chest set atop a chunk of carved stone. The front panel showed faint images of Christ's face, the strong brow and gentle gaze still discernible despite the centuries. The wood had a deep ebony sheen, inlaid with hammered bronze and silver, forming intricate loops reminiscent of Celtic interlacing. Patches of faded paint revealed faint outlines of Mary's sorrowful eyes, etched in a style reminiscent of the earliest Byzantine iconography.

Joseph's voice shook with both excitement and reverence as he described what he saw to Lavrov. "These images, Dr. Lavrov! There are early Christian images of Jesus and Mary!" He advanced, gingerly stepping over collapsed blocks of marble. "This style... the elongated fingers, the slightly enlarged eyes... The technique with the gold background behind Mary's face? This might be earlier than any known icon we have. Possibly late first or second century. This is an archeological gold mine!"

He reached out, not to touch the precious relic but to hover his fingers near an image of the Virgin holding the Christ Child. The paint, though chipped, retained a haunting vibrancy. Mary's robe folded with lines of gold that shimmered faintly, as though, even in the midst of ruin, the image preserved an echo of divine light. Joseph's heart pounded. Every academic fiber in his being wanted to examine each brushstroke, each hammered gold accent, if only to confirm whether these were among the earliest surviving Christian images. Next to Mary's image was the face of Jesus: symmetrical and kind, the large eyes seeming to gaze directly into one's soul.

Lavrov stepped up behind him, his own breath coming in taut bursts. "Professor Scanlon," he said brusquely, "I understand your fascination. But I must remind you—do you see the Keys? The reason we came, do you see them anywhere?"

Joseph tore his gaze away from the image. The question jabbed at the intense academic wonder he felt—still, Lavrov was right. Everything had led to this moment: the excavation, the cryptic references in Pope Gregory's letters, the hidden hints of Bishop Anastasius's cunning plan to protect the Keys of St. Peter. Joseph swept his headlamp slowly across the reliquary's broad top, then around the perimeter of the chamber. "I... I don't see them," he murmured. A wave of disappointment threatened. At that moment, his beam of light fell upon a small carved block of stone. There, nestled on the top, lay two golden lengths, ring-shaped handles catching the lamplight. And on the surface beneath, faintly etched, were the unmistakable words: "CLAVES PETRI."

Joseph let out a gasp that echoed in the hush. "There they are," he whispered in awe. "The Keys of St. Peter."

He approached slowly, feeling each step resonate through his entire body. The pillar on which they lay had a carved inscription around its circumference, each letter chipped and eroded. He recognized snippets of Latin references: "Tu es Petrus..." and "Super hanc petram aedificabo..." He whispered translations to himself: "You are Peter, and on this rock I will build..." The biblical allusions struck him deeply, stirring the old faith that had guided him since his youth.

In the faint glare, the Keys seemed humbler and more ancient than he had ever imagined. Solid gold, yes, but shaped like any typical set of Roman keys from the first century. Each was roughly six inches long and bore a characteristic L-shape: a straight shaft with a perpendicular extension—the bit. The handles (or bows) were ring-shaped, but unlike the typical rings of an average Roman key, these were elaborately wrought. Interwoven circles formed continuous loops, an infinity pattern that shimmered and twisted along the gold. As Joseph leaned closer, he noted how the designs appeared not hammered on, but seamlessly integrated into the gold's structure—a craftsmanship beyond what he believed common in the first century.

Where the bit began, the gold parted in a cruciform design, a geometric cross that extended or cut away from the central shaft, turning each key's bit into the shape of a cross. Every edge glinted with subtle ridges, as though the cross shape so there was no mistaking the importance.

Mesmerized, Joseph murmured, "Only the Cross of Christ can unlock heaven..." The moment crystallized something in him: centuries of theology and metaphors colliding with tangible reality. He couldn't tear his eyes from them. The shining gold against the ancient stone, the swirling dust in the lamplight, the hush in the air— it was all too holy, too charged.

He swallowed, mind reeling, remembering the warnings they had found in the old parchments: references to "evil spirits seeking a home" if the Keys were misused. In the quiet gloom of the chamber, he recalled lines from Gregory's letter: how the soldier from centuries past was said to be overtaken by darkness when he tried to cut them down. He trembled slightly, searching for his resolve in the faith he had practiced all his life.

Closing his eyes, Joseph whispered a prayer, his voice surprisingly steady in the vaulted hush: "Jesus, you gave these keys to St. Peter. I ask you to give me the humility and the grace to bring them back to his successor. Amen."

He reached out. Expectation, dread, and wonder coalesced into a single heartbeat. With cautious reverence, he lifted the pair of golden keys in his hand. The metal felt cold—yet he expected some kind of jolt, a surge of energy, perhaps. But nothing immediate happened. The dust-laden air remained still, the icons silent.

Lavrov's voice broke the spell in a sharp bark: "Hurry up Professor! I can't hold this open all day."

Joseph turned to see the Russian scholar's face lit by a single over-head lamp beam. Lavrov's eyes gleamed with triumph, his features taut with adrenaline. "I have them," Joseph said softly, cradling the keys. An unlikely sensation filled him—both awe and dread.

Lavrov nodded curtly. "Good. Then let's go. All this art you're so fascinated by can wait. We must get out of here now. We'll come back for the rest. But these Keys are the priority."

Joseph wanted to protest—he yearned to secure the icons, the earliest depictions of Mary and Christ. But he knew better than to argue. He gently set the keys into his excavation pack, tucking them in a padded compartment. The bag's closure gave a faint click.

When Joseph arrived to the entrance, Lavrov pushed the fulcrum extra hard creating space for Joseph to exit. The stone slab rumbled back into place, sealing the chamber once more. Dust showered from the top, and the heavy echoes of grinding stone reverberated through the passage, leaving them on the safer side of the partition.

A swirl of excitement lit Lavrov's voice. "We have them. Finally, after all these centuries." His triumph was tangible as he clapped Joseph on the shoulder.

He turned to Lavrov, "Let's hurry up and get out of here."

Abruptly, Lavrov caught Joseph's elbow, halting him. "One moment Joseph," he said quietly, voice taut with an edge Joseph had never quite heard from him. "I need to see the Keys. Now."

Joseph felt a sudden churn of alarm. "They're in my pack. Once we're up top, I'll pull them out. No reason to linger in this cramped—"

Lavrov cut him off by drawing a pistol from inside his coat. The muzzle pointed straight at Joseph's chest. For a moment, Joseph's mind reeled. He had known there was a lurking danger in dealing with these Russians, but he hadn't expected Lavrov—this polished academic—to brandish a gun at him.

In clipped, icy English, Lavrov said, "Dr. Scanlon, you've done amazing work, but your assignment has now come to its end. Hand me the Keys. Right this second."

Joseph's mouth went dry. Slowly he raised his hands, heart rattling with adrenaline. "Take it easy. Please, Dr. Lavrov, no need for a gun."

Every inch of Joseph's body was screaming with tension. He tried to keep his breathing under control. "Yes, yes," he continued softly, "They're yours. I have no illusions about them. I'll give them to you, no question. Let me just..." He slipped off his excavation pack, setting it on the ground in front of him. He unzipped it carefully, stalling for time, scanning the gloom for some possible ally or route of escape.

Lavrov advanced a single step, gun unwavering. "Do you think me naïve?" he demanded in a quiet, menacing tone. "I assure you, the gun is absolutely necessary. Now, drop the act, CIA Agent Scanlon."

Joseph's mind spun. "CIA? Dr. Lavrov that has been the worst joke since I arrived and I still don't think it's funny—"

Lavrov cut him off with a sardonic laugh. "I wish it was just a joke. God, how I wish. But I have it on reliable authority that you're a CIA informant. Oleg always suspected you. We've had your communications monitored from the start. At first, you were squeaky clean—strangely so. But after you visited your in-laws, Oleg picked up some interesting intel. While you were there at their home, he left his car and found a vantage point to keep you under surveillance. With a camera and telephoto lens, he took pictures of your rooftop meeting with Aziz Haddad. Oleg submitted the intel to the FSB in Moscow and after a few weeks we discovered that Haddad is a man with ties to the Chaldean militia. The same militia that fought not only ISIS but also the Syrian government, a government Russia supports. Our team started monitoring Haddad and they found him meeting with CIA operative, Agent Mark DeLuca. You have been feeding intel on our operation to the CIA this entire time! Admit it!"

At that moment, Lavrov's pulled out his radio. "Oleg, come in." "Here" Oleg responded. Lavrov grinned into the radio. "We have the keys." The voice responded, "Have you taken care of Scanlon?" Lavrov responded, "I'm in process now. I will be back to the surface in less than an hour" Oleg ended, "Be safe boss, over and out."

Joseph felt the blood drain from his face. So they knew. And from the beginning, he'd believed Lavrov was an unwitting academic with reluctant FSB ties. Yet here Lavrov was, gun in hand, spinning out Joseph's entire cover story.

"That's insane," Joseph insisted, forcing a shaky laugh. "You're letting Oleg's paranoia run wild. If there is a connection, it has got to be a coincidence. I told you, I was just visiting my in-laws—"

"I'm not a fool," Lavrov retorted, calm as a serpent. "And now, not even the CIA can protect you. Russia will reclaim her rightful place in the world, under President Volkov's leadership. The Western church has become apostate—pandering to homosexuality, transgenderism, institutional promiscuity. God has left the West. The only hope for Christianity in this next epoch will come from the Orthodox faith. Only President Volkov has the vision to restore the Russian Empire and the Russian Orthodox faith."

Joseph listened, stunned at the fervor in Lavrov's voice. In the musty corridor, the scholar-turned-fanatic pressed closer, the gun muzzle glinting in Joseph's lamp. "Not only will these Keys heal our president," Lavrov continued, "but they will imbue the Russian Orthodox Church with authority to bring Christ's reign to all nations without any of the decadent compromise of the Western Church."

Joseph tried to keep calm. "Lavrov... you have no idea what you're dealing with. The keys cannot be used ."

His words were cut short by Lavrov stepping even closer. The barrel of the gun was inches from Joseph's chest. Joseph raised his hands again, nonthreatening. "All right," he whispered, "All right. Let me show you." He reached into his pack, feeling the cold metal lumps. The golden keys.

Lavrov's eyes shone, entirely rapt. His voice trembled with unhidden longing. "Give them here."

Joseph gingerly set them on top of the pack. In the half-light, the Celtic-like interlace on the handles glimmered. The cross-shaped bits cast small shadows across the corridor floor. Lavrov inhaled sharply, as if physically struck by the sight. He lowered to a crouch, the pistol still angled at Joseph, and gingerly picked up the keys. The weight of them made him exhale in a small gasp.

Even from a step away, Joseph could see that Lavrov was en-thralled. The man's breath quivered, his eyes locked onto the gold. His lips parted as though he were gazing upon a relic of unimagi-nable worth. A certain mania flickered across his face—a primal hunger for power, but also something akin to spiritual reverence. He pressed his thumb over the cruciform bit, then traced the in-terlacing patterns on the bow.

Joseph tried to speak. "You have no idea what you're exposing yourself to. The parchment warns that misusing the Keys invites a darkness, an evil —"

Lavrov rose abruptly, cutting him off. His gaze bored into Joseph's, cold and certain. "Let's talk about the difference between you and me, Professor. You lie about your identity, you cheat on your pregnant wife—Oleg told me how he found Natalia in your arms—"

Joseph's eyes flashed in fury shaking his head.

But Lavrov continued, almost in a mocking litany. "A lying, cheat-ing failure of a professor who dares hold these Keys. And yet you handled them with no ill effect. If even you can do that, then how much more am I deserving? I am selfless, I am righteous, and Rus-sia is righteous. We shall be protected."

With that, Lavrov lifted the Keys out of the pack to the level of his eyes. He stared at them with trembling exultation, oblivious to Joseph's warnings. Lavrov's eyes widened with an almost otherworldly gleam as he held the keys aloft, their cold gold glinting under the dim light. His fingers cradled them with a reverence that bordered on obsession, each key a promise of power and secrets long hidden. A shiver ran through him, a ripple of pure delight that seemed to electrify his very soul. He marveled at the intricate designs etched into their surface, symbols whispering of ancient knowledge and untold dominion. The world around him faded into insignificance, all sounds muted, all sights dimmed, as his entire being focused on the keys' seductive allure. They were precious beyond measure, a treasure that transcended the mundane and beckoned him into a realm of limitless possibilities and the beginning of Russia's glorious revival. Lavrov's breath came in shallow gasps, exhilaration and awe entwining in an intoxicating dance. In that moment, he was both master and servant to the keys, a willing captive to their irresistible allure.

Then, in one horrifying instant, both men's headlamps started flickering simultaneously. The corridor plunged into strobing darkness. The beams of light fluttered like a malfunctioning strip light, revealing quick flashes of the stone walls in stark relief—on, off, on, off.

A sound—faint at first—rose from deeper in the tunnel, the direction leading back to the sealed chamber. A low whisper, like wind scraping across a thousand dried bones. A roiling shadow seemed to congeal at the very limit of their flickering lamp beams. The swirling darkness coalesced into a shape, then dissipated, then re-formed. The strobe-like effect twisted the perspective, making it impossible to gauge distance. But the presence was undeniably moving toward them.

Lavrov raised his pistol at the silhouette. "Stop!" he commanded, voice trembling between anger and panic. The shape advanced, a mass of swirling black vapor that seemed to devour the flickering light. Lavrov fired a single shot. The muzzle flash lit the corridor in a burst of orange.

"Stay back!" Lavrov bellowed, emptying the magazine in rapid succession. Bullets ricocheted off the stone or disappeared into that vapor with no visible effect. The muzzle flashes provided harsh snapshots: Lavrov's contorted face, the corridor's chipped walls, Joseph flinching, arms raised protectively.

Then, as the final round was expended, the black shape surged forward—like living smoke coiling around Lavrov. He staggered back, dropping the spent pistol with a clatter. "Scanlon!" he shrieked. "Help me!"

But Joseph froze. He recognized the sensation from the manu-scripts describing the Lombard who first stole the keys. Some vile presence, unleashed by the apparent pride and arrogance, was sweeping over Lavrov. Joseph scrambled backward. The swirling shadow clung to Lavrov's arms, his shoulders, writhing with pred-atory purpose.

Lavrov's eyes went wide with primal terror. He convulsed vio-lently, dropping to his knees. It was as though his body was a pup-pet controlled by unseen strings, limbs jerking in unnatural angles like a snake in agony. His back arched, his mouth open in a silent scream. Joseph watched in horror as the man's pupils dilated and a slow, unearthly hiss emanated from deep in his throat. Lavrov's convulsions intensified, each spasm more violent than the last, until his body finally went limp. He collapsed to the cold stone floor, utterly motionless. For a heartbeat, silence reigned in the corridor, broken only by the distant drip of water echoing in the darkness.

Joseph hesitated, his mind grappling with the grim possibility that Lavrov might be dead. The thought compelled him to inch closer, his heart pounding with trepidation. His headlamp flickered, casting jittery shadows that danced eerily across the walls. He knelt beside Lavrov, leaning in to check for any sign of breath. The eyes were closed, the face slack and devoid of its usual sternness.

Just as Joseph's face neared Lavrov's, the eyes snapped open. Joseph recoiled in horror, a strangled gasp escaping his lips. The eyes staring back at him were not the eyes of the Lavrov he knew. They glowed with an unholy luminescence, an otherworldly gaze that seemed to pierce through the very fabric of Joseph's soul. It was as if some ancient, malevolent intelligence now resided within Lavrov's once-familiar visage, watching him with a dark, inscrutable intent.

The corridor felt suddenly colder, the oppressive atmosphere pressing in around Joseph as he scrambled backward, his mind reeling with fear and disbelief.

Guttural words drifted from Lavrov's parted lips: "Furetur... mactet... perdat..." The Latin hammered into Joseph's mind: "Steal, kill, destroy..." He recognized them from the lines that Jesus spoke of the Evil One.

As Joseph retreated, the possessed Lavrov snapped upright. The strobing headlamps provided an eerie repetition of darkness and glare. The man's face was twisted, veins bulging at the temples. He advanced, chanting the unholy refrain, "Furetur, mactet, perdat... Furetur, mactet, perdat..." with each flicker of light. The golden keys dangled from his clenched fist, occasionally catching a flash of brilliance before disappearing in blackness again.

Joseph's survival instincts flared. He spun on his heel, lunging away. In the flicker of lamplight, the corridor's uneven stones snagged underfoot, sending him crashing to the ground. Pain shot through his knees and forearms. His excavation pack tumbled beside him. Adrenaline roared through his veins as he twisted onto his back, heart hammering.

Lavrov—no, the demon controlling him—pounced. They collided in a tangle of limbs. Joseph gagged as the man's hands, still clutching the keys, pressed against his throat. The key's cold edges dug into Joseph's skin, leaving lines that burned with friction. Through the strobe effect of the malfunctioning lamps, Joseph glimpsed the demonic mania in Lavrov's eyes—an unholy delight, as though it relished strangling him.

He tried to wedge his arm against Lavrov's chest, to push him off, but the man's strength was staggering. Joseph's fingers scrabbled against the stone floor. He felt the demon pressing the keys deeper into his neck, the ring-shaped handles grinding painfully into his collarbone. The choking pressure robbed him of breath.

In the chaotic flashes, Joseph spotted the Bible half-exposed in his pack, the carbon-fiber blade's handle popping out right next to it. It was nearly in reach—maybe a foot away. He stretched out his fingers, fighting the black spots forming in his vision as oxygen slipped away.

Memories unspooled in that suffocating haze, each one a fleeting glimpse of his life flashing before his eyes. First, his parents, their faces etched with love and care; then the tender warmth of his wife's touch on their wedding night; then his in-laws, their laughter echoing in the vibrant streets of Antakya. His mind drifted further back, to his mother's voice weaving tales of Saint Charbel casting out demons, the saint's voice resonating with the powerful invocation of the holy name of Jesus. Clinging to the remnants of his strength, Joseph summoned every ounce of will to speak. With a final, desperate breath, he croaked the name, "Jesus." It was barely more than a whisper, an exhalation of faith, but it was enough.

Even though the word spoken was without great volume, passion or strength, the effect was immediate and violent. The demon controlling Lavrov recoiled backward as though struck by an invisible force. Joseph gulped air, chest heaving, tears stinging his eyes. He managed to scramble sideways, near the pack. The demon-possessed man hissed, stumbling, yet already the dark force steeled him to attack again.

In the stuttering lamplight, Joseph saw Lavrov pivot, face twisting in renewed fury. The man lunged. Joseph frantically grasped for the handle of the carbon-fiber blade. But Lavrov's hand clamped over Joseph's mouth, intent on silencing him before he could speak the Holy Name again. The pressure on Joseph's jaw was excruciating; his lips were crushed together, preventing sound.

Summoning the last reserves of strength, Joseph found the handle and thrust upward with the blade. He felt the moment it met resistance, sliding into Lavrov's side, lodging between ribs. Lavrov shrieked, an unearthly wail that reverberated with layered voices. With the pressure off his mouth Joseph took a deep breath and then twisted the blade further and pulled it up into the lung. The screech transformed into a prolonged, hellish squeal, a sound not fully human.

Blood bubbled from Lavrov's lips, his chest convulsing. Seizing the chance, Joseph glared directly into the man's distorted features, addressing the malignant spirits that had claimed him. Regaining his composure over the creature, Joseph spoke with boldness "These signs will follow those who believe," Joseph gritted out, voice trembling but resolute. "In my name - the name of Jesus - they will cast out demons. I command you—spirits of murder, fear, control, hatred—leave this body now, in Jesus' name!"

Immediately, Lavrov's face twisted with new contortions, each functioning name of a spirit evoking flinches and jerks, as if the words themselves seared and bound the demons. The keys slipped from Lavrov's grasp, clattering onto the stone floor. The swirling darkness around him flickered, then peeled away. For a heartbeat, it seemed to coil and vanish into the deeper shadows of the corridor, as if banished by the invocation of Christ's power.

When the savage convulsions ended, Lavrov collapsed, no longer pinned to Joseph. Joseph rolled free, gasping, the blade still embedded in the man's side. Lavrov's eyes fluttered, wide with confusion. A wet gargle escaped his mouth—blood dribbled over his chin. The demon was gone. Only the man remained, undone by the mortal wound.

Joseph knelt at the side of the man who had, ironically, both led him to the Keys and attempted to murder him. Lavrov's gaze locked onto Joseph, desperation and regret shining in those final moments. The words in his throat were garbled by blood, but Joseph could sense the sorrow, the sudden clarity of the deceptions and strongholds of the mind that led the man to his fate.

Joseph swallowed tears. He recalled the weight of these Keys, the centuries of warnings, and the tragedy that played out time and again when men tried to exploit them. The most powerful reality that Dr Lavrov's face communicated was regret - deep and utter sorrow for what he had done. Joseph clearly understood that this man was expressing repentance. From that place, he spoke out "Dr. Lavrov, I forgive you. In Jesus' name, I release you of my anger."

Lavrov's eyes brimmed with tears. Joseph's own cheeks were wet as he prayed, the words spilling out from a place beyond reason, guided by the Holy Spirit himself: "Father, forgive this man... He didn't know what he was doing. Holy Spirit, comfort him. Mother Mary, pray for him now, at the hour of his death."

A gentle hush fell, as if the corridor itself recognized the solemnity. Lavrov's tense features relaxed, his gaze drifting, focusing somewhere beyond Joseph's shoulder. His chest rose once, shuddered, then stilled. The last of his breath escaped.

Joseph closed his eyes, stunned. He'd just witnessed a man possessed, delivered, and then dead in a matter of minutes. The unholy presence had vanished, but the dread still hovered in the stale air. Slowly, Joseph pulled his blade free, wiping the handle on his pants in a daze. He noticed the Keys lying just a foot away, splattered with a few drops of blood.

In the flicker of his lamp, Joseph gently retrieved them, folding them into his trembling hands. Now the corridor lay silent except for the rasp of Joseph's breath. With trembling reverence, he put the Keys back into the padded section of his excavation pack, zipping it carefully. He inhaled, trying to calm the riot of emotions.

Then a clarifying thought snapped him to reality: the FSB agents, perhaps a dozen, still waited outside. He rose, painfully aware of the throbbing in his bruised body, the sting on his neck from where the Keys had pressed, the trembling of adrenaline in his limbs. He stole a final glance at Lavrov's corpse. The man's wide eyes stared emptily at the ceiling. Joseph whispered a final farewell, crossing himself. Then he turned to face the darkness ahead.

A flicker of memory returned—the words from Scripture: "On this rock I will build my church, and the gates of hell will not prevail against it." Joseph couldn't ignore the bitter irony: they had literally braved a gate beneath the earth, unleashing darkness upon themselves. Yet in the end, Christ's name had prevailed. If God had protected Joseph thus far, maybe God would finish what He started in Joseph.

Down the final tunnel was the way out. And beyond that, his un-born child, his wife, and a mother whose fervent prayers had evi-dently shielded him from the darkest evil.

He steeled himself. Tugging the pack over his shoulders, put the keys back into the safe pocket of his excavation pack and whis-pered, "Let's go." The words were a vow as much as an instruction. With that word, he set off toward the uncertain light, toward the echo of voices, heart pounding with a dire mixture of hope and dread.

TWENTY-FIVE

The Escape Attempt

Joseph's chest heaved with ragged breaths as he sprinted through the sweltering darkness, the stale tunnel air pressing around him like a vice. His boots hammered the damp ground, echoing wildly off the stone walls. One thought looped through his mind: Get out. Get out now. The ancient labyrinth, carved in Byzantine times, seemed determined to swallow him whole, but he forced himself onward until the single pinprick of light ahead began to blossom—an opening. That was his salvation.

He burst through the low arch at the tunnel's end, stumbling forward into a spacious cavern lit by a few electric lanterns. Up above, at the edge of a rocky ledge, two silhouettes loomed—Dima and Yakov, scanning the darkness with anxious faces. They turned sharply when they saw him approach, startled by the clamor of his footsteps.

"Joseph?" Dima called, his voice bouncing off the stone. "What the hell is going on down there? We heard...shouting, gunshots, and crashes. Echoes everywhere."

Joseph lifted a trembling hand, pointing back into the gloom from where he'd come. "Pull me up—now!" he shouted, the urgency in his tone jolting both men to action. He lunged for the rope that hung from the edge of the ledge and tied in. Dima and Yakov grabbed the top and began hauling with all their might.

Adrenaline exploded through Joseph's limbs as he ascended. He risked a glance back and nearly choked on fear. Shadows writhed in the corridor behind him, half-seen nightmares lurking. The worst trap of all... The memory of it still scorched his mind.

At last, he clawed his way onto the ledge. Yakov seized Joseph's arm, pulling him fully out of the vertical passage. Collapsing onto his side, Joseph coughed up dust and tried to steady his breathing. Dima knelt close, shining a flashlight into Joseph's eyes. "You look half-dead," he said, eyebrows drawn in concern. "Is Lavrov behind you? Where's the professor?"

Joseph forced himself upright, though he swayed with exhaustion. "Still down there." His voice was hoarse. "We...there was a trap— like nothing I've ever seen. You need to get down there. I need to go get help."

"We'll get down there in a moment" He flicked a glance toward Yakov. "Come on."

"Wait—" Joseph swallowed hard, forcing steadiness into his voice. "I have to go back to the top. We need a real team, maybe medical supplies. As you head down there, be very careful when you get down there."

In the panic of the situation, neither Dima nor Yakov questioned Joseph further. They simply nodded, adrenaline bright in their eyes. "All right," Dima said. "We'll go. But Joseph, if you can, bring others. We'll need ropes, harnesses, maybe an electric pump for the water."

Yakov gripped Joseph's forearm, then turned on his heel. "Come on, Dima," he muttered, voice taut. "We need to first find secure locations to anchor our gear to rappel down. We need to start now."

Joseph watched them begin their rappelling preparations. A pang of guilt knifed through him—he knew that the so-called rescue attempt might be in vain. Lavrov is still down there...but he needed to get out of there and make sure that Dima and Yakov were preoccupied.

He spun away, panting, and forced himself into motion to exit the caves with the keys in his pack. The tunnel system branched in multiple directions; he knew the correct route to the surface. Summoning the last bits of energy, he dashed along a corridor lined with dripping stone. At a small alcove, he paused to rummage inside his jacket. His hand emerged clutching an old deck of playing cards, or so it seemed—the CIA's VLF transmitter disguised as a deck. Quickly, he thumbed the hidden switch on its side.

A tiny LED glowed once, signifying activation. Joseph's mind raced. They said forty-five minutes to scramble a helicopter if he signaled. He twisted the bezel on his wristwatch, setting an alarm for the same. "Forty-five minutes," he whispered. The harsh tang of dread filled his mouth: *Would that be enough time?*

Without further hesitation, he stuffed the transmitter away and tore down the corridor. Soon, the passage sloped upwards, and a damp breeze told him he was nearing the subterranean bridge. This was the precarious crossing that had claimed Elena and Mortem. Joseph's stomach twisted at the memory. The place was a byword for betrayal not hope.

He arrived at the yawning chasm, the subterranean dam's floodgate just visible as a shadowy mass beneath the walkway. Carefully, Joseph edged onto the first platform. No shift, no ominous rumble. He exhaled. The mechanism was designed for heavier loads, apparently. With just his body weight, it wouldn't re-trigger the watery doom they'd encountered.

Still, his heart pounded a furious cadence as he inched forward. Every footstep sent an echo bouncing into the darkness. *Don't look down.* But inevitably, he peeked. The memory of Elena's scream as she vanished over the side seared through him, but he had to focus. He forced one slow step, then another, distributing his weight across the precarious stone.

Halfway across, a wave of vertigo threatened to buckle his knees. Over the pounding in his ears, Joseph willed himself calm. He was alone. There was no team to help him if he fell. With a final burst of courage, he sprinted the last few yards, practically hurling himself onto solid platform of the other side. Again, no mechanism triggering at his weight. He climbed up into the entrance of the tunnel.

The narrow stony corridor that Joseph recognized from earlier explorations. He followed it, guided by faint touches of cooler air. He eventually emerged into a large cavern where dust motes danced in the beam of his flashlight. Giant stalactites hung from the ceiling like the fangs of some primordial beast.

In that vast, echoing space, the hush felt absolute—save for the drip of water from overhead. Joseph's own steps sounded alarmingly loud. He pressed on, weaving between jagged boulders until he found the final passage leading upward. This route, a winding corridor, had once connected the sublevels of St. Peter's Church with the deeper labyrinth. He took it at a half-run now, ignoring the burning in his calves.

Time blurred. By the time Joseph glimpsed the faint glow of sunlight reflecting on old stone, adrenaline coursed so powerfully that he hardly felt winded. He checked his watch: only thirty-five minutes had passed since he set the transmitter. The CIA had promised that if they were inbound, they'd arrive near the forty-five-minute mark.

Ten more minutes to wait. But wait *here*? He realized he was near the final steps that ascended into the room behind the sanctuary. That crypt opened into the old sanctuary, and from there out to the courtyard. If he waited unseen, maybe the CIA team would find him quickly. But a swirl of footsteps from the Church destroyed that plan: one of Oleg's men, a burly Russian security contractor brandishing an assault rifle, emerged from a side corridor and spotted Joseph in an instant.

"Ostanovit'!" the guard shouted, voice echoing. A stream of heated Russian followed, too fast for Joseph's limited vocabulary to parse.

"I need help!" Joseph yelled back in English, raising his empty hands in a universal sign of harmlessness. "Professor Lavrov is in danger—he's badly hurt! I have to get medical support."

"Why do you have blood?" the guard demanded, pointing at Joseph's shirt, which was stained a deep red around the collar and sleeves. His own words in Russian were incomprehensible to Joseph, but the meaning was clear from his outraged expression.

Joseph shook his head vigorously, stepping forward with feigned authority. "I'm going to get a rescue team. Understand? Res-cue. I am in command, stand aside."

The guard's brow knitted in confusion. He barked more Russian, still pointing at the blood. But Joseph pressed on, striding confidently past him as though outraged at being delayed. The guard hesitated, uncertain how to respond to this brazen attitude.

Inwardly, Joseph's heart hammered. He had no illusions about how precarious this was. But in the midst of crises, acting as though you are in charge can sometimes defuse confrontation.

The guard turned to follow, sputtering in Russian. Joseph repeated, "It's an emergency. A trap. Lavrov hurt. Move aside!" Then, without waiting for a response, Joseph pushed open a heavy wooden door leading to the lower crypt corridor. He marched through, ignoring the guard's protests behind him.

The corridor ended in the old chiseled steps that ascended into the portion of St. Peter's Church that was carved from the mountainside. Centuries-old stone walls soared overhead. Flickering lights and scattered crates told Joseph that Lavrov's security detail had set up some equipment near the entrance. The echo of voices drifted from the church's main chamber.

Climbing the last of the stairs, Joseph stepped into the sanctuary. The pillars rose around him, half-buried in the rock. The early evening sun glowed through a side aperture. He was nearly out. But upon setting foot past a broken marble screen, he froze at the sight: a courtyard beyond the church threshold swarmed with Lavrov's men—at least eight or nine of them. Full body armor, ballistic helmets, machine guns, and even a rocket-propelled grenade launcher were visible.

Armed to the teeth. Joseph's stomach clenched. If they saw him, they might seize him on the spot. But he had no choice. He needed out.

Taking a breath, he stepped forward. Immediately, Oleg—towering, grim-faced, and clad in tactical gear—rounded the corner with a few subordinates. The muzzle of a rifle glinted in Oleg's grip. Spotting Joseph, Oleg's eyes flared with surprise, then darkened with suspicion.

"What you doing here?" Oleg demanded in thickly accented English. He looked Joseph up and down, gaze freezing on the blood staining his clothes. "And professor—where Professor Lavrov?"

Joseph forced as much urgency into his voice as possible. "There was a trap at the end, the most fierce we encountered. Lavrov triggered it. I barely escaped. He's still down there, likely injured. We need immediate help—medical, extraction, anything!"

A flicker of confusion crossed Oleg's face. "We tried radio contact. He did not answer." Then, suspicion replaced confusion. "What did you do to him?"

"I didn't do anything!" Joseph nearly snarled. "He told me to run. If he's not responding, it must be that the tunnel collapsed around him. We have no time to waste. Let me pass so I can get help from the city—ambulances, rescue workers. The professor might still be alive."

There was a murmur among the security men. Some looked uncertain, as if they might actually let Joseph pass. But Oleg took a step forward. His voice turned low and menacing. "Shut up, you CIA liar."

Joseph stiffened, his pulse leaping. He had to salvage this. Quickly he started a frantic explanation, using broad gestures to keep Oleg's attention. "Listen to me—I know you think I'm connected to the CIA because of my brother in law but I have nothing to do with him! My family depends on this job. I'd never sabotage it. I need that million-dollar reward if we find the Keys. Why would I put all of that at risk? I've been risking my life down there. You think I want to sabotage the mission? No, I want to earn that money so I can take care of my pregnant wife. She's carrying my child, Oleg!"

Oleg's expression wavered. Joseph hammered the point: "If I messed things up, I'd lose the reward. My in-laws live here in Antakya. I'd be endangering them if I was double-crossing anyone. Why would I do that? I'm not insane."

There was a flicker of empathy in Oleg's eyes. Joseph continued. "You think I'd throw away a fortune that could secure our future? We're so close. We had to push deeper. The professor was ahead of me. Then the trap came. I only got out because he insisted I go for help. You need to get down there now. I'm the only one who can secure emergency services because I speak Arabic and none of them speak Russian. I'm the only one who can go out and get help. If we're going to save him—and get those Keys—we have to move and we have to go now. Oleg, if you don't let me go, Lavrov will die and it will be your fault. You're fault! Time is running out!"

A tense silence thickened. Oleg glanced at the other men, reading their uncertain faces. Slowly, he jerked his chin at the soldier next to him, who had been pointing a pistol at Joseph's chest. "Lower your weapon," Oleg muttered.

The man obeyed, albeit reluctantly. Joseph let out a silent exhale of relief. "Thank you," he said, voice still taut. "You have no idea how dire this is. If he dies, everything we've worked for is gone."

Oleg's scowl deepened, but he gave Joseph a brisk nod. "All right. Let's get a team ready. Dima and Yakov might already be in the tunnels, but we can send more men to them. You—" He pointed to a cluster of armed guards. "Grab harnesses, ropes, first-aid kits. Move!"

Joseph forced a grateful expression. "Yes, that's perfect. Meanwhile, I'll head into the city and secure local medics or an emergency response group."

He started toward the courtyard's exit, weaving around overturned crates and was passing the statue of St. Peter carved from pale stone, the apostle's right hand brandishing a set of stone keys. Joseph hurried past, heart pounding. He was nearly free.

At that moment, Oleg's radio crackled to life, halting Joseph in his tracks beside the statue. Dima's voice came through, tense and urgent. "Oleg, come in. Do you read me?" Oleg snatched the radio from his belt, eyes narrowing with suspicion. "I'm here, Dima. What's the situation?" There was a brief pause, punctuated by the distant rumble of the underground. "We found Dr. Lavrov," Dima continued, his voice grim. "He's dead. And the keys— they're gone. Listen, you need to stop Joseph Scanlon right now." The courtyard seemed to shrink around them as a heavy silence fell. Joseph and Oleg locked eyes, a silent battle waged in their gazes. Joseph shook his head slowly, a desperate plea. But Oleg's resolve hardened. "Shoot him," he ordered the soldier, voice like steel. The soldier, hesitation evaporating, raised his weapon, the barrel aligning with Joseph's chest once more.

Joseph's eyes fell shut. *This is the end.* A surreal calm came over him, the rush of fear so intense it almost numbed him. He heard the squeak of the soldier's glove on the pistol grip, the faint intake of breath before the shot.

CRACK!

A single report echoed off the courtyard walls. Joseph flinched, expecting agony—but he felt no impact, no pain. Confused, he opened his eyes. The soldier who'd been about to shoot him tottered on his feet, then collapsed, a crimson hole blossoming in his temple.

For a stunned second, Joseph could only stare. What followed happened in slow motion to Joseph. The courtyard exploded with shouts as every Russian pivoted, weapons raised, scanning the mountainous rock face above the church. A voice boomed down:

"Take cover, habibi!"

Joseph's heart soared at the familiar accent: Aziz. His brother-in-law, the crack sniper from the Chaldean militia. He and three other men perched high on a rocky outcropping, rifles glinting. Another shot barked from the mountaintop, forcing two Russians behind a low wall.

Joseph hurled himself behind St. Peter's statue, adrenaline flooding his veins. Gunfire erupted on all sides, bullets pinging off stone. The Russians sprayed bursts upward, muzzle flashes lighting the courtyard like staccato lightning. Joseph ducked, shards of stone chipping away from the statue with each ricochet. One high-caliber round severed the statue's right hand, sending the carved stone keys clattering at Joseph's feet.

He gritted his teeth at the savage onslaught. Over the deafening blasts, he heard a cry from above: one of Aziz's men had been hit. The man's agonized shout resounded against the rocky slope, and Joseph felt a cold dread coil within him. They were outnumbered, pinned down. This might be a short-lived rescue.

His gaze dropped to the pistol that had fallen from the dead soldier's grip. He snatched it, ducking as bullets whizzed overhead. He crammed himself against the statue's base, feeling bits of stone pelt his shoulders.

Aziz and his men took a moment's respite to reload. The Russians, emboldened, tried to maneuver around the courtyard's perimeter. Joseph spotted one agent creeping along the perimeter wall, aiming for a vantage point. Leaning out from behind the statue, Joseph steadied the pistol with both hands, inhaled, and squeezed the trigger once. The gun bucked in his grip. The man cried out, clutching his side, and dropped behind cover.

Aziz's shout ripped through the chaos: "Joseph, run! Get out of here!"

But Joseph couldn't. Bullets streamed across the courtyard. The Russians were hauling their wounded comrade away, returning covering fire so intense that crossing the open space was suicidal. Joseph was pinned behind the statue of St. Peter, the statues stone scarred with fresh bullet holes.

Then, from the Church entrance, another Russian soldier emerged carrying a massive riot shield. Bullets from Aziz's vantage pinged harmlessly off the heavy ballistic plate. A muzzle peeked through a slot, firing bursts that forced Joseph to flatten himself behind the statue. The shielded soldier advanced, step by relentless step, only about thirty meters away now.

Joseph's mind raced. The man was unstoppable with that shield, and Aziz's attempts to shoot him from above were futile. Could

Joseph surrender? If he did, Oleg would no doubt exact revenge for his soldiers deaths. The entire stand-off felt hopeless.

The situation looked lost. The shielded man advanced methodically, while other Russians fanned out behind him. In moments, they would be on Joseph, gun barrels pressed to his head. Even if Aziz and his men kept firing, they likely almost out of ammo. Joseph could sense the inevitability. He took a shaky breath, imagining the final bullet that might take him.

But then a strange noise—distant at first—caught Joseph's ear. It was a low hum that rapidly escalated into a thunderous roar, bouncing off the surrounding cliffs. The Russians paused, weapons half-lowered, as everyone cocked their heads to locate the source. It grew louder and louder, a mechanical pounding that rattled the courtyard.

Suddenly, from around the far side of the mountain, a sleek black helicopter streaked into view—dark as a raven, with a menacing turret protruding from its side. A Blackhawk. Painted matte to blend with the shadows, it soared overhead, the rotating blades beating the air like an oncoming storm. A door gunner manned a minigun, the barrel glinting in the last sunlight.

A loudspeaker crackled to life in Russian: "Drop your weapons! Lay down arms, immediately!"

For a split second, no one moved. Then Oleg roared, "Fire!" and the Russians unleashed a hail of bullets at the chopper. The muzzle flashes illuminated the courtyard in a frantic strobe.

Joseph pressed himself flat. The helicopter's side pivoted, and the minigun thundered in retaliation - the rules of engagement had been initiated. The roar was deafening, a metallic snarl that sprayed a stream of tracers into the cluster of Russians. Some dove for the church interior, others scrambled behind stone columns. Chunks of masonry exploded under the barrage.

Joseph seized the moment of confusion. He sprinted from behind the statue, weaving around fallen debris. The whoosh of bullets overhead made him flinch, but the Russians were too preoccupied with the helicopter.

He was ten strides from the courtyard's exit when Oleg, crouched behind a toppled column, noticed him. Briefly looking back, Joseph saw Oleg's face contort in hatred. He raised his rifle, finger on the trigger. Joseph's shoes skidded on loose gravel, sure that he wouldn't outrun a bullet.

Crack! Oleg jerked backward, a burst of red staining his chest armor. He staggered, rifle dropping from his hands. Joseph whipped his gaze upward toward the rocky ledge. There stood Aziz, rifle aimed, smoke curling from the barrel.

Joseph let out a breathless cry of mingled relief and triumph. "Aziz!" he shouted in near-disbelief. "I prayed for a guardian angel last night—thank God you answered!"

Aziz's laugh boomed across the courtyard, though Joseph could see only a fleeting grin from that distance. The older brother-in-law gestured for Joseph to keep moving. Meanwhile, the helicopter's minigun hammered the far side of the courtyard, preventing the Russians from regrouping.

Seizing his chance, Joseph dashed out the arched exit. At the base of the broad, rocky steps descending from St. Peter's Church, he nearly collided with Aziz and two surviving men from the militia. Their faces were grim, dust-streaked, eyes blazing with adrenaline.

"You all right, habibi?" Aziz panted, clapping Joseph's shoulder.

"Yeah," Joseph managed, though he could feel a tremor in his hands. "You came just in time."

Aziz nodded. "We'll talk later—this place is still hot. Let's go!"

Together, they sped down the winding mountain path. Overhead, the Blackhawk circled, unrelenting, pinning the Russians inside the church with suppressive fire. Joseph glimpsed muzzle flashes and saw a rocket-propelled grenade soar into the sky, missing the helicopter by a wide margin. The gunship's door gunner responded with a savage volley that peppered the stone façade.

At the mountain's base, a large green truck waited, engine idling. It looked battered, likely belonging to a friend of Aziz. He jerked the rear door open. "In—quickly!"

Joseph hauled himself in, collapsing onto a bench seat. Aziz's men scrambled in after him, slamming the door shut. The driver hit the gas, and the truck lurched forward, bounding over rough terrain. Over the noise of the engine, Joseph heard the helicopter overhead continuing to pound the courtyard, but with each second, the distance between them and the firefight grew.

As the truck sped off, Joseph felt a wave of dizziness. His body was coming down from the cataclysmic surge of adrenaline. His clothes were stained with blood, dust caked his skin, and every muscle quivered like a plucked string. But more than anything, he felt a bursting sense of gratitude for surviving.

They rumbled along a narrow dirt road, twisting away from the church's plateau. The roar of the helicopter receded behind them, echoing faintly in the mountain air. Finally, Aziz glanced over at Joseph with a crooked smile, wiping sweat from his brow.

"Ya akhi," he murmured, using the Arabic for "my brother," "that was too close. I don't think you'll ever doubt me when I say, 'I've got your back.'"

Aziz turned to Joseph once more, voice warm. "We have a safehouse in the city, courtesy of our friends at the CIA. You can rest there, figure out your next step. The chopper will land near there once they're done neutralizing those Russians. We'll meet the Americans, see what's next."

Joseph shook his head. "No. We can't do that. I'm changing the playbook. First, I need to get back to the compound and get my passports. Then I'm telling you the new plan." Aziz nodded his head and told the driver to get to the Russian compound.

TWENTY-SIX

Midnight Surrender

Joseph's heart pounded against his ribcage as he leapt down from the truck bed onto the packed dirt of the Russian compound. Night hung heavy over the rectangular building, the darkness broken only by the faint starlight and the distant glow of a single floodlight near the perimeter fence. The building was dark. Natalia was probably fast asleep. For a moment, he stood perfectly still, the acrid smell of gasoline and cold metal lingering in the still air. The truck's engine idled behind him, its rumble low and steady. Aziz, seated behind the wheel, caught Joseph's eye in the rearview mirror and offered a quick nod, urging him on.

He returned the nod and took off at a near-sprint, boots crunching on loose gravel. The compound rose in silhouettes. Its once-white stucco walls had turned gray with dust. Joseph slipped in through the side entrance, breath hitching in his throat.

The hallway was dark, illuminated only by a flickering emergency bulb at the far end. He passed door after door. The stale smell of old paint and sweat pressed around him like a heavy cloak. On any other night, there would be voices, footsteps, the clatter of late-night smoke breaks, or the hum of a TV in the common area. But now, every room seemed vacant, every corridor silent—eerily vacant, as though the building held its breath.

He sucked in air, scanning for motion. No sign of any of the men who typically paced these halls. The hush unnerved him. He crept up the stairwell, each step squeaking underfoot.

At the second floor, Joseph rounded the corner, heading straight for the room he'd occupied for months. The door bore the chipped, faded numbers 206. He hesitated, listening—still nothing but a faint rush of wind through broken windows. The entire building felt like a tomb.

He twisted the knob, heart hammering in his chest. Inside was an all-too-familiar space: an unmade cot; the small, battered desk; the dusty overhead fan that never quite worked. Moonlight seeped in through a tear in the curtain, revealing the edges of the bedframe, the faint silhouette of his packed luggage leaning against the wall.

He had prepared for this. "Any day could be my last," he'd told himself a dozen times. The question was never if, but when. Hurriedly, Joseph changed out of his blood stained clothing and into his best Turkish casual attire. He then grabbed his belongings, double checked that he had his passports, then flipped open the closet door, yanked the bag forward, and checked its contents.

A sudden hum of an engine outside made him glance over his shoulder. Perhaps another truck? He prayed Aziz would remain unseen. He slung the strap of the duffel over his shoulder, then paused. On the desk lay a stack of notes from the earliest digs—

Natalia's graceful handwriting in the margins. Part of him wanted to preserve them, but there was no time. Leaving anything behind was risky, but rummaging further was riskier. He inhaled, then exhaled slowly, stepping back into the hallway.

Downstairs. Out the lobby. Into the truck. The plan repeated in his head like a mantra. Already he could imagine the long, twisting roads that led to the city outskirts. Time was critical, especially since he did not know the outcome of the confrontation between the CIA and the Russians. Could the security team have made a pursuit behind them?

He hurried down the steps two at a time. The shadows cast by the single overhead bulb seemed to reach out, as if trying to snare him. At the base of the stairwell, an alcove near the cafeteria door gaped with darkness so complete it felt alive. Joseph's pulse quickened. He pressed on, sliding past the spot where, days ago, he'd last spoken to Dima about the excavation site.

The corridor ahead merged into the lobby. The tinted front windows displayed the faint reflection of streetlamps from outside, and the chipped tile floor glinted in shards of moonlight. He inhaled shakily and crossed the threshold into the lobby—a wide, open space with a defunct reception desk. Usually, it smelled of coffee or strong cigarettes.

As he made his way to the door—there was a silent, fluid motion that made him freeze.

Natalia stood there, pointing a handgun right at his chest 20 steps away.

Shock bolted through him. He nearly dropped his bag. By the dim glow from a streetlamp outside, he saw her face: eyes wide, beautiful as always, cheeks pale, with a look of intense pain. "Natalia," he breathed, mouth going dry. Her hair, always meticulously gathered, now fell in messy strands around her face, as if she'd sprinted here or wrestled with a choice too heavy to bear.

He made no move to step forward. "Natalia," he tried again, more gently.

Her hand trembled on the grip, but the muzzle stayed firmly aimed at his sternum. "Is it true?" she asked, voice raw. "Is it true that Sasha, Elena, Mortem, and Lavrov are dead?"

Joseph's chest tightened. He expected shock, fear, or confusion from her, but the sorrow and anger in her voice wrenched his heart. "I—" He drew a breath. "Yes, Natalia. It happened quickly. There were traps and no time to—"

She moved the gun in a quick, furious arc, cutting him off. "I knew something was wrong," she spat. "God, Joseph, just tell me... are you a CIA agent?"

His stomach twisted. The question he'd dreaded now hung in the air like a blade. He tried to keep his voice calm, reasoning. "It's complicated. Natalia, please, listen—"

She advanced a step, eyes fierce. "Don't lie to me. Don't dare. This entire time, I suspected you were more than just a curious professor." Her voice dropped low, trembling with anger. "I gave you the benefit of the doubt. I told myself you might have secrets, but you were here for the work—because you believed in the keys."

She shook her head, rage contorting her features. "My God, Joseph, what have you done? Did you kill them?"

Joseph swallowed, forcing composure and starting slowly pacing toward Natalia. "No," he said firmly. "I didn't kill them, Natalia. You need to trust me..."

She let out a trembling exhale, the gun unwavering. "Where are the Keys, Joseph?"

"They're safe," he replied calmly. "But they need to be taken to Peter's successor—just as they were always meant to be. What's happening here is bigger than you, me, Russia, or the CIA. I can't let them fall into the wrong hands."

She clicked off the safety, a subtle, chilling sound. Her lips pressed to a thin line. "I can't let you leave," she said, voice wavering between anger and desperation.

Joseph's heart hammered. In the gloom, her eyes glistened with unshed tears. He could see something swirling in them beyond mere duty to Russia, or fury at her lost colleagues. He saw heartbreak—the heartbreak of betrayal. They had spent months together, reconstructing parchment fragments, building an unspoken camaraderie that came from sleepless nights hunched over ancient words. He shared his life and his faith with her, a faith that he saw starting to come alive in her. Now all that trust had cracked.

He looked into her eyes deeply, feeling an ache in his soul. He saw months of shared triumphs and personal confessions, of frustrations and hopes. He saw longing for a different life, a life outside the shadow of this world. A life where she didn't have to brandish a gun at a friend she might have cared for.

"Natalia," he said quietly. "You have every right to be angry, to feel betrayed. But you need to let me go."

Her shoulders trembled, tears welling up. "I can't," she whispered.

He took another step closer, slowly, carefully. The muzzle of her gun was inches from his chest. A bead of sweat trickled down his temple. "Natalia," he began, voice hoarse, "please. I'm so sorry for the pain you are experiencing. I know you're scared. I'm scared too. But these keys belong to the Church, not any government. I'm sorry for the secrets, but it had to be done."

She shook her head, tears pooling. "You're not sorry. You only regret that I found out like this. You were going to vanish, letting me piece the shards of your betrayal together."

He took one more step, now close enough to see each tear trembling on her lashes. "Natalia, everything is going to be all right," he murmured, voice laden with earnestness. "I promise. God is going to bring good out of this if you let Him. But right now, you need to let me go."

The gun in her hands wavered. Her entire frame quaked with the effort of holding it steady. She took a shuddering breath. "I can't let you go, Joseph. I just... can't." Her eyes flicked downward, betraying the swirl of conflicting emotions. He dared to rest a gentle hand on the barrel of the gun, pushing it aside. "You can." He spoke with a warmth, as if consoling a distressed younger sibling. "You need to let me go."

Her gaze locked with his. Time seemed to still. There was such despair in her eyes, but also a flicker of reluctant acceptance. Like a dam breaking, she dropped her head, and tears slid silently down her cheeks. The weapon sagged in her grip. Finally, with a sob, she lowered it to her side, letting it clatter softly on the floor.

Joseph let out the breath he didn't know he'd been holding. The sorrow in her quiet weeping tore at him.

Unable to speak, she turned away, covering her mouth to stifle sobs. Joseph paused, wanting to offer more comfort, but he had no time. With cautious steps, he moved around her, bag clenched tight in one hand. A wave of guilt and pity flooded him, but he pushed forward. Every moment lingered like an echo in that dark lobby, the heartbreak too tangible to ignore.

At the door, he glanced back. She had sunk onto a tattered arm-chair, shoulders shaking. The gun lay forgotten on the tile. He parted his lips as if to say something—some final apology or prom-ise—but no words came. The best he could give her was a silent farewell.

Joseph stepped into the night. Immediately, the crisp air hit him. The truck's headlights shone like two searching eyes in the gloom. Gravel crunched as he crossed the compound yard to where Aziz sat behind the wheel. The big man leaned halfway out the window.

"Everything all right?" Aziz asked, brow furrowed.

Joseph hauled open the passenger door and threw in his bag. He climbed inside, breathing fast. "Drive," he said, voice tight. "We need to leave right now."

Aziz didn't wait for a second command. He shifted into gear, the truck lurching onto the pitted asphalt. They rumbled past the deserted guard post and out onto the open road, the compound dwindling in the mirrors. Joseph couldn't stop a final glance over his shoulder. The building, half-lost to the darkness, housed so many secrets and regrets—Natalia chief among them.

Aziz watched him with concern, but said nothing until they were well beyond the block, the silence broken only by the engine's roar. They drove on, passing rows of half-collapsed buildings. The truck's headlights illuminated the rubble where the quake had shattered entire blocks months ago. In the gloom, stray dogs roamed, their eyes glowing eerily as they watched the vehicle roar past. Joseph's mind drifted between the day's violence and the uncertain road ahead.

Aziz glanced at him. "What is your plan?"

Joseph exhaled. "I can't trust the CIA any more than I can trust the Russians. If the CIA thinks they can harness the Keys for their own ends, we'll be in the same place we started—just with a different government. I can't risk that. The keys belong to the successor of Peter only."

Aziz nodded vigorously. "So what's next?"

Joseph fixed his eyes on the road. "I need you to get a message to my dad. Tell him to call in the favor he's owed by Father Ryan at Notre Dame—we have to get the Keys to Pope Boniface directly, no middleman. My dad can make this happen."

Aziz arched a brow. "The Pope—going straight to the top, huh?"

Joseph let out a shaky laugh. "When you're dealing with the keys of Saint Peter, you might as well take them to Peter's successor, right?"

"True enough. So... how exactly do we get from here to Rome?"

Joseph retrieved his phone from his pocket, carefully sliding out the SIM card. "I'll need your help. First, this." He placed the SIM between thumb and forefinger and pressed it until it snapped in two. "No tracking me, no intercepting calls. DeLuca can't blow my plan if he can't find me."

He rolled down the window and flicked the remnants onto the road. A swirl of dust swallowed them.

"Next," Joseph continued, "I'm going to drive overnight to Beirut. Since I've visited so many times, and I'm in the system and have family in the North, I should have no trouble getting through. Once in Beirut, I'll hop on a plane to Rome with my U.S. passport. By the time anyone notices and tries to connect the dots, I'll already be through customs. With any luck, they'll be chasing illusions."

Aziz nodded, determined. "All right. But you're not going alone."

"What? No, that'll only make it more complicated," Joseph protested gently. "I have to do this swiftly, under the radar, and your family is—"

Aziz snorted. "Don't even start. You can't get rid of your guardian angel, brother. I already told you that. You might need me at the border or if things go sideways. We do this together."

Joseph studied Aziz's face, lit by the passing headlights. His sincerity was unwavering, the same fierce loyalty Joseph had come to admire. Despite the dread roiling in Joseph's belly, a small smile tugged at his lips. "All right," he conceded at last, voice tinged with relief. "I won't refuse you. Thank you."

Aziz dropped off the two other Chaldean troops he recruited at their homes. After an embrace and cash payment, Joseph and Aziz drive to the highway, the truck jostled violently over potholes. Aziz then took out and destroyed his cell phone's SIM card. Together, there was no way that their locations could be tracked. The headlights stretched into a yawning darkness beyond, revealing a battered sign pointing toward Beirut. Joseph squinted at the distance. Eight, nine hours if they pushed through the night. Possibly more if they had to detour.

He sank back into his seat, exhaustion finally creeping into his limbs. The day had been an avalanche of violence and heartbreak. The memory of Natalia's tear-streaked face floated to mind. In the rearview mirror, the battered outlines of Antakya receded slowly, silhouetted in the faint glow of distant streetlamps. The path ahead was uncertain—twisting mountain passes, border checks, and a plane from Beirut, if fortune allowed. But for the first time in days, Joseph felt a clarity in his soul: no governments, no agencies, only the lost keys of St. Peter - no, the found keys of St. Peter! The reality that he carried the keys in his excavation pack brought a wave of consolation over him as they drove through the night to Beirut.

TWENTY-SEVEN

Where Faith Takes Flight

Joseph had insisted on taking the first shift of driving, if only to calm his spinning thoughts. The headlights of the borrowed truck—its plates hastily swapped out in the last village—pierced the darkness of the mountain road. Aziz dozed in the passenger seat, arms crossed, his head occasionally tilting against the window. The dull hum of the tires on the asphalt, and the rush of the warm night air through a cracked window, provided the only soundtrack to their secret flight. They were leaving Turkish soil behind, heading south through the border checks into Lebanon, and on to Beirut's international airport.

Beyond the glass, stark moonlight illuminated silhouettes of jagged hills and clusters of scattered dwellings. Joseph noticed dim lanterns in the distance, lonely markers of people somehow living ordinary lives in these mountainous passes. He envied them. The mundane had slipped away from him in the last few days, replaced by frantic escapes, hidden relics, and the knowledge that entire governments were poised to do battle over two golden keys.

Aziz stirred, rubbing his eyes and glancing at the clock on the dashboard. "Three in the morning," he muttered. "We're making good time. You all right, brother?"

Joseph nodded, though his voice was tight. "Still awake. Not sure how much adrenaline I have left, but it's enough for another hour, maybe two."

Aziz checked the side mirror, scanning for headlights. "No sign of a tail." He twisted to see Joseph's face more clearly in the dim glow of the dashboard. "What's on your mind?"

Joseph flexed his fingers on the steering wheel. "I keep thinking about that last firefight. I can't shake the image of bullets ricocheting off the stone walls... you telling me to run... that helicopter overhead. Part of me wonders if the CIA just assumed we were captured—maybe killed." Aziz sucked in a breath. "We're nearly clear of this region. And once we get to Rome, it's sacred ground. They can't exactly storm the Vatican."

Joseph huffed a joyless laugh. "You think that would stop them?"

Aziz shrugged, stifling a yawn. "It's about moral lines. Even the CIA can't stage an international incident at St. Peter's Basilica. The press alone—" He broke off, rubbing the back of his neck. "Anyway, we'll get there safely. That's the plan, right?"

"Right," Joseph murmured, letting the conversation die.

They continued in near silence until the next checkpoint, a small crossing point guarded by a half dozen Lebanese officers. They were used to travelers passing from Turkey at odd hours—economic ties and daily trade had always made these borderlands fluid. With his Lebanese passport and the fact that Joseph had enough of his mother's look in him not to make him too suspicious along with his passing Arabic was good enough to get by. Every guard was polite, half-asleep, and hardly curious about two travelers heading for Beirut in the dead of night.

Before sunrise, Aziz took over the wheel so Joseph could curl up in the passenger seat and shut his eyes. Still, true rest evaded him. He dozed in nervous fits, hearing the roar of passing trucks and the subdued murmurs of local radio news. Every time he drifted off, an image of Salma with their soon to be born baby flickered through his mind—her exhausted face, the newborn's tiny fist wrapped around her finger. He longed to be by her side, not gallivanting across the Middle East.

They finally reached the outskirts of Beirut as pink light broke along the horizon, painting the Mediterranean Sea in subtle ribbons of rose and gold. Skyscrapers, half-finished and glinting in that new day's glow, lined the highway leading into the city center. The traffic here was already picking up: battered taxis weaving in and out, trucks loaded with produce, motorcycles darting unpredictably.

Aziz maneuvered the truck off an exit and turned toward Rafic Hariri International Airport. Large overhead signs in Arabic and English announced incoming flights. The terminal building loomed, a curved edifice of steel and glass tinted gold by the morning sun. They parked discreetly in a far corner of a short-term lot.

Joseph slowly unbuckled, gingerly stepping out. His entire body felt stiff from tension and insufficient sleep. Aziz hopped out too, stretching his back with an exaggerated groan.

"Right, let's see if our intelligence was correct," Aziz said, rummaging in his jacket pocket. "We have enough cash to buy the tickets outright."

Joseph nodded at the mention of money. "That's CIA money, though. You sure you want to blow it on plane tickets to Rome?"

Aziz's grin was boyish. "Let's call it poetic justice."

Together, they made their way across the lot and into the main terminal. The sudden blast of air conditioning reminded Joseph of American airports—sterile overhead lights, polished floors, the swirl of travelers from every corner of the world. Immediately, they spotted a row of digital departure boards. Aziz pointed.

"There: Beirut to Rome, direct flight, departing in four hours," he read, squinting at the overhead screen. "Looks open."

"Perfect," Joseph breathed. The next step felt surreal. He had grown accustomed to barbed-wire compounds and subterranean crypts; seeing a typical row of airline check-in desks felt almost jarring.

They approached the desk for the airline and quietly requested two one-way tickets to Rome. The attendant, hardly giving them a second glance, offered the fare total. Joseph felt a flutter in his stomach when Aziz calmly peeled off a thick stack of American hundred-dollar bills. The attendant counted them, raised an eyebrow, then forced a professional smile. Moments later, they both held boarding passes—an actual, tangible route out of this region.

"Four hours," Aziz said, tucking his wallet away. "We can breathe."

Joseph gave a shaky nod. "Let's find our gate."

They navigated toward security, passing restaurants and gift shops along the concourse. Their carry-on bags felt heavy: Joseph's large suitcase contained clothes, books, and a labyrinth of secrets. His battered excavation backpack weighed even more heavily on him, as it harbored something infinitely more precious.

Once they were through the checkpoint, they continued to Gate 26—a quiet corner with rows of molded plastic chairs. Only a scattering of early arrivals waited there. Aziz dropped into a seat, letting out a long sigh of relief. Joseph sat beside him, feeling tension drain from his shoulders.

For a few minutes, neither spoke. They were both exhausted from mental strain, from the last few days of madness. Finally, Aziz broke the silence with a gentle elbow to Joseph's ribs.

"Hey," he said, lips curling into a half-smile. "We made it. All that's left is to board the plane."

Joseph managed a small grin. "Yeah." He gazed out the tall airport windows, sunlight glinting off the wings of parked planes. "It's just—everything's changed, hasn't it? Feels like ages ago we were joking in your parents' living room about digging for relics for a living."

Aziz chuckled. "We've got quite the story. Better than anything we conjured up as bored young adults—though, come on, we were never that imaginative."

Joseph smiled at the memory. "I suppose not. We used to talk about 'adventure' in faraway lands, but this is... I never wanted the Keys of St. Peter to become a pawn in geopolitics."

Aziz fixed him with a knowing look. "You have a noble heart, Joseph. That's why my sister married you. And now you have a child—my niece or nephew. I can't believe I'm going to be an uncle again. But wait, let's talk about something important: godfather status."

Joseph laughed outright, startling a traveler two seats away. "You're not even subtle."

"Subtlety is overrated," Aziz retorted. "Come on, who else would be the kid's best role model? I'm the obvious choice. Your child's future depends on my sage wisdom and roguish charm."

"Ha!" Joseph shook his head with feigned indignation. "Not so fast, buddy. Henry Briggs back home might have something to say about that. And you're definitely lacking in the humility department—didn't you promise to read more biblical references about not exalting yourself?"

Aziz pressed a hand to his chest in mock offense. "I am the humblest man in the Middle East. The entire Chaldean diaspora, even."

"Sure, sure," Joseph teased. "Next you'll tell me you've parted the Red Sea."

Aziz roared with laughter. "Well, if I had the Keys of St. Peter, who knows what wonders I might do?"

Their amusement faded as the mention of the Keys brought the reality of their situation back. A few onlookers briefly glanced their way, but the men made no further mention, returning to safer topics. In that pause, Joseph tried not to dwell on the possibility that the CIA— or the Russians, or some other party—still might be tracking them.

Suddenly, two uniformed men strode toward them, wearing the navy-blue attire of Lebanese Security. Their expressions were unreadable. One approached Joseph directly.

"Pardon me, sir," the officer said. "Are you Professor Joseph Scanlon?"

Joseph's pulse jumped, but he tried to keep his face neutral. "Yes. May I help you?"

The officer's tone was cordial but firm. "Sir, please come with us to the customs office."

Joseph calmly produced two passports from his jacket—one American, one Lebanese. "I have dual citizenship. I haven't done anything illegal. Mind explaining what this is about?"

The second officer stepped forward. "Your citizenship isn't in question, Dr. Scanlon. Nonetheless, we require you to come with us. You're being compelled to attend an interview."

Aziz stood, tension clear in the set of his jaw. "If there's a problem, we can address it here. I'd like to accompany him—"

The officers shook their heads simultaneously. "No, sir. We need only Dr. Scanlon. This matter doesn't concern you."

Joseph sent Aziz a quick, reassuring glance. "I'll be fine," he murmured. "It might just be a formality."

He scooped up his large suitcase and shouldered his excavation backpack. A swirl of nerves twisted in his belly as he followed the two men. The short walk took them down a corridor behind the main duty-free zone, past a small administration hall. The hum of travelers and overhead announcements dwindled behind them.

In front of a nondescript door reading "Customs Office," one officer swiped a key card. Inside lay a small waiting area, fluorescent lights flickering overhead. Another door led to a private room. The men led Joseph inside.

The second door opened onto a cramped, windowless space with a single table. A figure in a black suit stood with his back turned, hands clasped behind him. He seemed to be studying a wall map of Lebanon.

Joseph's heart hammered. Something felt off. Then the figure turned. Joseph inhaled sharply.

Agent Mark DeLuca.

He wore that same practiced, almost fatherly smile that Joseph remembered from his forced "recruitment" days. His dark hair slicked back, crisp white shirt neatly pressed, tie a subdued navy.

"Joseph," DeLuca said warmly, stepping forward with open arms. "I'm so glad you made it out of that mess in Antakya. We were worried sick when you didn't show up to the safe house."

Joseph set down his suitcase but kept the excavation backpack on his shoulder. "Agent DeLuca," he managed in a steady tone. "What is this?"

DeLuca's eyes darted to the officers, who nodded and quietly left the room, closing the door behind them. "What is this? A rescue, maybe. Or a courtesy chat. Hard to say."

Joseph's posture tensed, though he tried to project calm. "You say you were worried. I never made it to your safe house. That's true. Let's just say I've developed some trust issues."

DeLuca chuckled lightly, as though Joseph had cracked a harmless joke. "Understandable. After the firefight, we secured the Russian compound. Helicopter dropped in the courtyard. The Russians put up a respectable fight but could not overcome our firepower."

Joseph's eyes widened. "A respectable fight? How long was it?"

"Long enough, Joseph. We interrogated everyone. No one would say where the Keys were. Although they knew they had been found, they all claimed they didn't know where they were. We assumed they were lying and had stashed them on the premise. For a while, we assumed you were taken hostage, or worse. Then we eventually made our way to the Russian compound and found Natalia. She told us you fled with the keys."

DeLuca spread his hands. "We cross-referenced her story with other witnesses. No one claimed otherwise. And when your phone didn't respond to any signals—nor Aziz's—it became clear you'd gone dark. I commend your thoroughness. But you see, I had a backup plan."

Joseph stiffened. "Backup plan?"

DeLuca's gaze dipped to the chain around Joseph's neck. The chain which held a small crucifix and a rosary medal. DeLuca smiled. "I like your devotion, Joseph. A man of faith is a man worth trusting, I always say. That's why we gave you that transmitter. The RFID chip, if you recall, was to mark you as friendly in case of a firefight. Turned out it was also a GPS device once activated. Rather advanced. We started tracking you the moment we learned from Natalia that you were out. And lo and behold, your signal popped up crossing the Turkish border into Lebanon."

Joseph's cheeks burned. "So you've been monitoring me this entire time."

DeLuca shrugged, unrepentant. "In fairness, we lost your signal for a few hours. Spotty coverage in those mountains. But once you hit the main roads, the device pinged again—just enough for us to guess you'd head for Beirut. Not too complicated to cross-reference flight schedules. And here we are."

Joseph felt a swirl of anger, betrayal, and a creeping sense of helplessness. "What do you want?"

Agent DeLuca took a slow breath. "We want the Keys, Joseph. You know the U.S. government can't let them roam free. Not after what we've seen. We must secure them."

Joseph's mind raced. If he refused, how far would DeLuca go? He tried to put on a brave face. "These Keys don't belong to any government—American, Russian, or anyone else. They're part of the universal Church's heritage. And they're dangerous in the wrong hands."

"Yes, we figured you'd say that." DeLuca sighed dramatically. "So let's try a different angle. You do realize that under Turkish law—section 2863 in the civil code, regarding the conservation of cultural and natural property—it's illegal to remove artifacts from an excavation site. The penalty can be quite severe including lengthy prison time in a Turkish prison cell. The CIA has helicopter resources to extradite you right back to Hatay province if we give them reason."

Joseph swallowed hard, picturing a lonely cell, the years slipping by as his child grew up without him. He pictured Salma, tears in her eyes, holding their baby alone. The harshness of it all nearly overwhelmed him.

"How about it, Joseph?" DeLuca pressed, stepping closer. "Are you prepared to spend your life in some Turkish prison, never seeing your wife or newborn child? All for two lumps of gold?"

A pulse pounded in Joseph's ears, a dizzying blend of rage and fear. He found it difficult to form words. Ultimately, survival instincts took hold. "I have the Keys," he whispered, his voice cracked with defeat.

DeLuca's eyebrows rose. "Where?"

Joseph exhaled, feeling a flash of self-loathing. "They're here. In my excavation pack."

His hand trembled as he set the backpack on the table and unzipped it. With the same care he'd shown in the catacombs, he searched around the pack for awhile. Eventually, he drew out two golden keys—heavy, ornate, glinting beneath the fluorescent lights.

DeLuca took them without ceremony, placing them into a molded, foam-lined evidence case. It clicked shut, sealed away. No prayers, no hush of wonder. Just the crisp sound of latches.

"Thank you," DeLuca said, sounding like a salesman finalizing a deal. "The United States government appreciates your cooperation. My superiors have instructed me to offer you five hundred thousand dollars in cash in appreciation for your role in vital national security and in exchange for signing another NDA to keep everything confidential."

Joseph stared at the sealed case of cash in DeLuca's hand. "I don't want your money," he croaked. "And I won't sign another NDA. I... just want out of this. I swear, I have no intention of going to the press or the world. The CIA can keep its secrets. I won't talk."

DeLuca studied him for a moment, then gave a polite nod, as if to say "Suit yourself." He extended a hand, which Joseph automatically, robotically shook. "You did well," DeLuca said, "even if it ended somewhat differently than we envisioned. You kept these out of Russian hands. That alone is a win."

The agent turned to leave, but paused at the door. He reached inside his suit jacket and withdrew a plain manila envelope. "For the trouble you went through. A personal gift..." he said lightly. "No strings attached." Then he stepped out, shutting the door behind him.

Joseph, numb, slowly opened the envelope. Inside lay thick wads of U.S. currency—he counted mentally, exhaling in shock. Likely a hundred thousand dollars, at least. Nausea coiled in his stomach.

He sat down in the lonely chair at the table, staring at the bare walls. The overhead lights buzzed. He let minutes slip by, trying to piece together how quickly everything had come to this moment.

Finally, Joseph shoved the envelope of cash inside his backpack. Collecting himself, he rose and stepped out of the customs room. No one stopped him in the corridor; the two Lebanese officers from earlier were gone. Without fanfare, he retraced his steps to the gate area, heart pounding.

Aziz was pacing near a vending machine. The moment he saw Joseph, he rushed over, face taut with anxiety. "What happened? You were gone forever!"

Joseph took a shaky breath. "It was DeLuca," he confessed, feeling drained. "The CIA had planted a tracker in my rosary chain. He demanded the Keys. He threatened me with prison for smuggling relics out of Turkey if I refused."

Aziz's eyes narrowed in alarm. "Habibi, tell me you didn't give them up."

Joseph's throat felt tight. "Aziz... I had no choice—" He paused, letting the last of his adrenaline fizz away.

A small, nearly imperceptible smile broke across his face. "I had no choice but to give him the wrong set of keys."

TWENTY-EIGHT

The Vatican

J oseph stared at Aziz who had confusion written on his face, "Let's start from the beginning. Years ago, after I defended my dissertation on the Keys of Saint Peter. My father, showed up with these two big golden keys—fully ornate, like something you'd see in a museum."

Aziz raised an eyebrow. "So he just... what, had them made for you?"

"Yeah, 3D printed." Joseph smirked at the memory. "Dad got the idea from some painting in the Vatican—'Christ Giving the Keys to St. Peter,' by Perugino, I think. My father took the image as a prototype, then convinced a friend at the Notre Dame IDEA Center to 3D-print them using a heavy tungsten-based polymer. Afterward, he painted them with a bright, metallic gold paint. They're bigger than the actual keys, the kind of dramatic relic you might see in an old religious painting. The detail's incredible: swirling designs near the bow of each key, so they look ancient. He gave them to me to celebrate my successful PhD defense—like a proud father awarding a medal."

Aziz chuckled, crossing his arms. "That's so your dad. Man loves big gestures."

A fondness flickered in Joseph's eyes. "Then, right before I left for Antakya, my wife—your sister Salma—dusted them off the display, and insisted I bring them along. She told me I should bring them as a constant reminder for why I was there. I was so scattered with everything when I got there that I honestly forgot about them."

Nodding, Aziz glanced at the open backpack.

Joseph let out a shaky sigh, the tension lifting from his shoulders. "Then everything happened so fast with DeLuca—being forced to cooperate. I was rummaging through my bag, fully intent on pulling out the real one from my padded pocket, when my fingers brushed that inside pocket. And I realized I still have these fakes! I intentionally maintained my depressed and defeated expression, pulled them out and handed them over"

Aziz let out a whoop of laughter, clamping a hand over his mouth lest someone hear. "You're telling me the CIA walked away with a couple of 3D printed souvenirs? That's absolutely priceless."

Joseph couldn't help a grin either, though his voice carried undertones of relief. "I was shaking the entire time, trying to appear calm. DeLuca just stared at them, muttered something, and left. Meanwhile, the real Keys—the actual Keys, the ones Bishop Anastasius stashed in Antioch centuries ago—were still right here." He dipped his hand into the backpack, rummaging past notebooks, battered tools, bits of cloth, and then parted a side flap. The glint of gold peeked through.

Aziz bent forward, breath catching. He saw them: the real Keys. If Joseph's father's replicas were impressive, these were beyond that—older, every surface exuding an almost tangible aura of ancient sanctity.

Aziz let out a low whistle. "Incredible. You did it, Joseph. Holy smokes, you were almost too casual about it. I can't believe you pulled it off."

Aziz clapped him on the shoulder. "It's official. You, my friend, have the best story to tell at parties from now on. 'Remember that time I tricked the CIA with 3D-printed keys...?'" He cackled, and Joseph had to put a hand on Aziz's mouth to hush him.

"Keep it down," Joseph pleaded in mock-seriousness. "We're not out of the woods entirely. But at least the direct threat from DeLuca is behind us. He's probably halfway back to Washington or wherever he needs to bring those decoys. Meanwhile, we have the real Keys."

Aziz shook his head, half in admiration, half in disbelief. "You do realize, if someone turned this into a movie script, nobody would believe it. Too convenient, too insane."

"Yet it's real," Joseph murmured, lightly running his fingertips over the golden bow. He felt a shiver, recalling centuries of legend, the shock of Pope Gregory's letters, the raw spiritual presence that saved him from Lavrov's illusions. "And they're safe now."

A short silence fell between them, rife with gratitude, relief, and an almost giddy sense of triumph. Joseph looked at his watch.

"Now that I'm not being bugged or monitored, I need to do some emailing. I have to let Salma know everything's okay."

Aziz gestured with a flourish. "By all means. Let me keep watch."

Joseph found a business concourse with complimentary computers. Now that the threat of CIA monitoring was over he logged onto his email and typed a message to Salma:

Subject: *Safe & Heading Home Soon*

My dearest Salma,

I'm so sorry for disappearing on you. My phone broke— under less than ideal circumstances—and I've had minimal access to anything safe or secure. But, my love, the mission is over. We succeeded! I'm finally free to come home and will tell you all the details. First, I'll have to make a stop in Rome—I'll explain everything once I see you. I won't have a functioning phone until I land stateside, but please don't worry. I'm healthy, I'm alive, and I can't wait to see you and receive our baby.

Yours always,

Joseph

He reread it, pangs of guilt welling up at how many times he'd been forced to keep her in the dark. But it would have to do for now.

Next, he composed an email to his father, Michael:

Subject: Flight and Arrival - Next Steps

Dad,

I'm free at last. I'll be landing in Rome (FCO) on March 19, early morning. I'm bringing Aziz, my brother-in-law and one of my greatest allies in this insane journey. We'll catch flight #AZ146 from Beirut straight to Rome. If you can set up the details, I'll fill you in fully once we're face-to-face. Let me know if anything changes—though I doubt it can, at this point!

Love you,

Joseph

He hit send. Within minutes, an email from Michael's account appeared in his inbox. It was terse but excited:

Joseph,

Everything's arranged. A driver will wait for you at Rome Fiumicino. Safe travels, son.

—Dad

Joseph snorted a soft laugh. "That was quick. Guess Dad's really on top of this." He shared the note with Aziz, who gave an approving nod.

"Your father's unstoppable, Joseph. We'll have a hero's welcome, I'm sure."

Eventually it was time to board their plane. As they checked in, they saw their names were on the first-class upgrade list. Joseph and Aziz exchanged a bemused glance, picking up their boarding passes from the desk. A short note accompanied them:

"Courtesy of M. DeLuca," scrawled in neat, slanted letters.

Joseph almost laughed at the irony: after everything, Mark DeLuca had arranged a comfortable flight. Perhaps it was an unspoken apology or an olive branch. Either way, Joseph accepted it.

The flight to Rome was, mercifully, uneventful. The plush seats in first class reclined nearly flat, allowing both men to collapse into exhausted slumber. Flight attendants offered them champagne, five-star meals, and warm towels, but they politely declined most of it in favor of rest. After weeks of tension—dodging bullets, booby traps, ancient curses, and global intelligence services— sleep was the greatest luxury of all.

When Joseph awoke near the end of the flight, he peered through the cabin window and saw the pale morning sun cresting the horizon. The plane's path angled gently, revealing glimmers of the Tyrrhenian Sea as they neared land. Aziz stirred beside him, rubbing bleary eyes.

"Morning," Joseph said, voice hoarse.

"Morning. Did we actually get eight hours?" Aziz replied, blinking.

Joseph checked his watch. "Something like that. Enough to feel human again, right?"

The plane's tires kissed the runway, and moments later they were taxiing to the gate. The usual bustle of disembarking followed, except this time, Joseph felt a surreal sense of calm. He was stepping into a final chapter of sorts—one that would lead to closure or, as he suspected, a new beginning.

They cleared customs with minimal fuss, retrieving their luggage from the carousel. He and Aziz stepped into the thronged arrivals hall, scanning the crowd. Sure enough, an Italian man with thick, dark hair stood near the edge, holding a sign that read JOSEPH SCANLON. The man wore a simple black suit, face solemn, eyes scanning for recognition.

Joseph lifted a hand, and the man strode forward, inclining his head politely. "Signore Scanlon?" he said, in thickly accented English.

"Yes, I'm Joseph," he replied. "And this is my brother-in-law, Aziz."

The driver gave Aziz a brisk nod, then pointed to a black sedan parked at the curb outside. He didn't speak more than a few words of English, but he insisted on loading their bags carefully. After verifying that both men had arrived, he opened the rear passenger doors and gestured for them to get in.

The city of Rome unfurled before them, a tapestry of ancient ruins and modern hustle. Once they merged onto the main road, the driver pointed out a few major sites, speaking in rapid Italian. Joseph couldn't parse every syllable, but he caught enough to follow the gist.

First, they passed the *Colosseum*: a monumental ellipse of stone rising out of the city's heart, the morning sun gilding its arches. Tourists swarmed around it already, cameras glinting. The driver slowed just enough to let Joseph and Aziz soak in the view. The imposing structure whispered centuries of gladiator battles and imperial might, a testament to Rome's layered history.

Next, they moved through winding streets until they glimpsed the *Pantheon*. Aziz pressed his face to the window, eyes wide at the stately columns fronting the massive dome. "It's bigger than I expected," he breathed, as the driver navigated the narrow roads. They caught only a fleeting look at the ancient temple-turned-church, but the echo of wonder lingered.

Finally, they skirted the *Castel Sant'Angelo*, that fortress-like silhouette on the banks of the Tiber. Once a mausoleum for Emperor Hadrian, it had morphed into a papal stronghold over the centuries. Its cylindrical bulk loomed against the sky, the statue of the Archangel Michael perched at the summit. Joseph recalled how this fortress once served as a sanctuary for Popes under siege. The driver gestured, presumably proud, repeating "Castel Sant'Angelo! Bellissimo!" with a grin.

Aziz pointed from the back seat. "I never realized how this city is basically a living museum. Everywhere you turn, there's something from a different era."

Joseph nodded, equally enthralled. He'd been to Rome once before, but not under circumstances anywhere near so extraordinary.

Their sedan rounded a curve, and suddenly St. Peter's Basilica rose before them. The expanse of St. Peter's Square opened like a grand theatre: towering colonnades lined the perimeter, saints carved in stone looming from the balustrade overhead. The central obelisk jutted skyward, flanked by fountains that glimmered under the morning sun. A swirl of pilgrims and visitors dotted the square, forming a mosaic of cultures. The sky overhead was a crisp blue, dotted by a few feathery clouds.

Aziz sucked in a breath, leaning forward in his seat. "My goodness... it's so... enormous." His voice held an edge of awe.

Joseph felt his pulse quicken, the wonder of the moment overshadowing any lingering fatigue. He noticed the basilica's grand façade, the Latin inscriptions, and the statues crowning the top—Christ flanked by apostles. The entire scene glowed with morning light, as though the city itself welcomed them with open arms. On the far side, the famed Swiss Guards could be seen in their striped uniforms, manning the security checkpoints.

Their driver, silent and efficient, guided the sedan around the perimeter, stopping at each checkpoint. There, Swiss Guards in bright Renaissance attire peered in, checked some form of credentials the driver produced, then waved them on. Joseph realized these were not the typical tourist security lines—some special arrangement.

At every point, gates opened like magic, the sleek black sedan gliding deeper into the Vatican territory. Eventually, they reached a heavily guarded area where the public foot traffic ended. Guards parted as if expecting them. Joseph and Aziz exchanged uneasy glances—this was more than a casual visit.

The car wound down a ramp leading to a gated garage. One wouldn't guess it existed unless specifically directed. The driver parked in a discreet corner, turned off the engine, and hopped out to open their doors. Joseph grabbed his excavation pack and stepped onto smooth stone floors, noticing the hush of subterranean air. This was a place rarely seen by outsiders. A set of bronze doors on the far side bore the papal insignia. The driver led them to those doors and offered a short, courteous bow, gesturing them onward.

They ascended a short flight of marble steps. Two papal aides, dressed in subdued black suits, opened the grand doors. Light spilled from inside, and the hush of thick carpeting muffled their footsteps. Joseph's chest clenched with anticipation. This was it— the final approach to the papal library, the seat of centuries of Church scholarship.

With only a moment's pause, the aides ushered them in. The interior soared overhead: a vaulted ceiling painted with delicate frescoes of biblical scenes and swirling gold trim. Dark wooden bookcases lined the walls from floor to ceiling, each shelf packed with ancient tomes and documents. Sunlight streamed through tall windows, dust motes dancing in the warm glow. The fragrance of old parchment and well-polished wood was almost intoxicating.

In the center of the room stood three figures. Joseph recognized them instantly: *Father Ryan*, wearing a broad smile; *Michael Scanlon*, Joseph's father, looking healthier than expected but still visibly drawn; and a man robed in white, with gentle eyes and a kind, unassuming posture—*Pope Boniface* X himself.

Joseph's heart skipped a beat. He barely registered the aides closing the library doors behind them. Without a word, he broke into a run, crossing the threshold to embrace his father. "Dad!" he gasped, arms going tight around the older man. He was stunned by how real Michael felt in his arms—warm, alive, not nearly as frail as Joseph had feared.

Michael chuckled, patting Joseph's back. "Son, you made it," he said in a soft voice laced with relief. "I had to call in a favor—Father Ryan here owed me, That's how I got to stand in the papal library." He coughed, but there was a beaming grin on his face.

Pulling back, Joseph gripped his father's shoulders, searching for signs of illness in his eyes. "I had no idea you'd actually be here. But I'm so glad," he murmured, swallowing the lump in his throat.

From behind, Father Ryan stepped forward, folding his hands in a cordial greeting. "My boy, you never cease to amaze me," he said, a teasing note in his voice. "I knew if anyone could unravel the mystery of the Keys, it was you. And it seems you've done just that." He gestured lightly. "We've followed developments from the moment you touched down in Turkey."

Joseph managed a sheepish grin, noting how Father Ryan's presence reminded him of simpler times at Notre Dame—a lifetime ago, or so it felt. Then he remembered whose presence overshadowed even that: the Pope. Turning, Joseph found himself face to face with Pope Boniface X. He felt an immediate desire to kneel, to show reverence, but also sensed the Pope's casual air as the older man offered a warm, paternal expression.

"Holy Father," Joseph began, bowing his head, "I'm honored... I—I hardly know how to—"

Pope Boniface X chuckled, stepping forward with outstretched hands. "Now, now, Joseph. Let's not stand on ceremony. I've heard so much about you, I feel we're already old friends." He gently clasped Joseph's hands. The Pope's voice was soft but resonant, carrying an unmistakable kindness.

Born Hector Ayala to a devout family in Monterrey, Mexico, Pope Boniface X became the first Mexican to ascend to the papacy, despite having no initial aspirations for the role. Embracing the position with remarkable grace, he adopted the papal motto "optimum veteris et optimum novi" (the best of the old and best of the new), a phrase inspired by Matthew 13:52: "Therefore every teacher of the law who has become a disciple in the kingdom of heaven is like the owner of a house who brings out of his storeroom new treasures as well as old." This motto perfectly encapsulates his vision for the Church—a harmonious blend of reverence for tradition and openness to contemporary movements of the Holy Spirit.

Pope Boniface X is widely regarded as a scholar and teacher, deeply appreciative of the Catholic tradition's rich tapestry while remaining vigilant to what God is doing in the present. He did his graduate dissertation on the second Vatican Council. His unique ability to merge the old and the new made him a reassuring figure for traditionalists who value historical continuity, even as he innovatively explored new avenues for the Church's mission to demonstrate the love of God through the power of the Holy Spirit. Under his leadership, the Church began to engage with previously unconsidered areas, seeking to evangelize and expand its reach in response to modern challenges.

Those who know him personally often speak of his keen sense of humor and enduring child-like faith. Despite the weight of his responsibilities, Pope Boniface X never lost his light-hearted spirit, endearing him to those around him and fostering a sense of warmth and child-like faith.

Joseph swallowed, adrenaline stirring within him. "Thank you, Your Holiness. I, well, I don't know where to start."

"I want to hear the entire story," the Pope said, eyes bright with curiosity. "From your dissertation on the lost Keys to your infiltration of that excavation. I've already received summaries, but I want the unabridged version, from your own lips."

Nodding, Joseph took a steadying breath. "All right," he said, glancing at Michael, who gave him an encouraging nod. Aziz stood nearby, trying to appear calm, though wonder shone in his eyes. The library's hush formed a cocoon of privacy.

Joseph launched into his account: he summarized how he'd first become fascinated with the legend of Pope Gregory the Great sending the Keys to Antioch. He described *Lavrov's offer* at Notre Dame, the overshadowing political tension with the Russians, and the CIA's recruitment. He recounted each step of the *excavation* in Antakya, how cryptic parchments guided them through labyrinthine tunnels beneath an ancient church. He spoke of the cunning booby traps from the Byzantine era, the sealed reliquary chamber deep within the mountain, and how Dr. Lavrov revealed his plan: to harness the Keys' healing power for President Volkov and thus resurrect a formidable Russian Orthodoxy under Volkov's prolonged life and the authority of the keys of St. Peter: of the *evil spirit* that overtook Lavrov—an echo of what happened to the Lombard soldier so many centuries ago—Pope Boniface stiffened, leaning in. Joseph recalled how he invoked the Name of Jesus in the face of that malevolence, barely escaping the labyrinth, of Aziz's rescue from near death at the hands of the Russian FSB agents. Then he explained the cat-and-mouse game with the CIA, culminating in the switch with the 3D-printed fakes.

Throughout it all, Pope Boniface asked quiet, clarifying questions: "And you say these parchments specifically referenced Bishop Anastasius by name?" or "So you prayed in that moment, and you saw the darkness recoil at the name of Jesus?"—all with a riveted calm that suggested deep faith and intellectual passion. Father Ryan and Michael listened attentively, occasionally exchanging glances. Aziz chimed in here and there, confirming details. Hours went by but no one moved.

At last, Joseph reached the final note: "That's how I ended up here, Holy Father. I'm convinced beyond doubt these Keys are the same ones entrusted by Pope Gregory - the lost keys of St. Peter. They belong, without question, to the Successor of Peter." His voice resonated in the hush. He reached into his backpack, and carefully unwrapped the gold glimmer. The true Keys of St. Peter now lay cradled in his palms.

With eyes shining, Joseph took two steps forward and knelt, raising his hands. "It is my honor, as a proud son of the Church, to place these in your care, Holy Father, where they have always belonged."

Pope Boniface's expression was one of wonder, like a child glimpsing a precious treasure. He reached out, fingers brushing the ancient metal. For a long moment, he simply studied them, turning them gently in his hands. Then he spoke softly. "Lost and found, so many times across the centuries...like each of us in God's eyes, is that not so?" He gave a tender smile and looked back at Joseph. "You've done what countless souls failed to do, my son. The Church owes you a debt."

At that, the Pope glanced at Father Ryan, Michael, and Aziz. "Would you kindly excuse us for a few moments? I'd like to speak with Joseph alone."

Father Ryan responded first, bowing with a respectful smile. Michael gave Joseph a gentle clap on the shoulder, his eyes brimming with paternal pride. Aziz offered Joseph a playful salute. They departed the library, leaving Joseph and Pope Boniface in the hush of ancient tomes.

When the doors closed, Pope Boniface set the Keys down on a velvet-lined table. Then he turned, eyes warm with gratitude. "Joseph, I'm deeply moved by your account. Thank you for trusting me enough to share it in full."

Joseph was about to protest—he was the one who needed to say thanks. But the Pope lifted a hand gently. "Before you speak, may I share a testimony of my own?"

It was so unexpected that Joseph blinked. "Of course, Your Holiness."

The Pope nodded, almost shy. "Ever since news of this expedition for the keys of Peter came to me, I've been sequestering myself in the Vatican Archives. I found those references to the Keys from the sixth century—Pope Gregory's letters, so rarely studied in detail. I even managed to get hold of your dissertation. I read it cover to cover. Multiple times, actually."

Joseph felt his cheeks warm. "I—I'm flattered, Holy Father."

"You wrote with such clarity and fervor, weaving theology, history, and a profound respect for the mystical. I realized you saw the Keys not just as an artifact but as a living sign of Peter's authority, bridging heaven and earth." He paused, gaze dropping. "Then something else happened. I began having dreams. Night after night, the same dream."

A tingle coursed down Joseph's spine. Pope Boniface continued softly. "In the dreams, St. Joseph, the patron of the universal Church, the terror of demons, would come to me and ask, 'Do you still entrust to me the intercession of the Church?' And in each dream, I found myself reaching into my pocket handing him the Keys of Peter as a sign of trust. The dream ended there. This happened three nights in a row, the last dream was just last night. And today—March 19, the Feast of St. Joseph—you walk in, physically carrying the Keys; your name is Joseph. Your story includes being a terror to demons"

Joseph's mind whirled and he could not respond.

Pope Boniface gave a decisive nod. "I know for certain what I must do. Joseph Scanlon stretch forth your hand."

Confused, Joseph complied. The Pope picked up the Keys, cradled them in both hands, and spoke with solemnity: "Just as my predecessor, Pope Gregory the Great, entrusted these Keys to Boniface, who in turn delivered them to a man of God for safekeeping, so do I, Pope Boniface X, now entrust these Keys to you, Joseph Scanlon." He pressed the Keys into Joseph's outstretched right hand. "I give you permission and extend my authority to use them and the power they contain as the Holy Spirit himself leads you. When the time is right, the Spirit Himself will reveal to you who you must entrust the keys to when your time has come."

Joseph felt his heart seize in shock. He tried to protest. "Holy Father, I—I can't possibly accept. These Keys—belong in the Vatican. In your possession. Who am I to—"

Pope Boniface's eyes sparkled. "Joseph, cautioning you not to argue with the Pope might seem comical, but trust me, it's better you don't. You see, you might hold the physical keys of Peter, but I still hold the spiritual keys of Peter. My keys are far mightier than any physical artifact. But as for these physical Keys of Peter? They've proven time and again how dangerous they can be if made too public. Let's not tempt fortune. Lavrov nearly succeeded in weaponizing them."

"But I... I'm just—" Joseph struggled.

"You're the man who risked life and limb to keep them out of hostile hands," the Pope countered gently. "You love the Church deeply, have demonstrated your humility, and yet stand outside the usual bureaucracies that might exploit them. You're the perfect person to keep them safe. If I keep them here, the rumor mill alone could incite half the world—Russia, zealots, other foreign powers. No, better you keep them. Be discreet."

Joseph stared at the ancient keys in his palms, mouth dry. "But what do I do with them? Am I supposed to hide them in a sock drawer?"

Boniface offered a cryptic smile. "I hear from Father Ryan that your father's in stage four cancer." His voice dropped to a near whisper, "If I were you, I'd start there."

Joseph blinked. "Wait—are you saying...?"

Joseph felt goosebumps prickle along his arms. He realized the Pope was entirely serious. The older man pressed a small button on the library's intercom, murmuring in Italian: "Per favore, chieda a Michael Scanlon di rientrare nella biblioteca." A moment later, the library doors swung open, and Joseph's father stepped in hesitantly.

Pope Boniface offered Michael a welcoming gesture. "Michael, I understand you have stage four cancer. Is that correct?"

Michael blinked, glancing uncertainly at Joseph. "Yes, Holy Father. Leiomyosarcoma, to be precise. It started in my digestive tract, now metastasized to the skin. I've developed these lumps across my torso." With a shaky sigh, he unbuttoned his shirt a bit, revealing several raised tumors, each discolored and swollen. "They're painful. Honestly, I was told I have months to live."

A hush fell. Joseph felt the weight of the Keys in his hands. Pope Boniface then nodded to the young professor. Joseph stepped forward, pressed the Keys gently against the largest lump on Michael's side. Then, closing his eyes, Joseph prayed.

"In the name of Jesus Christ," he began, voice wavering, "and through the healing power entrusted to these Keys, I speak to every tumor in this body—be healed in Jesus' name, for the glory of God! Every cancer cell dissolve, vanish, and never return right now in Jesus' name! Jesus, you gave Saint Peter the authority to bind and loose. Let these Keys manifest your healing power!"

As the prayer flowed, Michael shuddered, drawing a breath so deep it sounded like a sob. Pope Boniface stepped closer, and together they watched, hearts hammering. The lumps beneath the keys in Joseph's hand began to recede, shrinking as though deflated from within. The color of Michael's skin normalized in a series of moments, flush with healthy pink instead of diseased gray.

"I feel like my stomach is on fire!" Michael gasped, voice catching with awe. He pressed his own palm to the spot, as if to confirm. "It's... it's gone. The pain is gone. The lumps—"

Pope Boniface and Joseph exchanged a look of overflowing wonder. The Pope's solemn face cracked into a wide, jubilant grin. Without ceremony, he lifted a hand for a high-five, palm open. Joseph, half-laughing, half-weeping, slapped his hand in elation.

"¡Gloria a Dios!" the Pope exclaimed. In that moment, Aziz, Father Ryan and the other Vatican staff rushed in at the sounds of celebration to find the Holy Father jumping up and down—and Joseph with him. Joseph realized that he was not just celebrating a demonstration of Spirit and Power with the highest-ranking member of the church hierarchy - he was witnessing another child of God rejoicing in the Holy Spirit just like Jesus did after the disciples came back healing the sick and casting out demons in Luke 10. Centuries of solemn hush overshadowed by a glorious sense of God's presence. The feeling was indescribable: ancient volumes lining the shelves, the Pope in white vestments high-fiving the newly minted relic-bearer. Joseph let the Keys slip to rest in his palm, feeling their surprising weight, the once-lost relic shimmering with a renewed purpose.

In that instant, all words fled. The Pope's grin broadened. Joseph, panting with the rush of adrenaline, realized there was nothing more to say—only the knowledge that a new chapter in his life had opened, one where the Keys, the object of his academic study for years, were now fully entrusted to his care through the guiding of the Holy Spirit. And somewhere in the background, the choir of invisible angels were fully present and rejoicing with them.

The Pope looked at Joseph with joy and said, "You are now the 'Keeper of the Lost Keys."

TWENTY-NINE

New Life

The monitors hummed softly in the dim hospital room, a kind of mechanical lullaby. Outside the window, Chicago's skyline glowed against the night, all glass and steel and distant traffic. Inside, everything narrowed to the small bundle in Joseph's arms.

His son's fingers were impossibly tiny, curled around the tip of Joseph's index finger with surprising strength. A white hospital cap sagged over one eye. His breaths came in fast, soft puffs that rose and fell against Joseph's chest.

"Michael Peter Scanlon," Joseph whispered, the name catching in his throat. "Welcome, little man."

Across the bed, Salma smiled weakly, dark hair plastered back, cheeks pale with exhaustion and joy. "Say it again," she murmured. "I like the way you say his name."

"Michael," Joseph repeated, glancing at the sleeping figure in the recliner in the corner—his father, chin on his chest, an afghan from Joelle's couch tucked around him by some merciful nurse. "Michael for your Father. And Peter... for the keys that got us into this mess."

Salma's soft laugh dissolved into tears. "And out of it," she said.

They had dodged disaster more than once. The last trimester had been a gauntlet of hospital visits, monitoring, whispered consultations in hallways. There had been the scare at thirty-one weeks, the contractions that came too early, the night Joseph prayed the Rosary on the cold plastic chair, bargaining with God with the desperation of a man who knew what it meant to lose too much. In Antakya, he had asked heaven for protection in caves and catacombs. Here, the battleground had been a fluorescent-lit corridor outside the high-risk maternity unit.

He looked down at his son again. The little chest rose and fell. Alive. Here.

"Faith is not a feeling," he whispered, remembering the sentence that had steadied him on the eve of his departure, when he'd fallen asleep clinging to Salma and that single truth. "But sometimes," he added under his breath, "God gives you the feeling too."

Salma shifted slightly, wincing. "What are you thinking?"

"That this is... more than we ever dared to picture on those drives home," he said. He could still see her in the dim glow of the dashboard lights, tears slipping down her cheeks as she told him she didn't want to let him down. "We used to imagine this moment. Now he's here."

A nurse slipped in quietly, checking Salma's vitals, then Michael's. "Everyone doing all right?" she whispered.

"We're good," Salma said, a hand resting on her stomach where the incision pulled. "Just tired. But... good."

The nurse turned toward the mounted television. "Mind if we turn this on?" she asked. "Lots of news tonight. The whole floor's buzzing."

As she took the initiative and turned on the TV, Joseph barely registered the muted anchor in the corner—some generic world map graphic behind her, Cyrillic letters scrolling in a red band across the bottom of the screen.

Salma's eyes flicked over, unfocused. "What's going on?"

The nurse hesitated. "Russia," she said. "Something about their president. It's breaking news. The staff's been glued to it in the lounge."

Joseph's heart gave a strange, hollow thump.

The nurse raised the volume a notch. The anchor's voice cut through the gentle beeping of the monitors.

"...and announcing the sudden death of the Russian president earlier today. State television has confirmed that President Igor Volkov died from complications related to a long-term illness. In a brief address to the nation, acting President General Viktor Morozov pledged an immediate cease-fire on all Eastern European fronts and signaled a willingness to open talks with NATO leadership..."

Salma's head turned slowly toward Joseph. "Did she just say...?"

He nodded numbly, eyes locked on the screen. The camera cut to footage of soldiers embracing in muddy trenches, of families holding up phones in living rooms, faces streaked with tears. A ticker at the bottom read: MOROZOV CALLS FOR "NEW ERA OF PEACE IN EUROPE."

Joseph's chest tightened. In his mind, DeLuca's laptop flared to life again: casualty counts, burning cities, the warning that if Volkov died there might be a chance for peace—and if he was miraculously healed, they could be staring at another thirty years of war.

He saw Dmitri Petrenko's name in a casualty list that would never be shown. He saw Ivan screaming in the Antakya lobby—Proklyat Volkov! He sends our sons to die for his empire! He saw soldiers' faces, Russian and Polish and Latvian and unnamed, blurred together in a tide of grief.

He also saw a pair of golden keys on a velvet cloth in the papal library, Pope Boniface's weathered hands pressing them back into Joseph's own after a brief prayer.

"These belong to the whole Church," the Holy Father had told him quietly, eyes kind and fierce at once. "Not to popes, not to presidents. Guard them for us, Dr. Scanlon—far from the reach of empires. When the time is right, the Church will decide how to reveal them."

Since then, the velvet-lined box had been hidden in a fireproof safe beneath the basement stairs of his modest South Bend home, behind an unmarked panel only he and Salma knew about. The real Keys of St. Peter—entrusted to a professor who still forgot where he left his car keys half the time.

Salma's fingers found his, squeezing hard. "Joseph," she whispered. "You think...?"

"I don't know," he said. His throat ached. "But I know this: they didn't get the chance to use the Keys on him."

The thought landed with both weight and mercy. Joseph did not rejoice in any man's death—not even a tyrant's. But as Volkov's portrait flashed on the screen, framed in a black ribbon, he could not help thinking of the thousands who would not die now. Of boys like Dmitri who would live because a line had been drawn that could not be crossed.

"Lord, have mercy on his soul," Joseph murmured, surprising himself. "And on all of ours."

Salma bowed her head. "And let the wars end," she added quietly. "Please."

The nurse slipped out, leaving the sound low. After a long moment, Salma exhaled.

Outside, somewhere over the Atlantic or the steppes or the Baltic Sea, pilots were hearing the same news and recalculating flight paths that no longer needed to include bombing runs. Somewhere in Warsaw, a woman would wake up tomorrow without another siren.

Inside this room, a six-pound miracle flailed his arms and let out a thin, indignant cry.

Joseph rose to take him again.

Epilogue

Two months later, the bells of the Basilica of the Sacred Heart pealed across the Notre Dame campus, bright and insistent under a pale spring sky. Students spilled out of Sunday Mass, clusters of blazers and backpacks drifting toward the South Dining Hall or the library. On the basilica steps, Joseph paused, tightening the soft blue blanket around his son.

"Ready for your big moment?" he whispered.

Michael Peter blinked up at him from the crook of his arm, a tiny fist emerging from the blanket as if in answer.

Salma adjusted the diaper bag strap on her shoulder and smoothed the edge of her dress with her free hand. "He's going to scream through the whole baptism," she predicted, half-hopeful, half-terrified.

"Then everyone will know he has lungs," Joseph said.

Inside, the basilica was a little world of its own. Sunlight poured through stained glass—Christ handing keys to Peter, Mary in cobalt blue, saints in crimson and gold. The font's water shimmered under the overhead lights. Fr. Ryan stood beside it in a white alb and stole, grin wide. Just behind him, Aziz and his wife traded whispered jokes in Arabic, their children already smitten with the baby cousin they had met only the night before.

Joelle dabbed at her eyes with a tissue every thirty seconds. Michael, jaw set in quiet pride, stared on with the strength and resilience of a man fully healed of cancer. When he caught Joseph's eye, they shared a look that said more than any toast.

"You ready?" Fr. Ryan asked, opening his ritual book.

"As I'll ever be," Joseph answered.

The baptism unfolded in familiar cadences. The Sign of the Cross on the baby's forehead. The renunciations. The profession of faith. When Fr. Ryan asked, "What name do you give your child?" Joseph's voice didn't break the way he feared it would.

"Michael Peter," he said. "After his grandfather and the Apostle."

"And what do you ask of God's Church for Michael Peter?"

"Baptism," Salma said, steady and clear.

When the water finally poured over their son's head in three small streams, Michael Peter did scream, a righteous, outraged wail that filled the baptistery and echoed off the stone. Everyone laughed through their tears.

"Proof of life," Salma whispered, eyes shining.

Joseph kissed the damp curls, the chrism-scented crown, and closed his eyes for a moment. In Antakya, he had knelt in a cave that had once been Peter's pulpit. Here, in a basilica halfway across the world, his own child was grafted into that same Church. The continuity made his heart ache.

After the baptism, as friends and family crowded around with cameras and cell phones to get a picture of the new Christian child, Michael shuffled forward, laying a trembling hand on Joseph's head.

"I told you there was something rotten with that board decision," he muttered in Joseph's ear, half-proud, half-wry.

Joseph chuckled. "You also told me you were going to behave in retirement, remember?"

Michael snorted. "I lied."

He wasn't wrong. The letter had arrived from the university president just a week earlier, on heavy cream stock with an embossed seal. The language was carefully neutral—acknowledging "irregularities" in the deliberations surrounding the closure of the Late Antiquities program, announcing the resignation of Trustee Marvin Kozlov "amid ongoing federal inquiries," and expressing "regret for the distress these events caused Dr. Scanlon and his family." The real shock had come in the final paragraph: an invitation for Joseph to serve as the inaugural director of a new Center for Early Christian Studies and Global Catholic Heritage, with a mandate to steward both his Antioch discoveries and future collaborations with the Holy See.

"They never mentioned my involvement," Michael had said with mock injury when Joseph showed him the letter. "Not one word about my nosiness."

"That might have something to do with certain FBI agents dropping by their office," Joseph had replied.

Now, watching his father's hand rest on his son's head, Joseph felt the overlapping arcs of their lives—teacher and student, father and son, meddler and martyr—fold into something like harmony.

"Thank you," he said simply.

Michael squeezed his shoulder. "Just keep teaching the truth," he murmured. "And for God's sake, try not to topple any more empires before this one is out of diapers." Joseph chuckled, catching the glint in his father's eye and the unspoken nod to how, in their private shorthand, the Russian president's death still seemed to hang off those keys.

That night, after the party wound down and the last cousin left with Tupperware full of leftover pasta, the house in South Bend finally fell quiet. Salma put Michael Peter down in the bassinet beside their bed and, within minutes, was asleep herself.

It had been a long time since he went through his mail. He sat down and started sorting the stack that had piled up. Buried between bills and credit card offers was a letter addressed from Vatican City that made his chest tighten.

He hesitated, then opened it.

Your Excellency Dr. Scanlon,

In light of a recent rescript of the Holy Father concerning your new status in service to the Apostolic See, I write to confirm that the Directorate for Security Services and Civil Protection of Vatican City State has been asked to assume responsibility for certain aspects of your personal security and that of your immediate family.

Ordinarily, our mandate concerns the Holy Father and the territory of Vatican City State. However, at the express wish of His Holiness, and in close collaboration with the Pontifical Swiss Guard, we are putting in place certain extraordinary measures proportionate to the particular circumstances connected with your person and your recent service to the Holy See.

For obvious reasons, it would not be prudent to specify in writing either the full scope of your role or the considerations that have led to these arrangements. It is sufficient to note that the Holy Father desires that you should not be without appropriate support as you carry this responsibility in the midst of your ordinary life.

You may therefore expect, at the appropriate time, discreet contact from an officer attached to a special Swiss Guard liaison unit.

He will present credentials bearing my seal and the seal of the Governorate of Vatican City State. Until then, we ask that you continue to exercise the greatest prudence regarding your recent travels and any sensitive conversations, objects, or documentation that may be associated with them.

Please be assured of our prayers and our professional support as you balance this trust with your family and academic vocation.

In the service of the Supreme Pontiff,

Inspector General Carlo Benedetti

Director, Directorate for Security Services and Civil Protection

Commander, Gendarmerie Corps of Vatican City State

Joseph read it twice, then a third time, tracing the seals in the signature with his eyes. New status. Extraordinary measures. Swiss Guard liaison unit.

He felt suddenly very small in a world of forces that stretched from Langley to the Kremlin to the Apostolic Palace—and now, apparently, into his own front yard in South Bend.

He put away the letter and stared out at the thin sliver of city visible between brick buildings and let out a long breath.

"Special status," he muttered. "I'm just trying to learn how to change diapers."

Still, as he made his way back to the room and eased the door open on Salma and the sleeping baby, he knew something fundamental had shifted. The Keys in his basement safe were not just archaeological wonders. Somewhere in Rome, and in places far less holy, people were building plans around them.

As he gazed upon the miracle of Michael Peter, he considered all the years he had spent parsing footnotes and crossing continents in search of Peter's Keys, he could see now that the door they were truly meant to open was this one: a wife breathing softly in the dark, and a son who had unlocked in him a love fierce enough to stand against any empire. The world might someday remember him as the Keeper of the Lost Keys, but he knew better now—the real treasure was the warm, fragile body breathing beside his bed, the key that had just opened his heart more fully to the love of the Father. And as he turned out the light and let the house fall silent, Joseph understood at last that heaven's greatest secret had never been hidden in a Byzantine chamber, but entrusted, scandalously, to flesh and blood. In the years to come, whatever storms might gather around hidden relics and whispered Vatican directives, he knew his story would be measured not by the artifact he guarded, but by how faithfully he loved the small life that had just begun in the dark beside him.

———

Joseph Scanlon's story will continue...

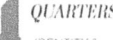

ENCOUNTER SCHOOL OF MINISTRY

ENCOUNTER SCHOOL OF MINISTRY

LEARN TO LIVE A SUPERNATURAL LIFE IN THE HOLY SPIRIT

"Truly, truly, I say to you, he who believes in me will also do the works that I do; and greater works than these will he do, because I go to the Father." – John 14:12

It is our mission to raise up disciples who are equipped to do "greater works," and it was the Lord's idea to use long-term discipleship for this training.

Designed and established from the heart of *Encounter Ministries*, this school draws from the richness of our Catholic heritage as we seek to **teach, equip, and activate** disciples to demonstrate the love of God through the power of the Holy Spirit in their spheres of influence. In conformity with the teachings and traditions of the Catholic Church, we offer students a dynamic 8-quarter training program designed to take you to the next level in your ministry.

encounterschool.org

QUARTERS

1. IDENTITY & TRANSFORMATION
2. HEARING GOD'S VOICE & THE PROPHETIC GIFTS OF THE HOLY SPIRIT
3. POWER & HEALING
4. INNER HEALING & FREEDOM
5. INTIMACY WITH GOD
6. ADVANCED MINISTRY TRAINING
7. POWER EVANGELIZATION
8. LEADERSHIP & DEPLOYMENT

435

www.ingramcontent.com/pod-product-compliance
Lightning Source LLC
Chambersburg PA
CBHW050915030726
47503CB00007BB/2302